Soul on th

Stephen Green

green.steve330@gmail.com

Copyright © 2023
All Rights Reserved

No part of this book may be reproduced or transmitted in any form or by any means, electronic or mechanical, including photocopying, recording, or by any information storage and retrieval system without the written permission of the author, except where permitted by law.

Soul on the water is a fictional story set against the backdrop of some real events and the dates when they occurred. The characters and their families are imagined, they bear no resemblance to anyone living or dead and any similarities are coincidental. The names of most venues and places are fictional, others are real when the same existing venue name and place have been used.

Contents

Dedication i
Chapter 1 1
Chapter 2 11
Chapter 3 23
Chapter 4 42
Chapter 5 52
Chapter 6 70
Chapter 7 82
Chapter 8 98
Chapter 9 109
Chapter 10 119
Chapter 11 123
Chapter 12 127
Chapter 13 137
Chapter 14 151
Chapter 15 168
Chapter 16 177
Chapter 17 185
Chapter 18 195
Chapter 19 200
Chapter 20 215
Chapter 21 224
Chapter 22 231
Chapter 23 239
Chapter 24 246
Chapter 25 255
Chapter 26 263
Chapter 27 273
Chapter 28 284
Chapter 29 296
Chapter 30 306

Chapter 31	315
Chapter 32	324
Chapter 33	331
Chapter 34	344
Chapter 35	357
Chapter 36	359
Chapter 37	361
Chapter 38	364
Chapter 39	369
Chapter 40	372
Chapter 41	375
Chapter 42	377
Chapter 43	379
Chapter 44	382
Chapter 45	384
Chapter 46	386
Chapter 47	389
Epilogue	397
Acknowledgements	400
About the Author	402
Motivation for Writing This Novel	403

Dedication

This book is dedicated to all homeless street sleepers and to those who are trying to make a difference to their lives.

Half of the profits from the sale of this book will be gifted to local homeless charities.

Chapter 1

Friday, 20th December 2019, 7.35 a.m. Cambridgeshire, England.

Alex and his friend Hamish stepped out from their club boathouse carrying their double scull over their heads and made their way steadily down a floodlit ramp. Water lapped around their Wellington boots as they placed their boat onto the river, part of a well-practised routine. Alex pushed back his thick dark fringe under his cap, stretched, and flexed his shoulders to warm up his muscles. He felt a rush of excitement as adrenaline pumped through his veins, and he inhaled the chilled morning air. Purpose-driven to be the first out on the water, Alex slapped his hands together. He knew that even in the dawn half-light, visibility would be good enough to check the direction and make good progress.

One of the other club members, Gordon Dullard, whose surname, Alex thought, matched his personality, followed them into the shallows carrying their oars. 'Thanks, Gordon,' Alex said with a contended grin to the wrinkled smiling face of the retired man, grateful that Dullard could always be relied upon as an early riser. Dullard held the boat steady for them in the swirling current as Alex leaned over the boat, fitted in each oar, and adjusted the lock collars on the rigging. The light from the boathouse illuminated their breath as a brood of inquisitive mallard ducks swam close, hoping to be fed.

Alex straightened up, rubbed his facial stubble, and gazed across the river into the shadows created by the imminent sunrise. His focus was suddenly snatched away by a light further along the embankment. He recognised the floodlight from the Cambridge boathouse as their university rowing teams got prepared. Determination fuelled him to beat them out onto the racing part of the river.

Stepping into the stern of the boat, he nestled into his seat, almost level with the deck. The two of them went into their routine of changing their footwear, putting on trainers, and fastening their feet before throwing their boots onto the ramp.

'It's damn cold,' Hamish said, trying to slap warmth into his shoulders and pushing back his dark hair. 'I'm ready.'

Alex hastily pulled his neoprene gloves on and made some further balance alterations with his rigging. 'My seat's snagging.' He frowned as he worked it back and forth on the runners.

'It'll be fine,' replied Hamish in his soft Scottish accent to the back of Alex's head. 'Nothing to worry about once the rollers have warmed up.' Dullard pushed their boat out into the river.

Alex synchronised the movement of his oar blades to cut into the water in timed precision with Hamish's as they rowed steadily north on the Great River Ouse. They reached the Cambridge boathouse as the women's rowing team of eight was getting ready in their boat. 'Hey,' he said, glancing around. 'You ladies need to get up earlier if you want to beat us out,' he smirked. The small coxswain raised her middle finger and sneered. Alex and Hamish chuckled as they continued sculling towards the straight part of the river. They passed the race marker starting point.

'Go...' Alex heaved back into his chest. 'Let's see if we can break our record.'

'We're at the half-kilometre stage,' panted Hamish, a while later. 'Up the pace to forty strokes.' Alex sliced his oar blades into the river surface and gulped down air as he pulled his oar handles hard into his chest, his seat sliding in unison with Hamish.

The sky slowly lightened in the dawn rays as the bow of their boat dipped in and out of the water, cutting sharply through the river current on each stroke of their oars as they headed towards the two-kilometre marker sign.

'Almost there,' said Hamish, glancing over his shoulder at the sign fixed to an old willow tree stump at the side of the river. A heron took graceful flight from it as they approached.

'And... stop!' said Alex. The pace of the boat fizzled away as their oars dragged across the water's surface. He felt his heart pumping as he slumped forward and caught his breath.

Their boat drifted in the current as mist veils wafted off their bodies in the still winter air. 'Look up,' said Hamish, pulling out a small towel from inside his top, wiping the perspiration around his neck.

Alex leaned back on the boat deck and absorbed the sunrise. Shades of orange and pink hues transformed the morning sky. 'Wow... That's priceless – something that money can't buy.'

'That's got to be the best we've seen.' Hamish slowly rowed their boat into the embankment as a white-beaked coot darted from the reeds.

Alex took hold of some stems to prevent their boat from drifting. 'What an incredible dawn. It really makes you feel alive.' He watched for a few minutes as the daybreak glow intensified across the hazy sky, caressing the underside of the clouds.

'Hey, look,' said Hamish. Suddenly, the women's team came into sight. 'Unbelievable pace.'

Alex wiped his face with his sleeve. 'And to hold that rate for almost seven kilometres.' The women's eight rowed past them at speed.

'That's impressive.'

'I think we've just seen the future women's boat race champions.'

Hamish flexed his tired shoulders as their boat bobbed in the wake. 'There's some fit-looking fanny in that team.'

'Don't you think of anything else?'

'You know me – single and free.'

Alex rolled his eyes. 'Are you working later?'

'My shift is from two to midnight. A&E will be heaving by the time I've finished.'

'I see we're both down for New Year's Eve.'

Hamish exhaled. 'No rest for the wicked. Evie won't be pleased.'

'You're right; she's not. But she understands – that's how it is as a doctor.' Alex gently rowed over to the other side and spotted a double scull appearing on the river. 'Look who's coming.'

'The Gormley brothers. Let's see if they want a race back from the one-kilometre marker.'

'Great idea.' Alex shaped his hands around his mouth as a loud hailer. 'You two up for a race? Usual wager, twenty pounds and a pint each.'

'If you want to throw away your money!' shouted back one of the brothers. 'That's fine by us!'

They gently rowed their boats back to the marker and lined up. Pressing their torsos into their bent knees and holding their oars in outstretched arms, they were ready for a race start. Alex counted down, 'Three... two... one – go!' They heaved away as hard as they could. The boats were side by side as they paced themselves back along the broad straight river, past a swan nesting in the reeds, some willow trees with their branches dipping into the water, and several moored narrow boats of various colours, shapes, and lengths.

They neared the finishing point with the Gormley brothers' boat half a length ahead. The gap between their boats closed as a narrow boat came towards them. 'The oars are overlapping!' Hamish shouted. Their oars suddenly clashed, and Alex and Hamish's boat veered away into the embankment.

The Gormley brothers laughed. 'Like I said, if you want to throw away your money,' one of them taunted as they continued sculling until their mocking voices faded.

Alex smacked the deck hard with his hand. 'That's the third time they've beaten us in a row. We need to commit to more training.'

'Let's start on the rowing machines when we get back.'

Alex folded his hands over his head. 'We'll get our own back next month in the races.'

6.50 p.m.

Robert Hardson's phone pinged while clearing the kitchen serving island after dinner at the family home in Richmond, Surrey. He checked the message.

'Is everything alright?' Annabelle asked, closing the dishwasher door. 'You look concerned.'

'It's work.'

'What is it this time?'

'I need to go in. The client wants a video conference at eight p.m.'

Annabelle frowned, 'It's almost seven. This was meant to be your afternoon off.'

'Remember, New York is five hours behind us. The meeting is scheduled for three… I need to go.'

Annabelle folded her arms. 'That's what you said last Thursday, but you got back very late.'

'I explained; I went for a drink with some colleagues… I won't be too late, I promise. I'll see you later.'

Robert entered his office at eight. His PA, Sophie, was standing in front of his desk, holding a file.

'You didn't need to be here,' he said, turning and hanging up his long coat and scarf on the back of his office door. 'But I'm pleased you are.'

She checked the time on her wristwatch, carefully placed the file down on his desk, and smiled. 'You still have a little under thirty minutes until your meeting in the Gateway conference room.'

'I know… and I think you know how I would like to spend some of that time.' He twisted the door latch behind his back until it locked.

Sophie leaned back against his desk and started to tantalisingly undo the buttons to the front of her green baroque pattern blouse, revealing her black bra. He watched her as he undid his tie and removed his suit jacket.

She stood straight, reached around, and unzipped the back of her knee-length skirt. 'It's been almost a week.' She wriggled the skirt off her slim, shapely waist and hips. It dropped to the floor, 'Mmm – stockings,' he said, as he undid his shirt.

Sophie smiled. 'I wasn't sure if we would get the chance to get close again before Christmas.' She stepped to one side of her skirt and reached down to pull off one of her high heel shoes.'

'Christmas has come early. You can leave your shoes on.'

'Naughty.' She undid the cuffs to her blouse and slid it off her shoulders.

He walked up to her and held her by the waist. She wrapped her arms around his neck, stroked his short grey hair back around his ears, and kissed him. He lifted her onto his desk. Parting her legs, she reached down and undid his belt and trousers, letting them drop to the floor. She unclipped her bra and tossed it away. Spreading her arms out behind her, she arched her back as he leaned over her chest and bit her breasts. Breathing heavily, she collapsed onto her elbows. Her neck was fully stretched, and her long wavy fire-red coloured hair fell back off her shoulders against his desk. He kissed her extended slender neck from her collarbone to her jaw and gently slid off her thong.

9.50 p.m.

Alex felt Evie take his arm as they walked down the exit stairs from the Arts Picture House out onto St Andrew's Street in Cambridge. He liked having her up close to him like this, just the two of them, like some impenetrable unit. They walked on the pavement back towards the city centre past some bars and restaurants full of people.

Evie glanced down to her side as they walked past a rough sleeper. She pushed her long, flowing dark hair back off her shoulders and pulled in the collar of her sheepskin coat. 'The critics slammed the film, but I thought it was really lovely.'

'I must admit, the guys at the hospital laughed when I told them we were going to see *Last Christmas*. But I actually enjoyed it – I even got a bit emotional at one stage.' The light from a passing car sparkled on a heavily studded left ear of a rough sleeper just ahead of them. 'Let's stop and speak to this woman at the shop entrance.' Alex crouched next to the young woman with short auburn hair and a nose piercing, sitting on a flat cardboard box reading a book. He knew from her slim elf-like face that she had a willow figure under the floral-patterned bed duvet that was wrapped around her. 'Hi, is there anything we can get you to eat or drink from the Express shop?' A small black terrier dog emerged from under the woman's duvet and snuggled beside her thigh.

The woman placed her paperback down on her lap. 'That's kind of you,' she said in a soft Irish accent. 'I'd love a latte. Maybe a hot chicken bap, please.'

Alex glanced around at Evie. She nodded and walked the short distance to the shop as he reached out to stroke her dog's head. 'Can I ask your name?'

'Rose, and this is Gertie.' Her dog sat up as he stroked it.

'How long have you been sleeping rough, if you don't mind me asking?'

'Eighteen months,' replied Rose despondently. 'It's the second time for me.'

'How come?'

'I had problems with my partner. Everything went wrong.'

He continued to stroke Gertie. 'What about family to support you?'

'They're the other part of the problem.' She coughed.

He admired her tough resolve. 'It must be really grim sleeping out here in all weathers – how do you manage and stay clean? Sorry, that was personal.'

Rose grinned, 'That's alright. There are a couple of charity hostels here in town that take us in on some nights. I get a bed, a shower, and hot food – generally once a week. They even wash my clothes.'

Alex was suddenly taken by surprise when Rose's tattooed hand clasped his hand and traced a line with her finger along his palm. 'Let's see,' she said. 'You're a Pisces. You feel comfortable in and around water.'

'Good guess.' He listened as she read his palm but then closed it after a couple of minutes and withdrew his hand.

Her gaze narrowed. 'What year were you born?'

'Ninety-two.'

'Four years older than me.'

Evie returned and offered Rose a chicken bap. 'Is there anything else I can get you?' Evie placed a hot drink down on the pavement. Rose shook her head as she tucked into the bap.

Alex stood. 'Do take care of yourself, Rose.'

Evie glanced around at him and then back at Rose. 'We'll leave you now to eat your food.'

He fought his instincts to stay longer as he felt Evie tugging his arm. They slipped away and started to walk home. 'I feel a little uneasy at leaving her alone,' he said, glancing back and seeing Rose eating.

'But she has her dog for company.'

'She was strange, but there was something else about her.' He exhaled.

'She looked so vulnerable, but you can't solve her situation.'

'Let's just hope that she doesn't land up being taken into A&E with a serious health issue.'

Chapter 2

Tuesday, 31st December 2019 – New Year's Eve, 7.35 a.m.

Alex's senses picked up on hearing Evie singing as he awoke. Rolling over, he pulled his pillow up behind his head. He thought she had a good voice, but it did grind on him some mornings when he wanted a lie-in, but not today.

'*I can feel a glowing sensation taking place…*' Evie sang, entering the bedroom in her pyjamas. 'Good morning, mon amour.'

He grabbed his phone off the side cabinet. Squinting, he checked for messages.

'I've made you a lovely cuppa.' She placed his drink down on the cabinet and knelt on the edge of their bed.

'You're exceptionally perky this morning.'

'You know I like to rise, sing, and shower.'

He nodded. 'What song is it?'

'Just an old tune from the Sixties.' She started singing part of the song again as it echoed through from the kitchen radio. 'Wonderful, it really helps me to start the day.' She straddled him, letting her hair fall on his face.

He smiled, 'I can tell you're feeling the vibes.'

'Exactly.' She kissed him on the lips. 'I'm just in a good mood,' she leaped off, grabbed her hairbrush, and went to the bathroom. Their Persian cat Cookie jumped up onto the bed and settled comfortably on top of Alex. Evie stuck her head back around the bedroom door, singing another part of the song. 'That was an intense night we had.' She winked and returned to the bathroom singing.

He nudged Cookie to one side, rolled off the bed, and went into the bathroom carrying his tea. 'Thanks for the cuppa.'

'What time is your shift tonight?' she asked from behind the shower curtain over the bath.

'I start at six.'

'They might need reminding that as a FY2 junior doctor, you shouldn't work more than ten hours.'

'You know how it is, they're just stretched at times.' He slid back the shower curtain as he sipped his tea.

'What do you want to do today?'

'I don't know, but I feel I need to get out in the air.' He watched her as she showered.

'It's meant to be sunny,' she said, rinsing her hair. 'Fancy a bike ride out somewhere?'

He put his hand onto her waist, as the conditioner suds ran over his fingers. She ignored his touch as he slowly stroked her bottom and thigh. He started to become aroused. 'A bike ride – why not. Where shall we go?' His groaning stomach suppressed his passion, and he retracted his hand.

Evie grabbed her towel. 'How about the tea rooms at Grantchester?'

Alex leaned back against the hand basin. 'I fancy somewhere different like that farm shop a few miles outside the city. It's meant to have a nice café.'

'Little Piggy's Farm Shop or something?' Evie dabbed her hair with the towel.

He went and got his phone and returned. 'It's open until four. We would have worked up a good appetite for lunch. Speaking of which – I'm hungry.'

12.15 p.m.

Alex was cycling along a track beside the main road, and Evie tried to keep pace at his side. The winter sun kissed the frosted landscape; silvery furrowed farmland lined their right side, and bare white woodland framed their left. He got out of his saddle and started pumping his bicycle peddles as they steadily ascended the Gog Magog Hills. 'Keep up, you're out of condition,' he said, breathing heavily and glancing around at the views of the open rolling countryside. He followed directions shown on a wooden sign, taking them off the track and along a country lane.

'I hope we arrive soon – my fingers are frozen,' Evie said, blowing warm breath onto her hand.

'Drips keep coming off my nose. But at least I'm wearing gloves.'

'Aren't you the sensible one?' Evie pulled a silly face.

Alex stopped, 'Here, take my gloves. You need them more than me.' He watched her put them on and then started cycling again. He caught sight of their destination a short time later. 'We're here at last. I think they have an outdoor clothing shop. I'll treat you to some gloves if they're open.'

After parking their bicycles in a rack near the farm shop, they walked into the half-empty café and glanced around at the Christmas decorations. A small fir tree laden with baubles stood proud next to the serving till as the waitress handed the change out to a customer. They got seated opposite each other at a table by a misted window.

'I've decided what I'm having,' he said, pushing the menu towards Evie, as the waitress arrived. They placed their orders, and the waitress left.

Evie started to giggle. 'Looking around at all the decorations in here, reminds me of playing the chocolate square race game after dinner at your parents.' She paused as she tried to compose herself.

'We all looked a right sight with chocolate streaks down our faces, but Mum was the worst.'

'Oh yeah. Your poor mum was hot and sweaty after coming from the kitchen. The mint chocolates kept melting on her forehead.' Evie laughed until she cried.

'Remember the one that slid down over her eye and got stuck on her cheek?' Grinning, Alex watched Evie wipe joyful tears from her face. Turning sideways, he wiped a patch of condensation from the window and peered through. 'The clothes shop appears open.'

The waitress arrived with their order of two toasted sandwiches and hot mugs of tea.

Evie stopped laughing and started to nibble at her sandwich. 'I was just thinking about that young homeless woman we bought food for when we left the cinema.'

'It's no life, sleeping in a cardboard box in a doorway.'

'I felt a little ashamed getting into our cosy bed that night.'

'I know what you mean.'

'We did what we could.' Evie reached over and squeezed his hand.

'All I could think about was her being alone with just her little black terrier,' he rubbed his stubble. 'It's hard to believe that she'd been homeless for eighteen months.'

'Her dog Gertie had such big sad eyes.' Evie cradled her mug in her hands as she sipped her tea.

He picked up his toasted sandwich and tilted his head. 'She was only twenty-four.'

'I struggle to understand how someone like her gets to that point where they're on the street?'

Alex raised his shoulders. 'You heard her. She hinted at really bad relationship stuff.'

'We should try and look out for her when we go into the city centre again.'

He rested his sandwich on the plate. 'People like her will often try anything to escape their desperate situation.'

'Like drugs.'

He nodded, 'Hyperthermia can also be another big problem for the homeless at this time of year.'

They finished their lunch, paid at the till, and walked to the outdoor clothing shop across the car park. He bought some gloves for Evie and a hat for himself. They left feeling content and walked over to a large metal-cladded animal barn that welcomed visitors with a money donation box. He slid back a wooden door and was hit by musky farm smells as they entered; hay, dampness, and animals. They casually strolled around the pens exploring the rare breeds of sheep and pigs.

He put his arm around her as they peered at some rare sheep breeds in their pens. 'How are the wedding plans going? Just over six weeks to go. It's a little bit scary, don't you think?'

She flinched. 'Don't say it's scary. It's the day after Valentine's Day – it's very romantic.'

'That's what I meant – not scary at all.' Alex bit his lower lip. 'But it's coming around quickly.'

'On a serious note,' Evie clasped her hands together. 'We need to discuss my wedding concerns.'

He rolled his eyes. 'Wait a minute... Look at the size of that big old sow.'

'Our guests' dietary requirements could be an issue.' Evie started to reel off a few of her worries.

'It says here she's called Polly,' he said, reading the information plaque. 'She's a Gloucestershire Old Spot. Look at all her piglets bundled together under the heat lamp. One, two... I count thirteen.'

'You asked me how the wedding plans are going and you're talking about piglets...'

'Look, you have to leave all your worries in Jenny's capable hands. After all, she's the wedding planner – isn't that what we're paying her for?'

'That's what Daddy is paying her for, amongst all the other costs. But some of our guests have complex dietary needs, not just the usual dairy or gluten intolerance.'

'Oh look,' said Alex, pointing. 'There's another piglet underneath with only its bottom and tail sticking out.'

Evie took a casual interest and counted. 'Fourteen piglets. It's a miracle it survives under all the others. Mummy pig looks worn out and is sleeping.' She walked over to the next pen. A large black pig's head suddenly lunged over the side rail snorting smelly hot breath in her face. 'Awwrrrhhhh!' she screamed.

He chuckled as he put his arm around her. 'It's alright.'

She tilted her head with displeasure at him. 'Another thing. Do we really need to invite so many of your so-called friends from the rowing and sculling club?'

'It's only to the evening bash.'

'I wish you wouldn't keep calling it – the bash.' She crossed her arms and sat down on a straw bale. 'It's our wedding. It'll be our most special and memorable day ever.'

Alex stroked his forehead as he sat down next to her. 'Remember what we agreed?'

She returned a reluctant nod.

'Part of that agreement was, that I was to leave all the arrangements to you. We sealed it with a kiss across the table.' He didn't care much for the big wedding of her dreams, but he wanted a family, ideally, two children. He recalled how pleased he was when she agreed to his proposal.

'I just want you to take more interest, that's all.'

'I trust you… And now you have Jenny the planner helping you… Just get it organised.' He got up, walked over to the next pig-pen with some saddle-back breed piglets, and leaned over. Evie slyly pulled a handful of hay from a bale. Seizing the moment, she stuffed the hay down the back of his shirt and fell about giggling.

He turned and gave a wry smile. 'At least you've lightened up.' He pulled the hay out from his shirt.

She grabbed some more hay and playfully flicked the strands at his face. He grabbed her by the waist and pulled her in close to him. Gazing into her green eyes, he could see the joy. He felt sure that all her anxiety and fears about having a baby and starting a family would fade once they were married.

Evie removed some loose strands of hay from his hair as she stared back into his glacial blue eyes. Leaning forward, they instinctively rubbed their noses together before fully kissing. He discreetly reached over the rail, grabbed a handful of animal pellet feed from a trough, and sprinkled it over her head as they kissed.

She lunged backward with a gasp and wagged a pointing finger. 'That's sneaky – I'm going to get you for that.'

He burst with laughter, turned, and ran towards the barn exit with Evie in hot pursuit. He glanced around as he ran out of the barn to see if she was catching up, but suddenly slipped on an ice patch and tumbled into a heap on the ground.

5.40 p.m.

Alex struggled to cycle along Hills Road as icy rain blew against him in the dark. The iridescent red and white car lights to his right created a barrier, preventing him from crossing. Head down, cycling erratically, he was progressing better than the traffic. Tired, he was lost in his thoughts and wondered how the homeless woman was coping outside in this weather. Steering off the cycle path, he cut through the flow of moving vehicles, but lost concentration. Suddenly, there was a squeal of brakes and a blast from a car horn.

'Up yours as well!' he waved his hand at the driver.

The driver opened his side window. 'Have you got a death wish, mate! You need to get working lights for your bike and use the cycle crossing.' The driver shook his head in disbelief.

Alex arrived a few minutes later, out of breath. He secured his bicycle outside the A&E department of the Royal Cambridge Hospital. Two triage nurses standing inside the entrance each forced a smile simultaneously as he entered. 'Hello, doctor,' said one of the nurses. 'We're already very busy.'

He nodded as he went past them. His shoulders slumped on seeing how crowded it was as he walked up to the reception desk to a round-faced, exhausted-looking woman. 'Hi, Alice. Can you brief me on who's on duty tonight and what area I'm covering, please?'

Sandra, the duty department manager with very short tailored brown hair, walked up behind him and tapped him on the shoulder. 'Good evening, Doctor Hardson. You will be working with Doctor Patel tonight.'

He frowned in frustration. 'You know I don't get along with Patel. He's arrogant and demeaning.'

'Be polite, stay calm and focused,' said Sandra clasping her clipboard. 'I need you to assess patients under his supervision prior to treatment in C and D areas. He's worked a double shift, and he's tired – that's why I need you with him.'

Alex rubbed his hair. 'But that's the second time this week.'

'We're up against it – we're all really busy. Doctor Bianchi is also on duty, you get on well with her, and six nurses are supporting you. Justine is the senior staff nurse on duty.' Sandra leaned over the reception desk and pulled the computer screen around. 'Look, we already have ninety-six people waiting and another twenty-eight in the treatment areas. We have requested a further three agency nurses.' She walked away.

An elderly grey-haired man walked over. 'Do you know how long I've been waiting?' said the man. 'I'll tell you – three hours and forty minutes, exactly.' The man lifted his arm with his other hand. 'I want to know, why is it taking so long to sort out my broken wrist?'

'Please be patient,' said Alex. 'It shouldn't be much longer.'

A nurse with neatly tied back long black hair hurried over. 'I'll let you know when we can take you through,' she said, leading the patient gently back to his seat.

'Hello, Doctor Hardson, good to see you,' said SSN Justine with a Jamaican accent as she arrived. 'I hope you're feeling resilient for a long evening.'

'Thanks,' he grinned.

Justine pointed to the screen. 'If you can attend to these two patients first, please. One is a cyclist hit by a car.'

'That could've been me tonight.'

'What?'

'Nothing, I just had a near miss with a car as I cycled here.' He coughed. 'I guess I'd better get started.' He turned and went to his locker, slipped on his teal-blue coloured scrubs, grabbed his stethoscope, and headed for the treatment areas.

'Doctor, over here,' shouted the straight-faced consulting Doctor Patel through his face mask. 'This gentleman has been in trauma due to a broken pelvis from a car accident. Quickly assess the patient.'

Alex felt around the anaesthetised patient's pelvis as a nurse held a breathing mask over the patient's face. 'Are there any other complications?'

'You tell me,' said Doctor Patel.

'There's a break here near the spinal joint. There must be a lot of internal bleeding. There's also a second break I detect at the pubis bone.'

'What needs doing?'

'I'm going to apply a pelvic binder and prepare the patient for anterior pelvic surgery.' Alex looked up and caught Patel's nonchalant nod, relieved that he'd proven his credentials.

'Good.' Doctor Patel started to walk away and turned around. 'By the way. You're doing the surgery. I'll see you in the theatre in ten minutes.'

8.50 p.m.

Alex pulled a small monkey hand puppet with googly eyes and a large pink mouth from his scrubs top and started to distract his distressed three-year-old little girl patient.

'Is she going to be alright, doctor?' asked the little girl's mother holding her daughter's hand.

'Absolutely.' He animated the puppet's mouth as if it was speaking to the little girl. 'Who's this sweet princess?' he said in a silly voice, bringing a smile to the little girl. He pulled in an examination light with his other hand, close to the side of the little girl's head.

'She was bouncing on the bed like a trampoline,' said the mother. 'She bounced off and hit the metal seam on the top of the radiator. I shuddered at the sound of the thud.'

'We need to get an X-ray. It's a deep cut, but I don't think her skull is broken. I like your funny little nose,' he mimicked through the puppet. The girl giggled.

Alex cradled her on his forearm as he carried her to the radiography department and continued to mimic silly voices through the puppet. The little girl giggled, and the mother laughed as she walked alongside him.

The X-rays were completed a short time later, and he applied a medical superglue to close the girl's head wound.

'Goodbye, Mr Mickey,' said the little girl waving to Alex and his monkey puppet as her mother carried her out.

Alex felt revived by the little girl's smile. Another one of those moments that made his work fulfilling. He grinned cheerfully as he animated the monkey puppet's arm waving back. He turned to the nurse as she walked up beside him. 'Who's our next patient, please, nurse?'

Chapter 3

Wednesday, 1ˢᵗ January 2020 – New Year's Day, 00.14 a.m.

Alex was stitching up a deep wound across the eyebrow of a middle-aged man with a shaven head. 'That must've been quite a nasty fall in the street,' he said, fighting back the feeling of sickness from the strong smell of alcohol and cigarettes on the patient's breath. He turned his head away. 'Is there any family who can pick you up and take you home tonight?'

The cubicle room curtain was suddenly pulled back, 'Happy New Year, Alex – I mean, Doctor Hardson,' said Doctor Hamish Campbell, resting a hand on Alex's shoulder and pulling him back to one side. 'I've got a date now with a nurse called Natalie,' he whispered. 'I hope to be raising something to see in the New Year. I'll leave you with your patient.' He gave a cheeky wink before leaving.

Alex rolled his eyes and went back to his patient. 'The nurse will give you some pain relief before you leave. No more drinks tonight. You need to rest.'

'Will the scar make me look hard-core?'

Alex grinned. 'Let's just say it'll make your face look more aesthetically distinguished.'

'I'll settle for that.'

Alex applied a dressing over the wound, and the nurse escorted the patient back to the waiting area. 'Who's next?' he asked Justine while washing his hands. She pointed to an open cubicle. He walked in with her to find a woman in a silver sequin party dress with blood-matted blond hair and severe bruising to her face.

'This patient has a suspected broken arm and ribs,' said Justine. 'We're taking her for X-rays shortly. She also had some bleeding to the side of her head and facial injuries, as you can see.'

Alex smiled at the patient. 'You poor thing, don't worry, we'll get you fixed up. Your name?'

'Amelia.'

He examined her injuries. 'There's a lot of bruising around your eye and upper cheek. Your left eye has almost closed up with the swelling. Nurse, can we get another icepack on that please.' He examined the tissue around her other eye. Can you explain to me what happened?'

'Of course, Doctor… Hard…som,' said Amelia, trying to read his name badge.

He gave a wry smile. 'It's Doctor Hardson.'

'Your looks match your name badge – you're very handsome, if you don't mind me saying. *Hic.*' She gave a pressed-lip smile.

'And is that an American accent I detect?'

'It sure is… *Hic*. Well, I sort of got pretty trashed at this party – it's New Year's Eve after all.'

'I can tell you've had a few drinks.' He folded his arms and grinned.

'Hopefully, you'll be able to fix this… very single… American girl, *hic*. So, will I be alright by the morning?'

'Sorry, I don't perform miracles.'

'Doctor Handsome, are you single?'

'Can you explain how you got these injuries, Amelia?'

'Well… I was at this awesome party in a huge country house. I was dancing to some swag music with a friend at a coffee table.

I remember downing a cocktail, which was probably a mistake... *Hic.* And then, I must have lost my balance and slipped or something.'

Alex continued to examine the patient as he listened to her babble.

'I remember waking up on the floor between the fire hearth and the table. Everything was blurry. There were lots of people buzzing around me,' she giggled. '*Hic.* I don't know why I keep laughing because everything really hurts, *hic.*'

'It's probably due to a mix of drink and shock. But if you remain in the wheelchair, Amelia, the nurse, will get you along to the radiology department. We need to clarify what we are dealing with, and then we'll meet again later.'

02.29 a.m.

Alex walked into the treatment room, rubbing the tiredness from his eyes with the back of his hands.

'Miss Hassle's X-ray prints,' said a nurse, passing them to Alex.

He immediately clipped the images up onto a backlit screen and smiled at Amelia. 'As suspected, your left forearm ulna bone is broken,' he said, pointing to the fracture. 'It will need to be set immediately.' The nurse pushed a trolley full of equipment up alongside Amelia.

Amelia flinched as the nurse applied a new dressing to the side of her temple. 'I just can't believe I've been so stupid. And oh boy, the pain.'

He examined her face. 'The nurse will get you some pain relief shortly. The bruising around your eye and to the side of your head will be visible for at least a couple of weeks.'

She frowned, 'Oh great, that's all I need – I'm going to look hideous.'

'Let's get that arm set,' he said, yawning, rolling up his sleeves. The nurse assisted as he wrapped wet *plaster-of-paris* bandages around Amelia's forearm. Alex became aware of her staring at him through her one good eye – he glanced around and met her gaze. He could tell that she was sensitive, despite her bravado.

'I'm sorry about being cheeky – calling you Doctor Handsome.'

He gave her a lopsided grin as he smoothed the plaster. 'That's okay. Once this is set, you'll be ready to go home.' He started to wash his hands while explaining about her aftercare treatment, 'You will get an appointment sent to you to have the cast removed and have an arm brace fitted.'

She nodded after each instruction. The soreness made her frown.

He typed in the treatment on a pad. 'It was nice meeting you, and do take care of yourself, Miss Amelia Hassle. Not wishing to overstate the obvious, but please remember that drinking and dancing on coffee tables do not mix. The nurse will give you some pain relief tablets on the way out.'

Amelia forced a smile. The nurse wheeled her out of the room. Alex refilled his glass of water and gulped it back before walking into another cubicle to see his next patient.

04.00 a.m.

Alex was putting his stethoscope back inside his locker when a nurse arrived. 'Doctor Carter has been delayed,' she said, holding the door. 'Doctor Ellis has asked if you could please examine another patient.'

Alex gazed up through heavy eyes, 'Can you please answer two questions about the patient? One, have they been drinking? And two, if so, in your opinion, is their injury drink related?'

'Yes, and yes…'

'Look, nurse, with all due respect – I've completed my hours following the rules for an FY2 junior doctor. I shouldn't go over, it's against the *Trust* rules. I'm tired of these wounded people.'

'But Doctor Ellis asked nicely if you could just plug the gap.'

Alex looked down at the floor and shook his head. There was a pause. He drew a breath and sighed. 'Alright, until Doctor Carter arrives.'

05.00 a.m.

Alex finally hung up his stethoscope and grabbed his coat. He walked out past security and unlocked his bicycle. The icy cold night revived him as he cycled steadily along Hills Road, leaving clouds of chilled breath glowing visibly under the streetlamps behind him.

Alex reached home, locked away his bike, and entered the stairwell that led to his first-floor apartment on Hampton Mews. He stealthily unlocked the front door at the top of the stairs. Cookie appeared as he crept through, greeting him with a meow and weaving through his legs as he removed his cycle helmet, scarf, and coat. He peered through the open bedroom door where he could just see Evie fast asleep on her side with only her head above the duvet. He withdrew back into the hallway and stripped off in the bathroom. Immersing himself in a hot shower, he sighed as the water flowed over his shoulders and washed away his work. Tiredness started to hit him as he dried himself. Slipping on his bed shorts while being careful not to wake Evie, he sneaked quietly into their bed, pulled the feather-down duvet up around his neck, and stretched out his feet and toes. His eyelids shuttered as he breathed out his remaining strength, letting sleep finally embrace him.

9.30 a.m.

Robert made himself a coffee at his home in Richmond and walked through the house to his office. Making himself comfortable at his desk, he carefully sipped the froth off the top. Sophie padded barefoot up to him, wearing one of his work shirts as a nightie, just as he opened the screen on his laptop. Her tousled hair tumbled over her shoulders as she sat across his lap, draping her arms around his shoulders. She placed a slow, silent kiss on the side of his jaw. He turned and gave a loving return kiss, but his gaze drifted back to his computer screen. Her eyes narrowed, and she rearranged herself with her legs fully astride him, blocking his screen. She unbuttoned the front of her shirt sensually as she gazed directly into his eyes.

He held her magnetic gaze. The desire grew within him. He drew a breath. 'I suppose the work can wait.'

10.26 a.m.

Alex's eyes flickered open. 'Urh. Please...'

Evie walked into the bedroom singing, '*Wake up, it's a beautiful morning…* Boo. It's ten-thirty – time to shine.'

He grimaced, 'Do you have to sing?'

'Happy New Year, Boo.' She leaned over and kissed him on the cheek. 'I didn't hear you come to bed.'

'I do try to be considerate,' he said with an exhausted sigh.

'Freya phoned earlier. Is one o'clock still alright to meet up, or should we make it later?'

'One's fine.'

'I'll get you a cup of tea.' Evie started singing as she went into the kitchen. '*I don't recall a time… so get up*, BOO!'

Alex dragged himself out of bed and into the bathroom, splashing his face with cold water. He joined Evie in the kitchen, wearing only his boxer shorts. She handed him a cup of tea. A Lionel Richie song – *Three times a Lady,* played on the radio. Alex took hold of Evie and swayed her around within the confines of their small kitchen. 'I've woken up now.' He arched her over.

'Okay, we need to stop,' she giggled and pulled herself free. 'There's so much to do, and the morning has almost gone.'

He sat down on a kitchen stool next to the serving island. 'It was exhausting last night; the injured punters just kept coming – there was little rest.'

'You sort of knew it would be like that – being New Year's Eve.'

He gazed out of the window and took a sip of his tea. 'I had to work an extra hour because Carter was late.'

Evie put on her kitchen pinny. 'It's not surprising it's getting busier in A&E – Cambridge is a fast-expanding city. Anyway, what're you having for breakfast? Or should I say brunch?'

He stared at her bottom as she bent over to get a pan out of a lower cupboard. 'Is your body on or off the menu?'

Evie straightened up a little and wiggled her bottom in reply. 'I can be on the menu tonight, but not now.' She glanced around with a broad smile.

'I'll settle for some scrambled eggs on toast.'

'I would like to try and sort out the seating arrangements for the reception with Freya after lunch.'

'Does that mean I'm entertaining little Charlotte?'

'Why not? She adores you.'

'That suits me.'

He remembered making iced biscuits with his niece while childminding for Freya. He wondered if he would be disappointed if his first child was a boy.

Evie stirred the scrambled eggs. 'I had a glass of wine with Becky in town last night.'

'I guess the conversation was all about weddings?'

'Of course.' She loaded his toast with a scrambled egg from the pan. 'Becky and Oliver's wedding is bigger than I thought. She now has a live band in the evening, along with the DJ.'

'Please don't go getting any ideas.' He pulled his plate over.

'And a toastmaster!'

'Far too pompous,' he said, chewing on a large mouthful of egg and toast.

Evie tilted her head. 'Ours will certainly be far more modest.'

He now feared that all conversations with Evie would somehow involve marriage up till their nuptials. 'Changing the subject,' he said. 'I just need to do my annual pleasantries this morning of calling around the family. I need to speak to Dad before his flight back to Mallorca this afternoon.'

'He's only been back in London two days,' said Evie as she picked up Cookie and snuggled her up against her face.

'He was only here for some big company acquisition thing that's going on.'

'Was your Mum seeing in the New Year with friends last night?'

'I think so.' He pulled his phone over and pressed his grandmother's contact number. 'Hi, Granny, it's Alex.'

Evelyn Hardson was breathing heavily. 'Hello, Alex.'

'Happy New Year, Granny.'

'Yes, yes. The same to you.'

'You sound anxious.'

'Percy is being very difficult – he won't go back in his cage.'

Alex put her on speaker and listened with Evie to Percy squawking and his grandmother calling out in despair. He grinned, 'Why did you let Percy out anyway?'

'For the obvious reasons – he needs exercise. And I still need to get ready. Havers is picking me up in thirty minutes.'

'Going anywhere special?' he struggled to hear above the parakeet's squawking.

'The Savoy. I'm meeting up with two old friends who were also High Court Judges. We're having a New Year's Day reunion brunch.'

'I guess I ought to say goodbye and let you get on.'

'Percy, you're being really naughty now. You need to get back into your cage!'

Evie put her hand across her mouth. Alex held back his laughter. 'Has Percy learned any new words?'

'He actually welcomes my housekeeper by name.'

'That's quite cool.'

'At last! Percy has hopped back into his cage.' Evelyn sighed. 'Alex, I really must go.'

'Sure, Granny. I hope you have an enjoyable brunch.'

Evie left the kitchen giggling as Alex immediately phoned his father.

'Hello, son. It's good to hear from you.'

'Happy New Year, Dad.'

'Oh yes, and a Happy New Year to you and Evie, of course. How is she?'

'She's fine but a little tense, perhaps. We're meeting up with Freya for lunch to organise the reception seating plan.'

'Give my love to Freya and little Charlotte, won't you?'

'Of course, but how's Mum?' Alex asked. 'It must have been really irritating to leave her alone in Mallorca and come back to freezing London?'

'I think your mother understands the importance of this acquisition deal to me and the business.'

Alex gazed out of the window across the silvery rooftops, 'What's the weather like in London?'

'There's a frost outside as I look across the garden. Hey, son, I don't want to sound rude, but I do need to get on before my airport taxi comes.'

Alex noticed an uneasy tone in his father's voice but dismissed it. 'That's fine, Dad. I'm going to phone Mum.'

'Do pass on my love to Evie. I'm very proud of you – you're doing an admirable job.'

'Thanks, Dad,' he mentally noted that his father didn't ask him to pass on his love to his mother.

12.10 p.m.

Robert was preparing to leave for the airport after arranging for a taxi pickup. He entered the bedroom as Sophie adjusted her green geo-patterned dress. His eyes flicked from side to side as he subtly scanned the bedroom and the en-suite, making sure nothing was out of place. He walked past her as she checked her look in front of the wardrobe mirror.

'Sophie, are you sure you have everything?'

'Of course – don't worry. As your PA, it's my job to be thorough with all your personal needs and affairs. It's a good job. I went around the room and found the condom packet from last night under the bed. That should have been your responsibility to dispose of – I believe?'

'Point taken – you're thorough.'

'I must say that the decor to the entrance hall downstairs looks amazing,' she said as she applied some eyeliner. 'There's something different about this bedroom compared to when I was last here.'

'Annabelle wanted a wallpaper feature wall, and the curtains are new. The decorators completed it a couple of weeks ago.'

'Well, I never. I guess I had other things on my mind to notice.'

'She's always making changes, the home here and the villa in Mallorca. She likes to express her creativity in design – constantly refreshing everything, especially the garden. After all, she's a kept woman, so she needs an interest.'

'I'm not sure I would want to be a kept woman.' She tidied his hair with her fingers. 'I like my independence – having a career and earning.'

'Annabelle has a good eye for design. I wish I had time to take more interest.'

'It looks amazing. In a way, I feel a little sorry for her.'

'Why?' He frowned. 'You know that she will have half of everything when I leave her. I just need to get the timing right, damage limitation as to who will get what at the end of the settlement.'

'I know, I shouldn't have said anything.' Sophie sat on the bed and slipped her shoes on.

'I'm not trying to fool her or anybody. She knows what drives me – the chase of getting the acquisition deal, that's my passion. I happen to make a lot of money for my clients and myself.'

'You sure do, Robert. It's a beautiful home.' She pulled out her phone, checked an image of the bed presentation, and then adjusted the position of some cushions. 'Just as long as you keep sharing the other kind of passion with me.' She turned and winked. 'And you keep your promise.'

Robert moved over to her and took hold of her hand. 'Don't worry, it'll be soon. It's just the timing.'

'I'm counting on it. I've attended to all your personal needs. Just remember your own words – I make you "feel alive."' She reached out and gently held Robert's neck between her hands. There was a moment of silence as she fixed her gaze on him. 'As you promised last summer, remember?'

His eyes narrowed with conviction. 'And, when that day comes, it will cause a lot of turmoil and hurt.'

'I know.'

11.50 a.m.

Annabelle sat alone on a metal swivel kitchen stool, enjoying a cup of lemon tea at Villa Francina, the Hardson holiday home in Mallorca. It was situated to the north of the island, near Port de Pollensa, and was owned by Alex's grandmother, Lady Evelyn Hardson. Even for the time of year, the day was warming under the bright Mediterranean sun. Annabelle wore a white and pink floral blouse with white linen trousers as she reminisced on her earlier FaceTime conversation with her daughter Freya and her granddaughter Charlotte. Smiling to herself, she didn't feel alone as she remembered teasing Charlotte and making her laugh. Sipping her tea, she peered across the kitchen at a row of family photos on a shelf. Her gaze moved over to a picture of when Alex was 11, and Freya was 13. It reminded her of enjoyable summer school holidays shortly after Robert's mother Evelyn had purchased the villa. She missed children being around her and longed to capture those holiday moments again, where she could make a fuss of her granddaughter. She knew that Alex also yearned to have children. The future for her family was full of hope and expectation.

Annabelle finished her tea and combed back her long wavy ash-blond hair with her fingers before gathering it into a tidy knot behind her head and fixing it with a comb slide. There was an emptiness within her that needed to be filled. She remembered how alive and happy she used to feel as she returned to making up some flower arrangements for the different rooms. Cut flowers lay spread out on the work surface in front of her; classical music played in the background as she started to make up two more bouquets before switching her attention to the sun-kissed garden view through the kitchen window. Emilio Sanchez, the freelance gardener, had just come into view, walking across the garden to attend to some large shrubs. Her gaze followed his movements – she started to study his physique as he pruned but wondered why he was working today. He was wearing his usual style of work clothes – shorts, a sports vest, and his well-worn trainers. She observed how his short black hair and tanned bare shoulders glistened in the sun. Forcing herself to look away, she admired her cut-flower displays lined up in glass vases on the worktop. She made some adjustments to the flower compositions but couldn't resist another quick look at Emilio through the window. It was only 15°C outside, but virile sweat gleamed on his muscular arms. Her thoughts strayed from being a loyal married wife to being entwined in his embrace, running her fingers over his toned body. She closed her eyes and imagined how he would respond with tenderness and passion.

'Don't be stupid,' she quietly told herself. Emilio looked around and caught her attention through the window, waving and smiling. She awkwardly waved back.

She resumed her flower arranging while he continued gardening, but it wasn't long before her focus returned to him. She was relaxed watching him through the window with her head now resting in her palm as she passively held pruning scissors in her other hand.

The garden was full of colour from exotic flower beds and shrubs, a testimony to their planting scheme and the time and care that had been spent on it. The grounds also boasted dramatic large structural cactus plants, such as her treasured agave weberi, in pots. She had spent a small fortune in garden centres where Emilio helped her select the right plants to match her designs. They would strategically position the plants, sometimes changing her plans after listening to his advice. They had created dramatic landscaping within the villa grounds.

Annabelle got down from her stool and opened her kitchen window. '*Buen día*, Emilio,' she said cheerfully. 'You look very hot – would you like a cool drink?' Although she valued Emilio's friendship, she reminded herself that he was contracted by Robert, not only as a gardener but also as a driver and handyman when needed.

'That would be very nice, *Señora* Hardson. Iced lemon *por favor*.'

She produced two iced drinks, passing one through the open window to him as he walked up to collect it. 'It's New Year's Day – I was expecting you tomorrow.'

'*Muchas gracias*. I cannot do the gardening tomorrow. I need to be elsewhere.'

'I see. How is the hedge trimming progressing? Are you managing to achieve the flowing shape that we discussed – like a cloth blowing in the wind?'

'I fink so,' he struggled with his English translation. 'It will take time, but it's beginning to look aethakicly pleasing.'

She giggled. 'You mean aesthetically pleasing – very agreeable.'

'*Si*, that's what I mean. Like your smile, *Señora* Hardson.'

'You flatter me, Emilio. Anyhow, you do look uncomfortably hot.'

'I'm working hard pruning,' Emilio said as he wiped his brow with the back of his hand.

Annabelle smiled. 'You are, and it's a lovely day.' She liked his smile and sense of humour.

'*Si*. Earlier, I just finished washing the car.'

She giggled. 'Oh, you have been busy.' Her mobile phone was ringing. 'Excuse, por favor.' She rushed to pick up her phone, and Emilio returned to his work.

'Hello, darling,' said Annabelle. 'And a Happy New Year to you and Evie.'

'What are you up to?' Alex asked.

'I'm just making up some flower arrangements for the rooms, and then I'm planning to go into Puerto Pollensa to meet Teresa for lunch. Your father is arriving back later this afternoon. What about you? And how is Evie?'

'We're fine. We're meeting up with Freya for brunch – Evie needs to sort out the seating plans for the wedding. Boring, but I know it needs to be done.'

'If I were you, just leave them to it and entertain Charlotte.'

'That's my plan.'

Annabelle walked out from the kitchen onto the veranda, holding the phone to her ear, and sat in her rocking chair. 'How's the job going?

'Mum, it is what it is – exhausting, but I try to make a difference, and I love most of the team.'

'Very admirable.'

'Did you stay up last night and see the New Year celebrations?'

'Teresa came around and kept me company. We had a relaxing girlie night in – we made dinner, had some wine, and shared gossip. She brought around a lovely dessert dish, and then we watched the fireworks over the London Eye on TV.'

'Sounds very pleasant. I can't help but think that it has only been a week since we were together as a family at Christmas.'

'I know.' Annabelle listened to Alex update her on the wedding plans, and then she noticed Emilio outside the veranda. She watched him, his muscles bulging as he repositioned a flowerpot. Something stirred within her.

'Mum, are you listening?'

'Of course…'

'So, what do you think? You know Evie values your opinion.'

Annabelle glanced around. 'Uh… I'm not really sure.'

'That's unlike you. Just make a decision – purple or white placement cards?'

'Oh… I think definitely purple script writing on the white card. Can you let Evie know that I'll text her an idea for the church pew bouquets?' She knew that purple heart lisianthus mixed with white and pink baby's breath flowers would look beautiful.

Alex checked his watch. 'Mum, I need to go now.'

'When are we going to see you both again?'

'Soon, Mum. I promise. I'll call again next week.'

'Alright, darling. But before you go, let Evie know that I've ordered a lovely lilac-coloured dress with purple shoes and a matching hat to match the bridesmaids' dresses.'

They said their goodbyes to each other. Annabelle left the veranda, walked back into her kitchen, and picked up one of her flower arrangements. She adjusted the odd flower, but her eyes were drawn to the window and Emilio pruning beyond. Carrying the vase of flowers, she walked through the villa to her bedroom and placed it on the window that faced the drive. Standing in front of her full-length fitted wardrobe mirrors, she critiqued her image – twisting one way then the other. 'Not bad for a fifty-eight-year-old woman – even if I do say so myself.' She stepped closer and checked her face, 'Mm... Too many laughter lines – there's a contradiction.' Unbuttoning her blouse, she let it slide back off her shoulders and made sexy, fun poses in the mirror, pushing out her chest. She removed her white sandals and slid off her white slacks, kicking them away so she only wore her underwear. Removing the comb from her hair, she shook her hair loose over her shoulders. Admiring her physique, she continued to make model poses in front of the mirror, sliding one foot up the inside of her leg behind her knee whilst maintaining her balance on one foot.

She was pleased that her healthy lifestyle practising yoga was helping to maintain her hourglass figure with a thirty-inch waist. She closed her eyes and imagined how Robert would sometimes embrace her, pulling her leg onto his thigh, kissing her neck until she surrendered. They would slump back onto the bed and lose themselves in the moment. Only now did she realise that she craved passion; she was like a pressurised container, but not sure when or who would release the pressure. She reminded herself that the last time that happened was a year ago.

'I'm still a young woman at heart. I have needs,' she said quietly.

Her thoughts of Robert and how he would physically interact with her started to morph into Emilio. She imagined Emilio's torso pressed into her back as he reached around and gently caressed her breasts while her hands reached around his body, pulling him into her. She simulated the movements over her body before becoming aware of a low distant tapping noise coming from the kitchen. It was Emilio's voice. She grabbed her bathrobe and returned to the kitchen to find him leaning on the open window frame.

Emilio held out his glass. 'Much thirsty – may I have another iced drink *por favor*?'

'I'll make two,' she said, taking his glass. 'We both need to stay hydrated.'

Chapter 4

Saturday, 4th January 2020, 09.10 a.m.

Alex had changed into his sculling kit and was sat on a bench with folded arms in the club changing room. 'You're late!'

'Good morning,' said Hamish walking in. 'Apologies, mate. I was working in Emergency until two this morning.'

Hamish quickly changed. They walked through to the boat storeroom, grabbed their Wellington boots from a locker, and removed their double-scull boat from the storage rack. They carried it upside down through the main open doors out into the air and down the ramp, placing it into the river. Dullard followed them down and held the boat steady in the water.

Hamish stretched out his arms and did some squats as the morning sun rose above the river mist. 'You know I wouldn't let you down, right!'

'I was beginning to have my doubts,' said Alex, rolling his shoulders to warm up.

'I'm freezing. The sooner we get going, the better.' Hamish stepped into the bow of the boat and adjusted the oar rigging until it was balanced. 'At least it's forecast to be sunny all morning with only a light breeze.'

Alex passed one oar at a time to Hamish and then nestled onto the sliding seat himself at the stern of the boat before following the same routine, changing his footwear and setting the rigging as Dullard passed the other two oars to him. 'Cheers, Gordon.'

'Let's start with a good warm-up,' said Hamish, 'before we pass the start marker.'

Alex nodded, and Dullard gently pushed their boat out into the river current. A gaggle of mallard ducks parted as the bow of their boat approached. Their oars simultaneously brushed into the surface water ripples as they headed north up the river.

'Only a few weeks to go until the big day,' said Hamish.

'Don't remind me,' said Alex, momentarily glancing around. 'She's already counting down. Watch out; we're drifting too close to the bank.'

'A wee more pace on the portside.' They passed the starting marker, both pulling hard back hard on their oars, racing down the river, passing under blades of light that were breaking through the gaps in the clouds. They were breathing heavily a few minutes later as they went past the two-kilometre marker. They eased off the pace and guided their boat into the embankment.

Breathing heavily, they rested as the sun rose in the sky, bathing the surrounding countryside.

Hamish caught his breath. 'What have you been up to this week?'

'We sorted out the seating arrangements for our reception.'

'Sounds like fun.'

Alex tucked in his oars. 'What about you?'

'I went out with that nurse Natalie on New Year's Eve, remember?'

'Dare I ask how that went.'

'What a crackin' body.' Hamish rubbed his hands hard together. 'We went to a couple of bars. She came back to mine for a nightcap, and one thing led to another – hey presto! Yeah, we fashionably toasted in the New Year!'

'What are you like? Anyway, shall we focus? Let's see if we can up our pace for the return so we're ready for the race with the Gormleys.' They rowed over to the other side of the river.

'Before we go, are you sure you're ready for all this tying-the-knot stuff?'

Alex shook his head. 'Come again?'

'You're looking stressed lately, and I'm not convinced myself that you truly love her.'

Alex twisted his head around and locked his gaze. 'What?'

'I know you have this arrangement to have children, but you've never actually mentioned that you love her – not once.'

'You're only jealous because your love life isn't exactly a glowing example of success.'

'I know that I can be a bit shallow with the women in my life,' said Hamish, correcting the alignment of their boat.

'That's an understatement.'

'But this is about you and the woman you're going to marry.'

'State the obvious.'

'Tell me. Have you actually told her in no uncertain terms that you love her?'

'Do me a favour and leave it,' Alex said, breaking eye contact. Silence fell between them, with only the sound of water ripples gently lapping against the hull of their boat, and some squawking crows were breaking the silence of the peaceful air. 'Let's just focus on the sculling.' Alex got ready with his oars.

'Ready?' Hamish asked. 'Racing pace all the way back.'

They both gritted their teeth, letting out their frustrations as they heaved back on their oars and sprinted back to the boathouse.

Two startled swans suddenly launched into flight at the midway stage, and a riverboat manoeuvred to get out of their way.

They slowed their boat as they neared the boathouse and caught their breath.

'How comes you're only interested in one-night stands anyway?' Alex asked, breathing heavily as they drifted.

Hamish sniggered. 'I don't want to make it complicated – as you know.'

'That's because you haven't found the right woman.' He exhaled.

'And I suppose you have.'

Alex leaned around. 'You should respect the way I feel about her.'

'And this feeling you have, is it love?'

'I'm so pleased I asked Sanjay to be my best man. No offence.'

'No offence taken,' said Hamish. 'I just don't want to tell you "I told you so" in a year's time.'

Alex narrowed his gaze. 'What do you base your assumptions on?'

'It's just... every now and then, the dynamics between you and her, they just aren't quite right.'

'This is coming from a man who only sees women as a form of sexual conquest and makes banter about how many dates it takes to get them into bed?'

'That's a little unfair, my friend,' said Hamish chuckling. 'After all, quite a bit of money is spent on the journey of getting the woman into bed – all the fine dining. Both sides are a winner in the dating game.'

'I've heard it all from you before.' Alex turned back around and watched a moorhen sitting on its nest among the embankment reeds. 'You're so shallow. You just haven't found the right woman.'

'I know you, and I know Evie.' Hamish started to row towards the boathouse ramp as Alex's oars dragged lifelessly in the water. 'I'm just saying, I don't think the two of you are right as husband and wife – mark my words.'

'You can be a right tosser sometimes. You gotta give me more than your so-called view on relationship dynamics…'

'Well… Evie seems uncomfortable when you're having fun around children, like your niece.'

Dullard handed them their Wellington boots and held their boat steady as they stepped out. There was silence between them in the changing room.

'That was a good practice today,' said Hamish, combing back his thick dark hair as he followed Alex out into the car park. 'We're almost ready for the competition.'

Alex despondently opened his Volvo car door. 'See you at work and maybe next weekend.'

'Alex, mate, I apologise for my comments earlier.' Hamish walked up close to him. 'I know I sometimes say the wrong things, but we're good, right?' Alex turned and leaned on his car door. 'You're my best mate,' said Hamish, placing his hand on Alex's shoulder. 'I'm sorry. Please let me make amends and treat you to a drink?' There was a moment of silence.

'Okay. A quick drink on you.'

11.15 a.m.

Alex stepped inside the door of the 17th-century Ferryman Inn and walked through a rustic oak lounge up to the bar. Soft ballad music played in the background. 'Two pints of orange juice and lemonade, please,' he said to the barman. 'And he's paying,' he said, gesturing to Hamish.

They carried their drinks to a small table to the side of an open log fire burning in a red brick inglenook fireplace. Sat in carver chairs, they sipped their drinks and gazed around at the paintings of wildlife scenes of the river.'

Hamish raised his glass. 'Here's to a good training session this morning and that stunning winter light.'

'Even if the conversation was quite irritating at times.' Alex tapped his glass and took a gulp.

'Mm – sorry, mate.' Hamish sat back and cringed. 'I can't believe how many serious cooking-related burns I've had to deal with over the Christmas period.'

'Burns and loads of deep knife cuts.'

'Not to mention other Christmas-related injuries, like falling off ladders and steps while fetching decorations down.' Hamish chuckled.

A woman came and stood near them. 'Hello, Doctor Handsome,' she said, smiling awkwardly at Alex. 'I know that's not your real name, and I'm sorry to interrupt your conversation.'

Hamish smirked. 'Doctor Handsome…' he slowly repeated, and gazed at Alex.

'It's Doctor Hardson,' said Alex, staring at the woman.

'Aha, sorry. I couldn't remember exactly.'

'I sort of recognise you and the American accent' His eyes suddenly widened. 'Oh yes, I remember now. New Year's Eve, the dancing on a coffee table, woman.'

She tilted her head and grimaced. 'I was that drunken crazy woman.' She pulled back the left sleeve on her loose-fitting jumper and showed a pink plaster-of-paris cast on her forearm. 'And you fixed me up.'

'Sorry. I didn't mean it like that,' he said. 'Wasn't it, *Eighties* music that you were dancing to before falling off... Amelia?'

'So, you do remember me.' Her eyes fluttered with shyness. 'I only just recognised you out of your scrubs. I was so trashed that night. And oh boy, I was so sore when I woke up the next morning after those painkillers had worn off. Anyhow, I just wanted to apologise for my behaviour that evening and to thank you again.'

'There's nothing to apologise for. After all, that's my job. Your left eye was almost closed up with swelling, so it's really good the inflammation has almost gone.'

'I've had a pack of frozen peas on the side of my face a few times.'

Hamish raised himself up out of his seat and stretched out his hand. 'His real name is Alex. And I'm Hamish, by the way. It's nice to meet you.'

'There's another side to me that isn't so crazy,' said Amelia in a quiet, reflective tone, looking softly at Alex. 'And it's a bit of a coincidence seeing you here, so I just thought I would say hello.'

'Well, it was nice meeting you again.' He nodded.

I don't suppose that you two would like to join us at the table over there.' She pointed to the window table. Her two friends smiled back.

Alex blinked nervously. 'I'm so sorry, but we're just finishing these drinks.' He felt Hamish tightly squeezing his leg under the table.

'That's a real pity, but I understand,' she said, nodding while clasping her hands together before returning to her friends.

'What's the matter with you?' said Hamish. 'We should join them, even if it's only for a few minutes.'

'I told Evie that I would be back for lunch.'

'We only need to stay for a short chat.'

Alex returned a disapproving gaze. 'Whenever there are attractive women involved, you just can't help yourself.'

Hamish grinned. 'With all that swelling and bruising – she's hardly attractive.' He picked up both their drinks and stepped out from the table, giving repeated eye signals and nods in Amelia's direction. Alex rolled his eyes and followed Hamish over to where she was sitting with her friends.

'We would love to join you after all!' Hamish announced as he arrived and sat next to one of them. 'I'm Hamish. I'm also a doctor. But perhaps not as good looking as my friend here – doctor handsome.' Alex pulled up a chair.

Amelia smiled. 'These are my friends, Avani and Lucy.' Avani pushed back her rich long black hair. Her skin tone matched her milk chocolate-coloured eyes. She beamed at Alex. They shook hands. Lucy turned her grey eyes towards Hamish, her brunette bob hugging her wistful-looking face.

'Can I get any of you ladies a drink?' Hamish asked, gazing at the small diamond stud that went through Lucy's nose.

'We're fine,' said Amelia, as they sat with their hot cups of tea and coffee while nibbling at toasted tea cakes. Her long wavy blond hair draped over her shoulders like a silk shawl as she sipped her tea and listened attentively to Hamish drone on about sculling.

'It's great for the mind and body, you know,' he explained passionately. 'You just feel so invigorated after a really good sculling workout – it beats the gym any day. And what brings you ladies out here today?'

'We've just been for a girlie riverside walk,' said Amelia. 'Like you – it's good to get out in the air after our week at uni.'

Alex kept checking the time on his watch.

'And what do you do at uni?' Hamish asked.

Amelia placed her cup down. 'We're all Ph.D. students studying natural life sciences. I'm researching the decline of the North American bullfrogs and toads.' She turned her head to Avani.

'And I'm investigating possible preventative measures to help prevent coral reef degradation.'

Lucy leaned forward. 'And I'm researching the impact that the thinning ice shelf of Antarctica has on the penguin populations. A lot of my studies are at the Scott Polar Research Institute – kind of boring to most people, I guess.'

'Sounds fascinating.' Hamish raised his shoulders. 'You're all aiming to make a positive contribution to helping the planet and wildlife.'

'Exactly,' said Lucy.

'Do I detect an Aussie accent?'

'Hell, yeah…'

Alex unconsciously tapped his finger on the tabletop and angled his wrist around, checking the time again. He looked up and caught Amelia's gaze. They exchanged smiles.

'So, like Amelia,' said Lucy, 'we both wanted to get a Cambridge Ph.D. and get a taste of living in the UK.'

'Wow!' Hamish nodded enthusiastically. 'But surely, the only way to study the North American bullfrogs and toads is to be researching the subject in North America?'

'I'll need to make a research field trip back to the States for sure – it'll give me an excuse to meet up with my folks in Wisconsin, but I don't have to be there. I had the opportunity to be at Cambridge – well, heck, I took it.'

Alex leaned on the table. 'So, apart from the possible effect of climate change decreasing the number of toads and frogs, is there anything else causing their decline?'

Amelia nodded. 'The loss of their habitat due to urbanization, demand for land and possible conflict between the wildlife over existing territory.'

'May I?' said Alex, stretching over and gently taking hold of Amelia's hand as the rest of the group talked together. 'Can you squeeze my hand?' He checked her strength. Looking up, he caught her gaze. Her wide hazel-coloured eyes momentarily locked with his. He awkwardly forced himself to break eye contact. 'That seems to be healing nicely. You'll soon have the cast off and an arm brace fitted.' He glanced at his watch again. 'Sorry, but I really must go.' Smiling gingerly, Alex slowly raised out of his seat. 'It was great meeting you all.' He walked to the door, leaving Hamish comfortably chatting with the women.

Chapter 5

Saturday, 11th January 2020, 9.05 a.m.

Alex flickered one eye open with irritation as his hearing senses connected to his environment.

Evie turned up the radio to an *Eighties* hit as she sang, *'Get up, get up, get out your lazy bed, before I count to three, get to it, Boo. It's gone nine a.m.'*

'Ugh. I didn't leave work this morning until two-thirty,' he said, reaching out and turning off the radio.

'I've got a lot on today, Boo, as you know.' She stood by the side of their bed with folded arms. 'I wasn't sure if you were going rowing this morning.'

'It's sculling, not rowing.' He pulled himself up and swung his legs out of the bed. 'Rowing has one oar per person, and sculling has two.'

'Whatever. You're still pulling at an oar.'

He rolled his eyes. 'I've arranged to meet up with Hamish.' Cookie jumped up onto his lap.

'And I'm meeting up with Becky, my mum, your sister, and the bridesmaids at Bridal Harmony Studio.'

'A busy day then.'

'I just hope the wedding dress looks and feels okay this time.'

He handed Cookie over to Evie on his way to the bathroom. 'What time are you leaving later for Becky's hen night?'

'I'm being picked up at eight. Shall we aim to eat at around six?'

'Yeah, that's cool. I'm meeting up with Sanjay, Spud, and Hamish after you've left,' he said, raising his voice from the bathroom. 'We're going to have a few beers, and Sanjay wants to go over some of the arrangements for my *stag* do.'

10.20 a.m.

Alex was sitting in the stern of a double scull as he started to row away from the clubhouse. 'It's a lot busier out on the river today compared to last weekend.'

'Aye, because of the clear weather,' said Hamish, holding a comfortable eighteen strokes per minute. 'The rain isn't due in until we finish.'

They rested after they had completed two kilometres. Alex leaned around. 'I've been meaning to ask. What happened with you and that group of Ph.D. students after I left you at The Ferryman?'

'I got a date with that Lucy. We met up for a meal on Thursday.'

'That was quick work. Was it back to your place afterwards for a nightcap?'

'I misjudged her – she wasn't interested. But she has agreed to meet up again this Thursday.'

'You're losing your touch,' Alex said, grinning.

'She's just playing hard to get. Thursday will be the day – once I've loosened her up with a wee drink or two.'

'I bet it won't happen. She's worked you out… Besides, she probably has a boyfriend already.'

'Let's just concentrate on our sculling. Look up – heavy rain is coming in.'

10.55 a.m.

Annabelle let the door slam shut behind her as she stepped into the Bridal Harmony studio. 'I hope you don't mind – I changed my plans to be here.'

Evie was startled. 'Of course not. We're pleased to see you, Annabelle.' She greeted her with a kiss on the cheek and introduced her to her friend Becky. Evie's mother also cheek-kissed Annabelle.

'Shall we start with the bride?' asked the seamstress. 'Then we can try on your outfit, Mrs Hawkins. Are the bridesmaids joining us for a fitting today?'

'Yes,' said Evie, 'but they're running a little late.'

Annabelle hung up her long camel-coloured coat and moved out of the way of everybody. She tried to distract herself by admiring the studio colour scheme, decorated in peach and a silver paisley-style feature wall with white furnishings. She thought it could be improved with some vases of flowers.

Evie went into one of the four changing cubicles and then re-emerged after slipping into her wedding dress. The seamstress maintained a smile as she checked the fit. Annabelle stayed out of the way as the others gathered around Evie and admired her dress.

'You've lost weight,' said Mrs Hawkins. 'The dress is too loose around your middle.' The seamstress put a tape measure around Evie's waist.

Evie nodded anxiously. 'I've been losing weight unintentionally – I've gone up a belt notch on my jeans.'

'This often happens – it's perfectly natural,' the seamstress remarked. 'Don't worry; I can make some alterations – we still have time.' She walked around Evie and ran her finger along some of the seams, giving all aspects of the dress an inspection. She took some more measurements and fitted pins to Evie's new size.

Becky tilted her head. 'At this rate, you could be down to a size eight on the day.'

'You'll be looking underweight if you're not careful,' Mrs Hawkins said, shaking her head. 'You need to be eating more seasonal food, not your usual rabbit-style diet.'

Annabelle looked on with mild interest as she inspected some other wedding dresses on display, but her thinking was elsewhere.

'And another thing,' Mrs Hawkins said. 'You know what your father would say: "You need a good roast dinner inside you at least once a week at this time of year."'

'Your dress is lovely,' said Becky. 'After all the excitement this morning – you'll be fired up for my hen night later.'

Evie beamed. 'I'm really looking forward to it.'

Mrs Hawkins ran her hand down Evie's forearm. 'I love the floral lace design on the sleeves and on the train.'

'I'm so pleased you like it, Mum. I wasn't sure about having a floor-length train, but I'm really glad I changed my mind from my original choice.'

'Mind you; I really liked that other dress that you first tried.'

'Oh, Mum – I just looked like a meringue in that. This is really me, don't you think?'

Mrs Hawkins smiled and nodded. 'It's beautiful.'

Annabelle wondered when Freya would arrive. She continued to keep out of the way as she loosely observed all the dress fittings.

The seamstress continued to examine Evie's dress. 'Because you've lost a little weight, the tulle sleeves come a little lower on the back of your hands. I'll just pin the new position for alteration.'

The manager returned with a tea for Annabelle. The group sipped their drinks and watched as Evie twisted one way and then the other in the mirror.

Evie glanced across the room. 'What do you think, Annabelle?'

'You look exquisite, Evie,' she said, feeling caught off guard. 'Alex will be bowled over when he sees you coming down the aisle.'

The seamstress made more adjustments. 'Are you happy with the shape across your collarbone?'

'It's just what I wanted. What do you think, Becky?'

'You look gorgeous. I love the trumpet shape styling before it tapers down to the centre of your chest.'

Mrs. Hawkins tightened her lips. 'A little too much flesh on show for my taste, but I suppose that's the fashion these days.'

Annabelle continued skulking around, taking a mild interest in the bridal display costumes.

The shop door burst open. 'So sorry we're late,' said Freya, carrying her daughter in one arm and closing the door quickly behind her with the other. 'Charlotte wasn't feeling well this morning, but we're here now. She's looking forward to trying on her pretty bridesmaid dress, aren't you, sweetie?' Charlotte nodded, then rested her head shyly back onto her mother's shoulder.

'Don't worry,' said Evie. 'We've just been having an easy morning chatting – they've been watching me try on my dress.'

Just then, the studio door burst open again. 'Hi – we're here at last,' Zahida said, clutching her daughter Zareen to her side. 'You wouldn't believe it – everything has gone wrong this morning.'

'It's fine – you can chill,' said Becky.

Zahida exchanged a warm smile with Freya as Charlotte wriggled to get down from her arms. 'Zareen darling, you'll be trying on your dress soon,' Zahida said.

Charlotte suddenly ran across the room and was swooped up by Annabelle.

Freya spun around. 'Oh, hello, Mum. I didn't know you were coming along.'

'I decided I couldn't miss seeing Evie and having a hug with my beautiful granddaughter.' She pulled Charlotte in close and gave her a kiss.

Freya placed her hand on her mother's arm. 'You look tired, Mum. Is everything alright?'

Annabelle forced a smile. 'It's just the cold weather.'

Evie's sixteen-year-old cousin, Katrina, the chief bridesmaid, arrived with a school friend and stole everyone's attention. Mrs Hawkins pointed Katrina to the dressing room where her dress was hanging.

Evie's dress was finally all pinned, and she slowly twirled, showing off the shape of her dress. The women beamed with approval. Becky helped Evie choose a floral hair comb for her veil. Zareen and Charlotte got changed into their purple-coloured silk dresses with help from their mothers. Each dress was adorned with a large bow at the back. The children giggled as they hopped from one foot to the other and spun around in front of a large dressing mirror. Katrina emerged wearing a long pleated maxi dress with a lace bodice and long sleeves made in the same purple material. She held out her hands to Zareen and Charlotte. They took hold of either side of her and did a practice walk around the room. The ladies clapped, and the bridesmaids took a bow. The mothers showed them how to curtsy, and they practised with each other. The atmosphere in the studio was full of joy and laughter. Annabelle pensively stood back and watched the bridesmaids perform.

'I feel like royalty,' Katrina joked. 'Does anyone know of a handsome prince who is available?'

Mrs Hawkins changed into her purple knee-length shift dress and a cream jacket with a fur collar for a final fitting.

Annabelle reminisced as she watched the seamstress make some alterations to Mrs Hawkins's outfit. Memories flooded back of when she was at a bridal boutique five years earlier when Freya was being fitted for her wedding dress.

Mrs Hawkins playfully showed off in front of the other women, teasing the hem of her dress up her thigh, seeing if it suited her above the knee. She searched her daughter's face for approval, but Evie raised a disapproving eyebrow and shook her head. Her mother released her hem and then tried on her cream-coloured wide-brimmed hat with a purple bow.

'Mum, you look great – you'll be upstaging me on my day.'

Mrs Hawkins started to fool around as if she was on a photo shoot, striking exaggerated model poses. Evie placed her hand over her eyes with embarrassment. The rest of the party laughed and giggled except Annabelle; she remained pensive.

Freya bounced Charlotte on her forearm, laughing at Mrs Hawkins. Then, she glanced around at her mother and walked over. 'Mum, are you sure you're fine?'

Annabelle wiped the corner of her eye with her finger. 'I just had to see you and Charlotte.'

Freya scanned the group to see if anyone was watching. 'Mum, what on earth is the matter?' She placed Charlotte down and put an arm around her mother.

Annabelle searched her handbag and grabbed a tissue. 'I'm just being silly.' She couldn't make eye contact with Freya and dabbed her cheeks.

'It's alright, Mum,' Freya whispered.

'This whole occasion reminds me of when I was with you at your dress fitting.'

Freya's eyes searched her mother's face. 'No one has noticed.'

'I'll be alright now.' She swallowed the words that were forming on her lips that she so desperately wanted to share, reminding herself that this wasn't the time or place. She pulled out her compact mirror from her bag, applied some lipstick, and fingered down some loose strands of hair.

Mrs Hawkins wound down her model posing routine. Freya examined her mother's face again as they joined the others.

'Is that the time?' Annabelle said suddenly. She walked over to the seamstress. 'Can I please have a spare piece of the purple material for colour matching.' She took the material and kissed

Freya on the cheek. 'I really must go.' She promptly left the studio without saying goodbye to the others.

7.56 p.m.

Alex glanced up at the clock on the wall as he washed up. 'Leave the rest of the drying up. Your taxi will be here soon.'

Evie folded her tea towel and placed it over the oven handle. 'I shouldn't be any later than midnight.' She headed to the front door, slipped on her high heel shoes, grabbed her coat, and checked her handbag for all the essentials.

A car horn beeped outside on the street. 'It sounds like your chariot has arrived,' he said.

'See you later, Boo. Have a nice evening.' She closed the door behind her and went down the stairwell.

He finished off the washing and drying up. Slipping on his jacket and hat, he also left their flat. Light rain fell as he navigated his way through the streets as if on autopilot. He thought about Hamish's remarks about his relationship with Evie. 'What is love anyway,' he said quietly. He knew they were good together, like a well-oiled machine, even if he couldn't bring himself to say the words, I love you. They shared everything and got on well – all apart from when she was in a bad mood and exercising her temper. Fury would be a mild word to describe how she reacted, but that was rare. He was confident that he would grow into loving her over time once they had started a family.

Alex's phoned pinged, and he read the text message. *We're at the bar.* A security man opened the entrance door for him at The Boatman's Rest bar. Thumping music pulsed through the bar area as he squeezed his way through the crowd to his friends.

Sanjay had a grin on his v-shaped face. 'Welcome.' He passed over a beer.

'Great. Where's Hamish?' Alex asked.

'He's running a little late.'

'Woman problems, I suspect,' Spud said through his bushy copper-coloured beard.

'You know what he's like,' said Sanjay.

'As my best man, how are my *stag* arrangements going? Alex asked.

'All sorted.' Sanjay ran his fingers through his slick wavy black hair. 'The paintball is booked up for the day, and dinner with axe throwing in the evening.'

'I knew you would organise it well.' Alex glanced up and admired the old university rowing boat hulls that lined the high ceiling of the converted old maltings building. 'Do you remember when we first came here after we formed up as a quad sculling crew?'

'Of course,' said Sanjay. 'And the four of us have managed to stay friends, despite Hamish being such a pain at times.'

'Speak of the devil,' said Spud as Hamish eased through the crowd to them. 'What took you so long?'

'I had some issues to sort out.' He rubbed Spud's cropped head of hair.

Alex tilted his head. 'The issues wouldn't happen to be a petit brunette trainee nurse by the name of Jessica?'

'Leave the poor man alone,' interjected Sanjay. He winked at the others whilst passing a beer from the bar to Hamish.

'Very funny,' said Hamish. The others chuckled. 'Anyhow, I'm here now and want to forget about working in A&E and girlfriends for one night.'

Alex smirked. 'Are Natalie and Jessica both history – now that we've met Lucy?'

'Who's Lucy?' Sanjay and Spud asked simultaneously.

'Hamish will explain later,' Alex grinned. 'Now that the four of us are here, time, I think, for a Scullerteers toast.' The four of them raised their glasses in unison. 'Here's to us, the Scullerteers.'

'All for one and one for all!' They chanted loudly in chorus and tapped their glasses together, spilling some beer before swigging the rest down until their glasses were empty.

'Line up four more, Sanjay,' said Hamish cheerfully.

'Hamish can then tell us all about the Jess and Lucy situation,' Spud said.

Hamish rubbed his dark facial hair. 'Not tonight. Let's talk sculling instead.'

'What a disaster that first practice session was,' Spud said. 'All the frustration of trying to synchronise our oars.'

Sanjay nodded. 'It was a complete mess.'

'Spud, you were useless,' said Hamish. 'You just couldn't get into the rhythm – getting your port side mixed up with the starboard.'

Spud frowned. 'I found it all very confusing.'

Sanjay passed around new full glasses of beer. 'It's a good job we all stuck at it. We need to win the Club M-four Challenge Cup, but we have to beat the Water-Cutters team in the semi-final next weekend.'

Alex nodded. 'We need to get in more practice.'

Sanjay held up his beer. 'If we beat them and go on to win the final, that'll be our wedding present to you.'

'That'll be the best present ever,' said Alex grinning.

'Perhaps we should arrange a practice session for Saturday fifteenth of Feb as well,' Hamish said, gazing at Alex. 'That'll give you an excuse not to turn up at your wedding.'

'Leave it out, Hamish,' said Spud interrupting. 'We're all out for a good time. Look around. We're surrounded by lots of great-looking totties!'

Sanjay rubbed the side of his face. 'I'm happily married.'

'No harm in looking at the eye candy even if you're in a relationship.' Spud grinned. 'As long as you don't touch.'

'Chance will be a fine thing for you, Spud, with that ginger beard of yours.'

'I'll have you know the women go for ginger these days. Just look at Prince Harry. Or is it just Harry? Anyway, ginger is fashionable.'

'Changing the topic,' said Hamish frowning. 'Are you sure about getting married?'

Alex narrowed his eyes. 'What do you mean?' The four of them stood huddled together as other drinkers swelled around them.

'I mean, to be direct. Are you sure about Evie?'

'We wouldn't be getting married if we weren't sure.'

'You say that, but marriage can bring a whole set of commitments and problems.'

'I'll be direct. You're talking garbage.'

Sanjay cocked an eyebrow. 'Let's talk about tactics to beat the Water-Cutters crew.'

Hamish raised his shoulders. 'Alex mate, you want the whole family thing – kids, right? But she doesn't.'

Alex's eyes flicked side to side at Sanjay and Spud. 'Have you all been talking about Evie and me?'

'Don't get us involved,' said Sanjay.

Spud frowned. 'We've noticed that she seems uncomfortable whenever you start talking about starting a family.'

Alex angled his head around at Spud. 'Evie and I have an agreement.'

'Ha.' Hamish shook his head. 'This so-called bloody agreement. What happened to wanting to start a family mutually through love as the foundation of your marriage?'

'And what're your views, Sanjay?' Alex asked. 'Don't sit on the sideline; give it to me straight.'

'Since you ask. I also have my doubts, ever since that time she ignored my girls when they went over to her.'

Alex shook his head. 'She's just a bit shy with children.'

Hamish rubbed the back of his head. 'She wants to get married for all the wrong reasons, and you're just blind to it.'

Alex took a gulp of his beer. 'I thought this was meant to be a fun night out. It's anything but.'

'It's just beer talk,' Spud said.

Hamish exhaled and wagged his finger 'I know I've had a few beers. But, all I'm saying is, you need to be really sure that Evie wants the same as you before getting married.'

Alex narrowed his gaze and drew a breath. 'I'm getting married in five weeks' time, and I don't need to hear this crap.' He nudged Hamish to one side and made his way through the crowd and out of the bar.

Cold rain fell from a black dismal night sky, reflecting how Alex felt inside as he made his way home. He was confident in his agreement with Evie and dismissed their doubts. He headed along Regent Street, but then he spotted the rough sleeper that he'd helped before, sitting in a shop doorway. He crossed over to the other side of the road.

'Hi, Rose. Do you remember me – Alex?' He crouched in front of her.

She raised her head from her slumped position. 'Of course. The man with the friendly eyes just before Christmas.'

He stroked Gertie's head. 'Can I get you and Gertie anything to eat or drink from the express shop?'

8.25 p.m.

Amelia, with her friend, Avani, went past the security bouncer as he held open the door to The Juicy Duck bar.

Her friend Becky started whooping when she spotted them and trotted over in her heels. Her sparkling tiara and bright pink-fitted sequined dress sparkled from the lights above the bar area. 'I'm so pleased you could make it,' she said, greeting Amelia with a hug and a kiss.

'Becks, you look fabulous!'

Becky wiggled her shoulders in a sultry manner and pointed to her *"Bride-to-be"* white sash. 'Only two weeks to go.'

'I can't believe how quickly it's coming around,' said Amelia, before she introduced Avani.

Becky took hold of Amelia's hand. 'Come on! I need to introduce you both to a few of my other lovely friends.' Becky trotted across the floor towards the bar. 'And these are my other good friends – Chloe and Evie. If I can leave you ladies to acquaint yourselves, I'll be back shortly.'

The group squeezed in close up to one side of the bar area. The barman walked over and took Amelia and Avani's drinks order.

'What happened to the side of your face and your arm?' Evie asked.

Amelia grinned. 'I had a mishap at a New Year's Eve party. Too much booze. I was dancing on a coffee table and lost my balance.'

'And you fell onto the floor,' Evie said.

She nodded. 'It could've been worse. The whole side of my face was really puffed out in a rainbow of colours.' The women frowned. Amelia rocked her head. 'Hey-ho – I consider myself lucky.'

'What brings you to England?' Evie asked.

'I came over to study for a Ph.D. here at Cambridge.' Amelia dreaded all the questioning and hoped Avani would interject.

'And how do you know Becky?'

'We met at Homerton College last September. We got to talking in the Buttery while waiting in the queue. I commented on how delicious all the cakes looked, and we joked about putting on calories just by staring at them. We sort of struck up a conversation and sat down together – we've been friends ever since.'

'Becky was with us this morning at my wedding dress fitting,' Evie said. 'Otherwise, we haven't seen each other in a while.'

'Hey, you're getting married as well – that's awesome.'

Evie enthusiastically continued to explain all her wedding and reception arrangements until all of Becky's friends had arrived.

'Down your drinks, ladies,' Becky announced. 'We're going.'

Amelia tucked in with the rest of Becky's party as the twelve of them headed out of the bar and further along the street until they reached the Evolution bar. Most of the women in the group were sensibly dressed, wearing coats in the freezing night air. Others jiggled from one foot to the other, trying to keep warm as they waited together outside. Becky went up to the front of the queue and spoke to one of the door minders, showing him a piece of paper.

Amelia discreetly pointed out to Avani and Evie a couple of women in stretch fabric dresses who shuffled past them, shaking with the cold. 'They're clearly not dressed appropriately wearing those tight strappy numbers.'

'The dresses just about cover their decency,' Avani said, tucking her hands into her coat pockets.

Evie folded her arms tightly. 'They must be freezing.'

Amelia tilted her head. 'If my dad saw me wearing that, he'd say, "Where's the rest of your outfit, girl?"' She mimicked her dad's voice. The women giggled.

'Neither of them is wearing a bra either,' Avani said.

'They just want to get all the guys' attention,' said Amelia, pulling up the collar of her strawberry-coloured coat. 'At least we've got self-respect and like to keep something for the imagination.' Amelia grinned. 'They're just advertising – hey guys, we're up for some fornication! Whoops, I said that out too loud.' The women in the group around Amelia giggled.

'Look!' Avani said. 'I think Becky has sorted it out – she's waving for us to come through.'

The group of women quickly moved forward and entered the nightclub bar. A waitress showed them through the busy bar area to a reserved high table which was at one end of the room. Disco music was pumping through the air from around the side of the main bar, where there was a dance floor. Amelia slipped off her coat and draped it on a stool as she stood with Avani and Evie on either side of her. Coloured lights pulsed through the disco entrance, and she could see groups of women dancing together.

'Girls, let's hit the dance floor to warm up while the waitress gets our drinks,' said Becky, pulling on her friends' arms.

'I'll just stand this one out,' said Amelia. 'My broken rib and arm won't let me do any sort of dancing.'

'I understand.' Becky trotted off towards the dance floor with the other women.

Evie walked back over and stood next to Amelia. 'I'll stay with you and keep you company – it's no fun being on your own. After all, it's not as if some handsome bloke is likely to come over and try chatting you up with your face looking like that.' She winked.

'Or some gorgeous woman.'

'Oh, I'm really sorry – I shouldn't have assumed that you were straight.'

'It's okay. I'm just messing with you.'

'Touché.'

Amelia smiled. 'It's really good to be out tonight and meet all you folk.'

'Tell me a little bit more about yourself?'

'I don't want to bore you.'

'Look, any friend of Becky's is a friend of mine. I'm doing dinner next Saturday evening. Come over if you've nothing arranged. Becky and her fiancé will also be there.'

Amelia brushed her hair over her shoulder. 'Are you sure?'

'Of course.'

Amelia nodded. 'Awesome. I'd love to.'

'Great. Seven o'clock?' Evie texted her address.

The area around their table slowly filled until it was almost heaving with people when two waitresses brought over two trays loaded with drinks for the group.

Two men hovered near Amelia and Evie. 'So, what happened to your face, darling?' asked one of them.

'Sorry, ignore my grossly crass friend,' said his mate, leaning over him. Amelia glanced at Evie and rolled her eyes. The two men started to introduce themselves.

'Right then,' said Becky as she returned from the dance floor, pushing in between the two men and grinning at Amelia and Evie. 'Pop these in your drinks, ladies,' she said, handing each of them a penis-shaped straw. 'This is where the fun really starts!' The women laughed out loud, and the two men uncomfortably drifted away.

Chapter 6

Saturday, 18th January 2020, 9.06 a.m.

Alex checked the time on his watch as he waited in his wellies at the water's edge. 'Where has that Scotsman got to?' He glanced over at the Water-Cutters crew as they made some final adjustments to their boat before the race.

'You sound very agitated,' said Spud, steadying their white-coloured quad boat in the slow river current as drizzle fell through the murky light. 'He'll be here soon.'

'He's always late.' Feeling exhausted from long hours at work and not sleeping well, he wondered if his family also had doubts about him marrying Evie.

'I hope you're not troubled because he was a bit belligerent last weekend?' Sanjay asked, holding the other end of the boat steady. 'We need to be focused if we're to win this race.'

'It doesn't sound as if you two have settled your differences.' Spud said, glancing around.

'Speak of the devil, and he's sure to appear,' said Sanjay. Hamish walked down the ramp from the boathouse.

'The devil says good morning to you all,' Hamish retorted. He high-fived Sanjay and Spud.

Alex ignored the pleasantries. 'Let's get going – we've wasted enough time, and we have a race to win.'

Dullard walked down the ramp and took over holding the boat steady as Sanjay and Spud climbed in at number two and three positions.

I apologise for what I said about you and Evie,' said Hamish, resting a hand on Alex's shoulder. 'I spoke out of turn last Saturday.'

'Just keep your negative thoughts to yourself in the future.'

Hamish held out his hand. 'I'm sorry.'

Alex hesitated for a moment before taking his grip. 'I accept your apology.'

The earlier drizzle had now turned to light rain as the Scullerteers and the Water-Cutters crews lined up side by side at the race start marker. The club marshal sounded an airhorn, and both teams heaved back hard on their oars.

The two teams were almost level at the halfway stage – with the Scullerteers slightly ahead, sculling with grit and determination.

'Let's up the pace to forty,' Alex shouted from the stern, as the sound of their oar blades slicing into the river echoed back on the heavy shrouded air. Their quad boat cut through the dreary grey conditions as they held their forty strokes per minute.

They were only three hundred metres from the finish marker when the Water-Cutters appeared to go up another gear. 'C'mon!' Spud shouted.

Another airhorn sounded as the Water-Cutters crossed the finish line, just ahead of the Scullerteers.

'And stop!' Hamish shouted. They hunched over, gasping for breath as they drifted on the river in the driving rain. 'They beat us again.'

Sanjay slapped the decking. 'We almost had them.'

Spud slumped forward. 'What happened to you three? I was doing all the heavy work back there.'

Exhausted, Alex twisted around and glanced back at his friends. 'Another lost opportunity, but I need to leave when we get back.'

Sanjay threw his arms into the air. 'Darting off is no way to finish the day.'

'Sorry, but I have to go.'

'What's so important?' Hamish asked.

'We have an appointment.'

'Oh, we… have an appointment?' Spud teased.

'What ever happened to – all for one and one for all?' Sanjay asked.

'Evie has arranged for us to have some more dancing practice…'

'Haven't you two got your wedding waltz sorted out yet,' Spud asked.

'That's why we need to practice.'

Hamish leaned forward. 'Perhaps you should consider not bothering with the dance if it's a problem.'

Alex glanced over at the Water-Cutters crew as they cheered and punched the air. 'Let's take it steady going back.' He pulled on his left oar to start pulling their boat around.

'Hang on!' Spud shouted, leaning around. 'I'm adjusting my rigging.'

Alex abruptly swung his torso around as he pushed on his right oar and unbalanced the boat. 'I thought you had…' The boat suddenly rolled over and plunged them all under the water.

Sanjay gasped as he surfaced. 'What the hell!'

Alex gulped air as he broke clear of the water. 'It's bloody freezing.'

Hamish wheezed in the air as he emerged. 'You idiots, I can't believe it… We've never capsized before.'

'Are you guys alright?' shouted the race marshal.

Snorting and coughing, the four of them managed to stand up in the shallow water near the embankment with their shoulders clear of the surface.

The Water-Cutters rowed back past them. 'You should rename yourselves – the scuttling-teers,' shouted one of the crew as they chuckled.

Alex and his friends clambered through the reeds up onto the riverbank, shivering and squabbling. All four stood in a row with their arms tightly folded and puffing as they stared at their overturned boat hull.

'Bollocks.'

'You frigging idiots.'

'What now?'

They finally got themselves organised, waded back into the river, and up-righted their boat. Shivering with cold, they gathered their oars and climbed back aboard. They sculled the two kilometres back to the boathouse, trying to build up their body warmth.

Arriving back exhausted, some club members sniggered as they helped them to get their boat out of the river and into the boathouse. The four trudged towards the changing room and the much-needed hot showers.

11.10 a.m.

Alex pulled his car up sharp in the dance studio parking bay next to Evie's car. 'Sorry I'm late,' he said as he got out.

'We've paid for this in advance,' she said, glaring daggers at him. 'And we've already lost ten minutes. You know this is important to me!' She turned and walked into the building.

'But…' He exhaled and followed her inside.

The two of them slipped off their coats in the dressing room and changed their shoes with no exchange of words. They entered a brightly illuminated dance studio with smooth wooden flooring and walked over to the dance instructor, Kofi, who was standing in the middle of the room, dressed smartly in black.

'Good morning,' Kofi greeted them with a broad smile. 'We'll start with a practice warm-up by doing some natural turns, then a change step, and then reverse turns.' Kofi walked over to a table in the corner where he had a laptop connected to speakers. 'If you could get into your hold position.' They could see their posture in the full-length wall mirrors as they got ready.

Evie wriggled and whispered, 'What's wrong with you this morning?' Frowning, she tried to pull his limp arms up into place.

Kofi walked back over, wearing his broad smile. 'Both of you need to get your postures correct. Remember – back, shoulders, and arms in the right frame. You both just need to come in together a little more with your right sides touching.' Kofi gently pushed their bodies together and corrected their arm positions and postures until he was satisfied.

Evie tried to smile.

'Cheer up, both of you,' Kofi joked. 'You're meant to be getting married in four weeks' time.' He gently raised Alex's head by lifting his jaw with the back of his hand. 'Extend your neck. That's it, much better.'

'I'm just a little tired.' Alex forced a smile.

Kofi withdrew out of the way. 'You'll both be wonderful in front of everybody once we've ironed out a few creases in your routine.' He walked back over to his laptop to change the music and looked up. 'No, no, no!' Kofi paced back over to the couple. 'Your bodies are parting again; come in together and hold the frame position. You need to always have your sides touching and lower your shoulders more so they're parallel with the floor.'

'There's so much detail to remember,' said Alex.

'Evie, you're looking elegant, but Alex, you're looking a little saggy in places.' Kofi pursed his lips. 'May I demonstrate with Evie?'

'Sure.' Alex stepped back as Kofi took his place, demonstrating the hold posture.

Kofi turned back towards Alex. 'Do you see? You've got to feel the energy that you're about to release. It's important that you feel good and you wear a smile.'

'I think I get it now.'

'So, the natural turns, then a change step. You must hold posture across the shoulders and remember your rise and fall as you move through the steps.' Kofi waltzed Evie along the studio as Alex looked on. 'So, if you both come together again, ready for a warm-up.'

Evie held her posture with a smile as she and Alex danced through the natural turn steps and then the change step, then the reverse step going anticlockwise. Alex kept looking down at his feet as Kofi called out instructions.

'Okay! A good warm-up,' said Kofi enthusiastically. 'Shall we try with your selected waltz music and start over here, remembering your steps going in and coming out of the corners.'

'You're not yourself this morning, Boo,' whispered Evie. She gazed directly into his eyes. 'You didn't ask me how my final dress fitting went.' They took up their start position and waited on Kofi to count them in.

Alex glanced around before his eyes came back and met hers. 'You didn't ask me how my morning went either. And as for this damn dance.' He glanced towards Kofi. She gazed at Alex with disbelief.

'I'll count you in,' Kofi called out. 'One, two, three.'

The two of them waltzed along into the first corner and turned. Alex stumbled as he came out of the corner.

'Stop!' Kofi smiled. 'We got our feet a little muddled, but not to worry – I'll count you in again.'

Alex's hands dropped to his sides as he let go of his hold and stepped back, shaking his head. 'Don't bother – I'm not up for this today.' He marched back to the dressing room.

6.55 p.m.

Amelia got out of her taxi with wine and flowers when she arrived at Hampton Mews. She climbed the stairwell to Evie's flat wearing a smile and pressed the doorbell.

'Come in, Amelia,' said Becky,' and meet everyone.' She took her coat and brought her through.

Amelia stood still at the entrance to the dining room, looking around at the other guests and feeling that her button-fronted raspberry-coloured cardigan and light-blue denim skirt were a good choice for the evening. Not knowing what to do, she was grateful when Evie arrived from the kitchen, came up to her, and kissed her on the cheek.

'My fiancé can't be with us tonight, but let me introduce you to Jenny – wedding planner extraordinaire, for Becky and Oliver's wedding next week, and also for my wedding in four weeks' time.' Jenny stood up and stretched out her hand. 'And this is Oliver.'

'Hi, Amelia. Pleased to finally meet you,' said Oliver. 'Becky has spoken quite a bit about you. I'm the only man here tonight.'

'Admit it, Oliver darling,' said Becky grinning. 'You love it when you're surrounded by women.'

'Okay, I admit it, my love.' Smiling, he stretched out his glass for a refill as Jenny topped it up.

'I must tell you about our wedding rehearsal at the church.' Becky beamed. 'It was two hours.'

'How did your rumba dance practice go afterwards?' Evie asked.

'It isn't quite nailed yet.' Becky glared across the table at Oliver. 'I wonder why.'

'That makes two of us who are having problems with our wedding dance!' Evie took a breath.

Jenny sat upright. 'It's just as well that I'm taking care of everything else with both your wedding arrangements.'

'Something smells good,' said Amelia.

'It's my take on vegetable cottage pie. I better get back and check.'

Amelia gazed around at the warm primrose and grey colour scheme, enhanced by softly flickering tealight candles dotted around. Evie gestured to Amelia to follow her into the kitchen. She breathed in the enticing smell of the cooking and admired the clinical décor of stainless-steel work surfaces.

'I'm so pleased you could make it,' said Evie, checking on her cooking. 'You look amazing.'

'I'm just pleased that all my facial bruising has now gone.'

'When's the plaster cast coming off?'

'Next week. I can then at least shower properly.'

'Oh, you haven't got a drink. Can you pour Amelia a drink, please, Jenny?'

Amelia returned to the dining room, and Jenny held up a red and a white bottle of wine. She pointed to the white.

'Have you got someone in tow, Amelia?' Jenny asked as she took a large sip of wine.

'Only an ex-boyfriend back in the States,' said Becky. 'We won't go there.'

Amelia rubbed the side of her forehead. She wasn't sure if she should explain, but it came out anyway. 'The ex is called Jake. I walked away from a difficult relationship last summer.'

'They were engaged and planning to get married,' said Becky. 'Sorry.'

Amelia looked up. 'I thought he really loved me, but I went around to Jake's apartment early one morning to pleasantly surprise him before he went to work.'

'She had a key and let herself in,' Becky said. 'I know the story.'

raspberry-coloured cardigan and light-blue denim skirt were a good choice for the evening. Not knowing what to do, she was grateful when Evie arrived from the kitchen, came up to her, and kissed her on the cheek.

'My fiancé can't be with us tonight, but let me introduce you to Jenny – wedding planner extraordinaire, for Becky and Oliver's wedding next week, and also for my wedding in four weeks' time.' Jenny stood up and stretched out her hand. 'And this is Oliver.'

'Hi, Amelia. Pleased to finally meet you,' said Oliver. 'Becky has spoken quite a bit about you. I'm the only man here tonight.'

'Admit it, Oliver darling,' said Becky grinning. 'You love it when you're surrounded by women.'

'Okay, I admit it, my love.' Smiling, he stretched out his glass for a refill as Jenny topped it up.

'I must tell you about our wedding rehearsal at the church.' Becky beamed. 'It was two hours.'

'How did your rumba dance practice go afterwards?' Evie asked.

'It isn't quite nailed yet.' Becky glared across the table at Oliver. 'I wonder why.'

'That makes two of us who are having problems with our wedding dance!' Evie took a breath.

Jenny sat upright. 'It's just as well that I'm taking care of everything else with both your wedding arrangements.'

'Something smells good,' said Amelia.

'It's my take on vegetable cottage pie. I better get back and check.'

Amelia gazed around at the warm primrose and grey colour scheme, enhanced by softly flickering tealight candles dotted around. Evie gestured to Amelia to follow her into the kitchen. She breathed in the enticing smell of the cooking and admired the clinical décor of stainless-steel work surfaces.

'I'm so pleased you could make it,' said Evie, checking on her cooking. 'You look amazing.'

'I'm just pleased that all my facial bruising has now gone.'

'When's the plaster cast coming off?'

'Next week. I can then at least shower properly.'

'Oh, you haven't got a drink. Can you pour Amelia a drink, please, Jenny?'

Amelia returned to the dining room, and Jenny held up a red and a white bottle of wine. She pointed to the white.

'Have you got someone in tow, Amelia?' Jenny asked as she took a large sip of wine.

'Only an ex-boyfriend back in the States,' said Becky. 'We won't go there.'

Amelia rubbed the side of her forehead. She wasn't sure if she should explain, but it came out anyway. 'The ex is called Jake. I walked away from a difficult relationship last summer.'

'They were engaged and planning to get married,' said Becky. 'Sorry.'

Amelia looked up. 'I thought he really loved me, but I went around to Jake's apartment early one morning to pleasantly surprise him before he went to work.'

'She had a key and let herself in,' Becky said. 'I know the story.'

'Oh boy,' Amelia said, shaking her head. 'I'm not sure which of us had the biggest surprise.'

Jenny put down her wine. 'Don't tell me...'

'He was in bed with her best friend Melanie...' Becky said. 'Sorry...'

'Oh no, that's so awful,' said Evie as she returned from the kitchen.

Jenny frowned. 'He must be an idiot.'

Amelia took a sip of her wine. 'I'd been having so many doubts about leaving America and coming to England, but he made it easy for me in the end.'

'This was the fresh start she needed,' said Becky.

'And as for Jake, I'm over him now and moving on.'

'And still searching for "the one?"' Evie asked.

'I guess so... The thing is I met...'

'Oh, my goodness!' said Evie, interrupting her. 'Excuse me – I should've taken my dish out of the oven.' She dashed into the kitchen. 'It's ready. If I can pass everything through to you, Becky, please.'

They all made themselves comfortable sitting down at the round table with a covering of white linen and a centrepiece of early spring flowers. Evie joined them at the table as Becky passed around the Parma-ham, melon, and salad starters.

'Well, this dressing you've made is delicious,' exclaimed Amelia. The starters kicked off numerous conversations around the table about healthy eating.

Evie cleared away the plates after they had finished. 'Becky, can you help me dish up, please.'

'Who's for a top-up?' Jenny refreshed everyone's glasses as Becky passed through their meals.

'I would like to make a toast,' said Oliver. 'To friendships – new and old.' They all raised their glasses. 'Furthermore! Here's to this time next Saturday when Becky will be my gorgeous wife.' She smiled and blew him a kiss.

'Also, to Evie and her future husband,' said Amelia. 'Sorry, I don't know his name.'

'Alex.'

'To Evie and Alex'. They raised their glasses.

'Thank you – all of you,' said Evie. 'Let's now eat.'

The conversation after dinner had turned to wedding planning, and Amelia decided to get up. 'Do you mind if I have a look around your lovely home?'

'Be my guest,' said Evie. 'You can change the music if you like in the lounge.'

Amelia left the others talking about their wedding plans as she left the dining room. Gazing around, she liked the style of their home. 'Neat,' she said quietly to herself. It was very much to her taste. Music played through speakers in a retro music centre from an iPod. She paged down the screen and found a country music song she liked and played it. There were shelves upon shelves of twelve-inch vinyl record albums, and she took an interest in the album cover designs. She recognised one of her dad's favourites, the Commodores. Her gaze fell upon a framed photo on a side table. 'Holy crap – doctor handsome.'

'What's that?' Becky said as she walked through and joined Amelia. 'Did you say "doctor handsome?"'

'No, no. Sorry… Mm, I was thinking out loud. What a handsome couple.'

'I agree, that's a lovely photo of Evie and Alex.'

'How come her fiancé couldn't make it tonight?'

'Staff shortages in A&E. They asked him to go in. Evie was quite emotional earlier – before you arrived. It didn't help that they had an argument after their dance practice earlier today. She wanted him to be here as a lead-up to his birthday on Wednesday. But, his work always comes first.'

Chapter 7

Saturday, 25th January 2020, 10.00 a.m.

Alex was buzzing with happiness when he got to The Caffeine Hub café, walking over to where Sanjay and Spud were seated.

'Can I get you a coffee, birthday boy?' Sanjay asked.

'That'll be great. My usual, please, Sanjay.' Alex sat opposite Spud as Sanjay went to the till and ordered a black Americano. 'I see Hamish is late as usual.'

Spud scratched his beard. 'I bet a woman is involved somewhere.'

Sanjay came back and slid onto the bench next to Alex. 'It's a damn shame we're not in the Club Challenge Cup final today.'

'There's always next year.'

'Changing the subject, guys,' said Spud interrupting. 'Have you heard the news about this Wuhan place in China?'

'No. What about it?' Alex asked.

'Well, it's gone into a lockdown thing, where the authorities are trying to contain a serious virus outbreak.'

'They have these sorts of problems in China,' said Sanjay.

'But they said that it could spread outside the country.'

'Don't worry – we'll be alright.'

'Here comes Hamish,' said Sanjay. 'He's got that look on his face.'

Hamish slid onto the bench next to Spud. 'How're we all doing?'

'Let me guess,' said Alex. 'You were with that new agency nurse Ellie last night, the one you've been sniffing around.'

'Actually, no,' said Hamish, smirking. 'I've finally cracked it with that lass Lucy, the Aussie totty. What a night!'

'Keep your voice down – we're in public, remember?' said Sanjay, gazing around.

'I already feel sorry for this, Lucy.' Spud rested his head into the palm of his hand.

Alex folded his arms. 'She'll soon be just another notch on your bedpost.'

'She was quite a vixen, well worth the wait. I'll just order my coffee, and then I'll tell all.' He winked at them before walking over to the serving counter.

Sanjay shook his head. 'I don't think I want to hear what he's got to say when he comes back.'

Alex shook his head. 'Nor me.' A waitress brought over his coffee.

'I'm interested,' whispered Spud. 'Even if you two aren't.'

Sanjay glanced around at the door. 'Zahida will be joining us soon.'

'I could tell you something even more juicy.' Alex sipped his coffee. 'Oliver's stag night.'

Spud leaned in closer. 'The groom of Evie's friend, whose wedding you're going to later?'

Alex nodded. 'You won't believe what happened.'

Hamish was returning from the counter when two nurses who were walking past the glass-fronted café recognised him.

'What a hot steamy… night of love…' Hamish said, interrupting and sliding onto the bench.

'Please spare us the details.' Alex glanced up, noticing the two nurses walking up behind Hamish.

'Oh, but I can't!' said Hamish. 'Lucy, what a woman – wow! She insisted on taking control on top, if you know what I mean, Spud.' He didn't notice his friends' eyes gawking over him. Both women were pursing their lips with folded arms.

'So, this Lucy was better than me,' said one of the nurses with long dark eyelashes and thick eyebrows.

Hamish spun around. 'Natalie. Oh, and Jess.' He held up his hands in surrender.

Natalie moved around to his side. 'You said you loved me, and you also told Jess the same – we got talking.'

'Natalie, I'm sorry.'

She dug her hands onto her hips. 'What a low life you are, Hamish Campbell.'

His eyes flicked from one woman to the other. 'Let me explain, please…'

The two nurses stood on either side of him with their eyes boring down. 'C'mon, ladies! We had nice times while it lasted. I took you both out on amazing dinner dates, and I paid for everything.'

Jess suddenly grabbed his coffee and threw it into his lap. He gasped. Both women smirked and walked out past Zahida, who had just walked into the café with her youngest daughter in a pushchair.

Hamish leapt out of his seat, puffing heavily as he scampered towards the toilet.

'I won't ask,' said Zahida. She leaned over and calmly kissed Sanjay on his cheek.

'There's never a dull moment when Hamish is around,' Alex said, grinning.'

11.40 a.m.

Alex was content sitting beside his niece Charlotte on the back seat, reading *The Tiger Who Came to Tea* picture storybook to her. Evie sat on the other side of Charlotte, gazing out the window.

The skies had cleared, and a low winter sun forced Freya to pull down her sun visor as she drove into Cambridge city centre. 'At least your friends have got a beautiful day for the wedding; the photos in the courtyard will look great.' She pulled the car up outside the gatehouse to St. Edward's College. Alex kissed Charlotte goodbye, jokingly pulling her nose as he got out of the car and pulled silly faces at her through the window. She giggled.

Evie had walked on a bit and then turned around. 'C'mon, Boo, we want to get good seats.'

Freya wound down her window. 'You're looking very relaxed. But in three weeks' time, it'll be your turn.' She winked as she drove away.

Evie started to walk back. 'Is there something wrong?'

Alex looked up and pressed his lips together. 'Everything is fine.' He walked towards her and took hold of her hand. They went through the gatehouse of the college and showed their wedding invitations to the porter, who directed them around the first courtyard to the chapel.

'You've not been yourself all week – are you sure everything is fine?'

He gazed around at the ancient architecture as the gravel crunched under their feet. She squeezed his hand as they entered through the stone arched porch into the ante-chapel with some other guests. Jenny was standing behind a couple of the ushers who immediately came forward to greet them.

'Great to see you both,' said Jenny, embracing Evie and exchanging a cheek kiss. 'Everything is going really well – the flower displays look wonderful, don't you think?' She took a cerise buttonhole from the usher's tray. 'Allow me.'

'It really does look so beautiful,' replied Evie, gazing around the decorated cloisters.

Jenny finished fitting the buttonhole. 'Wait until you see the displays in the chapel itself.'

One of the ushers handed an order of service to Alex and then fitted a buttonhole to his jacket before guiding them into the chapel. Alex's eyes were drawn to the vivid cerise pink aisle carpet as classical music gently played in the background. The usher stopped and pointed to a space on a pew about halfway down the aisle on the bride's side.

Alex grinned. 'Have you clocked Becky's mum in the cerise sombrero?'

'It certainly does make a statement.' She glanced around at the pink gerberas and lilies that were tied with ribbon to the ends of the pews. 'I love the flower displays.'

Alex gazed over at the bridegroom sitting with his best man. He thought about himself being in the same position as Sanjay, with only three weeks to go. He knew this was the deal he made with Evie if he was to have children and a family.

Evie sniffed the air. 'The scent of the lilies is strong.'

'They've really pulled out all the *bells and whistles* with the four-piece music group.' Alex watched Oliver lean forward in the front pew and put a hanky to his face, letting out three loud sneezes in succession.

'Oh, poor Oliver,' said Evie turning to Alex. 'He must have a cold,'

'He's certainly captured everyone's attention.'

The music group in the side chancel stopped playing and changed their music sheets. The female church minister waved her palms for everyone to stand. Oliver remained facing the altar as he blew into his hanky. The congregation started to turn and look towards the back of the chapel. The music group started to play *Sognatori Per Caso*. Jenny gently waved Becky and her father forward to begin their procession. Becky's two sisters and two little nieces followed as bridesmaids. Oliver tucked away his hanky as Becky and her father approached, placing Becky's hand into Oliver's.

'Welcome everyone on this cold but bright and sunny day to witness the marriage of Rebecca and Oliver,' said the minister, commencing the marriage ceremony. 'I will open with prayers. If you could all please respond using the bold type printed in the order of service.' The congregation followed the minister as she guided them through the prayers and the first hymn.

'You're singing out of tune,' said Evie, elbowing Alex in his side.

The minister continued through the preface of the marriage ceremony but had to suddenly pull back as Oliver sneezed. The minister composed herself, looked up over her glasses at the congregation, took a breath, and continued. Becky's older sister gave a bible reading at the lectern, followed by the minister's sermon about love and forgiveness.

Oliver sniffled as he took Becky's right hand and tried repeating the marriage vows after the minister. 'I Oliver…' He suddenly sneezed multiple times in a row. Pulling out his hanky, he dabbed his nose. 'I can't help it,' he whispered. 'You didn't tell me the displays had lilies – I react to the scent.'

Becky pulled him in close to her face. 'That's the problem when you don't tell me these things!' She turned briefly to face the bemused congregation and smiled.

'I think I've told you everything that could affect our wedding,' Alex said as he turned to Evie.

The ceremony continued with the wedding couple concluding their vows. The minister beckoned the best man to place the wedding rings onto the bible she was holding as Becky and Oliver knelt in front of her. The minister faced the congregation. 'Heavenly Father, by your blessing, let these rings be…'

'Achoo!' Oliver unexpectedly let out an enormous sneeze which caused both Becky and the minister to shudder. One of the rings tumbled to the floor, bounced on the step, rolled, and fell through one of the crypt grates.

Becky leaned forward. 'It's my ring that's dropped.' Her shoulders slumped. 'Typical, bloody typical!'

12.55 p.m.

Alex filtered out of the chapel with Evie at his side and beamed at Becky as he clasped her hand. 'Congratulations.' They cheek kissed. 'You look beautiful, Becky,' he said, shuffling past her and Oliver with the rest of the guests, out through the ante-chapel and into the courtyard.

Guests mingled in the winter sunshine on the broad gravel path between the grass area and the chapel as a photographer took snapshots. Becky slipped on a white faux fur bridal shawl around her shoulders as she and Oliver continued greeting the guests. Six hand-bell ringers stood in a line outside the master's lodge ringing out the *Wedding Bells* theme, the sounding chimes echoing around the courtyard.

'Mum, you're not allowed to throw confetti inside the college grounds,' said Becky, as her mother reached inside her handbag for another handful. 'You must wait until we're outside the gatehouse.'

'Surely some rules are meant to be broken,' she retorted, throwing some confetti.

'Thank goodness that all turned out well in the end,' said Evie, as she and Alex moved around the gravel path to stand opposite the bell ringers.

'Mm, that was so surreal.' Alex grinned. 'The best man standing up in the pulpit and asking if anyone had a large, bladed screwdriver in their car, so he could remove the grate to get to the ring.'

Evie chuckled. 'Thank goodness they managed to get it.'

He watched the photographer start to assemble the bride and bridegroom with the bridesmaids on the grass.

Evie pulled her jacket in close around herself. 'I wish they would hurry up with the photos.'

Alex's eyes narrowed. 'That woman walking towards us with her friend – I know her.' He wrapped his jacket around Evie's shoulders. 'What's she doing here?'

Evie glanced around at Alex and then turned her head back. 'Hello, Amelia, Avani. I wondered if you would be here.'

'We were late and slid in quietly,' said Avani. 'Just after the bridesmaids started to walk down the aisle.'

Evie turned to her side. 'Let me introduce you both to my future husband.'

'Hello, Doctor Hardson,' said Amelia. 'Pleased to meet you again.'

Evie gazed at her with bewilderment. 'You know my fiancé?'

'Well, sort of.' Amelia held up her braced forearm.

'Hm.' He coughed. 'Injury sustained by falling off a table, as I recollect?'

Amelia returned her gaze to Evie. 'Your fiancé kindly fixed me up on New Year's Eve.'

'But you didn't say that you knew my fiancé when you came to dinner last week?'

'I didn't know Doctor Hardson was your fiancé. Isn't it a small world?'

'I'm confused.' He rubbed his forehead. 'She came to dinner the night I was called in?'

'Yes, Amelia came to dinner,' said Evie, studying Alex with piercing scrutiny. 'If you had been there, well, we could've all listened as the two of you reminisced over the events of New Year's Eve.'

Avani leaned forward. 'The photographer is calling out for all friends of the bride and groom. Should we go up?'

'Good idea,' said Amelia. They walked towards the gathering.

Alex also started to walk over but stopped when he noticed Evie wasn't with him. She remained motionless and stared at him.

He knew that look and gazed back at her with imploring eyes as he held out his hand. She moved towards him and took his grip.

The photographer eventually finished taking all the photos. A wedding toastmaster in a bright red tailcoat and waistcoat came and stood in front of the master's lodge and announced, 'Do listen thus, one and all, it's now nearing the time to have a feast and a ball, so do follow me into the Great Hall.'

Becky and Oliver, along with a hundred and sixty guests and family, followed the toastmaster across the courtyard. The guests collected glasses of champagne and bucks fizz from waiters, checked the seating plan on an easel, and filtered into the Great Hall. They got seated along four rows of white linen-covered refectory tables that were decorated with cerise pink flower arrangements, stretching out from the top table. When everyone was seated, the toastmaster beat his ceremonial wooden mallet, and the hall fell silent. Everyone stood as the wedding couple took their places. The father of the bride stood and made a heartfelt speech to his daughter and son-in-law.

'Now we come to our star turn,' said the toastmaster. 'He'll make us laugh, he'll make us smile, but I'm sure it'll all be done in style.' He introduced the best man.' Liam wobbled as he stood up to applause.

'I've been watching Liam,' Evie whispered into Alex's ear. 'He's had at least five glasses of champagne.'

Alex glanced around as Evie watched Liam. He observed Amelia on the next refectory table as she fussed over a baby in its mother's arms.

Evie sniggered as she watched Liam prepare for his speech. 'I think he's full of Dutch courage.'

Alex looked over again as the mother passed her baby to Amelia to hold. He watched with interest as Amelia rocked the baby in her arms and then brought her face in close and pulled a joyful expression. The baby shrieked with joy, stealing everyone's attention away from Liam reading through some of the wedding cards. Amelia and the baby's mother beamed. Alex continued to watch discretely as she gently handed the baby back to the mother. Amelia turned to pick up her glass of bubbly and caught Alex's gaze, giving him a wry smile. He snapped his attention away. 'Liam is slurring his words.'

Evie rolled her eyes. 'I need some more champagne to numb me if he reads anymore.'

Liam swayed as he placed down the cards and reached to pick up a remote control for an overhead projector. A screen lit up behind the bride and groom. A friend switched off the lights. 'I thought I would start by showing you a montage of images of the bride and groom through the years.' Grinning, he first showed images of Oliver growing up. 'Now for Becky. This is her at the age of two.' The screen showed fun images of her growing up through the years.

He went through the presentation, then played a video clip of Becky celebrating with other teachers at a Christmas party while swigging wine from a bottle.

'How did you…?' Becky glared.

'I have contacts.'

'You wait!' she shook her head. The guests laughed.

The next slide read, *The stag night*. Oliver's jaw dropped. 'You gotta be kidding.'

Liam opened a link to another video showing Oliver in a pub, surrounded by his friends and having his shirt peeled off by a very large strippergram wearing a graduation mortarboard hat, black bra, suspenders, red high-heeled shoes, and a g-string. She sat Oliver on a chair, tied his hands with rope behind his back, and kissed him around his face, leaving rouge kiss marks. His friends could be heard cheering in the background.

Evie angled a sharpened eye at Alex. 'Were you also cheering?'

He grimaced. 'I was fuelled up on drinks.'

The video film showed the stripper-gram bending forward and wiggling her bottom in front of Oliver's face as he mimicked a licking action.

Becky turned her head from the screen and scowled in disbelief. 'Shame on you.' Oliver's face slumped into the palm of his hands.

Alex and Oliver's friends could be seen cheering as the stripper-gram unclipped her bra from the front and rubbed baby oil into her breasts. Crouching down behind him, she held her large breasts on either side of his head. Phone camera flashes lit the room. Standing up, she did a shimmy to another loud cheer. Oliver could be seen in a drunken state with disorientated eye movement. Liam stopped the video. The hall lights were switched back on to an equal mix of smiling and bewildered guests. Raising his glass of champagne, he toasted the couple.

Alex shook his head. 'Poor Oliver.' Sanjay would never stitch him up on his stag night, surely?

'I hope Sanjay doesn't have any similar ideas,' Evie whispered.

'I was just thinking the same.'

The toastmaster stepped forward. 'Please now welcome the bridegroom.'

Oliver dragged himself to his feet. 'That was unexpected, Liam. Ouch...' He exhaled and anxiously read through his speech. The speeches ended with the minister saying prayers and grace. The wedding breakfast was then served.

Alex occasionally glanced across at Amelia as he was eating. He was amused, watching her as she joked with the guests seated around her.

It was late afternoon; the waiters had cleared the tables to the sides of the room, and the musicians had been playing classical pieces for over an hour. Becky reappeared in a shimmering long white and silver evening dress with a low-slung back.

'Becky and Oliver are about to have their first dance,' announced the toastmaster. A female vocalist joined the musicians. Becky took Oliver's shaky hand as they walked to the centre of the dance floor. The couple got in hold as the guests assembled in a large circle around them. Amelia was wearing a velvet burgundy evening gown as she and Avani rubbed shoulders with other guests, holding their drinks. Evie held Alex's hand, almost directly opposite across the circle from them. Alex's gaze settled firmly on Amelia. A sparkle of light reflected from a silver pendant that hung around her neck. Her gaze briefly locked with his, and she confidently swept her long blond hair back over her shoulder.

Evie suddenly noticed Amelia staring and crooked her neck to look at Alex.

He flinched. 'What? I'm looking at Oliver and Becky like everyone else.'

Evie relaxed. 'Becky looks just radiant in that gorgeous dress, don't you think?'

'Definitely. But Oliver dancing the rumba, this is going to be interesting.'

The musicians started playing, and Becky and Oliver spiralled around each other as they started to dance. She flowed through under his arm to complete a graceful *alemana* movement. They went into another routine, but Oliver suddenly forgot his steps and missed connecting hands with Becky. She forced a crumbled smile but continued to dance. Oliver recovered and managed to finish without any further mistakes. The couple embraced to a loud round of applause. The music group continued to play as the guests mingled into the afternoon.

It was early evening when a band started playing some past hits from the decades. Guests were flitting to and from the dancefloor. Alex stood near Evie as she chatted to a couple of women whom she had met on Becky's hen night. Gazing around, he noticed Amelia along the hall in the *kiddies' corner*. She was the only adult playing table games with a group of children. He grinned with fascination as he watched her goofing around, making them laugh.

'Shall we take a seat over there?' Evie asked.

Alex blinked. 'Yeah, sure.' He followed her to a table.

More guests arrived as the reception rolled into the evening. Music pulsed, and coloured lights strobed across the floor to the beat as a DJ played an assortment of hit records. Evie and Alex were nestled at a table, watching the dancing as she chatted to a friend.

'I'm going to get a beer.' He stood. 'Another white wine?' Evie nodded, and Alex walked around to a sidebar that was out of sight to the hall and placed his order with the barman as he leant on the bar.

Amelia walked up and sat on a bar stool next to him. 'It's been a really cute wedding so far, don't you think?' She rested her black neoprene armbrace on the bar.

He turned around to meet her luminous glow of happiness. 'I guess so.'

'Very English; very much how I've always imagined a traditional English wedding would be.' She pushed her hair away from the side of her face, turned to the barman, and ordered two drinks.

'Traditional… What about the part in the chapel where the best man asked the congregation if anyone had some tools in their car to remove the crypt cover?' He glanced at her sparkling art-deco-style silver pendant earring.

She pivoted herself around and perused him with her soft hazel eyes. 'You English are so quirky. You guys appear to just bumble through situations in an eccentric yet charming manner.'

'Huh, really?'

'Well yeah. You take that time when we first met, Doctor Hardson.'

'Please, call me Alex.'

'Okay, Alex. When I was waiting to be seen in your hospital, well, it was just crazy in there, but in a pleasant and endearing manner.' She gave him a lopsided gaze. The barman slid her drinks over.

'Since we keep bumping into each other and you've made friends with Evie – please allow me to pay.'

'Well, I hope I'm still friends with Evie.' She sipped her drink. 'I've really got into these G&Ts since Becky introduced me to this British classic.'

'What's your default drink back in America?'

'Generally white wine, but it can be bourbon when I'm at home with family.'

He glanced at her armbrace. 'This may not be the normal environment to do a patient check-up, but may I examine your arm?'

'Sure.'

He carefully removed her armbrace. 'I couldn't help but notice you having fun playing with the children.' He gently examined the soft tissue.

'Well yeah, who wouldn't? They're just adorable. They brought out the little girl in me.' She flinched.

'Sorry. It does seem to be healing nicely. You'll need to keep the armbrace on for at least another two weeks.' He gently pulled in the Velcro fasteners.

Evie ambled up to him. 'Boo, I wondered where you had got to with my drink.' She turned to her side. 'And hello, Amelia.'

Alex got down from his stool. 'Sorry, I completely forgot. I was just checking how well her arm was healing as she is, uh… was my patient.'

Evie folded her arms. 'Is that appropriate to be examining a patient here?' Amelia eased herself away and left.

Chapter 8

Sunday, 26th January 2020, 08.00 a.m.

Alex pulled some of his sculling gear from their airing cupboard. 'Argh… My head is a little delicate this morning, and my throat feels as rough as the bottom of Percy's birdcage.' He pushed his trainers into his kit bag.

Evie was using her hairdryer as she knelt in her hallway with a purple towel wrapped around her body. 'Perhaps you should give it a miss for one weekend?'

Shuffling past her, he dumped his bag by the front door. 'My tea doesn't taste right.'

She carefully brushed her long wavy brown hair while checking her reflection in a small mirror propped up against one of her shoes. 'I tried to tell you to drink some water to avoid dehydration. You did knock back quite a lot of booze – was it four or five pints and some shorts?'

'You're in the way, Evie,' he said, squeezing back past her. 'Why are you drying your hair there?'

She applied a little bit of makeup. 'I didn't want to wake you earlier.'

'The evening was just the tonic I needed after such an exhausting week at work.'

Evie got up and went into the kitchen. 'I'll make us both a drink before you go.' She switched on the kettle and pulled a carton of milk from the fridge, and then made two teas. 'We should be thankful that you weren't sick – sitting on the toilet last night with your face pressed against the basin.'

He got the rest of his things together and took a sip of his fresh cuppa. 'Mm…That's better.'

Evie leaned back against her kitchen worktop. 'Are you sure about going sculling? You look washed out, and you haven't eaten anything.'

'I'll be fine once I'm out on the water.'

She reached out and held his hand. 'After yesterday's reception, surely it gives you confidence for our own wedding?'

'I guess so. Oliver's allergic reaction to lilies – that's one to remember.'

'That's why I need you more involved with the arrangements. Even if you could just check through some of the details with me, please.'

'I get the message. I'll have a look with you later.'

Evie smiled. 'Good. And ours should be just as lovely.'

He rubbed his mouth. 'I'm sure you're right.'

'I'm glad we're alright again after our argument last weekend. Once we're married, everything will be different.' She stroked the side of his face.

'In what other ways will it be different?'

Evie tightened the knot in her bath towel over her chest. 'We'll be more settled for a start – there'll be a sense of calm because we'll be married.'

'And what about our agreement on us starting a family once we're married?'

'Let's not go over that again.' She straightened up. 'I just don't feel ready to have a baby.'

'But will you ever?'

She turned and gazed out of the window. 'I'll be in a better position, career-wise, in the future. And then I could have up to a year off work on a good salary.'

'You know I definitely want children, right?'

She turned back to face him. 'You've made that clear. I understand. Your parents had you and Freya when they were young, but couples don't generally start families until much later these days.'

'You'll be a brilliant mum. Don't put it off, Evie.'

'Who's to say we can have children anyhow?'

'Remind me why we're getting married again?'

'That's not fair.' She took a breath and picked up Cookie. 'We're really good for each other – that's why we're getting married.'

He glanced away. 'I'm going sculling.'

She stroked Cookie's head. 'I know you've forgotten, but we were meant to go to church this morning for the final reading of our banns. I'll call the minister and make our excuses?'

He frowned and swigged back the rest of his tea. 'Thanks.'

'Give it a year or two, and I'm sure I'll get a promotion. At which point, we'll be in a much better financial position.'

He exhaled and put on his coat.

She walked towards their bedroom with Cookie in her arms. 'Don't forget our lunch in town before we have dance practice at two.'

'I'll be there.' He knelt by the front door and tied his shoelaces.

Evie walked into the hall wearing floral pattern knickers and a black bra. She leaned against the wall with her arms folded. 'I thought Amelia looked very stylish last night in her evening gown.'

He stood up and picked up his kit bag. 'I hadn't really noticed.' He pulled their front door closed as he left.

The winter sun illuminated the morning landscape as Alex drove north out of Cambridge into the flat Fenland area of Cambridgeshire. He caught sight of two large Red Kite birds of prey ahead of him, gliding over a woodland. He glanced up and watched their graceful circles against the backdrop of a clear powder-blue sky. Despite feeling delicate, he smiled to himself and thought of Becky and Oliver's wedding – his conversation with Amelia. But then, how much fun he had with Evie the rest of the evening.

He arrived at the clubhouse a few minutes later and walked into the changing rooms, and hooked up his coat. 'You're on time – what happened?'

'Aye. And good to see you as well,' said Hamish, pulling down his thermal top. 'An excellent day for sculling.'

'It's a bit crisp outside.'

'No hangover then after last night?'

'A little.'

Hamish grinned. 'I saw some images on Facebook of the wedding – some of the women looked stunning. Hey, I saw a picture of that American bonnie.'

'Amelia.'

'Aye. She scrubbed up really well, I thought, compared to when we met her at The Ferryman Inn. All that bruising had gone from her face. She looked amazing. Did you get a chance to have a chat with her?' Alex ignored him. Hamish squeezed his arm. 'Well, did you?' Alex nodded. 'I knew it.' Hamish patted Alex on the back.

'What are you implying?'

'I think you could be in there. I'm just saying…'

'I'm getting married in three weeks' time.'

'To the woman you love?' Hamish placed his hand on Alex's shoulder. 'Chill. Let's go out on the water.'

The river water lapped around their Wellington boots as the two of them adjusted the rigging set up on their boat. Dullard held their boat steady as they changed their footwear. He pushed their white double scull out into the river current when they were ready. Hamish sat in his usual position at the bow of the boat, wearing a sun visor as they rowed away north. A pair of mature swans with three grey cygnets cautiously swam around them.

'What a brilliant morning to be out here,' said Alex pulling back on his oars.

'Superb conditions. I would have felt gutted if I couldn't practise this morning,' said Hamish, slowly increasing the stroke pace.

'This is better than any holiday after a stressful week at work.'

'Aye!' Hamish heaved at his oars as the two of them settled into a balanced sculling rhythm, sliding in unison on their seats.

'Fancy a quick drink afterwards…' Alex gulped a breath.

'The Rusty Anchor… I've arranged to meet up with Spud there.'

'Okay...'

The two of them rowed at a steady pace up the Great Ouse River with the low winter sun on one side of their faces and a light icy breeze on their backs. 'Damn! It's the Cambridge team catching us up,' said Alex in the stern of the boat, facing back down the river. 'We'll have to move over.'

'No way – bollocks to them,' Hamish grunted. 'Let's just carry on.'

'We can't; it's the men's Cambridge eight. River etiquette, remember?'

'Move over,' shouted the Cambridge eight coxswain through his loudhailer.

'We need to pull in to let them through,' shouted Alex, pulling hard on his starboard oar as the Cambridge team bore down on them.

'Fuck it. Alright...'

'Poor river conduct,' shouted the coxswain as they rowed past. 'We have priority!'

Hamish let go of his oars and gave him a gesture with his forearm. 'Up yours.' They pulled as close to the riverbank as they could and caught their breath as their boat drifted slowly with the current. 'What do you make of this so-called *lockdown* in Wuhan, China? Do you think this new viral disease could affect us?'

Alex looked out across the water at the ripples as they glistened in the sun's rays. 'I think the Chinese have got it under control.' The sparkles of light were almost hypnotic as he gazed. The moment made him feel at peace, his mind drifting like the boat. 'I keep thinking about her.'

'Who, Evie?' Hamish started to ease their boat around over to the other side of the river under some hanging branches of a willow tree.

'You know who I mean,' whispered Alex.

'Whoa… The American bonnie – Amelia.'

'It's kind of weird how I feel.'

'I think this needs further discussion over that drink,' said Hamish breathing heavily.

'At least the sun's glare won't be in our eyes on the return.'

The two of them held a steady pace as they sculled back to the boathouse. They pulled up in the shallows. Dullard waded down the ramp in waterproofs and held their boat as they slipped on their Wellington boots and disembarked into the shallow waters.

One of the Gormley brothers walked over. 'When are we having this race that you two keep putting off?'

'We're going to have to let you down again as we've got plans,' said Alex.

'We're the fastest double scullers in the club, as you know. And to prove it, we wager two hundred pounds.'

'Some other time,' said Hamish.

'We don't want to take your money.' Alex grinned.

'If you two are so confident, let's double it and make it four hundred pounds, and you name the day of the race.'

'Why not make it six hundred, and we'll think about it,' said Hamish.

'That's a deal. And we'll make it official and arrange a marshal.' The Gormley brother walked off.

'What're you doing, Hamish? I was only joking when I said I didn't want to take their money.'

'I know, but I'm sure that we can beat them.'

'I'm not, and there's six hundred pounds at stake.'

Hamish raised his shoulders. 'We need to get the boat de-rigged, back into the rack, and down the pub.' They went through their routine, showered, dressed, and headed off to The Rusty Anchor in their separate cars.

'I'll buy,' said Hamish, leading the way through the quiet lounge up to the bar, where he ordered two orange and lemonades. 'So, what's the story from last night with Amelia? You didn't show much interest in her at The Ferryman Inn.'

'She looked like a million dollars, and she was brilliant with the small children, making them laugh. We got chatting, and I found her very…'

'Alluring.' Hamish chuckled. 'Oh dear, she's got you hooked.'

Alex's head slumped. 'We sort of connected.'

'Have you and Evie had a fallout or something?

'It's been awkward lately,' he said, scratching his chin. 'Everything that you had been saying to me about her went through my mind. I want to believe in Evie, but she's not interested in children.'

'You sound confused. Marriage has got to be for all the right reasons, especially love.'

'I don't want to talk about it anymore. How's your week been?'

'You mean, apart from the scene yesterday morning at the Caffeine Hub…' Hamish raised an eyebrow. 'That was bloody embarrassing.'

Alex smirked. 'That'll teach you to brag about your sexual conquests.'

'I don't need reminding, thank you.'

'So, how was the rest of your week?'

'A&E was busy yesterday and Friday.'

'Are you still going to be dating Lucy now you've scored with her?'

'Does it matter?'

'Just to remind you. She's good friends with Amelia.'

1.05 p.m.

Alex walked into the Grand Arcade and found Evie sitting in the café with a pot of tea. He leaned over and kissed her on the cheek as he sat down. 'Evie, I'm nervous about this dancing session. I made a hash of it last time – I'm struggling with the whole waltz thing, and I don't want to mess up on the day.'

She reached out and took hold of his hand. 'You won't, and I'm sorry if I've unloaded some of the pressure on you that I've been feeling.'

'I understand, but what makes you think I won't mess up?'

'Well, let's just say I have an idea.' She paused and tightened her hold on his hand. 'I've also been thinking about what you said this morning – about starting a family. I know how important it is to you, and I love you so much. So… I just wanted to say that I'm sleeping on it.' A waitress arrived at their table, and they placed their lunch orders.

They finished their lunch, and he put an arm around Evie as they left the café and walked to the dance studio.

Kofi was standing in the middle of the dance floor dressed in black. 'So, we're aiming to have a perfect waltz by the end of this session.' He shook hands with Alex and greeted Evie with a cheek kiss. He checked that they were in the correct start position and went to his laptop. 'If you start with some basic box steps in the hold position to warm up, please. Remember to rise on two.' They started to waltz. 'And one, two, three, one, two, three. And perfect. Now the box step with rotation. Well done, both of you, feeling the rhythm of the music. That's fantastic. I must say, it's great to see you both looking so relaxed; it makes such a difference to your dancing.' Evie and Alex smiled at each other.

Kofi restarted the music. Evie and Alex waltzed around the studio.

'Ouch.' Evie stopped, slipped off her left shoe, and rubbed her toes.

Kofi walked over to them. 'You will tread on Evie's foot if you let your right foot drift. Remember, Alex, your right knee has to brush against the inside of Evie's right knee as you waltz forward.' Kofi took Evie's place and went into hold with Alex. Evie watched as the two men waltzed along and into the corner of the studio; Kofi demonstrated how the underarm step was performed. 'So, I'll put the music on again. Just remember to lift your arm for Evie to walk under for the underarm step.'

The couple took up their start position as Kofi restarted the music. Alex felt at ease and comfortable as they waltzed successfully around the studio. He returned Evie's confident smile as they came out of an underarm step, but then he stumbled and lost balance.

'That was going really well until that point,' said Kofi. 'Remember the weight shift otherwise…'

'It's frustrating!' Alex interrupted. 'I know I'm getting there, but I keep messing up. I know I won't get it right on the day, especially with everyone watching.'

'Is it possible to simplify the waltz for us, please?' she asked.

Kofi rubbed his forehead. 'Well, you could just go into hold and dance around on the spot, then do a few underarm steps to add a touch of sophistication. Do you want to have a go?'

They both took up their start position. Kofi restarted the music. Alex settled into his own enjoyable dance style and started to lark around as his confidence grew. He supported her around her waist as she remembered her childhood ballet training; she arched her back right over and unfolded her arms like a flower opening to meet the sunshine. Giggling, she came up into an embrace with Alex. Kofi applauded.

Chapter 9

Saturday, 1st February 2020, 11.35 a.m.

Annabelle had caught the train up from London into Cambridge. She directed her taxi driver from the station to where she wanted to be dropped off, close to the city's market square, and made her way on foot to Picardo Cafe & Restaurant. Spotting Freya with Charlotte on her lap as she entered, she walked over and embraced her daughter before getting seated.

'I'm so pleased you could meet me,' said Annabelle, scooping up Charlotte onto her lap before ordering a pot of tea with the waitress.

'Mum, we always love to see you. But I hope you don't mind me asking, is everything alright? You look tired.' Silence fell between them as Freya waited for her mother's reply. 'You got a little upset when we last met at Harmony Studio.' Freya took a sip of her tea. 'And how is Daddy?'

Annabelle rubbed noses with Charlotte. 'And how does our Charlotte look in her pretty bridesmaid's dress? I suspect that you look like a beautiful princess.' The waitress returned with Annabelle's tea and took their brunch order.

'What's going on, Mum? I know when something is bothering you.'

Annabelle turned to meet Freya's gaze and drew a breath. 'That's why I wanted to meet up. Something has been troubling me for a while which I haven't shared with anyone.' She placed Charlotte into a highchair between them and started to secure her in place. 'I cannot bear the strain any longer. You're the only one I can talk to.'

'Go on.'

'To be direct,' she sighed. 'I think your father might be seeing someone.'

Freya's eyes widened. 'You think he's having an affair?' Annabelle nodded and watched Freya's eyes glance around the cafe. 'How, what...?'

'You must first assure me that you won't say anything of my suspicions to anyone, especially Alex.'

'Of course, but I can't believe it. I'm sure it's just a misunderstanding, or you're misreading the situation. He wouldn't be capable of such deception.'

'Let me explain,' Annabelle began. 'I think it all started after your father was working long hours last October. He was becoming distant, and he was too tired most of the time for any intimacy. No warmth. I just put it down to stress at work – he'd been taking on more clients, you see. I thought no more of it until...' The waitress interrupted as she arrived with their lunch order.

12.55 p.m.

Alex was treating a patient for a dislocated shoulder in an A&E cubicle. 'Nurse, can you pass me the syringe, please.'

Hamish walked into the cubicle. 'Can I assist?'

'Sure. I could always do with another pair of hands.' Alex injected a local anaesthetic into the patient's shoulder.

'Would you like me to hold down the patient's chest?'

'Please, Doctor Campbell. I'm going to push out and up on his elbow on the count of three. Ready – one.' Alex pushed. The patient groaned as Alex managed to pop the patient's shoulder back into place. 'Nurse, if you could please finish off here – all done.'

'Time for a bit of lunch,' whispered Hamish.

They headed to the food hall and ordered a burger and coffee each.

'Thanks for finding me. I needed the break,' said Alex, pulling in his chair. 'I couldn't believe that Sandra put me with Patel yet again. I swear she hates me.'

'I've found a way to play Patel,' said Hamish. 'You've just got to ask him about his family; take an interest. He loves talking about how well his two sons are doing with their education. He'll then be like putty in your hands.'

'I'll try anything if I can get him to speak to me with some respect.' Alex sipped his coffee. 'Changing the subject – how's your love life lately? Still seeing Lucy?'

'Aye. It's actually refreshing dating someone who isn't a nurse for a change. Speaking of which – Natalie just gives me the coldest stares every time she passes me in the corridor and grumbles unrepeatable expletives under her breath.'

'That's the price you pay.'

'Have you managed to get bewitching Amelia out of your head yet?'

Alex nodded confidently. 'I've thought about her occasionally, but I'm focused on marrying Evie.'

'What's changed? You were all topsy-turvy last time we spoke.'

'I know, but then Evie had a rethink about starting a family; she totally surprised me. I'm no longer feeling confused.'

'Pff… You do know that old saying – a leopard can't change its spots.'

'She changed her mind after thinking it through,' said Alex, leaning back. 'Don't make more of it.'

'Why don't you meet up for a discreet date with this Amelia lass? Just as friends.'

'There are several things wrong with what you're saying. Firstly, you want me to use Amelia. Secondly, I'll also be going behind Evie's back, and thirdly, she'll probably say no anyway. Evie has dumped her as a friend. Besides, I don't have Amelia's number.'

'I have her number,' Hamish said, getting out his phone. 'I got it from Lucy.' Grabbing the paper napkin, he wrote down the number.

'You're a sly dog, Campbell.'

Hamish pushed the napkin across the table. 'It'll be a good test of your love for Evie.'

4.05 p.m.

Alex got changed after he had finished his shift and emptied his pockets before transferring his scrubs into a hospital laundry basket. He pulled out the napkin with Amelia's number and stared with uncertainty at the digits for a moment, then saved the number on his phone. He wiped his forehead with the napkin and tucked it into his chino pocket.

A text message from Freya pinged through as he finished changing. *Call me.* He immediately phoned, sensing something was wrong. 'What, you need to meet me now? Okay, I'll see you there.' He got on his bicycle and cycled to the arranged meeting point at Lammas Land playground. There were only a few people there in the fading light. He spotted Freya and cycled up beside her. 'What's this all about, Sis?'

'I couldn't talk about it on the phone. In fact, I shouldn't be talking about it at all, as I promised.'

'Promised who?' He noticed the strain on Freya's face.

'Mum, I promised Mum,' she said, watching over Charlotte playing on a climbing frame. 'I met up with her earlier.'

'Mum was here?'

She nodded. 'I have to break my promise. It's so important that you know.'

'What're you talking about?'

Freya turned to face him. 'Mum thinks Dad is having an affair.'

Alex shook his head. Silence hung in the air as Alex processed her words. 'Never, I can't believe it.'

She stared at him. 'When I think back to Christmas, don't you think Dad was a little different – more distant towards Mum?'

'Mm... What has she told you?' His eyes met hers.

'You know Dad came back early from Mallorca just before the New Year? Then he flew back to join Mum before they returned together. Mum felt something was wrong in their home when she got back. She thought there was a subtle perfume scent on the bed, and she also found a long strand of red hair on her bedside table. She didn't sleep that night; she instinctively knew another woman had been in her bed, and the sheet had been changed. She also said that she has since smelt another woman on him.'

'Bloody hell... I don't believe it. What are we going to do?'

'I think we need to spy on Dad's movements.'

Charlotte came running over. 'That's a crazy idea,' he said, crouching down, sweeping her up, and spinning her around as she screamed with joy. After a few minutes, she ran back to the climbing frame.

'Mum said Dad was working at the office today. It's Saturday, which seems strange, don't you think?'

'Your point being?'

'Could you catch the next train into London and hang around outside his office? Follow him, see where he goes.'

'What? I've just finished work. Besides, Dad might have left by the time I get there.'

'Phone him beforehand. If you've missed him, get the train to Richmond anyway to see Mum.' Freya turned her gaze back to watching Charlotte. 'Mum will cook you a meal, but don't let on to her that we've spoken.'

He rolled his head back. 'I'm tired, and you want me to go to London.'

'Be guarded.' She turned to face him. 'Make Mum understand that you wanted to see her.'

'You've got this spying business all worked out, haven't you?'

'It's either that or we encourage Mum to hire an investigator.'

'Alright, I'll go. I'll let Evie know I'm going to see Mum.' He waved goodbye to Charlotte and cycled across town to Cambridge rail station, secured his bicycle, and within a few minutes caught the express train into London.

He was just ten minutes into his journey when he texted Evie. *Something has come up; I'm on the train to see Mum.* He sat back, scrolling through some of his phone messages and searched his contacts list, and gazed at Amelia's saved number. He thought about what Hamish had said, *"Why don't you meet up for a discreet date with Amelia, just as friends?"* He knew it made no sense, but his finger hovered over the dial button. The temptation to press the call symbol urged his fingertip forward.

'Just do it,' he whispered to himself and pressed the button. She picked up but, panicking on hearing her voice, he hung up. He released a long breath and relaxed back. *What am I doing?* His phone rang, and the screen showed Amelia's name. 'Heck.' Panicking, he pressed the decline button and exhaled a breath.

After a few minutes, he opened *YouTube* on his phone and put in his earbuds. He selected the women's quad sculling final video from the 2003 World Rowing Championships and settled back into his seat, trying to calm himself for the remaining journey.

On arriving at London Liverpool Street, he walked a few minutes from the station into the city. He stood across the street, opposite the illuminated entrance to the offices of Orion Hunter M&A, and phoned his father.

'Hello, Alex. It's good to hear from you. How are you?'

'I'm fine, thanks, Dad. I was thinking of coming up to see you and Mum this evening.'

'Oh, right, a bit sudden,' said Robert. 'I'm working at the office right now. The thing is, I'm trying to secure a deal. I won't be home until late.' His father made his excuses about needing to get back to work and ended the call.

Alex got out of the cold and walked into a glass-fronted café. He ordered a steak sandwich and a beer and settled on a stool at the window, looking directly towards his father's office entrance. He thought of the irony of eating a steak out on a stake-out. He texted Freya, giving her an update, and then he phoned Evie. She understood that he hadn't seen his parents in over a month.

Alex's empty plate and beer glass were collected. He wasn't sure how long he had been watching the entrance, but he felt heavy-eyed as he maintained his gaze. Stretching out his hands, he yawned and flexed his back in the seat. Suddenly he straightened up, like a rabbit in headlights, noticing his father leave the building. Alex jumped down from his seat and out of the café, making sure he couldn't be seen. He watched his father walk along the front of his office building until he got to the corner and waited. Alex continued to watch and wondered why he was hanging around. A red-haired woman approached his father and held out her hand. Robert grasped it. Alex continued to observe as Robert and the woman walked along the street together, her arm linked through his as a shoulder bag swayed around her side. Alex followed from the other side of the street, not quite believing what he was seeing. Crossing the street, he followed them, keeping his distance, hoping that his dad wouldn't signal for a cab. It felt alien to him, following his father around in the dark like a spy in a cold war movie.

His father and the woman unexpectedly stopped outside the entrance of a grand hotel. He noticed his father say something to her, they kissed fully on the lips, and then they stepped between the stone entrance pillars. The doorman opened the hotel foyer door for them. Alex walked up near the entrance and peered through the glass doors into the reception area. He could see his father, who appeared to be signing in and collecting a key. He felt as if something was wrenched away from his inside. The doorman took hold of the door handle to open it. Alex shook his head, turned, and walked back the way he came.

9.50 p.m

Alex knocked at his parents' house in Richmond. 'Great to see you, Mum,' he said, putting an arm around her and kissing her on the cheek.

'Come into the kitchen.' She opened the oven door. 'I've got your favourite pizza here ready to go in the oven, and there's a chilled beer on the table.'

'I'm not really hungry, Mum. I've eaten loads.'

'But I got it out ready for you after you phoned,' she said, picking up a glass of wine.

'Well, I guess I could manage a couple of slices.' He grabbed the bottle opener and popped the bottle cap.

'Have you spoken to Freya today?' she asked.

'No, should I? Is there some news?'

She placed the pizza into the oven. 'No, it's fine. I just wondered.'

'Where's Dad?'

'Um, working late again at the office.' She rolled her eyes. 'He phoned a couple of hours ago to say he'll be in later, and that he's eaten. I've made your bed up, by the way.'

'I'll probably miss him then – I've been at work since six this morning, and I'm absolutely shattered.' Annabelle settled herself onto a kitchen stool with her wine. 'How long has Dad been working on Saturdays?' he asked, taking a sip of his beer.

'It seems to go in phases.' She gulped some of her wine. 'He has been working late the odd evening since Christmas – he says he's really busy.' She pursed her lips. 'Just to make you aware, your father and I have an arrangement for when he's late – he sleeps in the guest room.'

Alex's heart felt heavy. He couldn't say anything; he'd promised Freya. The family had been let down by his hero. A headache had come on since he saw his father walk into the hotel with another woman. They both sipped their drinks and continued to make small talk with forced smiles.

Chapter 10

Saturday, 8th February 2020, 6.10 p.m.

Alex checked the time on his wristwatch as he sat in the passenger seat of Sanjay's car. 'That was a brilliant afternoon.'

'Truly excellent,' said Sanjay, yawning as he drove in the fading light to his home north of Cambridge. 'But I'm now desperate for a hot shower.'

'I hadn't realised how exhausting paintballing would be.'

'Did you notice that Hamish took a paintball hit to his vitals? He looked funny, with orange paint splattered around his groin.' Sanjay glanced around. 'Is everything alright? You seem a little distant.'

'Like I said, I'm just a bit exhausted.'

'Zahida will make us a hot cup of tea when we get back – she's made up the spare room for you.'

'Thanks again for organising today,' said Alex. 'I really appreciate everything.'

'You seem distracted. If it's wedding nerves, that's perfectly natural, you know.' Sanjay shared his memories of lost sleep before his marriage up until he reached his home and parked his car.

Alex pulled his overnight bag from the back seat. Sanjay walked into his home and embraced Zahida as she carried her youngest daughter on her hip. She kissed Alex on the cheek before he collapsed onto a kitchen stool.

8.30 p.m.

Alex walked towards The Frog and Lily pub. 'That hot shower was just the ticket.'

'And you're now ready for a good meal,' said Sanjay walking alongside him.

'And a few pints with the guys.'

'They've put us in a side room to the restaurant.'

'Understandable. Hamish's reputation must have preceded him.'

'You aren't so holier than thou yourself!'

'True.'

They walked into the bar area. Alex's friends turned with a loud cheer and raised their glasses.

Hamish stepped forward. 'I love this guy,' he said, pulling Alex in close and giving him a kiss on the cheek.

'How many drinks have you had?' Alex laughed.

Hamish grinned. 'Who's counting?'

Spud had two pints lined up on the bar, and Alex and Sanjay grasped them. A short time later, the whole group moved through to a side room, off the restaurant, and got seated. Sanjay sat to one side of Alex with Spud on the other.

Sanjay stood up from the table and tapped his spoon against his glass. 'Okay, we're going to adhere to our club conventions when dining out – that means phones switched off, gentlemen, and into the baskets in the middle of the table.'

Alex noticed two text messages and a missed call from Evie while his phone was on silent. 'I'll just be a minute.' Alex stepped outside and phoned her. 'Is everything alright?'

'You haven't replied to my messages. I wanted to speak to you – I haven't seen you for over a day.'

'I'm just here at the pub with the guys. I haven't interfered and tried to call you while you've been away on your hen night.'

'I wouldn't have minded. I love you, Boo.'

'Likewise, but I need to go. I'll see you tomorrow. Bye.' He ended the call, switched off his phone, went back inside and placed it in the basket when he got back to the table.

Sanjay looked across the table at an empty place and leaned in towards Alex. 'Couldn't your dad make it tonight?'

'To be honest, I told him not to come along. He'd be constantly on the phone and would struggle to fit in anyway.'

'Oh, okay.' Sanjay stood. 'It's now time for our competition,' he announced. 'Grab your drinks and follow me around to the axe-throwing room.' The group entered a long room with heavy netting lining the sides of the walls. Three red targets painted on wooden planks covered the far end wall. Several racks of bright steel axes on either side of the back wall were placed behind a white line on the floor. The group drew straws from Sanjay to decide on teams. He went through health and safety procedures and read from the notice board, *'No persons can throw axes if in an unfit state.'* His gaze fell on Hamish. 'Take note. Your axe must embed into the plank to score. Each of the small red circles is worth ten points.'

They started the game with Sanjay keeping score on a chalkboard.

Alex stepped forward when it was his turn. 'My top tip.' He felt the weight of an axe. 'Wrap both palms around the axe handle and launch it over your head.'

'Aye. Now imagine caressing the handle like it was the slim waist of this cracking lass Amelia,' said Hamish, just as Alex threw his axe. It bounced off the planked target hitting the rubber floor matting. Hamish chuckled. 'Did I put you off – sorry.' He winked.

The contest finished an hour later, with Alex's team losing to Hamish's team. They headed back to the bar with Sanjay buying everyone a drink.

'What was all that about earlier?' Sanjay asked, passing Alex his drink. 'Hamish going on about some woman called Amelia. The look on your face.'

'It's nothing, really. We met an old patient of mine...'

'What else are you not telling me?'

Alex wobbled and spilled some of his beer down himself. 'I'm pissed. Ask me again in the morning.'

It was almost midnight when Sanjay and Spud assisted Alex out of their taxicab at Sanjay's home. One under each of Alex's arms, they got him into the house and clambered up the staircase. All three started shushing each other, trying not to wake the children.

'Steady, all of you,' said Zahida appearing on the landing in her dressing gown. 'Don't fall.' They reached Alex's room, and she held open the bedroom door as they staggered forward and let Alex flop down onto the bed.

Sanjay wrapped his arm around her. 'We're drunk, tired, and exhausted.'

Spud put his arm around Sanjay. 'Copy that... Hic!'

'Spud. I've made up the sofa for you downstairs,' she said, pulling off Alex's shoes and covering him over.

Chapter 11

Sunday, 9th February 2020, 8.45 a.m.

Alex appeared downstairs, looking burry-eyed. 'Argh…' He eased himself onto a breakfast bar stool.

'Good morning. Not feeling so good by your expression,' Zahida said as she finished weighing out some cake mixture ingredients.

'No, but a cup of tea would be really welcome.' He peered around the lounge. 'Has Spud gone?'

'He left half an hour ago,' she said, putting on the kettle and making him a mug of tea.

'Ah… That hit the spot,' he said, sipping his tea as he leaned on the counter. Children's screams of joy echoed down the stairs. 'I've often thought that you speak wise words in conversations, Zahida.'

'You flatter me.' She stirred her rock cake mix.

'If you don't mind me asking. Did you and Sanjay always plan to have a family when you got married?'

'Where did that come from?' She chuckled.

'I'm just curious. You and Sanjay seem so happy and content. I know that you both had to overcome huge obstacles.'

'You're right there.' She raised an eyebrow. 'You mean with Sanjay having a Hindu mother but is an orthodox Christian through his Greek father? And me being a Muslim? We nearly never got married because of our different faiths.'

'Sanjay has mentioned it.'

'You know that's why we had to move away and settle in Cambridge. Did you know my father cast me out of the family?'

He shook his head. 'No.'

'They were very difficult times. We became even stronger as a couple, despite all the prejudices and adversity stacked against us.' Zahida's voice strained and her eyes welled up.

'Sorry, I really didn't mean to cause any upset.'

'I'm okay,' she said, swinging her gaze back to him. 'We did speak about having children, but that's not the reason why we got married.'

'Because you got on well…'

'We got married because we truly loved each other.'

'Of course…'

'I knew that Sanjay would always protect and care for me.'

'Would having a strong friendship have been enough to get married?'

She grinned. 'Love has to be at the foundation.'

Alex grimaced. 'But surely a couple could have a good working relationship without the love part?'

'That would be like building a house on sand.'

He rested his head in his palm. 'Mm…'

'This is really about you and Evie.' She placed a hand on his shoulder. 'Listen to your heart and let your soul lead you…'

Clasping his mug between his hands, he closed his eyes. His stomach churned, and his head throbbed as he wrestled with his emotions.

She went back to her rock cake mixture, adding an egg and some milk. 'Sanjay tells me that Hamish has got you all stirred up inside.'

Alex opened his eyes and put down his mug. 'He thinks he has my best interests at heart.'

She smirked. 'More like his own interests.'

'How do you mean?'

'I saw it for myself in the coffee shop,' she said, stirring her cake mixture. 'He's a collector of women's hearts and puts them in an old trophy box labelled "Used" – metaphorically speaking.'

'You're right. I've told him he's not exactly a shining example to give marriage advice.'

'But he might have picked up on some negative aspects in your relationship with Evie.'

'There is that.'

Zahida stopped stirring the mixture. 'Do you know – the one person I think Hamish truly loves is you.'

'He actually said that to me last night.'

She tilted her head as children's laughter filtered through from upstairs. 'Have you analysed your options with Evie? Sorry, I'm sounding like a scientist again.'

'I'm confused.'

'Well, the way I see it, you have two paths to choose.'

'And those are?'

'Fully commit to marrying Evie because you love her.'

'And the second?'

'One that is longer but leads to the same end.'

Alex rubbed his forehead and sat upright. 'The same end being marriage?'

'Well, yes, but with more time to evaluate everything. It's not too late to rethink.'

'My head feels worse.'

'I've just thought of a third.'

'Go on.'

'Just follow your instincts.'

Chapter 12

Wednesday, 12th February 2020, 10.30 a.m.

Alex stood waiting with his hands pressed firmly into his coat pockets at one end of a pedestrian bridge that arched over the River Cam in the city centre. A cold winter breeze cut through the warmth of the sun as he gazed around, taking in the view of a weir that controlled the river level. Tourists queued nearby to him at Scudamore's on Mill Lane to go on sightseeing punting excursions. He watched with vague interest as a group of twelve tourists covered their laps with blankets as they filled one large punt. Checking his phone for messages, he pulled his scarf in closer and looked up. There she was in a bright strawberry-coloured coat with a matching beret and gloves. Her blond hair bounced on her shoulders as she approached.

He was reminded of a piece of motherly advice – "Beware of women wearing red. It spells danger."

'Hi ya,' said Amelia as she walked up to him.

'You're late,' he said, grinning.

Amelia swept her hair off her face. 'I needed to be certain you arrived before I did.'

'Fair point, I guess.'

'I'm glad you finally found the courage to ask us to meet instead of hanging up all the time...'

'I felt awkward...'

'I had my reservations about being here.' She swept the hair off her face again. 'To be honest, I didn't expect to see you again as you're getting married on Saturday.'

'Perhaps us meeting isn't so wise after all.'

She tilted her head. 'I suppose there's no harm in us going for a walk and having a cup of tea, but I must be back for a lecture at two.' She raised her left arm. 'At least I have something to celebrate – no more armbrace.'

They set off following the river path as it meandered out of the city, past the Cambridge Canoe Club and then through Paradise Nature Reserve near Newnham, occasionally catching each other's slightly awkward gaze.

'Are you all set for getting hitched on Saturday?'

'I think so. Evie and the wedding planner have organised everything.'

'Is it a big wedding, like Becky and Oliver's?'

'No, we have just sixty guests, not a hundred and sixty like them.'

'Is it a church wedding?'

He nodded. 'That's what she wanted.'

'Uh ha. Will you also have musicians and a disco?'

'Can we change the subject, please... Why did you agree to meet up with me?'

'Ah, there's a question.' There was a moment of silence as her eyes rolled skywards. 'I enjoyed our brief conversation at the reception, and I felt disappointed it ended abruptly.'

'Is that it?'

'Well, yes, and the possibility that we would probably never see each other again, especially since Evie has dumped me as one of her friends. And it would be sad if I didn't get to see you one last time.'

He stopped walking as he digested her reply, and then she stopped. Their eyes met. He wanted to know how she felt about him, but he then looked around at the tree canopy. 'I enjoy being close to nature like this – walking through woodland.'

'This really is a beautiful spot, the way the winter sun comes through the trees.'

'This walk is just what I need at the moment.'

The pair of them started to walk on a little further, but then Amelia spotted some dead leaves shuffling under a fallen tree near the path. He followed her as she walked over to investigate. 'What's with all this creeping along?' he asked.

She looked around and picked up a stick, 'I've developed an eye for spotting these movements ever since I was a little girl.' She used her stick to carefully push back some leaves. 'Oh, hello, gorgeous.'

'A frog.'

'Correction. A common British toad,' she said, crouching down to examine it.

'How do you tell the difference? Oh, what... you're actually picking it up.'

Amelia stood still, holding the toad in her palm. 'Aren't you a handsome male toad with those golden eyes?' She brought the toad up close to her face and smiled as she stared into its eyes.

'Hopefully you're not going to kiss it because I doubt it will turn into a handsome prince.'

'Only toads have dry, warty skin,' she said, stroking its back with her finger. 'Whereas frogs are smaller in size and have long legs.' She glanced around at Alex. 'I know this is a male because the females are almost twice the size, which is unusual in the animal world. Surprisingly, they also don't hibernate in winter but burrow into compost and will emerge to forage in milder spells like today.'

Alex watched her with fascination, captivated by her care and knowledge as she reeled off lots of amphibian facts. He moved in closer.

The toad's eyes flicked towards him as she continued to gently stroke it. 'They also don't leap around like frogs but tend to crawl. They eat all sorts of things, but mainly slugs and worms. We're lucky to spot this one foraging.' She carefully placed it back down and covered it over again with leaves. 'Alex, can you pull out the small container of hand sanitiser from my handbag, please.' He passed it to her. 'They release poisonous secretions when they feel threatened.'

They went back to the path and continued their walk, leaving the nature reserve and going through Grantchester Meadows. He continued to take a keen interest, asking her questions. 'That's amazing,' he said. 'Over two hundred and thirty different species of those ugly critters in the world, including frogs and salamanders.'

'They're not ugly. Unfortunately, they used to get a lot of bad press. You take the fabled stories with witches and toads, the association with bad people. But, when you've studied these creatures as long as I have, you grow an affinity with them.'

They continued to walk along the riverbank and started to watch four students struggling to control their punt. Alex chuckled as he adjusted his scarf. 'You have to be reasonably skilled at punting to venture this far outside the city onto this natural part of the river. If my situation was different, I would like to take you punting sometime.'

Amelia turned and gave Alex a wry smile. 'Awkward.'

He nodded. 'Can you remember when you first took an interest in amphibians?' he asked, feeling relaxed with her.

Amelia adjusted her beret. 'I do have a vivid memory of one particular day in mind. I was with my family at a nature reserve by Lake Michigan. Would you like to hear how my interest started?

'Why not. Give me the full version.'

'Perhaps the shortened version for now.' Her eyes scanned the sky. 'It was two thousand and four; I was eight. I was sitting in the back of Dad's car. Barnabas, our Labrador, was sat between my sister Daphne and me. I remember it was a warm morning, and we were going to a church social gathering at a coastal park on the shoreline of Door County.'

'A church social?'

'Mmm.' She nodded. 'Anyhow, there were loads of frogs migrating across the road and getting squashed. Mom also tells this story. Only she says, "It was like the story from Exodus. The plague of frogs on the Egyptian people."'

'Crikey – a lot of frogs then.' He glanced around as they strolled along.

'There sure was. I remember screaming at my Dad to mind the frogs. He looked around at me and said, "It's okay, sweetie." He swerved – Mom yelled, and the tyres squealed. We almost had a head-on collision with another car.'

'Lucky for you and your family, he didn't. But did he squash any frogs?'

'I reckon so.'

They neared Grantchester Village, and Alex led her towards the recreational field. 'So, from that situation, you realised the impact urbanisation was having on parts of nature?'

She nodded. 'That's right... Also, on that same day at the park, a group of us, a few moms and kids, leaving the dads at the BBQ, went on a *Fairy Walk*.'

'Fairy Walk?'

'You know the type of thing – a path where all the bridges over the streams and ponds had pictures of fairies on them. I loved going there. The sound of croaking frogs everywhere – it's a wonderful experience.'

Alex rubbed his stubble. 'I thought you were telling the shortened story.'

'I am. Anyway – we found this really big bullfrog, about seven inches long. Everyone gathered around it.' Amelia giggled to herself. 'I remember that it suddenly hopped forward – it startled everyone, and they moved back.'

'The boys as well?'

'Even the boys. I stayed put. Everyone flinched when it hopped again – I remember laughing. I picked up a stick, flipped the frog over, and I rubbed its belly with the stick. I could swear the frog was smiling from having its tummy tickled.'

'I've never heard of such a thing.'

Amelia smiled. 'I guess it was seeing all those squashed frogs that day and the big awesome bullfrog that made me want to try and make a difference.'

'Very admirable.'

She nodded. 'Have you got a story as to why you became a doctor?'

'It just so happens that I have,' he said, opening a garden gate at the end of the recreational field. 'Let's get a hot drink first and a piece of cake.' They walked through a small apple orchard into a tearoom, purchased their teas and cakes from the servery, and sat inside at a small square table.

Amelia took off her coat, beret, and gloves. 'So, c'mon, what's your story?'

'It was two thousand and five – I was thirteen. We were at our family holiday villa on the island of Mallorca in the Med.'

'That sounds awesome. Does it have a swimming pool?'

'A modest one.' He swallowed back a piece of cake. 'I was with my dad in the car going to pick up my friend and his parents from the airport – they were coming over for a holiday.'

'And?' She bit into her cake.

'We were travelling down the island's main dual carriageway, passing the town of Inca. A car a few hundred metres ahead of us swerved. It crossed the path of a large truck, and there was a collision. The truck whiplashed over onto its side, crushing the car. Another car crashed into the truck. Dad pulled up and grabbed the first aid kit from the glove compartment. We ran to the scene. Dad and a couple of others helped pull a couple of people clear of their crumpled car – there was leaking fuel everywhere. They helped them onto the grass verge and then went back.'

'That must've been scary?'

'It was, and it wasn't. I started helping by applying a bandage to a woman's cut hand until an adult took over from me.'

'And that's what inspired you to become a doctor?'

'I reckon so. Dad said, "I think you'll make an excellent doctor." I remember it like it was yesterday.'

She finished her tea. 'I'm pleased we had this time together.'

'Likewise.'

'Evie is a very lucky woman.' She checked the time on her watch. 'I think we need to be leaving.'

'So soon.' He knew she had to be getting back, but he felt disappointed that their relaxed conversation was ending. It was the positive distraction he needed.

She nodded and pulled her beret over her head.

A cheerless grey sky had blown in, blocking the sun as they made their way back to the city by the same route, arriving back at the bridge from where they started.

She turned and looked deep into his eyes. 'I don't know what was going on today with us meeting up like this, but I really enjoyed our walk and your company.' She paused. 'You're a lovely guy, but I'm not sure we should do this again.'

He gave her a questioning gaze. 'Why not?'

She tilted her head. 'It just wouldn't be appropriate.' She leaned forward and kissed him on the cheek. 'I wish you well, Alex.' He just stared at her as she walked away. He pondered for a minute before he called the sculling club. 'Is there any availability on booking a boat today at three?'

2.50 p.m.

Alex arrived at the club, got changed, and collected his Wellingtons. Another club member helped him carry the single-scull boat out onto the water. Adrenaline powered him down the river. Out of breath and exhausted, he eventually stopped in the middle of the river and thumped the side of the boat.

'Why did I listen to Hamish?' He slapped the water. 'Bollocks! I shouldn't have met up with her…' His boat drifted in the river current. Reaching behind him, he got out his phone, put in his earbuds, and selected his favourite Eighties soul music tracks. He slumped forward and tried to find peace.

5.10 p.m.

Amelia was sitting alone at a table in the college Crocus Café reading when she caught sight of her friend. 'Lucy, over here.'

'I'm pleased I've seen you in person,' Lucy said, taking a seat opposite Amelia and placing down her tray of food. 'I was thinking of going into town for a drink tonight. Fancy coming along?'

'Why not. I could do with a quiet drink.'

'Quiet – that doesn't sound like you.'

'I met up with Hamish's friend, Alex, today.'

Lucy grinned. 'Oh yeah? The bridegroom to be on Saturday.'

'The very one.'

'Why…?'

'He called me and asked if we could meet.'

Lucy leaned forward. 'And you agreed. What's going on?'

Amelia's eyes went wide. 'I wish I knew.'

'He didn't seem interested in you when we all met at the Ferryman Inn?'

'I know, other than examining my arm. I agreed because I can't stop thinking about him.'

Lucy drank some water. 'It all makes sense now why Hamish asked for your number. He wouldn't let on why.'

'Alex has such comforting blue eyes and a reassuring soft voice. His touch aroused me when he examined my arm.'

Lucy giggled. 'What?'

'It was like the only healing I ever needed. I knew he was spoken for, but I couldn't resist taking the chance and meeting up with him. I didn't flirt, I swear.'

'Oh, Amelia.' Lucy rubbed Amelia's forearm. 'You need to find a boyfriend that's single and free.'

'I know.' Her shoulders slumped. 'It's been over seven months since I've had any interest in men. Jake was the last. Alex has reawakened sensations in me that I thought were lost forever.'

'You hardly know this Alex. So, just let it go.'

'Easier said than done.'

Chapter 13

Saturday, 15th February 2020, 3.50 a.m.

Alex awoke in a hotel room and checked the time on his phone. 'Ugh…' Yawning, he got out of bed and went to the ensuite to relieve himself. 'Are you awake?' he asked Sanjay, coming back into the twin bedroom.

Sanjay turned his head. 'Mm-hmm.' He pushed himself up into a sitting position. 'What is it?'

Alex sat on his bed. 'It's about Evie finding that napkin in my pocket with Amelia's phone number.'

Sanjay turned on his bedside light. 'What's done is done.'

'Yeah, thanks, that doesn't help. I still can't believe she phoned the number and recognised Amelia's voice. She just ranted at her. She thought it was her that gave me the napkin.'

'Crap happens.'

'Is that your answer?' Alex shook his head. 'You're meant to be my best man, the one out of the two of us that should be thinking straight and finding a way out of this mess for me.'

'What mess?' Sanjay asked, pushing out his arms. 'You both had an argument about it, and you promised not to see or speak to Amelia again. She promised Evie that she wouldn't see you either. Evie forgave you. Surely everything is resolved?'

Alex sighed. 'I suppose when you put it like that.'

Sanjay shrugged his shoulders. 'Alex mate, you're getting married in around ten hours' time. You and Evie have been planning this wedding for months. You've both been living together for three years – you must know if it's right or not? I don't see the problem.'

'The problem…'

'You even said last night that you've sorted out your differences. "I'm not going to see Amelia again; I'm going to marry Evie." Those were your words, which is the right answer because you and Evie are both good for each other.'

'I know in my head you're right, but I have this sense of uncertainty.'

'My alarm is set for eight. That gives us four hours – can we go to sleep now?' He switched off his bed light.

Alex got into bed and pulled the duvet over his head as he tried to get back to sleep.

11.50 a.m.

Alex and Sanjay had parked the car at St. Mary's and walked down Church Lane towards a pub.

'I don't like the look of that gloomy sky,' said Sanjay, looking up as they walked around a cricket field towards the Cricketers Arms pub.

They got themselves seated at the window alcove table with two pints of beer when Hamish and Spud suddenly stepped through into the lounge. Alex caught sight of them in their wedding finery, buttonholes proudly displayed. Hamish and Spud turned to face him and immediately launched into a well-rehearsed song at high volume, startling the other drinkers. *"Alex is getting married in three hours'! Ding dong! The bells are gonna chime. Pull out the stopper! Let's have a whopper! But get him to the church on time!"*

Some customers in the pub who recognised the *My Fair Lady* tune started clapping along to the rhythm. *"Alex's gotta be there in three hours', spruced up and looking in his prime. Girls, come and kiss him – show how you'll miss him. Hopefully, we'll get him to the church – on time...!"*

They sang two rounds before the four friends embraced each other. Two buttonholes were pinned on Alex and Sanjay's suits. They ordered some beers and sandwiches, which arrived shortly afterwards.

Sanjay raised his glass as they sat around the table. 'I would like to make a Scullerteers toast.' They raised their glasses. 'All for one! And one for all!' they chanted, chinking the necks of their glasses together and simultaneously taking a swig.

'Guess what, guys,' said Spud. 'We're all going to meet Hamish's girlfriend, Lucy – she's coming to the reception later.'

'Bloody hell,' said Sanjay. 'You must be getting serious with her.'

Hamish looked daggers at Spud. 'I asked you not to say anything. Can't you keep a secret?'

Spud grinned. 'Evie has promised to introduce me to her teacher friend.'

'But she's a professional woman,' said Hamish. 'What will she see in a builder bloke like you?'

'Oh-ha bloody ha. With my muscles, she'll know she's met a real man. And, I drive around in a mighty new Ford Ranger pick-up.'

Sanjay rolled his eyes. 'That's right, we forgot about your penis extension.' They laughed. The beer flowed; another round was ordered. 'Alex, it's good to see you relaxed.' Sanjay put an arm around him.

The banter carried on for a while. They joked about the time they capsized their quad-scull boat a few weeks earlier.

Sanjay put his empty glass down and checked his wristwatch. 'Well, it's come to that time. The taxi will be here shortly. You two need to get the order of services and buttonholes to the church. Jenny, the wedding planner, should be there waiting.'

'Bravo, Sanjay, for arranging this pre-marriage drink,' said Hamish, nodding. 'Alex's last as a bachelor. Thank goodness you didn't take any notice of me acting like an idiot for the last few weeks – shouting my mouth off about Evie.'

Spud stared out of the window. 'The rain has got heavier.'

Hamish stood. 'The taxi is here.'

Sanjay paid the bill, and then the four of them went to leave. A married couple looked up from their table and started to sing, *Get him to the church on time.*

Hamish and Spud instantly joined in the singing. They linked arms with Alex and led him out of the pub singing at the top of their voices. *"He's getting married in an hour! Ding dong! The bells are gonna chime…!"*

The taxi drove the short distance to the church. Alex and Sanjay hastily raised their umbrellas as they stepped out into the rain. 'Here I go,' said Alex, pulling in his coat and walking up the gravel path.

'Damn the weather,' Hamish shouted as he and Spud hastily collected the service booklets and buttonholes from his car before pacing towards the 16th-century church porch. They halted as they stepped inside. 'Whoa…'

'It looks stunning, doesn't it,' said Sanjay turning around.

'Blimey,' said Spud, his mouth gaping open. 'It's amazing.'

Floral garland displays decorated an arched door frame. Raised pillar candles stood on either side of a heavy oak door entrance, bathing the flowers in gentle light.

The door creaked as Alex pushed it open and walked through. The central aisle was lined with tall candle-stands with crowns of lit candles aloft. Spotting Jenny near the altar, he walked towards her. Sanjay, Hamish, and Spud waited by the entrance gazing at the church adornments. Tea lights and candles burned angelically on each windowsill, illuminating the church from the dismal grey day outside the windows. Candlelight swept across white stone walls and shone into the vaulted timber ceiling. The air was filled with the fragrance of flowers drifting from the garlands adorning the ends of the pews.

'Hello, Alex,' said Jenny as he walked up to her. 'I hope you like what you see.'

'You and your team have done a marvellous job,' he said as gentle classical music played in the background.

Sanjay joined Alex and caught Jenny's attention. 'You've created something quite magical here.'

'Evie will be really delighted,' said Alex, seeing guests were arriving.

Spud elbowed Hamish. 'We'd better start handing out the buttonholes and order of services.' They started to show some of the guests to their seats.

'Zahida has arrived,' said Sanjay, noticing his wife walk in carrying their little girl. 'I'll be back in a jiffy.'

'The scent isn't too strong, is it?' Jenny lifted her nose to the air. 'I recall the problem the lilies caused at Becky and Oliver's wedding.'

'I can't fault anything,' Alex said, gazing around the illuminated scene.

'We switched the church heating on early this morning to make it feel warm and cosy, but I used a little scent trick to create the pleasant fragrance. The team placed essential oils behind the radiators and in the garland displays,' said Jenny, looking pleased with herself. 'We think it helps create a sense of tranquillity for everyone.'

'It definitely works,' said Alex, watching the guests starting to stream into the church.

Alex noticed his parents with his grandmother, Evelyn, taking her seat between them on the second row. Annabelle blew him a kiss. He could feel his heart beating strongly – as if it wanted to push out of his chest. Sanjay walked towards him, holding his wife's hand. 'Hi, Zahida,' said Alex. 'I guess Zareen is with Evie?'

'Yes, they should be in the car on their way right now.'

Jenny straightened Alex's buttonhole. 'Your ushers look very smart and appear to be enjoying themselves organising the wedding guests. If I didn't know better, I would say they've had a sneaky tipple earlier. I'm just going to check on the service with the minister.' She peeped at her watch. 'But other than that, we're good to go in a few minutes when the bride should arrive.' She walked away.

Zahida turned to Sanjay, giving him a bright-eyed gaze. 'Can you give Alex and me a couple of minutes together, please, my love?' Zahida glanced around and noticed a quiet spot out of sight of everyone in a side transept. She tugged on Alex's sleeve, and he followed her. She turned to him and took hold of both his hands in hers. 'Remember our conversation from last Sunday? I sense that you still feel knotted up inside. I can see it in your eyes.'

He frowned and nodded. 'I guess I just have to accept the situation.'

'Take a slow breath in and hold. You need to be in the moment right now and listen to your heart.'

He stared at the tiled floor. 'Evie has been alright, but…'

'Do you love her?'

He pressed his eyes shut. 'I'm still not sure if I'm marrying Evie for the right reasons. It's more about what she wants.'

'Search your feelings and let your soul guide you. It's not too late; you're not married yet. I think you need to have an open, honest, but brief conversation about having children before the ceremony.'

'She'll be here soon.'

'The timing isn't good.'

He bashed his forehead with the palm of his hand. 'I've left it too late.'

Zahida stepped in close to him and placed a calming hand on his shoulder. 'Remember, you're about to get married with love embedded as the foundation of your marriage. So, is it about love or having children?'

'I really don't know anymore.'

'Evie has come this far. She'll want to marry you today, no matter what.'

He closed his eyes and breathed deeply for almost a full minute before opening them again. 'I'm going to have a conversation alone with her in the wedding car.'

Zahida nodded. 'Listen to what she says, and then let your soul lead you.'

A steely determination descended upon him. He straightened himself up, drew a breath, and walked out of the side transept, past the confused faces of Sanjay, the minister, his grandmother, and his parents. He was almost marching back up the aisle past a packed congregation and went out through the porch past Jenny. He almost barged past Mrs Hawkins as she walked up the gravel path with the bridesmaids. Hamish and Spud were holding umbrellas over them and glanced back around with baffled gazes as Alex went past. Looking puzzled, Freya snatched an umbrella from Spud and followed.

Sanjay grabbed an umbrella at the porch door and gave chase. 'What's going on, Alex?' he asked, catching him up by the lychgate, his face full of bewilderment as Freya stood beside him.

'I need to speak to Evie alone before the ceremony.'

Mrs Hawkins arrived. 'You should both be inside with the vicar.'

'If you can just give us a moment, please,' Sanjay said.

Mrs Hawkins walked back halfway up the path towards the small group of worried faces.

Alex stood silently with Sanjay as the bride's white vintage Rolls Royce wedding car came up the road and stopped in front of the gates. Evie's father stepped out and put up an umbrella. 'You're meant to be inside, Alex.'

'I need to speak to Evie alone in the car.'

Mr Hawkins looked back at his daughter.

'What's happening?' Evie asked as Alex stepped past her father and into the wedding car, pulling the door shut behind him.

He reached over his shoulder and tapped on the glass screen behind him. 'Start driving, please.' The chauffeur hesitated. Alex tapped the glass harder. 'Please just drive! Take a circular route for a couple of minutes.'

Evie gazed anxiously at Alex as they headed off. 'I'm now scared, Boo. I don't understand.'

Alex sat on the bench seat opposite her and took hold of her hand. 'It's about us having a baby.'

'I can't believe we're going through this now...'

'We had an agreement and that was to immediately try and start a family.'

'When I'm in a better position at work – that's what we agreed.'

'I didn't agree to that.'

'I thought we'd sorted this all out. It makes sense to wait,' she said as her eyes filled with tears.

'It makes sense to you, maybe, but not to me!'

'I love you with all my heart,' she said through trembling lips.

'But I'm not ready for this.'

'You do love me, don't you?'

His gaze locked with hers. 'I care for you a lot, but I cannot go through with this wedding, not now.'

'What are you saying?' A teardrop fell from her watery eyes.

'You've gone steaming ahead with all of this and dragged me along with this charade. I need to feel I'm getting married for all the right reasons.'

There was a minute of silence as the car drove around. Evie's lips shivered. 'Alright. Let's start trying for a family on our honeymoon.' She started to sob as she waited for some form of acknowledgment, her eyes full of desperation as she gripped his hands.

He looked for sincerity in her watery eyes. Heart racing, he'd made his decision.

A crowd of friends and family had developed outside the church porch and on the road in the rain as the wedding car arrived back, pulling up beside the lych-gate. Evie's father opened the car door, and he was shocked by Evie's distressed state; she was sobbing, her eye makeup running down her cheek. Sanjay opened the door on the other side. Alex stepped out past him, giving him a nonchalant glance.

'What's happening here?' Annabelle asked as she paced up to Alex and grabbed his hand.

Robert rushed over and gripped Alex's shoulder. 'Son, what's going on?'

'What have you done!' Evie's mother screamed.

Alex pulled his hand away from his mother's and then shrugged off his father's grip as he backed away from the car and the crowd. Guests were staring; everyone was trying to make sense of what was happening. Alex gazed obstinately around at the sea of faces and then spotted Zahida standing passively with her two daughters under the church porch as he backed away from the scene.

'Where are you going?' Sanjay shouted.

Alex turned into the rain and walked briskly down the lane.

5:50 p.m.

Alex was soaked through in his wedding suit and feeling numb. His head was slumped down as he almost dragged his feet along the south side of the Thames embankment towards Hammersmith Bridge. He rose off the path and was crossing over the middle of the bridge when he looked up at the figure standing still facing him. 'What the hell are you doing here?'

'Looking for you, man,' said Hamish.

'I'm not good company to be with.' Alex turned and started walking back the way he had come.

Hamish caught up. 'Please, just talk to me.'

Alex stopped and turned. 'How did you know I was here?'

'Freya had an inkling.'

'Aha. Are you on your own?'

'She's on her way, and so is Sanjay and Spud. But can we please just stop and talk?'

Alex sat down on a dry part of the pavement and rested his head back against the metalwork of the bridge wall. 'What's there to talk about?' he said, pulling in his knees and folding his arms.

'For a start, you're soaked through,' Hamish said, sitting down next to him. 'You'll catch pneumonia if we don't get you out of that suit and into some dry clothes.'

'Don't care. Talk about something else.'

'Where did you go? We went to Cockfosters tube station and back to the Cricketers Arms looking for you.'

'I just got on a bus that came along.'

'That's why we couldn't find you.'

'Did everyone just go home after the upset I've caused?'

Hamish glanced around. 'The minister and Jenny made an announcement, and about half went home. The rest of us went to the hotel and had some the wedding breakfast.'

'So, you had a lovely meal and a joke at my expense?'

'It wasn't like that. The atmosphere was very subdued. A lot of your guests were hungry. It was a collective idea and the right thing to do.'

Alex rubbed the back of his head. 'I'll have to reimburse Evie's father for everything he has paid out.'

'I think your dad has promised to sort it all out.'

'I do feel for Evie after what I've done.'

'Mm... By the way, Sanjay has your phone; you left it in your coat back at the church.'

'Has anyone heard from her?'

'She called your phone when we were at the hotel. Sanjay answered, and she asked where you were.'

'What did he say?'

'The only thing he could, that he didn't know, and she then hung up.'

'Did Freya say what gave her an inkling that I would be here?'

'She explained about a time when you split up with an old girlfriend, and you used to walk the four-mile Oxford Cambridge boat race route from Putney Bridge to…'

'Chiswick Bridge every day for a couple of weeks,' Alex said. 'Sometimes more than once a day.'

'And here we are on Hammersmith Bridge,' said Hamish. 'Is this some sort of de-stressing mechanism?'

'Something like that, I guess.'

'They should be here soon. We started off at different points to cover the boat race route on both sides of the embankment after Sanjay dropped us off. As soon as I recognised you, I phoned her.'

'I can't believe that I've done what I've done. I've mislaid my moral compass.'

'Don't talk crap,' said Hamish, putting an arm around him. 'Your moral compass has just had a wobble.'

'I could stay at the family home tonight.'

'A wise decision.'

7.35 p.m.

Alex walked into the kitchen-diner at his parents' home after he had a bath. 'I feel a lot better.'

'So, it looks like my old dressing gown fits you,' said Robert, pouring Alex a beer. 'And help yourself to pizza; we ordered a selection.'

Annabelle poured herself another glass of wine.

Hamish sat back comfortably, eating pizza. 'I'll have another beer, please, Mrs Hardson, if you're offering?'

Spud gave Annabelle a thumbs up for a beer as he had a full mouth of pizza.

'I'm going to be heading off now,' said Sanjay wiping a napkin across his mouth as he rose to his feet. Alex also got up, and they embraced. 'I'll call you in the morning.' Alex nodded as they released their embrace. 'And if Evie calls, please speak to her.'

Alex's head slumped. 'I feel awful; I wouldn't know what to say.'

'I'll see you to the door,' said Freya. 'Are you okay to be driving back?'

'I've only had a small beer. I feel fine.'

Freya walked through the house with Sanjay and held the front door open. 'It's been a strange, horrible day,' she said, unaware that Alex had followed her and was on the other side of the open hall door listening.

'At least Alex is alright,' said Sanjay. 'And, hopefully, Evie is as well with her family. I'll phone in the morning to see how he is.'

'Thank you for everything that you've done. And thank Zahida for looking after Charlotte tonight.'

'Of course, I will,' Sanjay said as he started to walk away.

Alex withdrew back into the kitchen diner. Freya waved to Sanjay and closed the door. She went back inside and reassuringly patted Alex on the back as she leaned over him and picked up her wine from the table.

'What a day,' said Robert. 'Here we are, eating pizza. But today has cost me a bloody fortune now that I'm paying for the whole wedding that never happened. Money down the drain.'

'Well, I'm sorry!' Alex snapped back as he slammed his tumbler glass down hard on the table, almost smashing it as beer exploded out. His nostrils flared as he stood. 'All you bloody care about is money and shagging your fucking bit on the side!' He walked out of the room.

Chapter 14

Sunday, 16th February 2020, 4.40 a.m.

Annabelle had laid awake for ages. The occasional vehicle went past on the other side of the Green, with its lights creating shadows on the walls that morphed into haunting images of the previous day. Alex's anger in the kitchen and the scene outside the church were fixated on her mind. She decided it was no good and prised herself up, switched on her bedside light, and started reading her book. Heavy-eyed after a time, her eyes closed, and she fell asleep.

'Mum, are you awake?' Freya whispered, gently tapping on Annabelle's bedroom door.

Annabelle shook herself conscious. 'Come in.' She forced herself up and placed her book down. 'I must have drifted off.'

'I've made a pot of tea,' Freya said as she pushed open the door. 'I've hardly slept.'

Annabelle took off her reading glasses. 'Me neither.'

'Sorry, it's only five-thirty if you're wondering.'

'The time doesn't matter – I'm pleased you're here. That was a dreadful scene yesterday.'

'Well, it was all going to come out sooner or later,' Freya said, placing down the tray on the dressing table. 'It was especially awful with Alex's friends witnessing everything.'

'What must they think of this family? What a shambles at the church and searching around for him along the river. But I do wonder if it really is all over between those two?'

'I guess we might find out later. But what about you, Mum?'

'I'm trying not to think about it.'

'I hate him!'

'Shush now. Don't speak like that. Remember, he's still your father. You should always love him.'

'That was until you shared your suspicions with me. What he's done, well, it's unforgivable.'

'Hush. You don't love someone for thirty-six years and then suddenly stop loving them overnight because they've lost their way.'

'Don't you? I thought that's exactly what you do. You should divorce him.'

'I can't. Well, not just yet, anyway. I'll give him a chance to redeem himself, and then if it doesn't work, I might consider what you say. But I really don't want to think about divorce right now.'

'I don't believe you – he doesn't deserve a second chance. Just think about it. If you divorce him, you could have this house, be financially secure, and hold your head high.'

'That's enough.'

'But, Mum, you need to think about it.'

'Listen to me,' Annabelle said, straightening up in bed. 'She's probably young and only sees the exciting side of him. I bet she hasn't witnessed his mood swings when he's stressed. Or washed and ironed his clothes.'

'Oh, come on. She's probably the sort of person that pays for someone to do all the ironing – like you should have done years ago.'

'I actually find it relaxing. Take last week. I was doing the ironing while watching TV. If I was sitting down, I would've probably fallen asleep.'

Freya leaned back against the dressing table and shook her head.

Annabelle sighed. 'Alex should not have spoken in that way – your father meant it in a manner to make light conversation.'

'I can't believe you're defending him.'

'He wouldn't have wanted to upset Alex. You also made the situation worse by getting Alex involved. And by what you said afterwards.'

'Oh, when I said, "We know you've been having an affair – you've been lying to Mum." Yes, I remember exactly what I said.'

'Keep your voice down. I can't tell you how shocked I was.'

'I know – you dropped your glass of wine.'

'It was very nice of Spud and Hamish to clear up all the mess.'

'You almost passed out – Spud caught you,' said Freya, picking up the hairbrush on the bedside table and gently brushing her mother's hair.

'Mm, I guess I've known for a long time, but I've just been in self-denial. Do you think I made it easy for him and his floozy by making him sleep in the guest room?'

'Don't be daft. You did the right thing. Besides, he'll be staying in a hotel from now on.'

'It appears he knows a few intimately.'

'At least there won't be an atmosphere with him not being here.'

'Will you stop calling your father "him?" You always called him Daddy.'

'Not anymore. Especially after he ranted at me and Alex – accusing us of spying on him. And what he said about you in front of everyone was unforgivable.'

Annabelle interrupted. 'You mean that I'm "always too tired for sex?"'

Freya nodded. There was a moment of silence. She put down the brush and poured the tea.

'I'll make a case up for him with clean clothes after breakfast.'

'No, Mum. He needs to sort out his own things. And then don't let him back in the house.'

9.45 a.m.

Annabelle was feeling more relaxed as she sat with her elbows resting on the table, sipping tea and chatting to Freya opposite her. She felt reassured by Freya's presence. Putting down her tea, she went through to the front reception room and glanced through the gap in the door before going back and taking her seat opposite Freya. 'Alex is just lying back on the sofa watching TV.' They both cradled their mugs of coffee in their hands and continued dissecting every part of the previous day's events.

Annabelle went to the window after she heard a car drive down the side of the house and then returned to her seat. 'It's your father. I'm feeling alright, strangely enough.'

Robert let himself in and walked slowly into the kitchen. 'I've just come by to collect some things.'

'Okay,' said Annabelle. Freya ignored him.

'I understand how you both must feel.' He stepped a little further into the kitchen, rubbing the back of his neck. 'I reacted badly last night, and I'm sorry for what I said.'

'I appreciate your apology,' said Annabelle. 'But I'm not sure you're being genuine, Robert. Is your apology meant to excuse the double life that you've been living – all the lying and sneaking around? And I don't know how long it has been going on for.' She released an exasperated breath. Freya remained motionless, with her eyes fixed firmly on her mother.

'But...'

'What's her name, this floozy of yours?' Annabelle asked.

'She's no floozy. Let's not talk about her.'

'Why not? Don't you think you at least owe me the right to know her name? I will find out sooner or later, possibly in court sorting out our divorce.'

'Her name is Sophie.'

'Whatever.'

Robert's eyes narrowed. 'Are you thinking about divorce?'

'Well, isn't that what you want?'

He drew a breath. 'I guess.'

'You guess! Either you do, or you don't!'

'We're all feeling a bit bruised at the moment, and now's not the time to discuss this.'

'I just thought you could've gone about it in a more dignified manner, been more open and honest with me rather than go behind my back.'

Robert cringed and folded his arms tightly. 'It was about getting the timing right. The impact it would've caused on Alex's wedding wouldn't have been fair.'

'Huh, being fair!' Her gaze bore into him. 'Do you think the timing was right when you brought your floozy back here to my home and slept with her in my bed? Answer me that! And don't deny it.'

Silence fell upon the room for a while.

'I'll go and pack some things.' He turned and went back through the hallway.

Annabelle rushed to the door. 'And Robert,' she shouted as he walked up the stairs. 'Leave your house keys before you go!' She closed the door and resumed her position at the table.

'Well, that was unexpected,' Freya said. 'I thought you were going soft on him earlier.'

'His attitude triggered something within me. I can think clearly now, but I couldn't last night with all the arguing and shouting.' Annabelle pursed her lips. 'At least your father was calmer today. You don't think I was too harsh on him, do you?'

'Not at all. I still don't even want to face him. I was tolerating him for you up until last night.'

'I understand, but he's your father. And what I said earlier still stands – I haven't given up on him yet.'

'I'm going to phone Granny and explain to her about his affair after he's gone.'

'I suppose she needs to know, and I can't face telling her.'

'Once she finds out, she'll be straight on the phone to give him a hard time.'

'She may not thank you for it.'

'I know how to manage Granny.'

12.35 p.m.

Robert was in the process of unpacking his things in his hotel room when his mobile rang. 'No, don't come up; I'll come down and meet you in the lounge. I'll only be a few minutes. Order some wine for us both.'

Sophie was sitting back in a chair reading a magazine when Robert joined her and hugged her. 'Steady,' she said as Robert took a large gulp of his drink. 'I take it this morning didn't go too well?'

He grimaced. 'No.'

'Just try to relax and tell me what happened. Did you manage to stay calm this time?'

'Freya couldn't face me. And Alex ignored me.'

'It must be so tough, my love, but you have to expect this reactional behaviour. They must all feel very hurt and concerned about their mum and what the future holds. But they'll get over it in time. They cannot change the fact that you're their father – that won't change no matter how hurt they're feeling. Just be patient.'

Robert ordered another glass of wine. 'Bella was completely different – very defensive and determined; she caught me off guard. I haven't witnessed that side of her for many years.'

'As I say, they're all feeling a little emotionally hurt. It's come as a complete shock to them all. But we know time is a healer.'

Robert folded his arms. 'You're right. They'll come to accept the situation in time.'

Sophie rested back in her chair. 'How did you break it to her?'

'Well, to be honest, she asked me if I wanted a divorce.'

Sophie narrowed her eyes. 'Oh, so you didn't ask her. What was your answer?'

'Look, one step at a time. I've just moved out of my own home, which I'll no doubt lose in a divorce settlement – not to mention a lot of my financial investments. That's the sacrifice I'm making – isn't that enough?'

Sophie smiled. 'Yes, of course, my love. Let's not talk about it anymore today.'

He exhaled. 'Let's make a toast,' he said, taking a breath and raising his glass. 'Here's to us and our long weekend in Heidelberg.' Robert took Sophie up to his room after lunch. As soon as they stepped through the door, he grabbed her, kissed her passionately, and started to undress her, letting her dress fall to the floor. She undid his shirt and trousers, helping him out of them before the two of them slid onto the bed in just their underwear. He removed her bra and kissed her breasts. She slipped off her knickers as they slid between the sheets.

'What's the matter? You've become distant.' She lay silently alongside him, stroking his chest.

'I'm sorry.' He let out a long deep sigh. 'I guess I've got a lot on my mind.'

'Well, let's try and fix that,' she said, moving her hand down and gently stroking his equipment. Seconds later, he was fully aroused again.

'You're amazing; you really know how to turn me on.' He tilted his head back, breathing deeply as her thigh glided over his loins. Straddling him, she guided him into her.

9.20 p.m.

Alex was sitting opposite Freya on an express train from London to Cambridge. He was watching YouTube clips on his phone of last year's World Sculling Championships. Freya was reading an article from the Sunday Times magazine.

'I'm still not sure I've done the right thing,' he said.

Freya rested her magazine on her lap. 'It should never have got to this stage. I also keep wondering about Evie as well and how she must feel right now. I considered her to be a good friend.'

'I know, I messed everything up.'

'But it obviously didn't feel right for you. Any ideas on what you'll do next?'

'It's Evie's home. I'll have to move out. Can I stay with you for a while until I get myself sorted?'

'Of course. I'm pleased you asked. Charlotte will be ecstatic.'

'Great – thanks.'

'Have you spoken to Evie?'

'No,' he said, rubbing his forehead. 'I almost feel ashamed to speak to her after what I did. She's tried calling three times.'

'I understand that you possibly feel like lying low, but you must call her back.'

'Maybe later.'

'Do you think she could be back at your flat?'

'I expect she's still with her parents. My idea is to stay at the flat tonight and sort out a few things that I'll need. I'll get a taxi over to yours in the morning and stay until I can get a rented flat arranged.'

Freya placed her hand on top of his. 'Is it really final?'

'I think so... But I'm not sure.'

'What has happened that has made you feel like this?' Her phone started ringing, and she pulled it out from her handbag. 'It's Evie.' Their eyes locked. 'I should answer it. 'Hello, Evie, how are you?' Freya grimaced at her own words.

'As well as can be expected after yesterday, I suppose,' said Evie in a shallow voice. 'I've been trying to speak to Alex, but he's not answering. Does Sanjay still have his phone?'

'No, Alex has it now,' said Freya frowning as she turned to face him.

He buried his head in his hands. 'I'm not ready to talk to her,' he whispered.

'He's very upset about what he did and cannot bring himself to talk about it.'

'I see. We have got a lot to sort out. When you speak to him, please explain that I still love him.'

'Yes, of course. I'll ask him to phone you tomorrow if that's alright?'

Alex's face emerged from behind his hands only to shake his head at Freya.

'Where's he staying?' Evie asked.

'I'd rather not say. You both need to rest and take five – he'll phone you in the morning, I promise. I must be going now. Bye, Evie.' Freya hung up. 'What else was I meant to say?'

'Okay, Sis. I'll phone her in the morning.'

The train pulled into Cambridge Central Station. They both got in a taxi and went to the apartment at Hampton Mews.

'Have you got your keys?' Freya asked.

He nodded. 'You sound like Mum.'

'Huh. At least it doesn't look as if Evie is back,' she said, staring up at the windows. 'And now that you're back, I won't need to feed Cookie.' Freya winked and gave him a reassuring smile. 'I'll phone around eight.'

Alex watched the taxi drive away and then went over to his street entrance door. Feeling edgy, he quietly let himself through into the stairwell and deliberately avoided turning on the light as he softly made his way up the stairs to his apartment's front door. As he neared the top, Cookie put her head around the side and meowed loudly, startling him. He lurched back. 'Whoa…' He tumbled head over heels down the stairs into a knotted heap at the base. Cookie meandered down the stairs as he lay groaning and greeted him by brushing her side against his shoulder.

'Cookie, you could've killed me,' he said through crumpled lips. The side of his face was pressed against the tiled floor. He forced himself to sit up with his back to the wall and felt down his side, assessing his injuries in the dark. Stretching his arm out, he switched on the stairwell light. Blood was on his fingers from an abrasion to his head. He flexed his shoulder; it was sore to touch, but he could tell it was not broken. Looking up the stairs, he gathered his strength and, with purpose, slowly crawled to the top. Cookie went through the front door cat-flap ahead of him. Wincing with soreness, he got onto his feet and unlocked the door.

He put his head around the door and switched on the light. *Good, she's not here*, he thought as he stepped through, rubbing his back and hip. Cookie peered up at him as he waddled into the bathroom and had a pee. He ran a bath, peeled off his clothes, and eased himself into the hot water with a sigh. Feeling the warmth cocoon him, he rested his head back on the edge of the bath. Tiredness gripped him as he closed his eyes.

Alex had almost gone to sleep when he heard Cookie meow. He knew that particular meow, and his senses were alert. His eyes sprung open, and he sat bolt upright, causing water to splash onto the floor. He noticed Cookie slink past the open bathroom door, and then he heard a key in the lock and the front door opening.

'Boo, are you here?' Evie asked.

'Shit!' He gritted his teeth as he scrambled out of the bath, closed the door, and locked it. 'Yeah, I'm here!'

'I just want to talk to you, please,' she said from the other side of the bathroom door.

'I'll be out in a moment.' He quickly dried himself, put his crumpled shirt and trousers back on, and slowly opened the door.

'It's alright – you don't have to look so worried,' she said with Cookie nestled under her chin. 'I'm not going to rant at you or anything like that.' He just stood there. 'Oh, my goodness. You've got a nasty graze across your cheek. You need a dressing on that.'

'It's really nothing.'

'Can we talk? I just want to try and understand what happened.'

'I guess I owe you that,' he said, rubbing his hip. 'Shall we go in the lounge?'

'Great. I'll just speak to Dad; he's waiting outside. He won't go until he knows I'm settled.'

Alex went and got changed in the bedroom and limped into the lounge a few minutes later to find Evie sitting on the sofa with two cups of steaming hot tea on the table.

'Is your father picking you up later?' he asked, grimacing from pain as he sat down opposite her.

'No, I'm planning on staying here.'

'Ah.'

'I guess you intended to do the same?'

Alex nodded. 'I'll move out. I just need to pack a few things.'

'You don't have to move out. Just wait until we've talked about yesterday and where we go from here.'

He nodded. 'I'm actually glad that we're having this conversation now face to face.' He leaned forward to pick up his mug of tea.

'I explained to Dad that I wanted to try to sort this out. We could go back to living how we were. I still love you.'

'I'm confused about a lot of things, Evie.'

'Just be open with me. I thought we were happy up until yesterday. I was hoping it was just wedding nerves.'

Alex felt prickly when he caught her gaze. 'I'm not sure how to say this... but I think we should have a break and go our separate ways for a while.'

'Go our separate ways.' She sprung to her feet.

'Just to see how we really feel about each other.'

'But I explained to you that I've changed my mind. I'm prepared to try and start a family for you!'

'Well, that's just it, you see. I don't want you to do it just for me – it should be what you want as well.'

'But I've agreed to what you want.'

'I've thought long and hard about this during the week. I'm sorry that I've left it so late. All the effort and planning that went into the wedding. I feel really bad about what I did.'

'Surely we can work this out!'

He shook his head. 'We both need some space.'

She crossed her arms, and her gaze was like a hawk. 'This is my apartment. You'll have to move out. In fact, go now!'

'Alright,' he said, pushing himself to his feet. 'I'll just pack a bag.'

'You need to go now. Just go!'

'Be reasonable; let me pack some clean clothes. I'll only be a few minutes.'

'I bet that American bitch has something to do with this. There's something you're not telling me!' He frowned. 'I thought as much!' she said before pacing into the bathroom. She grabbed his toothbrush and threw it at him. 'Just go!' She stood to one side and pointed to the door.

Alex picked up his phone, hobbled to the door, and pulled on his coat.

Evie's father held open the front door. 'I heard everything. If I hadn't turned soft in my old age, I would probably punch you in the face right now. You deserve it for the way you've messed my daughter about.'

Alex cautiously edged passed him.

'Go, just sod-off. If I see you again, I promise that I won't be responsible for my actions. I'll put you in that A&E department of yours as a bloody patient. Do we understand each other?'

Alex nodded and limped down the stairs, step by step.

Her father looked down at him from the top of the stairs. 'And to think that a waster like you was going to be my son-in-law – huh!'

Alex didn't look back as he limped out of the ground floor entrance, pulling his coat in and turning up his collar against the cold. He stopped at the road entrance to Hampton Mews and went to phone his sister. But knowing that she'd only just picked up Charlotte from Zahida's home, he tucked his phone away and decided to go to the nearest pub just a few minutes' walk away. Hurting physically and emotionally, he entered the pub clutching his side.

A barman was polishing some glasses with a tea-towel as Alex walked up to him. 'You're lucky; you've just caught last orders,' said the young barman with a goatee beard. 'What's your poison, anyway?'

'Something to warm me up and to numb some pain.'

'I reckon that'll be a double whisky. Nasty graze you've got there on the side of your face.'

Alex nodded. Easing himself onto a barstool, he phoned Hamish.

'Aye, what's up?'

'Can you put me up on your sofa, just for tonight, please?'

'I thought you were staying at your flat.'

'Evie came back shortly after I got in. I explained why I thought we needed to have a bit of space. It all turned sour.'

'What happened?'

'She told me to go. She wouldn't even let me pack a few things. Can I crash on your sofa?'

'Ah, the thing is,' Hamish said. 'I have Lucy around.'

'Please? You owe me this. I can't ask my sister.'

'Bollocks, okay... I'll speak to Lucy after we've done the deed.'

'What.' Alex gasped. 'Look, I'm in The Black Swan, and they're closing shortly. Please hurry, do the deed, and get here.'

'Ah, so you also want me to pick you up.'

'I'm in no fit state to drive. And forgot to pick up my car keys from the apartment.'

11.55 p.m.

Alex was waiting at the pub entrance, smoking a joint. He had bought some weed off the barman for what they had agreed was medicinal purposes. Hamish pulled up in his car and opened the door. 'I've been waiting ages,' Alex said, taking a last drag from the joint and then flicking it away as he got in. 'It's only a ten-minute drive – what's taken you so long?'

'I had to gently persuade her out after we'd done the deed. She was suspicious at first when I told her that I was picking you up. Hey... is that weed I can smell?'

'Yeah,' said Alex, grinning. 'Good stuff, actually – it's helped take my mind off the pain. It's been years since I had a joint.'

'What've you done to the side of your face? She didn't hit you, did she?'

'Long story – it can wait.' Alex slumped his head back against the seat headrest.

Hamish parked his car a short time later on the road near his block of flats and helped Alex up the stairs.

Alex flopped onto the sofa. 'That hurt.'

Hamish removed some of Alex's clothes. 'Oh, that's not good,' said Hamish. 'The bruising across your shoulders and back. You've taken quite a bashing – you could've been killed.'

Alex laughed. 'It would've been Cookie's fault.'

'Seriously, you may have a cracked vertebra or something else. I'll examine you properly in the morning.' Hamish started to make up a bed around Alex. 'I'll leave you some Panadol by the side here with some water. Do you hear what I'm saying?' But Alex was already asleep.

Chapter 15

Monday, 17th February 2020, 6.29 a.m.

Robert was standing in his boxer shorts by a window in his hotel room, watching as the winter dawn was breaking, staring out onto the London street scene below as it came to life with people. He was thinking of his home that he might not access again.

Sophie stirred from her sleep in the bed. 'You're up.' She pushed her hair off her face and propped herself up. 'It's only six-thirty.'

'I automatically get up early during the week, generally before six.'

'Is everything alright?' She pulled the sheet up around her naked body as she sat up on the edge of the bed.

'It's the start of a new life. Things can't go back now to how they were before Saturday.'

'Would you want them to?'

'Of course not. What's done is done.' He gazed out of the window.

'I'm really looking forward to seeing Heidelberg.'

'Yes, but we still need to be careful,' he said, turning around to face her. 'We can't let our work colleagues suspect anything. You're my PA; we need to keep things professional.'

'Being discreet is my business. Speaking of which, don't forget you've got a lunch appointment today at the Savoy at one o'clock with your mother.'

'Great, that's all I need. She'll be aiming to give me a difficult time.'

'But you're a grown man?'

He turned to face Sophie. 'Hey, you don't know my mother – she's formidable. She still talks to me like I'm her little boy. In fact, she thinks more of her parrot than she does me. She and Freya are especially close. And Mother always makes sure she has the last word on everything. I don't know anyone who has got the better of her yet. She likes to try and control all our lives, she's got nothing better to do, and she's got worse since Dad died. He knew how to pacify her superior tendencies. At the age of eighty-five, her mind is still as sharp as a razor with a tongue to match.'

'I wish I could be there supporting you.' She padded over to him, letting the sheet unfold itself off her body as she pressed her naked form against his back. He could feel her sensual warmth radiate into him, and he caught his breath. She released her hold and ran her fingertips slowly down over his arms, making him tingle. Her fingers entwined in his, and she took a firm grip. He knew the signal, and he let her take control. She eased her grip and placed his palms on her thighs.

Robert's breathing hastened. 'You know we have to go into the office separately this morning. We cannot risk any gossip.'

'Shhh...' She kissed his back as her right hand moved around and slipped inside his boxer shorts. 'I remember,' she whispered as she caressed his equipment. 'Discreet is the word.' He became fully aroused. Her free hand pulled him around, and they locked together, kissing.

6.34 a.m.

Annabelle had been lying awake for ages. The house felt unusually quiet and empty. Now that the dawn was breaking, she decided to get up and make a cup of tea. She grabbed her book from her bedside table and went downstairs to the kitchen, made a pot of tea, and watched the sunrise from the kitchen window. A new day. She wondered what Robert was doing – if he was with his floozy. Endless thoughts filled her troubled mind as her tea went cold between her palms. She went into the front drawing room, switched on the reading light, and curled up in her favourite chair. She checked her watch. Teresa should have just taken off from Mallorca. She picked up her book and tried to read, but her eyes grew heavy, and she drifted off to sleep.

Her senses were jolted by her mobile ringing on the side table. 'Hello, Freya.'

'Good morning, Mum. Did you manage to sleep alright?'

'Not brilliantly, if I'm honest.'

'Me neither. Kept thinking of you and going over the weekend again. I'm just sorry I couldn't be with you last night.'

'Have you spoken to Alex this morning?'

'I've tried, but his phone must be switched off. I was going to arrange a time for him to move in today. Charlotte's very excited.'

'I've been thinking of calling Mrs Hawkins. I thought we could intervene and help smooth things out.'

'Don't get involved,' said Freya. 'You've got enough worries of your own. You need to take care of yourself and start by having a nice healthy breakfast, and then perhaps make a list of things to do, places to visit for when Teresa arrives.'

Annabelle checked the time on the mantle clock. 'Her plane should've just touched down. I'll take your advice. Speak to you later. Bye, for now, darling.' She compiled her *to-do list* in the kitchen while preparing a fruit salad in a bowl. Afterwards, she had a bit of a clean-up around the home, showered, and dressed.

8.30 a.m.

Annabelle was walking through the hallway of her home when she heard her door chime. She opened the front door and embraced Teresa. She immediately got a little tearful.

'Hey, what's all this?' Teresa asked.

'Oh, nothing, but it's so good to see you. Come through. Would you like some tea?'

'Forget about the tea, girl – we need something much stronger.'

'Perhaps you're right.' She wiped her eyes. 'I've booked a table at the Ivy for lunch. We can catch up over a glass of wine.'

'That sounds wonderful.'

'I thought we could go shopping this afternoon, then maybe cook something together tonight, and watch a movie.'

'Even better,' said Teresa. 'Just like good times when our men weren't around. Sorry, I didn't mean…'

'That's fine – I'm just about getting my head around things.' Annabelle smiled weakly. 'Is it too early for a gin and tonic, do you think?'

'Definitely not – I'm on holiday, remember?'

6.50 a.m.

Alex groaned when he moved. Soreness and stiffness had set into his back, shoulders, and side. He decided to just lie still. His eyes searched around Hamish's open plan lounge-kitchen, and then he noticed the small side table next to him with a note, some Panadol, and a glass of water. Grimacing, he manoeuvred himself to take the medication and rested his head back. It wasn't long before he drifted back off to sleep.

'Alex, time to wake up, mate,' said Hamish, sitting down next to him.

Alex jolted awake. 'Ah, what time is it?'

'It's almost ten. How're you feeling?'

Alex started to push himself up into a seated position with Hamish's help. 'I think I need more pain relief.'

Hamish passed him two more and a glass of water. 'Let's examine you. I probably should have taken you to A&E last night, but I thought better of it with your breath smelling of weed and drink.'

'I just need some rest.'

'An examination first.' Hamish helped Alex to his feet and gave him an examination. 'You'll live. No real major damage, but your shoulders and back are heavily bruised. You're going to be sore for a few days.'

'Thanks for putting me up, but I need to phone Freya, and then I'll get out of your way.'

'You're not in my way. Lucy is coming around. Why don't the three of us go out and have a lazy brunch together?'

'You know what, I've seen a change in you since you've been with her,' he said, starting to get dressed. 'Your previous relationships don't normally last this long.'

'That's because she's a bit different – refreshing and fun...'

'Yeah, she's good.'

'How about you and Amelia?'

'Please don't go there.'

'As a good friend, I just want to see you happy.'

'I appreciate everything you've done for me, but I'd be on the rebound, and that wouldn't be fair on her.'

'You could just ask her out for dinner. It could simply be a friendly date, no more in it than that. It will help keep your mind off Evie.'

'You don't give up, do you.'

'Hey, you know me.'

11.05 a.m.

Alex was enjoying a relaxed coffee and a light brunch at the Caffeine Hub. 'Despite my body aching like hell, I feel much more relaxed today.'

'That's great, man,' Hamish said, sitting opposite him with his arm draped casually around Lucy's shoulder. 'While you were having a quick shower, I booked a double scull session for this Friday morning. That's if you feel up for it?'

'We'll see.'

'I figured that you need to be doing something positive, keep active and busy now you're not on your honeymoon.'

Alex rubbed his shoulder. 'Like I said, we'll see.'

'I've also arranged with Spud and Sanjay to have a quad session on Saturday.'

Alex grinned. 'I'm not sure I'll be fit enough.'

Hamish turned to Lucy. 'Has Amelia mentioned anything to you about Alex?'

Lucy's eyes went wide. 'I cannot divulge.' She leaned into him. 'I do need to catch up with her. I'll arrange that when she gets back from visiting her parents.'

Alex straightened up. 'Is she going back to America?'

Lucy nodded. 'She's leaving from Heathrow sometime tomorrow. Her father isn't well.'

12:57 p.m.

Robert stepped out from his taxi at the Savoy Hotel, smartly dressed from work, wearing a grey three-piece suit with a light-blue silk tie. The head waiter at the restaurant reception desk escorted him to Lady Hardson's table. 'Hello, Mother,' he said, taking his seat opposite her. The waiter tucked the chair in behind Robert and laid a napkin over his lap.

'I'm impressed, Robert; you're on time,' she said, touching her silver-coloured bobbed hair and straightening her black dress jacket. She gazed around at the waiter, catching his eye before flicking her gaze to her empty glass. The waiter refilled it with sparkling water. 'Thank you.'

Robert smoothed out a ripple in the white linen tablecloth in front of him. 'I'll have the same, please.'

Evelyn narrowed one eye. 'Nothing stronger? That's unlike you.'

The waiter handed him a menu. 'I'll also have a small ice-cold Heineken,' said Robert. 'Thankyou.' His gaze shifted to his mother's large silver brooch, a serpent in the shape of a letter *E* with red jewelled stones as eyes.

Evelyn twiddled with the pearls around her neck. 'Shall we order and eat, and then we can discuss why I wanted to meet with you? In the meantime, tell me how work is going.'

Robert smoothed the tablecloth again after their plates were cleared. 'So, you've spoken to Freya. What did she have to say?'

Evelyn levelled her gaze at him across the table. 'What do you think she might want to speak to me about?'

'That's hard to say. Possibly, her concerns for Alex's wellbeing – especially after the fiasco on Saturday.'

'Unlike you, Freya had a frank, honest conversation with me. Now let's cut to the chase – you need to tell me what's been going on?'

'Oh please, Mother. You've been a retired high court judge for fourteen or fifteen years. But before you judge me, wait until you've heard my side of the story.'

'Well, that's what I'm waiting for. Just the truth, then I'll make a judgement.'

Robert narrowed his eyes. 'I guess Freya explained that she thinks that I'm having an affair with another woman?'

'Are you?'

'It's just a misunderstanding – they've jumped in before they know the full facts.'

'Now you're speaking like a proper defence. Go on – explain the full facts, as you put it.'

'Apparently, I've been seen going into a hotel with another woman on my arm. I have been seeing someone, but I wouldn't call it an affair because we haven't been doing anything sexual. I've been faithful to Bella. But now she's talking about divorce.'

Evelyn held up her finger. 'So, to briefly sum up – you admit you're dating another woman behind Annabelle's back. You've been lying to her, but you say that you haven't had sexual penetration with this other woman.'

He nodded.

'I'm almost afraid to say it, but you're guilty!'

'What, how?'

Evelyn waved the waiter over with the coffee trolley. 'Under the law, you're guilty because an extramarital affair doesn't only have to be a sexual relationship. It can also be a romantic friendship between you and another without your spouse knowing.'

Robert rolled his head as the waiter served the coffee.

Evelyn's commanding eyes narrowed on Robert. 'Listen carefully. I'll be direct; you've had your fun with this woman, but now it's time to end it before it goes too far.'

'But you haven't…'

Evelyn threw out the palm of her hand. 'I haven't finished. You'll need to follow my advice. Take Annabelle out to dinner at a neutral location, somewhere romantic, and ask for forgiveness.'

'Next, you'll be expecting me to beg her to come back?' His gaze fell on his mother's serpent brooch.

'Exactly, that's what you need to do. Make her feel special again…'

He exhaled as he stood. 'I'll pay the bill, Mother. But we're done here.'

Chapter 16

Tuesday, 18th February 2020, 8.25 a.m.

Alex had been awake for a couple of hours, propped up on his pillows, staring at the morning light coming through the gap in the curtains. He was torn between thinking about Amelia and what he'd done to Evie.

'How're you feeling this morning?' Freya asked, entering his room and placing a cup of tea down by the side of his bed.

'Still sore, but at least I've got my overnight bag back from Sanjay and some new clothes. I still can't believe Evie wouldn't let me pack a bag.'

Freya sat down on a chair. 'Well, you've told me before that she can be feisty at times. But in her defence, I might well have reacted in the same way after what you did.'

Alex pushed himself up. 'My head is all over the place – I still feel confused. We've had some fun times living together, and now it's over.'

Freya sighed. 'This is just the guilt talking. Did you sleep well?'

'I did, actually.'

'There you go; if you really weren't sure, I suspect you wouldn't have done. So, what're your plans for today?'

'You've been great putting me up, but I need to start looking for another place to live. I need to contact Evie about getting my car keys and my bike and collecting some stuff. That's if she's approachable?'

'I'm already ahead of you on that one. I phoned her yesterday. She was sort of okay-ish with me. I hope you don't mind, but we came to a compromise because she doesn't want you back in her flat.'

'What's the compromise?'

'Zahida and I are going around there this morning, and we're going to box up your stuff. She said that her friend Becky would be there.'

'Good, so I don't have to see or speak to her.'

'Not quite,' said Freya, grimacing. 'Part of the arrangement is, we have to leave all your stuff outside the flat for you to collect. She wants to say goodbye to you in person.'

'I guess that's fair enough. I'll ask Spud if he can take some time out from work this afternoon.'

Freya stood up. 'I better get ready as Zahida will be around soon.'

Alex smiled as he got out of bed, finished his tea, picked up his phone, and scrolled to Amelia in his contacts. He pondered for a moment with his thumb hovering over her name, thought better of it, and then showered.

He returned later with a towel around his waist and kept glancing at his phone as he got dressed, then picked it up, took a breath, and phoned her. 'Hi Amelia, it's me, Alex. Can we talk, please?'

'Aren't you meant to be on honeymoon with your wife?'

'Evie and I split up.'

'You're kidding me. She made me promise that I wouldn't speak to you again.'

'I know,' he said, grimacing. 'But it doesn't matter now.'

'Please tell me that you didn't break up because of me?'

Alex walked slowly up and down in his room. 'Sorry... you might have had something to do with it, but you're not the main reason. Shit, that didn't come out right. Look, can we meet up, please?'

'I'm not sure that's wise. But where are you staying?'

'With my sister, here in Cambridge.'

'Alex, the thing is – my dad's not well, and I'm leaving for the airport. I just can't think straight, and I'm not sure I need another worry at this time. I'm sorry, but I must go.'

10.30 a.m.

Alex and Zareen's younger sister lay on the lounge floor pretending to be patients. Two dollies lay beside him as he got out his phone. Charlotte and Zareen played doctors and nurses using Charlotte's playset.

'You won't get better if you don't lay still,' said Charlotte. The girls adjusted the blankets around each of their four patients' and started using the play stethoscope on the dollies.

Alex seized his chance and phoned a Cambridge florist. 'I would like to send a single pink rose, please, with a simple message, but it must arrive in the next hour. I'll pay the extra. She lives in the city in one of the college dorm rooms.'

Freya came home and walked into the lounge, followed by Zahida. 'And you're still playing doctors and nurses,' said Freya smiling.

'How did it go?' Alex asked as he sat up.'

'Sort of okay. We had enough flat boxes and got everything packed up. We stacked them just outside the front door on the landing with some of your clothes on hangers draped over the top.'

'Is there a problem?'

'We felt obliged to have a cup of tea when Evie offered. The four of us sat in the lounge, but it felt really difficult under the circumstances.'

'Quietness filled the room for a while as we just sipped our teas,' Zahida added.

'I broke the silence,' said Freya. 'I asked her what she was going to do next.'

'And…' said Alex.

'She's going to keep herself busy assessing students' GCSE coursework before she goes back. She needs to keep her mind off things,' said Freya. 'They were her words.'

'She was quite despondent,' said Zahida.

'Did you manage to get my car keys?'

'Sorry, but no,' said Freya. 'Evie wants to be sure that she has a chance to speak to you in person. She thinks that you might just take your things and go.'

11.30 a.m.

Annabelle walked along Richmond High Street with Teresa at her side checking out boutiques, popping in one after the other. 'What a horrible, dull, grey day,' said Annabelle. 'I wish you could've brought some of the Mallorca sunshine over here with you.'

'My blood has got too used to the Mediterranean climate.' Teresa tucked her scarf around her neck. 'I forgot how damp and cold this country can be in winter.'

'Well, you have been living there a few years now. But thank you for being here; you're just the tonic I need to cheer me up.'

'I'm just being myself.'

'That's what I need, you being yourself – forever young at heart.'

'You give me too much credit – my heart may be young, but my wrinkly skin tells a different story.'

'You look great. You glow with sophistication.'

'Ha.' Teresa adjusted her fur hat.

'Hey. This looks like a really fab shoe boutique,' said Annabelle staring through the shop window.

'Let's have some fun. You should get some chic new shoes and spend some of Robert's money.'

Annabelle suddenly froze. 'That's a good point – he may have cancelled my credit card.'

'Surely he wouldn't be such a bastard. Let's find a stylish pair of shoes to test it.'

The two of them spent almost an hour casually chatting and trying on shoes before Annabelle settled for two pairs and some suede designer boots.

'Phew, the card still works,' whispered Annabelle. 'That might have been embarrassing.'

'Not at all. We simply would have made our excuses and walked out. What shall we do next, continue shopping?'

'Well, there's nothing else I need.'

'Nonsense, woman,' said Teresa, standing back, eyeing Annabelle all over. 'Your Radley handbag is looking a bit tired these days, if you don't mind me saying. Let's go and look at getting you a new one. Then it'll be time for lunch, which will be on Robert – I think.' Teresa grinned.

'Maybe you could give me some advice over lunch, just in case he does go and cancel the credit card. I haven't got a lot of my own money.'

2.45 p.m.

Alex sat in the passenger seat in Spud's pickup, just outside Evie's flat at Hampton Mews. 'Thanks for helping me out at short notice.'

'That's what friends are for.'

'I've got a bad feeling about this.'

'Run through the plan with me again,' said Spud.

'Everything is stacked outside at the top of the stairwell. We'll load up the pickup, and then I'll go in, have a chat with her, and get my keys.'

'And you're going to give me the keys to get your bike from the lockup.'

'Precisely. I'll then drive my own car back to my sister's. Got it?'

Spud nodded. They went in and loaded up most of the boxes into the pickup.

Alex pressed the doorbell. 'Hi, Evie.' He walked tensely through as she held open the door. 'Where are the keys to the lockup and my car keys?'

'That's all you care about, isn't it?' She dug her hands into her hips. 'That and your stupid rowing. You could have asked me how I was?'

'Of course. That was thoughtless of me – sorry.'

'That's all you have been is thoughtless. You've only cared about yourself.'

'Wait. I thought we were going to have an amicable chat?'

'Amicable? After what you've done…'

Alex backed out of the front door. 'Evie, be reasonable. Please, can I have the keys?'

Spud came up the stairs and froze behind him.

'Here you go.' She threw the lockup keys down the stairwell.

Spud trotted back down, grabbed them, and retreated to the lockup. Alex backed himself away halfway down the stairs.

Evie stood beside the remaining two boxes on the landing. 'Going behind my back and seeing that American bitch just before we were getting married. I can't believe you could do that to me!' She bent down and started pulling books out of one of the boxes and throwing them at him.

'Hey – that's my stuff.' He shielded his face. 'Just calm down!' His body absorbed the ferocity of flying books and other objects as he backed down the stairs. He turned and hurried out to the pickup as Spud placed his bicycle in the back. Evie walked out with his radio alarm clock in her hand.

'Spud… Quick,' Alex shouted. 'You better go.'

'Good idea,' replied Spud, pushing up the tailgate as Evie walked towards them with gritted teeth and eyes blazing. Spud sped off. Alex dodged the alarm clock as it hurtled towards him and smashed into the ground.

'Please, Evie. That's enough.'

'You've turned out to be a lowlife cheating toad!' she said, breathing heavily. Neighbours started to pull back their curtains to peek out to see what all the shouting was about.

She stopped a couple of metres from him. He knew that hawkish stare when she was calculating her next move. He just stood and watched as fury spun her around, and she paced over to his car. 'Evie, please don't…' he said. She stabbed his car keys into the front light and the wing panel several times before slowly dragging and twisting them along the full length of the car body, scoring the paintwork. She dropped the keys to the ground and walked back into her flat. He walked over and picked them up. Standing still, he gathered his thoughts. He knew there was still a sealed box of his stuff remaining on the landing, and he cautiously returned. As he bent over to pick it up, a searing pain shot up his side, making him drop to his knees. He could hear Evie sobbing inside as he rubbed his back. Wincing, he lifted the last box and forced himself to his feet. His knuckles hovered in front of the door. He wanted to try and have a rational conversation but knew it wouldn't work. He lowered his hand and hobbled down the stairs towards his car.

Chapter 17

Wednesday, 19th February 2020, 4.55 a.m.

Robert awoke in his hotel room bed on his side, snuggled into Sophie's back. Trying not to wake her, he carefully untangled himself from her and the bedsheets, picked up his phone, and went into the ensuite, closing the door quietly behind him. He sat down on the toilet and checked his phone; four missed calls. He read a text from his mother:

I suspect u r avoiding answering my calls. Annabelle has been a loyal good wife to u. End this nonsense with your plaything by this Sunday. Otherwise, there will be consequences. X.

He texted a reply; *Hello Mother, I'm NOT about to end it, and don't threaten or JUDGE me!*

It was almost a couple of hours later when he was having breakfast with Sophie in the hotel café when his phone pinged, and he read the text.

I'm happy to meet with u for lunch today at the Savoy again. I've booked a table for 2 pm. X.

'Everything alright?' Sophie asked. He nodded and continued with his breakfast.

1:20 p.m.

Annabelle walked through Richmond Park with Teresa by her side as they both sheltered under their umbrellas from the rain.

A sudden gust of wind blew Teresa's umbrella inside out. 'This is why I don't visit London in the winter. I know you wanted to be out in the fresh air, but really?'

'We'll soon be at The Roebuck,' said Annabelle. 'I thought you would enjoy all the daffodil borders – they usually look so colourful and vibrant.'

'You know what I think? You need to get away from London and from Robert. Come back to Mallorca with me and stay for a while. At least think about it; the island's sun and warm temperature will lift your spirits.'

'That would be just running away from facing up to what's going on.'

'You're overthinking it. Besides, I could do with your company.'

'Are you still lonely? Michael has been gone two years now.'

'It's really hard. I've not forgiven that inconsiderate husband of mine for dying of a heart attack while playing golf.'

'It was a shock.'

'It still makes me angry and upset that he didn't take his medication. Otherwise, he would still be alive.'

'I'm sorry,' said Annabelle, putting an arm around Teresa. 'You seem so self-assured – as if you've moved on.'

'Let's change the subject, please.'

'What to?'

'Back to Mallorca. Come on; the change will do you good.'

Annabelle shook her head. 'It doesn't feel right to just go.'

'You'll be involved again in my social scene, and you'll have your gardener popping over. What's his name again?'

'Emilio.'

'What do you say?'

'There's a lot going on in Alex's life,' Annabelle said as they continued walking side by side. 'I feel I need to be here for him.'

'Nonsense, he's a grown man for goodness sake – he'll work it out. Besides, he's got your gorgeous Freya supporting him.'

'Perhaps we can discuss this later after we've eaten.'

'Okay, deal,' said Teresa, tucking in her scarf. 'So much for a lovely walk around Richmond Park; the weather has rather put a damper on it.'

They reached The Roebuck and were seated at their reserved table, and promptly ordered.

'The smell of vinegar – just wonderful,' said Teresa, shaking salt onto her gourmet fish and chips. 'This is what you need inside you on a day like today. Not that super-food salad you're having.'

'Oh, go on then, let me pinch a chip,' said Annabelle, reaching over to Teresa's plate. 'I hope you enjoy what I've planned for after lunch.'

'No more walking, I hope.'

2.05 p.m.

Robert arrived at the Savoy wearing a charcoal-coloured suit. He was shown to his mother's table and sat opposite her as the waiter tucked in the chair behind him.

'A little late,' said Evelyn. 'A good choice of tie; it nicely matches your pocket square.'

'Thank you, and that's an interesting brooch you're wearing. A lizard with emerald eyes. I don't recall seeing that before.'

'It's clever, don't you think, how it's been shaped into the letter *E*. I've had five different silver ones made by a designer jeweller.'

Robert turned to the waiter. 'I'll have a small beer and a sparkling water, please. Shall we order?' He knew what he was having. Evelyn nodded, they placed their orders, and the waiter left.

Evelyn rested her clasped hands on the table. 'Do you love this woman?'

'Here we go again.' He rested back in his seat. 'She's fun, and she makes me feel young.'

'This sounds like a midlife crisis. To just discard Annabelle seems so very cruel – all because she doesn't make you feel young? Don't you think that you should grow up and act your age?'

'We've grown apart,' he said, glancing away. 'She isn't the same woman anymore – not the one I married.'

'We all change over time.'

'But she's taken no interest in me for a while now. It's all about the décor of the home, plants, and other stuff.'

'That's you just making excuses.'

'It's not. Sophie really does make me feel alive.'

'This is utter nonsense. It's not too late to turn this situation around.'

'What makes you think I want to? I'm happy at the moment, and I quite like living in a hotel.'

'This plaything of yours is a gold-digger – she'll find another sugar daddy in the future.'

'Her name is Sophie. She's not a plaything nor a gold-digger.'

Evelyn raised her eyebrow disapprovingly. 'You're being naive. Just come to your senses before it's too late. Like I said to you before – make Annabelle see that it was all a huge mistake.'

'This conversation is going around in circles.'

Evelyn looked over his shoulder with a smile. 'Here's lunch. Let's continue our discussion after we've eaten?'

3.00 p.m.

Annabelle and Teresa's taxi pulled up outside Kew Gardens. 'Here we are for my surprise. I've got tickets for a special orchid festival,' said Annabelle. 'It's celebrating Indonesia's immense biodiversity.'

Teresa tugged at Annabelle's coat when they reached the exhibition hall. 'Come over here and look at these.' She led her to a display. 'Aren't they incredible? Just look at the detail and colours.'

'Oh my, they're so beautiful.'

'Wow, I'm so pleased we came – it's just amazing.'

'I knew you would love it – that's Kew for you.'

Annabelle turned to face Teresa. 'I've been thinking a lot about what you said earlier. On reflection, I would love to come back to Mallorca with you.'

5:08 p.m. USA Central Time Zone.

Amelia walked through the arrivals gate at General Mitchell International Airport, Milwaukee. She heard her name being called and turned to spot her sister Daphne in the waiting crowd.

'Hey, so awesome to see you again, Sis,' said Daphne, hugging Amelia.

'Your baby bump has really grown since you sent me those pictures. Are you on your own?' said Amelia.

'Yep, Greg couldn't get off work. Never mind, it's fine. But what's all this?' she asked, pointing to a pink rose that Amelia was holding in a clear plastic container.

'Ah, it's from a friend. I've found it strangely comforting on the journey here, and the lovely message really touched me. But it's all a bit awkward.'

'Hmm... tell me more on the journey home.'

'How's Dad?'

Daphne pursed her lips. 'I'll explain all in the car as well. How was your flight?'

'Long, almost fourteen hours with the stopover in Detroit. But at times when I thought of Dad, I found myself clutching my rose.'

Amelia had been sitting quietly in the passenger seat, having caught up with her sister on family matters, digesting the news on their father's illness and some town gossip. Her rose rested on her lap in her hands, and she watched the taillights of other cars in the dark and started to get sleepy. Daphne remained focused, driving north on Interstate 43 by Lake Michigan. Snow-lined road edges glistened in the car headlights. Amelia was half-listening to the radio music as her sister was humming along.

Daphne switched the radio off. 'The temperature has been below minus seven degrees today and is set to drop to minus seventeen later. You'll have to dig out some of your old winter clothes while you're here; that fashionable red coat just won't hack it.'

'I've got a thick warm coat at home.' Amelia lifted the lid off the plastic container and smelt her rose.

'You were going to tell me more about this friend.'

'Okay, but don't go gossiping to Mom or anybody!'

'Hey, of course not. What's his name?'

'Alex. He's twenty-eight, but like I said, it's awkward.'

'Start at the beginning – how did you first meet?'

Amelia described the time she was taken into Emergency, and he treated her. She went on to explain the coincidence of meeting him again at a pub, then at a friend's wedding, and how he didn't go through with the marriage. 'So, that's it really,' said Amelia, tilting her head. 'I don't know what went wrong or why he and Evie didn't get married.'

'But how did you leave it?'

'He contacted me yesterday asking if we could meet up again. I did ask him if the breakup was because of me. All he said was, "You're not the main reason." So, I made my excuses. I sort of cut him short.'

'So, let me get this right. You've only spent a few hours in each other's company, and he possibly ditched his bride for you.' Daphne glanced across at the plastic case. 'And he sent you that lovely rose.'

'Yeah, that's about the sum of it. But he's kind of cute, and he's well-jacked.'

Daphne chuckled. 'A super fit guy, hey. So, what's the message?'

Amelia pulled out the card and read it. *"Dear Amelia, I long to see you again and hope that we can still be friends. Love and affection. Alex. X"*

'He sounds smitten. What was your reply?'

'I haven't replied yet.'

'Why not?'

'I don't want to be known as a marriage breaker.'

Daphne glanced around. 'Is he handsome?'

Amelia grinned. 'He sure is… And there's more to the story of how we first met.'

'Go on.'

'I was trashed and kind of flirty at the hospital on New Year's Eve. I called him Doctor Handsome.' They giggled.

'Text him with a "thank you."'

Amelia wrote a reply text. *"Thank u for my very beautiful rose. I'll be in touch when I return to Cambridge."*

'I've also got some news. I promised I would pass on a message to you to stop him harassing me with notes and texts.'

Amelia frowned at her sister. 'Not Jake the cheat?'

'He split up with Melanie and wants to meet up with you with no conditions attached. He asks if you'll give him just thirty minutes of your time.'

'I'm pleased that it hasn't worked out with Mel. I knew it wouldn't. She's got the looks, but I knew she wasn't right for him. He's the last thing on my mind at the moment. But I'll think about it.'

7.50 p.m.

Amelia jumped out of the car as soon as Daphne pulled up in front of their parents' home. She walked past the snow piles by the side of the drive and immediately got tearful as her mother greeted her with open arms by the front door.

'Hey, you need to be cheerful when you see him, you hear?' said Connie with a smile. 'He's really looking forward to seeing you. He's resting in the sitting room.'

They walked through, and Amelia sat down on the armrest next to her father, who was dozing, his head tipped slightly forward. She took hold of his hand; he stirred and met her gaze. Grinning, he leaned in towards her; Amelia almost flopped on him as they hugged. Daphne then joined in. Connie walked over and smiled as she rubbed Bradley's shoulder.

'Greg,' said Daphne. 'Can you get us all a drink, please? Amelia and Mom will have a bourbon, and I'll have a juice.'

'No tears, pumpkin,' said Bradley as he held Amelia's head gently between his hands. 'I'm going to beat this cancer, so don't fret.'

Amelia nodded. 'I've been in shock since Mom told me at the weekend.'

'Never mind all that,' he said. 'You're here now. How long are you staying, cos we've got to make it special, and I've got something planned.'

'Just five full days. So, what've you got planned?'

Bradley beamed. 'A fishing trip. It'll be just like the good old days – ice fishing in Green Bay. It's all booked for the day after tomorrow. Your uncle is meeting us there, so it's five of us, including Daphne and Greg. Your Mom doesn't want to go.' Bradley gazed teasingly at Connie.

Connie straightened up. 'Ah, but I'll be baking the fish for our Friday night supper.'

He turned his gaze back to Amelia. 'It's going to be a great five days.'

Chapter 18

Thursday, 20th February 2020, 6.30 a.m. USA CTZ.

Amelia heard noises on the bedroom landing. Detaching herself from the cosy comfort of her duvet, she switched on her bedside light, slipped into her fluffy slippers, pulled her dressing gown around her, and opened her door. Daphne was opposite the bathroom leaning back against the wall.

'It's Dad,' Daphne whispered. 'He's been like this since his treatment started. Mom is in there helping.'

'Are we going to be able to cope with Dad on this fishing trip tomorrow for the whole day?'

Daphne pursed her lips. 'I'll speak to Mom later and get an idea of what to expect. He's so looking forward to going; please just go with it. Besides, Uncle Dex and Greg will be there to help.'

Amelia nodded. The bathroom door latch pulled back from the other side. Bradley gave a subtle wink as he stepped out. 'Apologies for being in the bathroom too long.'

'We're fine, girls,' said Connie, following him out. 'By the way, I've got someone coming out to fix the downstairs restroom tomorrow while you're all out fishing.'

8:15 a.m.

Amelia was drying dishes after breakfast. 'Dad looks so frail compared to when I was last home.' She stacked another plate on the table.

Connie finished washing up and pulled off her washing gloves. 'I just pray that this time next year, he'll be given the all-clear, and then we can get back to being normal.'

'Don't you think the fishing trip should wait until then?'

'He's got his heart set on going.'

Daphne walked into the room and started putting some plates away into the cupboard. 'Greg's getting the fishing bait from the store on his way home.'

Connie untied her apron. 'I'm leaving all the equipment for you girls to sort out with your father.'

Amelia placed the towel over the oven handle. 'That's fine, Mom. Could I borrow your car this afternoon? I need to visit the County Parks Department in Sturgeon Bay to do some research.'

8:54 p.m.

Alex parked his car along the street to The Boatman's Rest pub in Cambridge. Spud stepped out and ran his finger over the gouge Evie had made along the side of the car. He then jogged and caught up with Alex and Sanjay just as they walked into the pub. They spotted Hamish with Lucy and Avani.

'Nice to meet you again, Avani,' said Alex, shaking hands with her and introducing Spud and Sanjay.

'I hear you're researching ways to prevent the decline of coral reefs,' Spud said, leaning in close to Avani.

She nodded and started to enthusiastically explain her research as the others listened, and Sanjay took drinks orders before going to the bar.

Sanjay returned with a tray of drinks. 'It's quiet in here tonight.'

Hamish grabbed his beer. 'Aye, but it'll be heaving tomorrow night and Saturday.'

Alex picked up his alcohol-free beer. 'Take it easy, Hamish, we've got a sculling session in the morning. I think my back has recovered enough.'

'That abrasion you've got on the side of your face will take a while to heal,' said Sanjay.

Alex nodded. He'd hoped that it would be healed in time before he started back at work on Monday.

Hamish raised his glass. 'To the Scullerteers! And to good friends!' All six of them tapped their glasses over the centre of the table.

Lucy sipped at her cocktail and turned to Alex. 'Have you heard from Amelia?' He glared across the table at Hamish.

Hamish shrugged his shoulders. 'Lucy is Amelia's good friend, so I couldn't lie.'

Sanjay tilted his head at Alex. 'What's going on with you and this other woman?'

'It's not quite like that,' said Alex. 'I've explained why it hasn't worked out with Evie.'

'But I thought there was still a possible chance of you two sorting out your differences, despite how Evie has reacted. To be honest, you both just need to let the dust settle. After all, it's only been five days since you were going to marry her.'

'I like Evie,' said Spud.

Hamish put his hand up to Spud's mouth. 'Shush... not helpful.'

Sanjay inclined forward. 'Seriously, Alex, I'm saying this as a friend. You need to have a cooling-off period without other women involved.'

Alex sighed. 'We're just friends.'

Hamish nudged Sanjay's shoulder with his elbow. 'Go easy.'

'You didn't help matters,' retorted Sanjay, before turning back to face Alex. 'I really thought that all your reservations were just pre-wedding nerves.'

Alex cast his eyes down and stared at his drink. 'I don't want to talk about it right now.'

Lucy leaned forward. 'Alex, I know it's none of my business, but Amelia is a good friend, and we don't want to see her hurt.'

Alex nodded. 'I'm not out to hurt anyone.'

10.30 p.m.

Alex dropped Sanjay and Spud home but then took a detour back into the city rather than going to his sister's. He pulled into The Black Swan car park just before last orders and texted a message before walking into the pub. The barman with the goatee beard clocked him. Alex waited at the bar until he was served a whisky. The barman discretely glanced around before slipping Alex a small plastic bag. Alex slipped it into his jacket pocket as he pushed some cash across the bar, knocked back his whisky, and left.

He decided to drive to a cash machine in the city centre en route to his sister's house. Driving down Hills Road, he spotted a homeless woman sitting on a makeshift bed of cardboard and blankets with her black dog beside her. Realising who it was, he pulled his car over. Popping into the nearby express shop, he bought two takeaway teas.

'Hi, Rose,' he said, standing over her. 'Tea.'

'It's good to see you, Alex,' she said, looking up. 'It's been a while.'

He crouched and stretched out his hand. 'There's been a lot of stuff going on.'

'Like what?'

He exhaled. 'It's not important. How have you been since I last saw you? Are you still managing to get the occasional respite off the streets?'

'Me and Gertie have been coping despite it being a hard winter. The days are getting a little longer.' She cradled her tea between her fingerless gloved hands. 'I twisted my ankle a couple weeks ago; it's taking its time to heal.'

'How're you now?' He listened to her as he slowly drank his tea and realised that his situation and his stresses were very mild in comparison.

Chapter 19

Friday, 21st February 2020, 7.50 a.m.

Alex was waiting by the boat rack in the club boathouse when Hamish joined him. They followed their usual routine, carrying their double scull over their heads towards the open doors.

'How are you feeling?' Hamish asked.

'I'll let you know once we're sculling.'

They walked out of the boathouse into the morning sunshine. Their attention was stolen by a swan gliding down with its wings fully stretched and feet extended towards the water as clouds drifted behind on the breeze. They stepped into the shallow water in their boots and lowered their boat. Dullard held their boat steady for them as they adjusted the boat rigging.

The Gormley brothers walked over. 'No more copouts, you two. We'd seen that you were booked in for a practise session this morning and have arranged with club members to be marshals for a race.'

'It's not convenient today – were not ready,' said Alex anxiously.

'Like we said, no more copouts.'

'Which one is your boat?' Hamish asked. One of the Gormleys pointed to it at the other end of the ramp. 'Okay, were up for this race.'

'Remember the wager,' said one Gormley brother. 'Six hundred pounds.'

'You'll have to give us fifteen minutes to get sorted and warmed up.'

'Ten is long enough.' The Gormley brothers left and went back inside the boathouse.

'We're about to throw away three hundred pounds each,' said Alex. 'I'm not fit enough to race.'

'You've got plenty of nervous energy to burn off,' Hamish said, glancing around. 'You'll be fine. We're gonna win.'

'Huh.' Alex shook his head. 'Only by a bloody miracle.'

'I need to go to the loo and get some water.' He walked off and left Alex setting up his rigging.

Alex climbed into the stern of the boat ten minutes later, slipped on his trainers, and, with Hamish in the bow, set off, sculling towards the start line.

They lined up next to the Gormley boat with a club marshal watching on the embankment, his arm raised and ready with an air horn. The marshal counted down, blew the horn, and both crews heaved away, sculling north up the Great Ouse River.

'Let's up the pace,' Hamish panted as the Gormley boat was half a boat length ahead.

'More pace,' said Alex, breathing heavily as the Gormley boat got a full length ahead at the halfway stage.

Both boats were matching each other's stroke rate at the 1500-metre marker, the crews sliding in unison on their seats with their oar blades slicing through the water.

'We're gaining on them,' panted Hamish.

Alex was fighting soreness in his back and pain in his shoulder with less than five hundred metres left. 'Go for it,' he shouted.

'We're almost there!' He gulped in air and forced his whole body to respond as he glanced around, noticing the stern of the Gormley boat slipping back.

Alex and Hamish's double scull crossed the 2000-metre marker finish line, one metre ahead of the Gormleys' as the marshal's air horn sounded.

'We did it,' said Hamish, slapping the water.

'I can't believe it,' Alex said, his voice straining as he leaned back, exhausted, every inch of his body throbbing. He reached around and gripped Hamish's hand. 'That showed the gormless Gormleys we're now the club champions. And they owe us six hundred quid.'

Hamish rowed into the riverbank. The Gormley brothers started to slowly row back to the boathouse. Alex gazed around as he caught his breath and listened to the different morning bird songs. He felt the peace of the moment touch him before a shrill of a blackbird reconnected him back to the present.

'How's your back?' Hamish asked.

'Really sore, but it was worth it.'

Hamish chuckled. 'I feel dead.'

'I haven't got any energy for the return.'

'I'm enjoying soaking up this moment.'

'Let's just hang out here for a few minutes.' Alex pulled out a small pouch from his training shorts pocket.

'What've you got there?'

He rolled a weed joint, lit it, and took a deep drag. He passed it to Hamish without glancing around.

Hamish took it from him and dragged a lungful. 'Bloody hell, mate. Any more of that, and we'll be crashing into other boats.' He took another drag and started coughing as he passed it back.

They both sat in their double scull, sharing the joint, gazing around in the cool light of the morning as the occasional boat passed them. Hamish struggled to focus after a while and slumped forward. Alex rested back on his elbows, put in his buds, and played a mix of Eighties soul music. His eyes closed, and their boat started to drift on the water.

A few minutes had passed, and Hamish heard some shouting. He tapped Alex. 'There's an angry man on a large boat coming at us.'

Alex laughed. 'Who cares.'

Hamish rowed their boat clear just as the boat passed. The angry man continued shouting river etiquette rules at them. Alex took a breath, and they casually sculled back, chuckling every time they accidentally let their oars clash together.

'Gordon! Boots, please.' Alex shouted as they approached the club boathouse.

'Where is he?'

The starting marshal walked down the ramp with their boots. 'Well done. The Gormley brothers were off the pace. You were lucky to win.'

'What do you mean, lucky?' Alex scorned. 'We beat them.'

The marshal was a little taken back by their carefree attitude as he passed them their Wellingtons. Hamish slipped his on and went to step out of the boat but stumbled and fell forward into the water. The boat swayed back and tipped Alex backwards into the water. They both laughed at each other as they stood. Some club members watched them with bewilderment. Still laughing, they both eventually got the boat out of the water and back into the boathouse. Giggling at each other, they de-rigged the boat with the help of another club member before getting changed.

Alex grinned at Hamish as they sat opposite each other in the clubhouse, drinking coffee. 'This is just what I needed today – it's made me feel normal again.'

Hamish rubbed his face. 'I wouldn't quite call it normal if you've taken to smoking weed.'

Alex shrugged.

Hamish leaned back, stretching. 'So, where's this room you're viewing tomorrow?'

'Green Street, right in the heart of town.'

'What's the set up?'

'The room is a good size from what I can see on the internet. It's a two-bed first-floor flat – the owner lives there. So, if I take it, we'll share the lounge, bathroom, and kitchen.' Alex put down his drink and narrowed his gaze. 'What did the marshal mean, being off the pace?'

'I have a confession.'

'What about?'

'When I went off and left you before the race, and while the Gormleys were on the rowing machines warming up, I paid a friend to nobble their boat.'

'What…'

'Look. There was no way I could let them win – we would never have heard the end of it. Besides, you're not fit. I just arranged to have the odds of the race evened up.'

Alex rolled his eyes. 'So, we cheated to win.'

Hamish grimaced. 'Only technically. We'll only take a hundred pounds off them. That's how much I offered my friend. No names mentioned.'

'How did he manage it?'

'He's got a tube of work-hardening resin in his locker. He smeared some around the swivel gate pivot pins on the riggers. It only took a minute.'

Alex shook his head. 'I guess they thought their arms were just tiring and wouldn't have noticed anything was wrong when the swing of their oars started to stiffen.'

'Exactly...'

10:00 a.m.

Robert was in a meeting at his business office, Orion Hunter M&A. He was sitting at one end of a large, oval, glass table, with five colleagues to one side of him and three people representing a client on the other. 'Could you please start your proposal for the merger,' said Robert to his female colleague. A screen lit up as she pressed a remote control.

The door opened, and Sophie walked over to Robert, leaned over, and whispered in his ear, 'Your mother has just come into the building. She's on her way up.'

Robert stood. 'Excuse me, and please carry on with the presentation. I'll be back shortly.' He followed Sophie out of the room and closed the door behind him. 'Why the hell didn't they hold my mother at the reception?'

'There was nothing they could do. The receptionist told her that you were in an important meeting and cannot be disturbed, but she just walked towards the lift. The security guard was going to stop her, but the receptionist waved them away to prevent a scene.'

Robert exhaled. 'I'll handle this – don't say anything.'

Sophie listened through her headset as she took her seat behind her desk to one side of the entrance door. 'I've just had a message that she's approaching. Security is following her.'

Robert opened the door and watched his mother walk towards him across the large open-plan office, past rows of people working at desks. 'Hello, Mother. Please come in.' He closed the door. 'To what do I owe this honour?'

'Oh… I just realised that this must be her,' said Evelyn craning her head around at Sophie.

'Good morning, Lady Hardson,' said Sophie as she stood up and removed her headset.

'Mother, don't start anything. Not here,' said Robert, moving within arm's reach of her. 'I have an important client in my office.'

Evelyn studied Sophie with piercing scrutiny. 'You're very pretty, I must say, and your dark orange suit really does compliment the colour of your hair.' Evelyn sat herself down, crossed her legs, and rested her handbag on her lap. 'I can see why Robert is attracted to you.' Sophie's face flushed with embarrassment as she hesitantly sat back down, put her headset back on, and perused some paperwork.

'Let me take you to another room with more comfortable seats and have some refreshments brought to us,' said Robert, moving to the door and clasping the door handle.

'Actually,' said Evelyn, turning her penetrating gaze back to Sophie as she stood. 'I've seen all I needed to see. I think I'll leave.'

Robert started to open the door, and Sophie swallowed down a short breath and exhaled.

'One final thing,' said Evelyn. 'The real reason why I'm here.'

'And what's that?' he said, closing the door again.

'She needs to leave the room first.' Evelyn glanced towards Sophie.

'She's my PA,' said Robert. 'She's going to stay.'

Evelyn narrowed an eye at him. 'Just don't do anything silly with Annabelle's credit limit on her card.'

'You know that I'm not that sort of person.'

'Just checking that we understand each other.' Evelyn stepped forward, and Robert opened the door as she walked past him.

8.10 a.m. USA CTZ.

Amelia sat next to Greg in the back of her father's pickup as Daphne drove north through Door County with Bradley in the front passenger seat.

Crossing over Sturgeon Bay Bridge, she gazed out across the horizon beyond the ice shelf of Green Bay to where the sea met the sky. Her mind was focused like the vibrancy of the winter sunlight; she wanted the fishing expedition to be special for all of them.

Daphne glanced over. 'Dad, you said it was a surprise, but I need to know where I'm heading.'

Bradley grinned. 'We're going to Sunset Beach near Fish Creek. I've only fished there once before, with your Uncle Dexter when we were teenagers.'

Amelia leaned forward. 'I get it – we're going down memory lane with you and Uncle Dex.'

Bradley turned his head. 'Sort of, but I really wanted us to do some unforgettable fishing there as a family.' He coughed. 'Look at that sky – we have perfect conditions to make it a very memorable day. I checked on the fishing website yesterday; the ice is thick enough – at least six inches.'

Greg checked his sat-nav. 'Twenty miles to go.'

8.35 a.m.

Amelia jumped out of the cab as soon as Daphne parked up next to Uncle Dexter's pickup on the east side of the bay. She clapped her hands together. 'Uncle Dex,' she said, embracing him. 'I've missed you so much.'

'Last August it was,' he replied.

'We're going to have a great day, unc.' She clenched her fist. 'It's been a while, but I'm aiming to beat you.'

'Hey-hell. No chance, Missy.'

They all suited up with their insulated winter wear, unloaded their pickups, and put on their backpacks. They carried fold-up chairs and equipment as they walked at Bradley's pace down through the snow-covered ground to a jetty.

Bradley caught his breath as he stood on the jetty. 'I'm fine,' he kept replying as Amelia checked again on how he was feeling.

She watched Daphne hold her tummy with both hands. 'How's the baby?'

'It's going mad inside with all this activity.' Daphne took a deep breath.

Bradley and Dexter stood for a short time, pointing to different locations in the bay. They agreed on the spot where they had fished when they were teenagers and headed onto the ice to the exact spot, two to three hundred yards out. There were a few other people out fishing who appeared to have been out since dawn with tents set up on the ice. Greg checked the condition of the ice as he walked just ahead of them, but not beyond the point of the safety markers. They settled on a spot, unloaded their backpacks, and set up their chairs. Dexter started drilling a ten-inch diameter size hole through the ice with an auger tool, cranking it around by hand and dumping the ice to the side. Bradley set up his rod, got himself comfortable in his chair, and lowered the line down through the ice. Dexter drilled the second hole a little way along for Daphne. Puffing, he handed the auger tool to Amelia.

'I'll fish over there on the other side of Daddy,' she said. Greg and Dexter headed back to the pick-ups to collect more equipment. 'I'm all set up over here.' Amelia relaxed back in her chair as Daphne loaded her hook up with bait before lowering it through the ice.

Dexter and Greg returned a short time later, pulling a sleigh loaded with a BBQ, a stand, another chair, and a small fold-out table. Once set up, they joined the others.

Amelia and Greg sat listening to music through their earbuds while they waited. It wasn't long before Dexter and Bradley had caught three whitefish between them, reeling them in through the ice hole as the others gathered around before laying them out on the ice. Their lengths were the size of Dexter's forearm.

'But who's going to be the first to catch a large walleye for lunch, I wonder?' Amelia grinned.

'I bet that'll be me,' Bradley joked, 'or your uncle.' He chuckled and coughed.

Dexter reset his rod and adjusted the sensitivity on his bite indicator. He left his rod and checked on the condition of the BBQ coals, which had just started to whiten. He poured out a couple of hot chocolate drinks from a flask and offered one to Bradley.

'I think these youngsters have lost touch,' said Dexter.

'Practise makes perfect,' replied Bradley, coughing. 'But isn't it just brilliant to be out here, though?'

'It sure is. We should have done this sooner.'

Amelia discreetly took out her earbuds and listened to every word from just a few yards away.

'I've been sitting here lost in my thoughts, thinking about old times,' said Bradley. 'That first time we fished out here overnight by ourselves.'

Dexter chuckled as he sipped his hot chocolate. 'I remember. Pa couldn't believe it when he turned up the next day and saw how many fish we caught.'

'That's why I wanted my girls out here with me, so they have similar memories.'

Dexter squeezed Bradley's shoulder. 'Don't talk as if you won't be around to do this again.'

'But the reality is that I might not be,' Bradley whispered. 'The disease has started to spread again. Put it this way, it doesn't look good.'

Amelia heard enough words. She drew a breath and lost her focus. Tears pricked her eyes.

Bradley and Dexter stood for a short time, pointing to different locations in the bay. They agreed on the spot where they had fished when they were teenagers and headed onto the ice to the exact spot, two to three hundred yards out. There were a few other people out fishing who appeared to have been out since dawn with tents set up on the ice. Greg checked the condition of the ice as he walked just ahead of them, but not beyond the point of the safety markers. They settled on a spot, unloaded their backpacks, and set up their chairs. Dexter started drilling a ten-inch diameter size hole through the ice with an auger tool, cranking it around by hand and dumping the ice to the side. Bradley set up his rod, got himself comfortable in his chair, and lowered the line down through the ice. Dexter drilled the second hole a little way along for Daphne. Puffing, he handed the auger tool to Amelia.

'I'll fish over there on the other side of Daddy,' she said. Greg and Dexter headed back to the pick-ups to collect more equipment. 'I'm all set up over here.' Amelia relaxed back in her chair as Daphne loaded her hook up with bait before lowering it through the ice.

Dexter and Greg returned a short time later, pulling a sleigh loaded with a BBQ, a stand, another chair, and a small fold-out table. Once set up, they joined the others.

Amelia and Greg sat listening to music through their earbuds while they waited. It wasn't long before Dexter and Bradley had caught three whitefish between them, reeling them in through the ice hole as the others gathered around before laying them out on the ice. Their lengths were the size of Dexter's forearm.

'But who's going to be the first to catch a large walleye for lunch, I wonder?' Amelia grinned.

'I bet that'll be me,' Bradley joked, 'or your uncle.' He chuckled and coughed.

Dexter reset his rod and adjusted the sensitivity on his bite indicator. He left his rod and checked on the condition of the BBQ coals, which had just started to whiten. He poured out a couple of hot chocolate drinks from a flask and offered one to Bradley.

'I think these youngsters have lost touch,' said Dexter.

'Practise makes perfect,' replied Bradley, coughing. 'But isn't it just brilliant to be out here, though?'

'It sure is. We should have done this sooner.'

Amelia discreetly took out her earbuds and listened to every word from just a few yards away.

'I've been sitting here lost in my thoughts, thinking about old times,' said Bradley. 'That first time we fished out here overnight by ourselves.'

Dexter chuckled as he sipped his hot chocolate. 'I remember. Pa couldn't believe it when he turned up the next day and saw how many fish we caught.'

'That's why I wanted my girls out here with me, so they have similar memories.'

Dexter squeezed Bradley's shoulder. 'Don't talk as if you won't be around to do this again.'

'But the reality is that I might not be,' Bradley whispered. 'The disease has started to spread again. Put it this way, it doesn't look good.'

Amelia heard enough words. She drew a breath and lost her focus. Tears pricked her eyes.

'Of course, I'm trying to stay optimistic, and so are the oncology doctors,' said Bradley. 'But I'm also preparing myself for the worst. This is like a sort of *bucket list*, but I'm mindful of Connie and how she'll cope if I don't make it. I'm relying on you and Ruby supporting her.'

Dexter patted Bradley on the shoulder. 'It goes without saying – I'm surprised you feel you need to say anything.'

Bradley nodded. 'I'm sure pleased you're coming back to have a fish supper with us tonight.' They clasped each other's hands and smiled.

Amelia glanced around. She wanted to go and hug her father but felt numb.

'I won't be coming back if we don't catch any walleye,' said Dexter.

'I've got a bite!' Daphne shouted, startling all of them. They hurriedly gathered around as she slowly pulled a whitefish through the ice. Amelia started whooping.

It was mid-morning by the time they had all managed to catch something, with Greg being the last to catch a whitefish.

Dexter called out to Greg. 'We're going to the hut to use the restroom. Can you watch over my rod?' Dexter put his arm around Bradley as they walked steadily towards the hut set on the ice, just over a hundred yards away. They had been gone a few minutes when Dexter's line alarm went off. Greg trotted over and took control.

The two women watched Greg struggle with the rod as smoke from the BBQ coals drifted behind them.

Greg turned to the women. 'This is something bigger than a whitefish!'

Amelia walked over. 'Hopefully a walleye. Can I have a go?' Greg nodded as she took the rod from him, taking up the strain as the rod bent over from the pull on the line.

Amelia was still trying to reel the fish in when both Daphne and Greg also got bites on their lines. Dexter was supporting Bradley back across the ice when they noticed all three of them were standing and working their lines. There was a bite on Amelia's line just as they arrived, which Dexter just got to in time to bring in a small whitefish.

Bradley walked over and knelt down beside Amelia. 'Come on, pumpkin.' He coughed. 'Just tension the line a little more.'

Amelia worked the rod in and out towards the hole. She breathed heavily but could see on her father's face how much it would mean to him if she brought in the catch. 'Daddy, am I doing this right?'

'You're doing great, pumpkin. Do you need Greg to take over?'

'I've got this sucker,' she said, heaving at the line. She finally managed to reel in a walleye, almost a metre long, through the ice hole. She supported the fish on her knee and posed for a photo. 'At least that's lunch sorted. Just remember that I beat you, Daddy, and Uncle Dex.'

It was just past midday when Daphne pulled in another whitefish. 'I'm hungry... How about lunch?'

'Time to start cooking,' said Dexter. He prepared half a walleye with butter and lemon juice, then grilled it on the BBQ, accompanied by small boiled potatoes. They dished up and added some of Connie's homemade coleslaw and bread onto their plates. They sat around the table, tucking into their fish lunch with their forks while laughing at some old family stories.

Amelia and her family carried on fishing after lunch for a few hours. She thought of her past love life with Jake as she watched, in an almost meditative state, the fishing line disappearing through the ice hole into the freezing water. She thought of her new life in England, her new friends, and him. The light had started to fade when she peered up towards the warm setting sun and thought of the one who sent her the rose. She smiled to herself.

'Should we call it a day?' said Daphne as she reeled in her empty line.

'Hang on!' shouted Dexter. 'I've got a bite. It's a big one.' They gathered around him.

'Look at that rod bend,' said Bradley. 'It must be a walleye.'

'Walleye, walleye, walleye...' Amelia chanted. The others joined in with her.

Dexter managed to bring in the second walleye and final catch. They packed up their camp and wrapped up their walleye catches. Having loaded up the sleigh, they made a couple of trips back with all their gear to their pick-ups.

Bradley had an arm around Greg's shoulder as he trudged back through their tracks up the embankment. 'I have to stop,' said Bradley.

Amelia came back down the embankment and hauled her father's arm over her shoulder. 'You can make it, Daddy, C'mon,' she said, pulling her father forward along with Greg on the other side of him before they made it back to his pickup.

Amelia drove Bradley's pickup back home, with Dexter and Greg following in his truck.

Connie held open the door for them when they all arrived back at the family home in Maplewood.

'Hey, Momma,' said Amelia. 'This girl caught the first walleye all by herself.'

'And your reward is to help me bake it.'

'That sounds great.' She helped her mother make dinner. They prepared the largest walleye of their catch in herbs and baked it in the oven with roasted vegetables.

Connie raised a toast over dinner to the restroom cistern finally being fixed after six years. Further toasts followed; Amelia's walleye catch, Greg's helpfulness, Dexter's stories, Bradley's jokes, and Daphne's success in managing to catch the most whitefish, even though she was five months pregnant.

Chapter 20

Saturday, 22nd February 2020, 9.10 a.m.

Alex was sitting in the lounge on the sofa at his sister's home with Charlotte on his lap, who was applying some of Freya's old makeup to his face. He hadn't noticed Freya to his side peeking around the kitchen door as Charlotte smeared eyebrow pencil on him.

'Don't forget lipstick,' he said before he puckered up.

'Keep still,' Charlotte said, giggling.

Freya walked into the room, sniggering. 'You're looking very Groucho Marx-ish,'

Alex held up a compact mirror and checked his look, and laughed. 'More blusher, I think, Charlotte.'

Freya sat on the arm of the sofa. 'They've been discussing this latest Coronavirus outbreak on the radio, the Diamond Princess ship in Japan. It's scary – fourteen dead and hundreds infected. It's starting to spread everywhere.'

'I did hear the bad news.'

'Do you think there's a possibility of you treating infected people?'

'Only if it became a pandemic.'

'The experts say that pandemics come around roughly every hundred years.'

'I know where you're going with this. The last one was the Spanish flu pandemic a hundred years ago, killing over fifty million people.'

'Just be careful, as you might be on the front line against it in a couple of months or so.'

'I'm sure it won't get that bad,' he said as Charlotte dabbed some blusher to his cheek.

'Don't forget to put some nail varnish on his fingers, sweetie,' said Freya returning to the kitchen.

He was at the kitchen table a short while later, still wearing makeup and having a cup of tea, when Freya sat opposite him.

'I'm struggling to look at you,' she said. 'You do look a bit creepy.'

'I've just been thinking about Mum again, going off to Mallorca and leaving the house empty.'

'It's a shame you couldn't take her up on her offer and live there for a while.'

'I know, and I so wanted to… But that idea just isn't practical unless I move my job to London.'

Freya nodded. 'I recognise your situation. But I can understand Mum not wanting Dad moving back while she's away.'

11.30 a.m.

Alex arrived at the street door to the property he had an appointment to view a few minutes early and stared up at the decorative metalwork supporting some window boxes before ringing the bell.

A short, slim man in his mid-twenties with spiky dark hair opened the purple-painted door. 'Hi. You must be, Alex. I'm John. Please come on up.'

Alex followed him through a hall, up some stairs, along a landing, and through into the flat. 'Do you get much noise in the evenings from the restaurants below?'

'Some, but it's not really a problem.'

Alex stood in the middle of the lounge and looked around. 'It's cosy and very spacious. I like the feature Victorian fireplace and the room décor.'

John pushed open another door. 'This is the room, right next to the bathroom.'

Alex walked in and gazed around at the small double bed, a desk, and an old walnut-veneered wardrobe. 'It's just what I need – comfortable with plenty of storage space.'

'It's a little old-fashioned, I know, but I'm pleased you like it. The floral furniture belonged to my grandmother, who used to own the flat. She passed away last year.'

'I'm sorry to hear that.' Alex pointed to the bed.

John chuckled. 'No, she was in a care home. This used to be my room. Have a look around, and I'll wait in the lounge.'

He joined John after a short while and settled back into a floral patterned winged chair. 'I'm happy with the rental costs and conditions.'

'Could you tell me a bit about yourself?'

'I'm a junior doctor.' Alex knew that John was assessing his suitability as he continued to speak about his job. 'I do sometimes work unsociable hours.'

John frowned. 'Being a doctor, you're potentially in a high-risk category for catching this coronavirus if it gets any worse.'

Alex rubbed his chin. 'We've discussed the disease at work. The government is monitoring the situation. I think it'll be fine.'

11.40 a.m.

Annabelle had spent the morning packing her bags with Teresa's help. They were both sitting in her kitchen having lunch and discussing where they were going out afterwards. Annabelle's phone rang. She looked up at Teresa with wide eyes. 'Hello, Evelyn,' said Annabelle. 'So, you're in the neighbourhood.' Her posture tightened. 'Okay, I'll see you in a minute.' Annabelle put her phone down. 'Robert's mother is going to be here shortly.'

'I remember her, the retired high court judge?' Teresa said.

'I'm not in the mood if she's going to lay down the law to me about divorce and all that stuff.'

Evelyn arrived in her chauffeur-driven car. 'Tea?' said Annabelle as Evelyn followed her into the kitchen.

'Yes, that would be good,' said Evelyn. 'A weak Earl Grey please – no sugar or milk, remember.'

'I'll make it,' said Teresa turning to the cupboard.

'I wonder if we could have a private conversation?'

'It's alright,' Annabelle said, glancing at Teresa. 'I'll make the tea.'

Evelyn sat herself down and waited for Teresa to leave the room. 'I made this trip to see you because Freya informed me this morning that you were going to Mallorca tomorrow. I thought it important that we should have a conversation before you left.' Evelyn softened her gaze. 'I would like you to know that I'm very disappointed with Robert and that I'm here to give you my support.' There was a moment of silence between them. 'I also want you to know that whatever your feelings are for Robert, please don't give up on him, even though he's done this awful thing.'

Annabelle poured out two teas. 'Did you manage to have a word with him about my credit card?'

'Yes, and you need not worry.'

'Thank you.'

'If you could just see your way to giving him a chance, should he attempt to win you back?'

'Now that everything is out in the open, I'm sort of getting used to Robert not being around.'

'We can work together on this – you are a lovely daughter-in-law.' She paused. 'I know over the years we haven't always seen eye-to-eye, but I've become very fond of you, as you know.'

Annabelle frowned. 'Really, I didn't know.'

'Yes, yes, yes, but never mind that now. I'm asking if you will give him a second chance, should he ask?'

Annabelle's eyes flicked around the room. 'Well, it depends. To start with, he needs to give up this woman he's seeing.'

'Of course,' said Evelyn.

'But that would just be the start. It would still be very difficult for us to patch up our marriage as my trust in him has been shattered.'

'I know it must be extremely difficult for you, but I'm hoping that it won't come to a divorce.'

'I feel totally betrayed. I need to have some time away and think things through.'

'So, you're going off to stay at Villa Francina tomorrow. How long for?'

Annabelle took a breath. 'The foreseeable future. I hope you don't mind?'

'I see.' Evelyn nodded. 'I haven't been to my villa in years. You can use it at your leisure. On condition that I have your reassurance that you'll consider trying to salvage your marriage with Robert.'

Annabelle closed her eyes and nodded.

Evelyn gave a hint of a smile. 'Now we have a ladies' understanding, we should stay in touch. I'll do my bit here in London pulling Robert's strings, but I need you to be mindful about forgiveness – when and if the moment comes.'

'Thank you for the use of the villa.'

'Well, I must be going now.' She rose from her seat, quickly walked across the kitchen, and opened the door to find Teresa leaning against it, who almost lost her balance. Evelyn cocked her eyebrow and then walked past her to the front door. 'I'll be in touch, Annabelle.'

7.30 p.m. USA CTZ.

Amelia had borrowed her mother's car and made the relatively short drive from Maplewood to the coastal town of Algoma on Lake Michigan. She parked in the parking lot of a popular trendy restaurant just off the harbour. She remembered having eaten there before with Jake and, recognising his car, walked over. Jake stepped out, holding a bunch of flowers.

She wedged her hands into her coat pockets. 'If the flowers are for me, Jake, I'm not sure about taking them. Please remember, I only agreed to see you because Daphne said you wanted to explain something important to me. There is no more us.'

He looked awkwardly at the flowers, then placed them back down on his car passenger seat and closed the door. 'Can we at least go inside and talk? I've taken the liberty and booked a table.'

She nodded and followed him into the restaurant. They were shown to a reserved table, and the waitress took their drinks order.

Amelia gazed around. 'It must be at least a year since we last came in here together.'

'Exactly one year, well, give a day. It was on Saturday, February twenty-third. I can recall the evening – we arrived around the same time, much like this evening. We sat on that table over there.'

'I've agreed to meet you,' she said, clasping her hands together. 'But I should be at home with my parents. My father's not well, and I'm only in the country for another two days. What's so important that you wanted to speak to me?'

Jake straightened himself up. 'Can I just say that I'm so sorry to hear about your father and that my prayers are with him? But, I wanted to talk about us.'

'There is no us,' she said, picking up the menu. 'There, I've decided what I'm having.' The waitress returned with their drinks and stood poised to write down their meal order. 'The beer-battered cheese curds with roasted vegetables, please.' She handed the menu to the waitress, then kept glancing down at her watch and unconsciously tapping her finger on the table.

Jake sighed and put the menu down. 'I'll just have the same, please.' The waitress left.

'If my father knew I was meeting you after what you did, he would have argued that I must be mad. I don't know what I'm even doing here. What is it you want from me, Jake?'

'I did say that there were no strings attached.' His lips crumpled. 'I wasn't sure if I would ever have this opportunity again to sit down with you. But I would like to sincerely apologise for all the hurt I've caused.'

The tightness in Amelia eased. 'You made me believe in you, that I would be the only one you would ever need. I put my trust in you, and you went with my best friend.'

He frowned. 'I was a complete dipshit for doing that. If only you knew how much it haunts me still. I know it doesn't matter to you now, but for the record, Mel just turned up at mine, and then she came onto me.'

'But you could've pushed her away if that was the case.'

Jake frowned. 'I know.' He sighed and shook his head. 'If only I could take it all back.'

Silence fell between them, and they sipped their drinks until their meals arrived. They passed polite compliments about their food dishes.

She gazed at Jake as she finished her meal. 'Tell me, how is your family – keeping well?'

'Yeah, they're fine. They miss seeing you; they really liked you.' He sighed. 'Pa called me an idiot after we split up.'

'Your parents are lovely.'

'Yeah, they're good. How is life in England – at Cambridge?'

She felt pensive that he was leading her into discussing her personal life. She had her answer ready; she was focused on her Ph.D. They reminisced about some fun moments that they had shared together when they were dating, and then she realised that the restaurant was virtually empty of customers and it was getting late.

'Another drink?' Jake asked.

'I gotta shoot. Let's split the bill.'

'I've already taken care of it,' he said, grabbing her coat before she had time to reach it. He held it for her as she slipped her arms into the sleeves. They walked out together and stopped in the middle of the parking lot.

Amelia looked up. 'I had a lovely evening, thank you.'

Jake grinned. 'Does that mean we're at least friends again?'

She momentarily glanced away before her eyes settled back on him. 'Let's just say I'm pleased we've had this chance to find peace between us.' They held each other's gaze. 'Perhaps I will take those flowers if you're still offering them?'

Jake turned and fetched the bouquet from his car and smiled as he passed them to her.

'Thank you, they're lovely. She gave a wry smile and walked to her car. She was startled when he dashed past her and held her car door open as she stepped in and got seated. She wound down her door window. 'You asked if we are friends again. Well, this evening was a start.'

Chapter 21

Sunday, 23rd February 2020, 6.20 a.m.

Annabelle sat in the airport departures lounge café gazing out of a smoked glass window. 'The rain is very heavy outside.'

Teresa sat adjacent to her as she checked her appearance in a compact mirror. 'Despite the gloomy weather, it's really good to see you looking so relaxed.'

Annabelle smiled. 'I do feel more positive. I was apprehensive about leaving the house when you first suggested it, but my home has felt tarnished ever since that woman has been there.'

'That's the spirit, my girl,' said Teresa clasping Annabelle's hand. 'We'll have a nice relaxing day together with a drink later at mine, before going to the villa tomorrow.'

Annabelle raised her cup of tea. 'I'll drink to that.' Her phone buzzed with a text message. 'It's Alex wishing us a safe journey.' She chuckled. 'He wishes that he could join us and escape.'

'You did offer him the full use of the house.'

'That idea wasn't realistic. Besides, he would've been lonely, and he needed his friends around him at this time. Work will help take his mind off things. But I also wonder how Evie is coping – I would've loved her as a daughter-in-law. I thought she and Alex were in love. I still don't understand what happened between them.'

9.05 a.m. USA CTZ.

Amelia arrived in the upstairs bathroom as her father was bent over the toilet pan, being sick and coughing. 'Do you think it's wise for us to be going to church today?' she asked, passing her mother a glass of water.

Bradley wiped his mouth with a hand towel. 'We're going,' he said, coughing.

'Okay, Daddy, I'll be ready. But we need to be leaving in around thirty minutes.'

Amelia drove her father's pickup in the morning sunshine along snow-edged roads the few miles to their church near Forestville. She glanced at the outside temperature on the dashboard, reading -2°C.

'I know I went to bed early last night, but I didn't hear you come in,' said Bradley turning to Amelia. 'You said you were meeting a friend and that you would be back before ten.'

She glanced around, only now noticing how thin and pale his face appeared. 'I stayed out a little longer than I planned.'

Bradley grinned. 'Male or female?'

'Don't be so nosey,' said Connie from the back seat. 'She's all grown up.'

Bradley shrugged his shoulders. 'Just curious. I can't help looking out for my girl.'

Amelia glanced around. 'An old high school friend; we were catching up.' She felt awkward and turned away to hide her blushing.

Connie leaned forward. 'I was concerned as the temperature was forecast to drop to minus seventeen degrees. I didn't sleep until I heard the car pull in. Your Daddy was snoring. I'm surprised you didn't hear.'

'What, me?' he said, smiling before he went into a prolonged coughing spell. 'This damn chemo-treatment will be the death of me if the disease doesn't kill me first.'

'Don't talk like that, Brad,' said Connie. 'The oncology doctor said that you'll have good days and bad days. A pattern is emerging.'

They arrived at their church and pulled into the car park. Bradley noticed some folks were staring when Connie tried to help him down from the cab. Bradley nudged her away and started to walk towards the church entrance leaving Connie motionless.

Amelia walked up and put her arm around her mother. 'Don't take it personally, Mom. You know Daddy is a proud man.'

'I know,' Connie said, wiping a tear from her cheek. 'But it still hurts to see him like this. I still cannot believe this has happened to us.'

'I know, Mom.' She hugged her mother. 'But Daddy is a fighter. He'll beat this, and he'll do it for us, not for himself. We best catch up now.'

Bradley neared the steps of the church and got stuck trying to lift his leg. Amelia and her mother held back as they approached. Friends entering the church put their shoulders under his arms and assisted him up the steps.

Connie and Amelia sat on either side of Bradley on a pew bench. They gently assisted him when they stood for hymns.

At the end of the service, many of the congregation were having refreshments with homemade cakes and biscuits. Bradley was speaking to his friends when the church pastor walked over. 'It's really good to see you, Brad. How are you?'

'A little tired this morning, but no more than that.'

The pastor glanced over at Connie and read her eyes, then turned back to Bradley. 'My prayers are with you both. If there's anything I can do, just call me any time. It's also good to see you again, Amelia. It's been too long.'

'I know. I'm enjoying being back, catching up with my folks and the church family. I enjoyed your sermon about the holy spirit, especially how God's holy fire can remould our hearts through prayer.'

The pastor nodded. 'I think the whole world is going to need God in their lives more than ever in the months ahead if this Coronavirus goes pandemic.'

Bradley grinned. 'Everyone is making a big thing of it. It'll all blow over soon.'

'I just hope you're right, Brad,' said the pastor. 'Take care now.' He turned to speak to some other members of the congregation.

Amelia noticed her mother standing on her own and joined her. 'Thanks for intervening on the way here.'

'I noticed the flowers in the vase this morning. Were they from Jake?'

'Please don't say anything to Dad. This was all Daphne's doing.'

'How did the evening go?'

'Surprisingly well.' Amelia half-smiled. 'I didn't want to be there at first, but he was the perfect gentleman, very apologetic for everything, and we sort of got talking. I felt comfortable with him again.'

'It's your life,' said Connie picking up a biscuit. 'Just be careful. Remember, he broke your heart.' They both stared pensively at each other. 'Look over there at your father speaking to his friends. He's smiling again; you can see he's happy. That's why we needed to be here today.'

Amelia was driving back home a short while later. 'Daddy, has anyone been direct and asked you…'

'Asked me what?'

'If the chemotherapy doesn't work, what then?'

'It's in the Lord's hands. I'm praying to live to see my first grandchild born in four months. My next target, God willing, would be to see one of my girls married.'

Amelia forced a pressed-lip smile. 'Sorry, Daddy. But Daphne and Greg seem very happy just living together, and don't get your hopes up for me.'

1.58 p.m.

Alex sat in the back of Freya's car as the tyres crunched the gravel on Zahida and Sanjay's drive. Sanjay invited them into the lounge and served them pre-dinner drinks. Charlotte joined Zareen as they pretended to bake on her play cooker.

'Something smells really good,' said Alex trying to get a peek into the kitchen.

'That'll be Zahida's roast chicken. It's a family recipe from back home, coated in a yogurt spice with my special stuffing mix.'

'Sounds delicious,' said Freya.

The seven of them, with Zareen in her high chair, and their youngest sitting on Sanjay's lap, were soon sat around the dining table, tucking into their starters and homemade bread.

The table was cleared afterwards, and Sanjay tapped his spoon on his glass. 'Before we serve the main course, I would like to make a toast.' They held up their glasses. 'To a friend, who at times can be a real pain in the backside, especially when it comes to his own wedding day.' Alex grimaced; his gaze dropped to the table. 'Nonetheless, he's also a good reliable friend. He had a crap start to the week – he's still bearing the grazes on his face. But the week has ended positively. To Alex and a bright start in his new home.' They toasted.

'Thank you,' Alex said as he raised his glass. 'You've all been so supportive. Cheers!'

'Time to celebrate and enjoy the food,' said Zahida rising out of her seat. She brought in the roast and placed it in front of Sanjay. He carved the two chickens as Zahida served them up onto plates.

They finished their meal and started talking about future plans for their homes and holidays. The children left the table and returned to playing in the lounge.

Alex noticed that Freya appeared melancholy. He waved his hand in front of her face. 'Let me guess – Mum?'

'She doesn't deserve what Dad has done.'

Sanjay stood. 'Can I get anyone anything stronger?'

Alex nodded. 'I'll have a whisky.'

Freya leaned in towards Alex. 'You're being sensible, aren't you? Remember that you're starting back at work tomorrow, and that's your fourth.'

Sanjay poured out a whisky. 'Now there's been a few cases of Coronavirus reported, do you think it'll spread to Cambridge?'

Alex took his whisky and leaned back. 'In my opinion – probably. The virus is now out and spreading. I can see my job getting very interesting – for all the wrong reasons.'

'There are now thirteen confirmed cases in the UK,' said Sanjay. 'Four from the Diamond Princess cruise ship.'

'That's what I mean,' said Alex. 'It's concerning.'

Zahida tapped her spoon against her wine glass. 'All morbid subject talk is banned.'

'You name a different topic of conversation then.' Sanjay grinned.

'Since we're celebrating Alex's new home,' said Zahida focusing on Alex. 'Have you heard from your new friend, the one that's gone back to America?

Alex shook his head.

'What, not even a single text?'

He shook his head again.

Chapter 22

Mallorca. Monday, 24th February 2020, 7.06 a.m.

Annabelle awoke early at Teresa's home. She sat up on the edge of the bed, brushed her long hair, tied it up, and set it in place with a comb. She pulled up the blind and pushed open the window. Leaning on the window ledge, she breathed in the morning scent of the Aleppo pine trees that stretched down to the shoreline. The moment evoked her sense of freedom as she gazed out over the Bay of Pollensa at the anchored yachts with the view of the mountains beyond. Feeling the chill in the air, she dragged herself away, slipped on her cardigan, went through to the kitchen, and made herself a cup of lemon tea. She checked her phone; no more messages since the two she had received from Freya and Alex last night. She grabbed her book along with her shawl and went out onto the veranda, making herself comfortable in a reclining chair.

'Ah… chilly, but still pleasant enough,' said Teresa joining her. She pulled her dressing gown up around her neck and inhaled. 'I'll never tire of that wonderful morning scent of the pines and the sea air.' She sat in the other recliner. 'Being here has obviously done you some good already – you're positively glowing.'

Annabelle placed her book down. 'I do feel strangely calm.'

Teresa sipped her tea. 'You're welcome to stay as long as you would like.'

'That's really kind. Could I stay until I'm settled?'

'Of course.'

'Maybe we could cook something together later?'

'That's a fab idea. I'm really pleased you're here keeping me company.'

'Likewise.'

'As you know, I feel as if I've been losing my mind at times, ever since Michael died.'

'You cover it up well with your humour.'

'I try. But enough about me. What're you thinking?'

'Once I'm settled and made the villa my new home, who knows, I may not want to go back to London.' Annabelle raised her gaze to the sky. 'I can't explain it, but I feel cleansed and renewed.'

'That's encouraging talk,' Teresa said, slapping her hands together. 'Good for you. I'll walk over to the villa with you this morning. We should then go into Puerto Pollensa to have lunch.'

'Okay. I'll call Emilio to see if he can meet us at the villa.'

Teresa teasingly raised an eyebrow. 'That'll be a visual treat.'

Annabelle laughed. 'What are you like?'

They set off, crossed the coastal road, and followed the path through the pines that wound between the road and the shoreline. Annabelle half-listened to Teresa talk about some of the ex-pat gossip as she gazed up at the beams of dappled light breaking through the branches of the crooked Aleppo pines. It was as if all her troubles were being shed behind her on the woodland path. Her gaze searched for the birds she could hear singing but couldn't see. Further on, the gentle sound of shallow waves lapping against the rocky shoreline soothed her. She glanced around and caught sight of some borage plants gleaming in the sun rays coming through the pine canopy. 'What beautiful blue, star-shaped flowers.'

'You haven't heard a word I've said, have you?' Teresa joked.

They both grinned and continued along the main path before taking a detour until it came out up by the roadside, almost facing the entrance to Villa Francina.

Annabelle knew why Evelyn bought the villa. Its large imposing rustic gates mounted on stone pillars – a statement of strength.

They crossed the road, and Annabelle went to a hidden nook in the stone wall, where her fingers found a small plastic bag with keys. After opening the gates, they both walked in under the wrought Iron archway and up the stone path with its evergreen shrub-lined borders. She checked the condition of some of her large agave cactuses in pots before stopping at the porch entrance. Memories of Alex and Freya sitting inside on the built-in benches playing during family holidays came flooding back to her like it was yesterday, and her stomach knotted. She reminded herself that, in reality, the villa was Evelyn's property.

Teresa waited patiently, then Annabelle unlocked the door, and they walked in together.

'Ahh, it's just as I left it,' said Annabelle looking around.

'Well, there's a surprise,' Teresa joked, pulling back some curtains and letting the light flood into the lounge.

Annabelle walked through the rooms smiling. 'I'm feeling surprisingly comfortable here. I didn't think I would be – without Robert.' She heard a vehicle pull into the side entrance.

'It's Emilio,' said Teresa.

Annabelle walked down to meet him. '*Buenos días*, Emilio.'

He gave her a polite hug and immediately burst into enthusiastic chat in his broken English about the progress he had made on the grounds, showing her and Teresa around. Annabelle was captivated by his passionate ideas. Teresa followed them from a short distance.

His arms were very animated as he discussed his improvement ideas before they arrived back at his van. Emilio said goodbye, shaking hands with Teresa and kissing Annabelle on both cheeks.

Teresa tilted her head towards Annabelle and nudged her shoulder. 'C'mon, don't tell me you haven't imagined being intimate with that hulk of a gardener. I could see the way you looked at him.'

Annabelle grinned and shook her head. 'He's like studying an attractive painting in an art gallery.'

'Don't tell me,' said Teresa, smirking. 'No matter how much you enjoy looking, you wouldn't dare touch.'

'He's at least ten years younger than me.'

'But you would, wouldn't you?'

'I don't know what you're talking about.'

'I think you do.'

10.15 a.m.

Alex unloaded his things from the back of Spud's pickup on Green Street as a murky grey morning coated the city of Cambridge with drizzle. 'That's the last box,' said Alex as he and Spud lumbered up the stairs from the street entrance into his new home. John, the landlord, disappeared into the kitchen and made everyone a cuppa.

Spud collapsed into one of the floral-decorated chairs. 'A little effeminate for my taste,' he whispered as Alex joined him.

'Shush...' Alex narrowed his eyes. 'It's clean, it's a central location, and it's a reasonable price.'

Spud sat back. 'I'm just saying.'

John walked back into the room carrying a tray of refreshments with cake and placed it down on an occasional table. 'All settled in?'

'It's perfect; I'll be quite content here.'

John made them feel welcome as they sat back and enjoyed their teas. But suddenly, flashing blue emergency lights illuminated the lounge window. They stood up and looked down through the window at an ambulance that had pulled up close behind Spud's pickup on the single cobbled road. There was a short burst of a siren.

'You need to go,' said Alex.

Spud dashed down to his pickup and sped off.

Alex texted him. *I owe u a couple of beers.*

'Another tea?' John asked.

Alex nodded and relaxed back into the chair as John went into the kitchen. He found himself reflecting on what Zahida had said over dinner; about contacting Amelia. He wondered what time of the day it was in America, and then he used the internet on his phone to check; it was early morning.

He decided to text her. *Hi Amelia, I hope u and your family r well. Would u like to go out for dinner when u return? Alex.* He pressed *send* and immediately cringed. He somehow knew she wouldn't reply and started to think of Evie.

13.50 p.m. USA C.T.Z.

Amelia dried up another plate after lunch. 'That was a lovely farewell lunch, sis.'

'Oh, and by the way,' said Daphne doing the washing up, 'Greg says goodbye and safe journey back. He's looking forward to another adventure out on your next visit home.'

'Be sure to pass on my thanks, and we should try to do another family expedition somewhere,' she said, looking across to the hallway door. 'I'm a little concerned, though. Mom's been up there a while helping Daddy. I should go and check on things.' Amelia put down the tea towel and went upstairs. She returned after a couple of minutes. 'Dad's zonked and having a lie-down after being sick again. Mom's sitting in her chair beside him.'

'That seems to be the routine now.' Daphne pulled off the washing-up gloves. 'I meant to ask, how'd it go Saturday night with Jake?'

'Yeah, fine; I said I would stay in touch.'

'Well… Your attitude has changed. I'll say no more…'

Amelia continued drying up. 'Mom is worried about me getting involved again.' She paused and leaned on the worktop. 'I also received a text from Alex.'

'The well-jacked, super fit doctor guy.'

'The very one. He'd like to take me out for dinner.'

'That's cool. You could just play them both and see how it works out.'

'Not very ethical, but I might just do that.'

13.57 p.m.

'Hi, Alex,' said Alice at the A&E reception desk as Alex returned to work after his holiday.

'What's with the long face?' he asked. 'I'm fine to start work again.'

'It's not that…'

'I'm sorry that the evening reception got cancelled.'

'It's not that either. Sandra, the duty manager, is coming over. I think she wants to speak to you in private.'

'Welcome back, Doctor Hardson,' said Sandra. 'I need to have a word with you in my office now, please.'

'What's this all about? he asked, feeling Sandra's discomfort as he sat across the desk from her. 'I'm meant to be starting my shift.'

'You won't be starting back at work today.'

'Why?'

'There's no easy way to say this. Evie is here in the hospital. She took an overdose of sleeping tablets. I'm so sorry.'

'What?'

'Her parents should be here soon.'

'Is she alright?'

'She's stable.'

'Thank goodness.' Silence filled the room for a moment as he digested the news. 'It's my fault.'

'Fault is not the issue right now.'

'I didn't think she'd do anything like that. She didn't mean it – surely? A cry for help?'

'Her friend found her – she'd taken the whole packet. The ambulance crew did an excellent job. It was touch and go at one point. So, it definitely wasn't a cry for help.'

'Shit.' He slumped down and buried his face in his hands.

'You need to go home for the rest of the day. Take a couple of days off. I'll be in touch.' She wrote some notes in a planner.

'Do you know the name of the friend that found here?'

She flicked through her paperwork. 'Rebecca Reynolds.'

'Becky, that makes sense.'

'And, Alex, don't go getting any ideas about seeing her on your way out. You know it wouldn't be appropriate – it could make the situation worse.'

He nodded. 'I guess you'll arrange for a primary care physician to evaluate her mental state.'

'Of course.'

Grim-faced, Alex went straight to his bicycle and cycled out of the hospital grounds to a woodland park. He sat on a trunk of a fallen tree and got out a pouch of weed, and rolled a joint. He tried to smoke away his worries before getting back on his bike and erratically cycling home.

He sat alone in his new room for the rest of the day and thought about calling Becky but got drunk on a bottle of whisky instead.

Chapter 23

Friday, 28th February 2020, 7.44 p.m.

Amelia glanced at her watch as she was in a video conversation with Jake on her phone. 'Hey, that'll be great if you give me a call again in a couple of days,' she said, trying not to give the appearance of feeling rushed and mindful that she had run out of time to do her hair.

'I look forward to seeing you again – bye for now,' he said.

'Bye, Jake.' She kept her goodbye minimal and charming enough but was calculating her minimal time to get ready. Placing her phone down, she rushed to her limited wardrobe and deliberated between her red and blue dresses as she alternated holding them up under her chin in front of the mirror. She went with the red. She plonked herself down and speedily applied her makeup whilst glancing at her watch. She checked her look. 'Done!'

She pulled on her red coat and slipped on her black shoes, and was out of the door. Following directions on a Google-maps, she walked through Cambridge city centre with her red umbrella shielding her from the light rain. Turning a corner, she walked up a bricked paved street and instinctively recognised the silhouette figure waiting outside the wine bar.

'These are for you,' said Alex, stepping towards her and presenting a bunch of flowers.

Amelia returned a half-convincing smile as she took them. 'Thank you, how lovely.' Something sank inside her. 'A whole bunch of red roses this time.'

He grimaced. 'Sorry; it's too much, isn't it?'

Smiling, she tried to lift her spirit. 'I've still got the pink one you sent me. It has travelled home to America and back again.' They gazed at each other in brief silence.

'I wasn't sure if I would ever see you again, to be honest...'

'Likewise.'

'But, it's lovely you could make it.'

'You're getting very wet standing there.'

He relaxed. 'Let's go in.' He held open the door for her.

John spotted Alex and immediately came over. 'And you must be Alex's friend, Amelia,' he said, motioning them towards a small reserved table near the wall. A small arrangement of carnations was in the centre, and a tea light burned to one side. John took Amelia's umbrella and coat and then pulled back the chair for her, giving a quick thumbs up and a wink to Alex out of sight of her as she sat down. John left them with a menu and went to serve at the bar.

'Very good service here,' she said.

Alex glanced around at John. 'He's my landlord and new flatmate who part-owns this place. He's alright – very genuine, and he serves up a good helping of dry humour to make people smile.'

'It's good to have folks like that around you.'

'Definitely. I promised that I would try out the place.'

'Something to celebrate this evening – your new home.' She gazed down at the menu. 'I'll just stick to having a Sauvignon Blanc, please.'

'And I'm going to have a beer before we order our food. It's a very limited menu.'

'Hey – I'm sure it'll be good.'

Alex gave John the nod, and he immediately made his way over. He took their order and joked with them about the ambulance scenario on Alex's moving-in day. Amelia giggled.

'Could you look after the flowers for me?' she asked. John took them.

'You look amazing, by the way,' said Alex.

'Thank you, but you know it wasn't that long ago that you were about to marry Evie.'

He gulped. 'Let's not talk about that, please.'

'I do feel a little awkward with the red roses – especially as they're generally given to loved ones on Valentine's Day, which was the eve of your wedding.'

'Sorry, it was a bad idea.'

'Alex, I really do like you. But I didn't know when I met you that you were about to get married. I'm just conscious that you're on the rebound.'

He frowned. 'Just hear me out. I know we've only spent a short time together, but I really enjoyed it and want to get to know more about you.'

John arrived with their drinks. 'You both need to switch those pensive faces back to being happy this instant, you hear me?' They both returned a small smile, and John disappeared to the bar.

'The thing is…' said Amelia. 'I've got to focus on studying for my doctorate. So, can we just be friends?'

Alex rested back in his seat. 'I'll drink to being friends.' He raised his glass.

Amelia raised her glass. 'Awesome. Good friends.'

He grinned and put down his glass. 'How was your visit back home?'

Amelia proceeded to explain about her father's lung cancer, the treatment he was having, and the side effects. She glanced away and smiled as she tried to capture the memory of happy family moments.

'Are you alright?'

'Mm-hmm. You've asked all the questions so far,' she said. 'What've you been up to this week?'

'Wait until we've ordered.' He examined the tapas menu and placed their order with John. 'I should tell you the story of my sculling challenge in the week,' he said. 'How Hamish organised it and how we won. I'm ashamed to say we cheated.'

'That's really bad...' She frowned.

He nodded. 'And what about you?'

'I'll tell you the fun narrative which involved a fishing challenge.'

They shared their experiences with each other over dinner but omitted their former partners from everything. They finished their meals and enjoyed conversation until it was late.

'I think John is waiting for us to go,' she said, looking around at an almost empty place. 'You know what?'

His eyes locked with hers. 'No. What?'

'I do think you really could be a toad.'

'Come again?'

She grinned. 'It's a compliment…'

'How's that a compliment?'

'Toads have the most attractive eyes and a calm nature.' She smiled. 'Their skin is also beautiful to stroke.' She raised herself out of her seat.

Alex was digesting her answer as John fetched their coats and walked back holding the flowers. Alex noticed Amelia grimacing at them. 'The thing is, John,' said Alex. 'We'd really like you to have the flowers as a thank you for looking after us this evening.'

'I'm just doing my job – I couldn't possibly.'

'Please?' she said. 'I'm absolutely sure.'

John held open the door as she and Alex left. Amelia linked her arm through his as they made their way through the streets.

8.40 p.m.

Robert and Sophie wheeled their cases through Arrivals at Frankfurt Airport. They caught the train to Heidelberg and got a taxi to their hotel in the heart of the old town. He stepped out of the taxi onto the medieval cobbled market square and stood for a moment and admired the illuminated ancient stone architecture of the hotel from the up-lighting, capturing its magnificence. Sophie walked around and held his arm. They walked up the steps and into the hotel. They quickly unpacked in their room and went back down to the hotel bar for a drink before dinner.

'We're early; our reservation isn't for another half hour,' said Robert checking his watch.

Sophie ordered their drinks. 'Well, we have time to relax here by the bar.'

Robert's phone buzzed; he glanced at it, and switched it off. 'It's Mother; she's called three times.'

'I understand how you feel. I felt so awkward that time I met her. I just wanted the ground to open up and swallow me.'

'That's the effect she has on people.'

'She didn't give me a chance, no pleasantries; she just shot me down.' The barman passed them their drinks.

Robert picked up his glass of wine. 'I think it comes from years of putting lawyers and barristers in their place.'

Sophie sipped her wine. 'Hmm… but surely you don't have to listen to her?'

'I can't say why, but she's got a hold over me.'

11.15 p.m.

Alex walked Amelia back to her college and stopped outside the entrance with its ancient insignia coat of arms displayed above the porch.

'Well, this is me,' she said, holding out her hand. 'I had a lovely evening thank you.'

He took her hand. 'What're you doing tomorrow?'

'I haven't got anything arranged.'

'How about coming punting with me?' he asked, still holding her hand. 'We could go up to Grantchester. I'll bring a picnic lunch.'

'I'm not sure.'

'It'll be good fun. C'mon.'

'Why not. Text me tomorrow.'

'Until then,' he said, releasing her hand. He strolled back home as if he was walking on a heavenly cloud as he cherished her touch.

Light rain was still falling when he decided to sit down at a park bench only a short distance from his flat. He pulled out a small pouch from inside his coat pocket and, shielding the contents with his fingers, rolled himself a joint. He lit it, leaned back, and as he puffed, he thought of her qualities; the way she made children laugh, her fun, carefree attitude, her honesty, her sensitivity to nature. He reminisced about the time she stood across the dance floor at Becky and Oliver's reception, looking glamourous in her burgundy-coloured evening gown. He smiled to himself until he finished his joint. Feeling euphoric, he pulled a small metal hip flask from another pocket and swigged back the whisky contents until it had all gone. He rose unsteadily to his feet and stumbled home.

Chapter 24

Saturday, 29th February 2020, 8.20 a.m.

Alex carried a bowl of cereal and a cup of tea into the lounge and carefully placed them onto the occasional table as he sat down in his dressing gown. He texted his sister. *Gd morning, sis. Have u got Becky's number?*

Yes, why?

Is it convenient to speak?

I'll call u in 5 mins.

He stopped eating his cereal when his phone rang. 'Hi, Sis. It's about Evie. She tried committing suicide and was taken to A&E.'

'What! Oh, my goodness. Is she alright? When did that happen?'

'Last Monday, the day I was moving in. Becky discovered that she'd taken an overdose and called nine-nine-nine. But I don't know any more than that.'

'I could try calling Becky and discreetly ask how Evie is and see what she says.'

'If you wouldn't mind, please.'

10.00 a.m.

Alex sat at his sister's kitchen table while she made him a coffee with Charlotte on his lap. 'Did Becky say anything about Evie when you spoke to her?'

'Hm… recovering.' Freya took hold of her daughter's hand. 'Charlotte, sweetie. Can you go and play, please, while Uncle Alex and I have a chat?' Charlotte jumped down off Alex's lap and ran into the lounge.

'Did you get any more details?'

'I did. Becky was surprisingly open with me.'

'Please tell me everything.'

'Evie is under medication and has an appointment back at the hospital tomorrow with a psychiatrist. She's been signed off work for four weeks.'

'So, she's convalescing.'

'Her and Becky had been out for a walk together around Trent Park.'

'That sounds more positive. But did she say what happened?'

Freya nodded. 'Becky had gone around last Sunday night to keep Evie company and stay the night. But Evie was in a poor state; she didn't look well. The place was in a complete mess and smelt stale when she'd arrived. Bins hadn't been emptied, and no washing up was done.'

'She should've stayed with her parents.'

'Becky noticed patches of blood on the sleeve of Evie's blouse. She managed to get her in a hot bath and washed her hair. She'd been self-harming. There was a row of laddered cuts down her forearm.'

'Oh, shit.' Alex shook his head.

'Becky was woken in the night by Evie sobbing and went in to check on her. She was meant to go back to work the next day. First day back after half term.'

'Of course.' Alex buried his head in his hands.

Becky got her to take one of her sleeping tablets, but not thinking, left the packet on the bedside table.'

'Evie must have taken the rest of the packet when Becky had gone back to bed – right?'

Freya nodded.

'What have I done? Evie could have died.'

Freya knelt down and hugged him. 'But she didn't, and now she appears to be on the mend. Her friends and family have pulled in around her.'

'I've been having a good week getting my act back together, and poor Evie – it's been like a nightmare for her.'

'You can't blame yourself.'

'Who else is to blame? I'm responsible. I was moving into my new home, giving another woman a bunch of red roses while Evie was in my A&E department having her stomach pumped.'

'Please don't,' Freya said.

'It never occurred to me she'd do anything so desperate as attempted suicide.'

10.35 a.m.

Robert stood just inside the hotel reception area, killing time reading The Times.

Sophie walked out of the elevator and put on her coat as she joined him. 'You've got a stern face. What're you reading?'

'It's about this virus that's come out of China – it's getting serious in Europe. There's a list here of the situation in different countries. It shows Italy at the top with hundreds of infections and twenty-one deaths. The World Health Organisation is concerned that it'll turn into a pandemic.'

Sophie opened her handbag. 'If this virus starts to spread through the community back home, could that cause a problem for your son?' She took out her compact mirror and checked her makeup.

'Potentially, but let's hope they contain it.' Robert folded away his paper. 'The plan today is to visit the castle, take in the views, and walk around the park gardens.'

They both followed a tourist map to the Kornmarkt in the old town, bought their tickets, and took the funicular railway up to the castle.

Sophie read the tourist guide as they approached the castle gate. 'This is Elizabeth Gate built by Friedrich the Fifth for his English princess in sixteen hundred and fifteen. She became the Queen of Bohemia.' Robert nodded with mild interest.

They entered the cellars. Robert stared up at the royal crest on a giant wine vat. Sophie walked up to him continuing to read from her guide. 'This is the Heidelberg Tun. It holds over fifty-eight thousand gallons of wine.'

'We could hold a party for hundreds of guests every night for years.'

They finished viewing the castle from the inside and walked around outside, posing for selfies in the cool air. The sun glistened in the background off the rooftops far below in the old town.

Robert put his arm around her as they walked around the castle gardens. 'It's a good thing that we're not in the tourist season – there's hardly anybody around.'

Sophie spotted a bench in a secluded part of the garden. Removing her hat, she rested in the sunshine. Robert joined her and pulled her in close, stroking her hair and her neck. They leaned into each other and kissed. She rubbed his groin area while he reached inside her coat and started to fondle her breasts. She took hold of his hand, got up, and guided him to a shaded area behind some large oak trees. Leaning back against a tree, she opened her coat and undid the buttons on her cardigan and blouse. He unfastened the front of her bra. She pulled him closer, unzipped his trousers, and started to rub his equipment.

'Wait, not here…' Breathing heavily, he took hold of her wrist and pulled her hand away. He pulled up his zipper and tidied himself up.

'What's wrong? You've liked it when we've done alfresco sex before.'

'Well, that was before I had separated from Bella.' He scratched his head. 'We don't have to do it like this anymore – it's different now.'

'But it's erotic, exciting, and it'll make this place even more memorable.' She fastened her bra.

Robert frowned. 'I really don't need to have sex here to make it memorable.'

1.05 p.m.

Alex climbed into a punt with his picnic bag. Evie was out of his thoughts as he held out his hand. Amelia took hold as she stepped in and quickly took a seat. He clenched his hand, feeling the warmth from her touch. The assistant at Granta Punts handed Amelia a couple of blankets.

'This is a strange boat,' she said, spreading the blanket over her lap. 'It reminds me of when I went out fishing in a boat this size with my Uncle Dex. It was on a small river where the fish actually jumped out of the water into your boat as you powered along.'

'Really?' he said, taking the punting pole from the assistant.

'Yep, really! Go on YouTube. I started screaming when one landed on my lap. The boat was strewn with fish flapping about everywhere.'

'I didn't know there were such places or fish.' He punted out onto the river and towards Grantchester along the River Cam. He punted for half a mile past Sheep's Green and the nature reserve where Amelia had discovered a toad. She rested back in her seat, enjoying the views while listening to the gentle sound of the water lapping against the wooden punt as the grass-lined banks of Grantchester Meadows slipped past them.

'It's such a lovely sunny day and surprisingly mild for the time of year,' she said, gazing up as he stood on the back of the punt, pushing the pole into the water.

'You sound very English with that comment.' He pulled the pole back out of the river, running it up between his hands as water dripped onto his pumps and the rear decking.

She beamed. 'You make it look so easy, but I guess there's a knack to it?'

'I've punted a few times – practise makes perfect, as they say.' He grinned as he pushed the pole into the water. 'It's quite relaxing but also a good workout – like sculling.'

'That's your weekend thing, isn't it?'

'Yes, but not this weekend. I'm with you, much prettier company than the guys.'

'Thank you, but won't your friends be disappointed?'

Alex shrugged. 'They'll cope for one day.'

He punted past the cricket green at Grantchester Village. 'I'm going to push on a bit further.'

He found an embankment around a corner of the river away from the public paths that had a grass verge and woodland. He wedged the punt up against the bank using the pole and sat down opposite her. He opened the picnic hamper, pulling out some containers of food, plates, napkins, glasses, a bottle of gin, and some tonics.

'All this food looks lovely. A proper English afternoon tea with nice little cut sandwiches and scones. I can see there's some thought and planning gone into this.'

'I'm pleased you like it,' he said, pouring out two glasses of G&T. 'My sister helped, so I can't take all the credit, but the idea was all mine.' A blackbird chirped away from a branch above them.

She patted the space next to her on the seat, and he moved over. They were shoulder to shoulder, and she adjusted the blankets, pulling them up onto their chests.

'A toast,' he announced, holding up his glass. 'Here's to punting and picnics.'

'I'll drink to that.'

'A top-up?' He poured more gin into her glass.

'Whoa... That's quite a full glass.'

'So, you're not driving, and I can't exactly get a ticket for being drunk when punting.' He grinned. 'Hang on, let me get a selfie of us if that's okay with you?' He held up his phone in front of them and pulled her in close. 'Say cheese.' He pressed the button. 'That's a great one.'

They continued drinking and nibbling on food as they chatted about experiences. Amelia felt very relaxed and was soon a little woozy. He suddenly went vacant.

'Is everything alright?' she asked, leaning into him. 'You seem a little distant.'

'Sorry,' he said, shaking his head and turning to face her. 'Just some news I received earlier.'

'Nothing upsetting, I hope.' She stroked the side of his face.

His skin tingled, and their gazes locked. He leaned over her, and their noses were almost touching. They held their position, feeling each other's warm breath on their mouths. He ran his fingers down the side of her cheek and stroked her hair. She tilted her head back, and he moved to kiss her exposed slender neck. His hand started to wander and find its way inside her coat.

She took a breath and slid to one side. 'Hey, I think we need to be going back now.' She sat upright. 'And besides, I need the bathroom.'

Alex pointed to the woodland. 'You can always take a wild wee.'

She grinned, then shook her head. 'I've had a lovely day so far. Let's not spoil it. We're meant to be just friends.'

They packed away all the picnic things, and he started to punt back. She occasionally glanced up at him as he punted along the river until they arrived back at Granta Punts. He held her hand, steadying her as she stepped off the punt.

'Thank you for a lovely picnic.' She kissed him on the cheek. 'I've really got to bail.' She turned and walked away.

'When are you free to meet up again?'

She turned and smiled. 'I don't know. Call me tomorrow if you want.'

Chapter 25

Sunday, 1ˢᵗ March 2020, 5.30 a.m.

Alex fidgeted around, trying to get to sleep. Eventually, he gave up, punched his pillow, and got up. He threw back the curtains, put on his dressing gown, went to the kitchen, and made himself a half mug of tea. He seized his bottle of vodka and topped up his mug. Grabbing his coat and slipping on shoes, he left the flat holding his drink, walked to the end of Green Street, crossed the road, and sat down on a wet bench near the porter's lodge to Sidney Sussex College. Mixed emotions surged through him. He took a swig of his cocktail tea, pulled out his pouch, rolled himself a joint, and smoked it in the cold half-light dawn.

Sipping the last of his drink and taking his last puff, he tried to block thoughts of Evie and savour his punting trip with Amelia.

After a while, he ambled back home and stumbled around between the toilet and his room before putting in his earbuds. Woozy and feeling free-spirited, he moved around his room to the music. He spun around, trying to dance but bumped into his boxes and furniture before eventually collapsing onto his bed and falling asleep.

7.50 a.m.

Robert had been awake for ages, propped up in bed wearing his hotel bathrobe as he worked on his iPad.

Sophie stirred from sleep next to him. 'Hmmm... that was a great night, just like it was when we first met – all over the room and the bed.' She stroked her fingers down his chest as he remained focused on his screen. She snuggled up to him, sliding her thigh over his tummy. She continued to stroke his chest and then moved her hand onto his equipment.

'I must get this report completed today.'

'But it's Sunday morning. Time for relaxing.' She stroked his penis playfully. 'We need to wake up my pleasure fella, and bring him back to his morning glory.'

Robert tried to carry on working.

'Hey, he's starting to stand to attention.'

'Sophie... I really must get this completed.'

She slid completely over on top of him, kissing him around his cheeks. Her hair flopped over his face.

'What's wrong with my pleasure fella? He's gone all floppy again.'

Robert gently pushed her off, sat up on the edge of the bed, and pulled his robe around him. 'I must really get on with this report.'

'What's the matter with you lately?' She kneeled on the bed. 'You were acting strangely in the castle gardens yesterday, now this!' She got off the bed and pulled the sheet around her. 'You used to love being risqué, like on my desk and on your office floor. You said that's why you would leave your wife because she's boring, whereas I excite you. But now I'm beginning to wonder.'

Robert's eyes struggled to meet hers. 'You do excite me. It's just that I have a lot on my mind.' He exhaled. 'It was really good last night, but I have to work when the need arises – that's what pays for everything.'

'I'm going to shower.' She turned and slammed the ensuite door shut behind her.

Robert closed his iPad and picked up his phone, dialled, and waited slightly anxiously.

'Hello, Mother… I know I haven't answered your messages or calls this weekend.'

'Have you dumped your plaything yet?'

'Can we change the subject, please? You can be so blunt at times. No, I haven't.'

'I thought not. You've often struggled to do the right thing when it really mattered, even from an early age. Because of that, I've already written you completely out of my will.'

'What! You've cut me out of everything?'

'I did warn you. Now, pay off your plaything, and I'll amend it.'

'Mother, you're not going to force me to give her up.'

'And there's this unethical business matter of when you organised the merger with that mining company last year. It would be a shame if the press got to hear…'

'You wouldn't. Mother, Mother? Are you still there?'

9.15 a.m.

Alex got up from bed. Feeling half-conscious, he ambled into the kitchen.

'There's fresh coffee in the jug – help yourself,' said John, fully dressed and having his breakfast. 'Sleep alright?'

'Eventually.' He poured himself a coffee and proceeded to make scrambled eggs on toast. 'What are you up to today?'

'Well, since you ask. I've decided that the lounge chairs look a bit dreary. I'm going to give them a makeover and paint the woodwork.'

'What colour?'

'I'm undecided. Something bright and cheerful. I'm going to the DIY store after breakfast.'

Alex nodded. 'Sounds like a good plan.' He pulled his phone out from his dressing gown pocket and texted Amelia. *Would u like to meet up for a walk and lunch? 10.30? X.*

A reply came back almost immediately. *Can u make it 11.20? Meet me outside St Bene't's. I'm going to church. X.*

Alex's eyes went wide. 'Church.'

John looked up from eating his cereal. 'Everything alright?'

'Sorry, just thinking out loud.' Alex texted a reply. *See u then. X.*

Alex had been waiting outside the porch entrance to St Bene't's Church as the congregation trickled out into the sunshine.

Amelia spotted him as she came out. 'You could've come inside out of the cold and had a hot drink with cake.'

Alex shrugged.

'Oh, I get it.' She tilted her head and smirked. 'You do realise that Christians are just normal people. Hopefully, it's not a problem because this is me.'

'It's not a problem.'

'Good, because I've got a lot to pray about with what's going on in my family. It's part of my life.'

He nodded. 'Zahida, my friend's wife, is Muslim. I don't understand her faith, but she's normal.'

'So, are we going for this walk around Cambridge?'

'Absolutely.' They headed off through the ancient city, past some of the churches and university colleges. He looked down with surprise as she linked her arm with his.

'Just friends, remember,' she said.

They walked around Jesus Green, and then they followed the river around to Midsummer Common. They weaved through the streets to the spring garden displays on Christ Pieces.

He turned to her. 'A question. Do you see yourself having a family in the future?'

She chuckled. 'I couldn't imagine not having children. I look forward to the day.'

He smiled. 'This might sound like an old cliché, but would you like to come back to see my new place, and I'll make lunch.'

'What sort of lunch?'

'One that suits you. There's a local deli nearby.' He walked her to the deli and bought some freshly baked bread, cheeses, and cold meats before heading to his home. 'This is it,' he said, unlocking the purple street door. They walked up the stairs and entered his flat. There was a smell of paint, but John wasn't to be seen, and there was some furniture missing. Alex looked out of the kitchen window and could see John painting the chairs in the rear courtyard and went down to join him.

'What do you think of my handiwork?' John asked as he stood up from painting the legs of one of his chairs. 'Do you like the colour?'

'Well, they're certainly looking bright and cheerful,' said Alex.

'I think the colour primrose works, don't you?'

'It's perfect. A good springtime colour. Are you painting anything else?'

John frowned. 'I was considering painting the street door as well.'

'It's your door; why not. We've been to the deli. I'll make us all some lunch while you're finishing off your furniture.'

'Instead of the whole door,' said Amelia interrupting. 'What about creating a small shape or pattern on the door?'

'Like what?' John tilted his head.

'It could be something personal to you.'

John's eyes suddenly widened. 'I've got it. My grandmother lived here with her beloved cat Bessie. But how do I get a yellow Bessie on the door?'

Amelia placed her hands on her hips. 'Have you got a printer?'

John nodded.

'Leave it to me; I'm good at artwork.' She went on John's computer and printed off a cat silhouette on two pieces of paper – almost life-size – and cut out the image. She taped it on the bottom of the door as Alex and John watched. 'I'll need the quick-drying white primer to start,' she said. 'And have you got an old shirt?'

John went and found an old long sleeve shirt and passed it to her. 'Are you sure it will look alright?'

'Trust me.'

John helped Amelia get set up with brushes, paints, and old newspapers before she started painting. He quickly cleaned down an old table and chairs in the courtyard before Alex appeared with the lunch. John passed around blankets that they put over their laps. All three of them ate lunch in the chilly spring air as they discussed ideas for redecorating his wine bar.

'Changing the topic,' said Alex. 'This Covid-19 is becoming more of a concern – forty-seven dead in China, according to the news on the radio this morning. That's even with the area in strict shutdown. Italy has twenty-nine dead and over a thousand cases. There are reports of it across Europe.'

'It's coming this way,' said John staring at Alex. 'How do you think it might affect you?'

Alex shook his head. 'It's manic enough in casualty. We don't need extra pressure from a contagious virus. I'm not sure if the hospital or the staff could cope.' He checked his watch as they finished their lunch.

'Are you alright for time?' John asked.

'My shift starts at three. I need to be leaving soon.'

'I'm happy to stay and paint,' said Amelia.

'I'll go and make another pot of tea,' said John.

Amelia returned to the street door. Crouching down on her knees, she continued applying paint with a small art brush. Alex brought out two cups of tea and stood on the cobbled pavement.

'Thanks for the tea.' She placed her mug down on the doorstep. They both took a step back and viewed her artwork. She put her arm through his. 'Honest opinion?'

'You really want my honest opinion?'

She quickly swung her hand around with the paintbrush and dabbed white paint onto his nose and across his cheek. He stepped back, spilling his tea, and stood, mouth wide open. She collapsed in fits of laughter.

Raising an eyebrow towards her. 'There's clearly another side to you.'

Chapter 26

Friday, 6th March 2020, 10.30 a.m.

Annabelle was sitting adjacent to Teresa at the kitchen table at Villa Francina, reading while having a cup of tea. She rested her English newspaper on her lap. 'I'm getting worried about what's going to happen here in Mallorca with the Coronavirus situation. It appears to be escalating in Italy, with a hundred and forty-eight deaths now. Spain and the UK have also recorded their first deaths.'

'Too gloomy.'

'The Italian government has advised people to wear masks, but the British government says that they won't provide protection with this sort of virus.'

Teresa looked up from her magazine. 'Enough talk about potential pandemics. I just love reading all the gossip about the movie stars, and I love the wedding photos.' She sipped her tea.

'Perhaps I also need a lighter read.'

'Try *Homes and Gardens*.' Teresa gazed out of the window. 'I can see the difference you've made in the garden already since you've been back. All the flower borders look glorious, and your flower displays inside look beautiful.'

'Thank you. It's a joy being back here. I've no regrets.'

Teresa smiled. 'I knew it would be the *tonic* you needed. I'm going to go now. So, I'll see you later at seven. Remember, you're bringing the dessert.' The two women stood and hugged.

Annabelle watched from outside as Teresa walked down the path in the bright sunshine, got into her car, and drove off. She then knelt to smell the scent of her white flowered Sarcococca shrub. Smiling, she returned to the kitchen and continued reading. A short time later, a familiar car horn sounded. She went to the window and then walked down the path. '*Buenos dias*, Emilio. Is everything alright?' she asked as she shielded her eyes from the sun.

He got out of his van. '*Si, Bueno*. I've come to work on garden.'

'But you were here only yesterday. I thought you were contracted to do just one day a week by Robert?'

'I've some spare time, not so busy at moment. So, I have come at no extra cost.'

Annabelle beamed. 'Well, if you're sure. We can take a walk around the grounds and talk about ideas.'

Emilio walked over to an area on one of the lawns where there was a large dip. 'I had this idea. We could create a large flower island here.' He crouched down and knifed out a plug of earth in the dip and rubbed it between his thumb and finger. 'Do you see how the soil is moist compared to elsewhere?'

'I understand, moisture-retaining soil. But how much of this area would you use?'

Emilio pulled off his T-shirt and dropped it. He paced across the area and stopped. 'Twelve metres.' He pointed out the distance back to his shirt.

'It's a rather large area.' She struggled to maintain eye contact and not look at his body. 'Will it take a long time to complete? And then there's the cost.'

He paced around the area with excitement, explaining his scheme. Annabelle watched him, thinking how entertaining he was; his hands were very animated as he pointed out where different types of plants could be positioned for height and colour. Half-listening, she struggled not to gaze at his toned body every time he looked away.

Emilio stopped and turned to her. 'A beautiful shrub and flower island. Imagine it.'

She snapped herself out of dreaming. 'Yes… But I'll need a plan drawn up with a list of plants and pictures attached. I'll need a quote from you for Robert to approve, understand?'

Emilio nodded and put his tee shirt back on. They continued to walk around the grounds discussing other ideas. They made their way over to the villa to examine the condition of the window boxes below the leaf-green-coloured shutters. Emilio used his secateurs to quickly deadhead some red geraniums. They walked around the villa and arrived back at the porch, and stopped to check on the array of potted cactuses before Emilio joined her in the kitchen for a cool drink. She got some A3 paper and colouring pencils. Sitting side by side, they started researching plants using her laptop and sketching out their design ideas. Her hand brushed over his. And suddenly, he took hold of it. She froze. They turned and faced each other. He leaned forward; she didn't back away. She breathed in his manly odour; it started to arouse a hunger within her. She didn't move as he kissed her tenderly on her cheek, then lower on her jaw, on her ear, and on her neck. She tried to compose herself but felt unable to resist his loving attention. Her lips found his, and their arms locked around each other. Their kissing increased with intensity. She felt like a teenager again as she let her pent-up lust flow unhindered. They stood up. Her chair fell over. She pulled off Emilio's tee shirt while he undid her blouse and groped her breasts. They kissed passionately as she pulled him towards the bedroom. She lost her blouse on the way, and then she undid his shorts in the hallway as he stumbled out of them. They made it into the bedroom, where they flopped side-by-side onto the bed. Their hands were all over each other. She felt his bulge. He undid her trousers and pulled them off. They rolled around in an embrace on the bed in their underwear. She pulled off his briefs, and they lay kissing with his leg inside hers. Emilio's fingers found their way into her knickers.

But then, something seemed wrong to her. 'No, stop,' she whispered, pulling his hand away. Her panting slowed as she sat up.

'What's wrong?'

She pushed her hair back to one side. 'Nothing… Everything is just perfect, but I can't do this. Maybe if we weren't here in my bed and we were at yours, or…' Her gaze went to the window.

He immediately stood up, grabbed her hand, and tried to pull her towards the open door. She shook her head, picked up his briefs from the floor, and prompted him to put them back on. He pulled them up.

'Just hold me, Emilio. Please…' His bulging muscular arms embraced her. She nestled the side of her head under his chin as she held him, not wanting the moment to end.

She stroked his hair around his ears. 'You're a gorgeous man.'

Emilio shook his head. 'You're a beautiful woman.'

'Thank you, it's been a long time since anyone has said that to me.' She tried to remember when Robert had last said it to her. 'This moment has been very special. I wanted to make love, but I'm a married woman, and at this moment in time, it would be wrong.'

He exhaled.

She showed him to the shower in the guest room, passing him a clean towel from her cupboard. She showered in her room and smiled at herself in the mirror as she got herself dressed. They made their way to the kitchen, and she made them both cold drinks.

Afterwards, she walked with him down to his van. She reached out with both her hands and took hold of his. 'You're very special to me, a very dear friend.'

'I would like to be more.'

'Maybe in the future. I haven't asked if you have anyone in your life. Actually, don't answer that. I'm just pleased you're here as a friend, and I can trust you.'

7.30 p.m.

Annabelle was on the veranda at Teresa's home. 'The table is laid,' she said.

'The paella is almost done,' Teresa called out from the kitchen.

Annabelle poured out two glasses of white wine and carried them back through to the kitchen. 'Let's have a toast,' she said, passing a glass to Teresa. 'Here's to being in the moment and living life to the full.'

'I'll drink to that.' They raised their glasses together. Teresa tilted her head. 'There's something different about you this evening. I can't put my finger on it, but you're positively glowing.'

'I'm just happy.' She looked away.

'Something has happened since this morning?'

Nothing has happened.' Annabelle blushed.

'If I didn't know any better, I would say that you're in love.'

'How ridiculous.'

'Has Emilio been around?'

Annabelle looked up. 'Alright – I'll explain.'

8.30 p.m.

Alex waited in the dark outside the entrance to Amelia's college when a text message from Freya pinged through on his phone. *Becky says that Evie is making progress, but we should try and arrange a meeting with u both.*

Ok, but let's talk first. He tucked his phone away, and then he saw Amelia walking towards him in her red coat. Unaware of his presence, she stopped momentarily under the entrance light and carefully arranged her hair around her red beret; he was captivated. It was like a touch of déjà vu – where had he witnessed this scene before? He dismissed the feeling and started to walk slowly towards her. She spotted him as he emerged into the light. He turned out his elbow as she approached, and they walked into town with their arms linked.

John had reserved a table for them at his wine bar and promptly served them when they arrived, lighting the candle on the table before he went back behind the bar.

'To us,' said Alex raising his glass. She looked at him questioningly. 'I really enjoy us spending time together. I know it hasn't been long since I was with Evie. But, we've both moved on.'

'There's something you should know. I was engaged not so long ago myself, but I was badly let down. It was that old cliché; my fiancé slept with my best friend. I've struggled to move on trust-wise.'

'I see... I knew about your engagement; Evie mentioned it. Do you still keep in touch with him?'

'I do. He wants us to be back together again, and he's prepared to wait for me until I return to the US, but I've promised nothing in return.'

'It sounds as if I've got competition.'

Her gaze searched his. 'The thing is, we're both emotionally damaged, and I'm nervous about getting involved with you so soon after your breakup. It's all that rebound stuff.'

'So, are we dating or not?'

'Let's just go slowly.'

'Of course.'

'To be honest, I thought I'd got over Jake. But I met up with him when I was last back home, and I felt very confused about my feelings – even though he hurt me. I can't switch off from those past emotions.'

Alex held her gaze. 'So, you're still recovering as well. What a pair we make.'

'It's difficult as I feel that we get on so well. Alex, if only we'd met without all this emotional baggage.'

He reached under the table, found her hand, and gently squeezed it. Their fingers entwined as they drank.

'I can't help feeling some responsibility for your relationship breakdown with Evie,' she said. 'On top of all that, I'm worried about my father and family.'

He knew he couldn't explain Evie's suicide attempt as he listened to Amelia talk about her family concerns and describe her father's illness. 'It must be very difficult for you, being on this side of the big pond. You probably feel helpless.'

'That's it precisely.' Her eyes glazed with emotion.

He gently squeezed her hand again. 'I'm here if you need someone to listen – you can lean on me.'

'Thank you.'

He took a breath. 'So… how do I win your heart?'

'Just be like good fruits of the vine.' She held her glass.

He narrowed an eye. 'Did you mean to say wine?'

'Of the vine. They're Christian qualities referred to in the Bible, of love, joy, peace, patience, kindness, goodness, and faithfulness.'

There was a moment of silence. 'But surely that's what relationships are anyway?'

'Jake is a Christian and goes to church, but he failed to show self-control and be faithful when he slept with my best friend. Do you see my point?'

Alex gave her hand another gentle squeeze. 'You can trust me.'

'I hope so.'

Alex observed an engagement ring with a trio of three small diamonds hanging on a gold chain around her neck. 'I hope you don't mind me asking, but is that the ring?'

'Oh no,' she chuckled. 'It was originally my grandma's; she gave it to Mom, who gave it to me. I feel I've got part of Grandma close to my heart.'

They slowly finished their drinks and then went and found Alex's favourite steak restaurant opposite King's College.

It was late when he walked her back to her college, stopping outside the entrance gate. She kissed him on the cheek and turned to leave but then spun herself around and planted a firm kiss on his lips; his hands didn't get a chance to move from his coat pockets. She walked away past the porter in his bowler hat. Alex watched her go under the porch before he turned and started walking home. Further along the avenue, he was going to stop at his now-familiar favourite bench and wondered if Rose was bedded down on Hills Road. He took another detour through the streets and almost fell upon her as he walked around a corner.

'Rose, it's okay, it's me,' he said, emerging into the street light.

She was half asleep and sat herself up in her makeshift cardboard bed. 'What're you doing here at this time?'

'I just thought of you and wondered if you would like to share a puff?'

She chuckled. 'Sure, why not.'

He sat himself down beside her, stroked Gertie, and pulled out his pouch from inside his coat pocket. 'Life is really shit at times, and I just don't like to think of you living your life like this.' He rolled a cannabis joint, lit it, and passed it to her.

She took it and inhaled. 'There's nothing you can do. It is what it is – crap.'

He took the joint as she passed it to him and took a drag. 'Maybe we can just chat for a while, please? You're a good listener.'

She chuckled. 'What am I now – your psychiatrist? Shit, pass back that joint.'

'I feel as if we have an affinity.'

She laughed. 'Is that what you call our relationship? I'm the one who's a fecking headcase and needs a shrink – not you.'

'You'd be surprised.'

'You're right – I would be.'

He took back the joint and had a drag. 'I've badly hurt someone, and I'm sort of messed up in the head.' She leaned over and rested her hand on his shoulder. 'I couldn't imagine you hurting anyone.' She took the joint. 'I can tell your character. You're compassionate and tough.'

'I wished.'

'What's troubling you? Who have you hurt?'

He rubbed his stubble. 'I've dumped my fiancé, she tried to commit suicide, and I feel really bad. I've got a new girlfriend, who's unsure about me, and I'm a bit confused about everything.'

'It sounds like you're a bit of a lost soul.'

He sighed, got out his whisky flask, and took a swig. 'I also still have feelings towards my old fiancé.' He passed his flask to Rose.

She took a gulp. 'I know you like being in and around water. Commit your soul and swim hard with just one of those relationships. Otherwise, you'll sink.'

Chapter 27

Saturday, 7th March 2020, 00.15 a.m.

Alex was in a stupor as he fumbled around trying to unlock his street door. He eventually got the right key into the lock and stumbled into the hallway. His movement triggered the motion sensor for the light. He lumbered up the stairs and scrabbled with his keys, accidentally dropping them. He slid down the door trying to reach them, and fell asleep.

'Alex, Alex, it's me,' said John, arriving home a short time later and finding Alex curled up at the base of the front door. 'Let's get you inside.' He helped Alex through and into one of the lounge chairs. He got some water and held it up to Alex's lips.

'Sorry,' Alex mumbled, trying to grab the glass. It dropped, and it smashed on the floor.

John fetched the dustpan and brush. 'Your breath reeks of weed and alcohol.'

'It helps take away the stuff that's inside my head.'

'You look like shit. I'm genuinely concerned that you've got a drug problem.'

'I'm meant to be a doctor – worrying, isn't it?'

'I only let you have the room because I thought you'd be responsible.'

Alex rubbed his face. 'I am most of the time.'

'But it's happening daily. I've noticed the smell of weed in the mornings and evenings. Does Amelia know?'

He shook his head. 'No...'

'You're going to lose her if you don't sort yourself out and stop this path of self-destruction.'

'I'm not like this when I'm with her.'

John stood in front of him with folded arms. 'I bet. She wouldn't approve, and then she'll be gone.'

'I know.'

'Don't mess it up. I'll help you if you want.'

Alex pushed himself to his feet and embraced John. 'Thank you.'

'Let's sit you back down. I'll get you a tea and run you a bath with some bubbles.'

Alex's hand shook as John helped steady the cup of tea to his lips. John started to help Alex get undressed and then prepared a bath.

'You know my sexuality,' John said as Alex walked naked into the bathroom. 'And yet you have all your bits on full display.'

'It's okay; we both have the same plumbing, and you know my sexuality.'

John passed Alex the soap. 'Mmm…' John left the bathroom as Alex flicked some bath water at him.

8.00 a.m.

Robert was lost in thought as he had breakfast with Sophie in the hotel café.

'Wake up. You're doing that dull thing again,' said Sophie sitting opposite him.

'I've got a lot on my mind – sorry.'

Chapter 27

Saturday, 7th March 2020, 00.15 a.m.

Alex was in a stupor as he fumbled around trying to unlock his street door. He eventually got the right key into the lock and stumbled into the hallway. His movement triggered the motion sensor for the light. He lumbered up the stairs and scrabbled with his keys, accidentally dropping them. He slid down the door trying to reach them, and fell asleep.

'Alex, Alex, it's me,' said John, arriving home a short time later and finding Alex curled up at the base of the front door. 'Let's get you inside.' He helped Alex through and into one of the lounge chairs. He got some water and held it up to Alex's lips.

'Sorry,' Alex mumbled, trying to grab the glass. It dropped, and it smashed on the floor.

John fetched the dustpan and brush. 'Your breath reeks of weed and alcohol.'

'It helps take away the stuff that's inside my head.'

'You look like shit. I'm genuinely concerned that you've got a drug problem.'

'I'm meant to be a doctor – worrying, isn't it?'

'I only let you have the room because I thought you'd be responsible.'

Alex rubbed his face. 'I am most of the time.'

'But it's happening daily. I've noticed the smell of weed in the mornings and evenings. Does Amelia know?'

He shook his head. 'No…'

'You're going to lose her if you don't sort yourself out and stop this path of self-destruction.'

'I'm not like this when I'm with her.'

John stood in front of him with folded arms. 'I bet. She wouldn't approve, and then she'll be gone.'

'I know.'

'Don't mess it up. I'll help you if you want.'

Alex pushed himself to his feet and embraced John. 'Thank you.'

'Let's sit you back down. I'll get you a tea and run you a bath with some bubbles.'

Alex's hand shook as John helped steady the cup of tea to his lips. John started to help Alex get undressed and then prepared a bath.

'You know my sexuality,' John said as Alex walked naked into the bathroom. 'And yet you have all your bits on full display.'

'It's okay; we both have the same plumbing, and you know my sexuality.'

John passed Alex the soap. 'Mmm...' John left the bathroom as Alex flicked some bath water at him.

8.00 a.m.

Robert was lost in thought as he had breakfast with Sophie in the hotel café.

'Wake up. You're doing that dull thing again,' said Sophie sitting opposite him.

'I've got a lot on my mind – sorry.'

Evelyn's car pulled in outside the hotel where Robert was staying. Her driver, Havers, stepped out, walked around, and opened the rear car door, stretching out his gloved hand as Evelyn took hold of it. The hotel doorman held open the entrance door and gave Evelyn a polite nod as she walked through, past the reception, and into the café.

Robert looked up as Sophie coughed, almost choking, and caught the look of shock on her face looking over his shoulder. He twisted around. 'Mother, what on earth are you doing here?'

Evelyn's eyes suddenly focused like a praying mantis at Sophie. 'If you would excuse us, I have some important business to discuss with my son.'

Sophie looked at Robert. He frowned and exhaled. His gaze gestured towards the exit. Sophie got up, threw her napkin down with disgust on the table, and walked away.

Evelyn took Sophie's place. 'A nice warm seat. Just what I need on a cold day like today.'

'How did you know…'

'That you were staying at this hotel. As a Lady Justice, I occasionally just call in a favour here and there – you must know I have my contacts.'

'You're a retired Justice!'

'We never truly retire; it's in the blood.'

He noticed a large silver brooch on her jacket of a rhinoceros beetle with a purple gemstone eye.

'Anyhow,' she said, relaxing back. 'I'll get to the point.'

'Please do.'

'I've given Annabelle the full use of Villa Francina for as long as she wants.'

'Let me get this straight. So, you've cut me out of your will, you've threatened to disclose some dubious information about me, and now Bella's got free use of the family villa.'

'You ceased to be a member of the family in my eyes when you had a marital affair.'

'Is she there now?' Evelyn nodded in reply. 'How long has she been there?'

'Almost two weeks.'

'So, I've been staying here when I could've been back living in my own home.'

'And you thought it would be appropriate to take your plaything,' said Evelyn, pointing over her shoulder, 'back to her home? Now listen to me. Freya and Alex don't want anything to do with you because of your betrayal. Is that what you really want?'

'Of course not, but they'll...'

'Furthermore, Annabelle has been a loyal wife to you. She's been by your side for the last thirty-plus years. You may say that she's changed, blah, blah, blah...'

'But...'

Evelyn held up a finger. 'I haven't finished. We all change, but we talk to each other, try to work things out, and make compromises.'

'But she hasn't been interested in sex for a long time.'

Evelyn sighed. 'Neither would I have been interested in making love with your father if he'd kept talking about business and how much money he'd made – I can't think of a worse turn-off.'

'Mother! There's more to it than that.'

'Think of all the hard work she's put into the family. The love and commitment she's given you over the years. I'm sure she still loves you.' He found his attention drawn to her brooch as he listened, only now just seeing the letter *E* in the shape of the insect. 'You've had your fun with what's-her-name back there.'

'Sophie.'

'Pay her off with a year's salary and a little sports car, but make sure your plaything signs a non-disclosure agreement.'

'What do you mean? Just like a business deal?'

'Exactly, because it won't last with her. She'll take your money and be gone. I've seen her sort so many times before in court – she's a gold digger. She knows how to win your heart by satisfying you in bed.'

Robert's eyes narrowed. 'I wish you wouldn't speak like that.'

Evelyn raised a questioning eyebrow. 'Why? That's what she is, and we both know it.'

Robert glanced around the café.

Evelyn's shoulders relaxed, and she smiled. 'Charm Annabelle back. You two belong together. She's attractive, she's sophisticated, and she's elegant. Go and see her...'

'Let us just say that I'll try what you've suggested. Do you really think she'll take me back?'

Evelyn checked her watch and picked up her handbag. 'You need to try. I'll speak to Annabelle, and then I'll call you.'

'I won't give up Sophie just yet, because Bella's heart may have hardened towards me.'

Evelyn frustratingly rubbed her forehead with her fingers. 'Take a leap of faith, Robert, lose your plaything. I'll even buy her a new car myself.' Evelyn took her phone out of her handbag.

'Mother, as I've said before, you don't have to talk to me like I'm still your little boy. I'm sixty.'

Evelyn dialled her driver. 'You'll always be my boy; that's the way it is between a mother and her son. Oh, hello, Havers. I'll be out the front in two minutes.' She turned her gaze back to Robert. 'Besides, all men are boys – they never really grow up.'

10.30 a.m.

Alex scurried down the ramp from the boathouse. 'Sorry I'm late,' he said as he quickly slipped off his Wellingtons and threw them to the side. Dullard held the quad boat steady in the current as Alex got seated in the stern and pulled on his trainers.

'You look like crap,' said Hamish. 'And you've been holding us all up.

'You're late for everything recently,' said Spud.

'We're meant to be a team,' said Sanjay. 'All for one and one for all – remember?'

'Like I said, sorry.' He hastily set his rigging. Sanjay, Hamish, and Spud waited with oars ready to pull away. 'I'm ready.'

Dullard pushed them off, startling some ducks. They warmed up, finding their rhythm as they sculled towards the straight part of the river. They passed the start marker. Hamish called out pace until they finished at the two-kilometre point and rested by the reeds at the embankment.

'That was hard,' said Alex, slumped forward, breathing heavily and sweating after the others had caught their breath.

'You really look and sound out of condition,' said Sanjay. 'Even if we had won the M-Four Challenge semi-final, we'd never have stood a chance of winning the final with you being so unfit.'

'I bet this new woman is sapping all of his energy,' said Spud.

Sanjay nodded. 'We only used to have this problem with Hamish. It's now like role reversal.'

Alex's friends made jokes at his expense. Alex ignored them, his thoughts drifting between Amelia and Evie. Breathing in the cool air, he watched the clouds drift overhead and the branches of the nearby trees sway in the breeze. That's when he suddenly noticed a silver turquoise flash of colour dart from a willow tree into the water. He watched as it surfaced and flew back into the trees. He smiled; the moment lifted his soul.

'Kingfisher!' shouted Spud, pointing.

'Alex,' said Hamish. He turned around. 'I'm going to your landlord's bar tonight. Do you want to come with Amelia?'

8.05 p.m.

Amelia was keeping a check on the time as she spoke to Daphne on her phone. 'Daddy has lost how much weight?'

'Another twelve pounds since you last saw him.'

'But, we know he's a fighter.'

'We're praying the chemo works.'

'It's no wonder he has no appetite and feels sick with those toxic chemicals in him. I'll get a flight back home.'

'No, don't,' Daphne said with a firm tone. 'Dad wouldn't want that.'

She hesitated. 'Alright... if you're sure.'

'In the meantime, how're things going with you and Jake?'

'We've spoken, and I've said I would meet up with him next time I'm back.'

'And what about Alex?'

'It's still early days with him. Look, Sis. I've really gotta shoot; I'm already late.' She ended the call and bolted through her college to where Alex was waiting outside.

They walked to John's wine bar and found Hamish and Lucy already seated at a table with drinks. John brought over two glasses of red wine as they got comfortable.

'Why the serious face?' Hamish asked.

Alex gritted his teeth. 'The World Health Organisation is about to announce a Coronavirus pandemic alert. We know the importance of wearing masks around infected people. Look around – do you see anyone wearing one?'

'Relax.'

'We should be wearing them; they are in Italy.'

'But the government advice is clear – the wearing of masks by healthy people isn't recommended.'

'Can we change the conversation?' Lucy asked.

'Sure. Explain to them how Avani was asking about Spud last weekend,' said Hamish, nudging Lucy. 'Apparently, she likes a man with a ginger beard.'

'What! Are you suggesting setting them up on a date?' Amelia asked.

'Why not?' laughed Hamish. 'Most unlikely pair. She's intelligent and attractive, and Spud is well… Spud.'

Alex chuckled. 'He's reliable and good fun.'

The four of them chatted and finished their drinks before they went to a steak restaurant. The drink flowed as they ate. Hamish got louder as he told stories from the A&E department. Obscenities started to flow as he drank.

They had finished their meals and it was late. Alex felt awkward from the bad language and got up from his seat.

'Tonight is on me,' he said, returning to the table. 'I've paid the bill.'

They said their goodbyes and left. Amelia held onto Alex's arm as they weaved unsteadily through the Cambridge streets back to her college. He didn't notice Rose sitting quietly with Gertie at a shop entrance as he passed, but she noticed him.

'Would you like to come back to mine for a cuppa?' Alex asked.

Amelia stumbled in her high-heel shoes and fell on one knee. 'Hm, not sure.' She giggled. 'It's very late, and I'm wrecked.'

'Just for a drink, and then I'll see you home.'

'Okay, but just one.' They weaved back through the streets to his flat. 'Look,' Amelia said, pointing to the bottom of the door. 'That's my painting of good old Bessie.'

He held Amelia's hand as he guided her unsteadily up the stairs. She dragged off her shoes when they entered his flat, and he looked in on John's room. 'John's not back yet.'

Amelia went to the kitchen, put on the kettle, and placed a couple of tea bags in the teapot. 'Is there any chocolate in this place?' She opened a cupboard and immediately spotted a bottle of gin and a bottle of whisky. 'Let's have a wee dram instead.'

'I'll get the glasses and ice.' He concentrated on holding the bottle steady as he poured out two nips of whisky.

She linked her arm through his, and they simultaneously knocked back their drinks. 'Another?' She wiped her mouth with the back of her hand.

He coughed and nodded. 'I'll put on some music.' He went to his room and played some Motown on his phone. The soul music drifted through the flat.

Amelia had poured out another two nips and was sitting comfortably in the lounge when Alex returned. 'Ah... my mom sometimes listens to this stuff when she's not listening to Country.'

'I really love seventies' and eighties' Motown.' He walked into his room. 'Come and see my vinyl collection.'

She giggled. 'Not that old chestnut.' She got up with her glass of Scotch and walked into his room.

Wobbling, he lifted down a box from his wardrobe and opened it on the floor. She sat on his bed, watching as he showed off some of his favourite albums. He sat close to her with a worn cardboard cover of a Lionel Richie album.

'That's one of my mom's favourites,' she said, pointing to a track.

He found the song on his phone and played it. She leaned back on her elbow, listening. 'It does touch the soul.' She giggled.

He leaned back, matching her posture. 'I don't want to sound cheesy, but you must realise that you've captured my soul.'

She stopped giggling and stroked his hair. 'I think we could be good soul buddies for each other.'

He leaned over and kissed her. She let herself fall back onto the bed. She let him slide off her jumper and undo her blouse. Her bra was off a few minutes later, and she started to become aroused as he stroked her skin. She pulled off his jumper.

'The door and the lights,' she said softly.

He closed the bedroom door, switched off the lights, and whipped off his shirt. Their naked torsos embraced in passion. He tried to undo her jeans, but she pushed him away. His masculine aftershave aroused a craving within her. She gave in a while later, and he pulled them off. He slipped off his jeans and glided back onto the bed. They rolled around, kissing and touching intimately. She stretched out her neck to his loving kisses and sighed as his fingers slipped inside her panties. He slid them off with no resistance and then slipped off his own briefs. He moved around on top of her until both his legs found their way between hers. She gripped his hips and held him back as they tenderly kissed.

'I love you,' he whispered. She loosened her grip, and he merged into her.

Panting for breath, she soaked up the blissful sensation as he gently made love to her, almost to the rhythm of the music. She suddenly felt unsure as he started to climax. 'You've got one on – haven't you?'

'What... Ahh...'

'Hell, no!' She pushed him off to one side. 'What were you thinking?'

Chapter 28

Sunday, 8th March 2020. 6.45 a.m.

Alex's eyes slowly fluttered open. He immediately rolled his head around and met Amelia's smile. She lay on her side gazing back at him.

He rubbed his eyes. 'How long have you been awake?'

'Only a while.' She reached over and stroked his hair. 'I got up and made myself a tea.'

He propped himself up on his elbow. 'You should have woken me.'

'You looked so peaceful – I've just been watching you.'

He took hold of her hand and kissed it. 'My head is a bit tender.'

'Mine too.' She smiled. 'What happened last night? We were just meant to be soul buddies – good friends.'

'It would've been perfect if I'd…'

'Been wearing some protection?'

'Sorry – I'm out of practise using those things.'

'We both got swept away in the moment. It shouldn't have happened so soon.'

He grinned. 'I'll make sure that I'm using a condom next time.'

She immediately sat up, whipped her pillow out from behind her, and whacked him over his head. 'Don't push your luck. We both had too much to drink, and my guard was down.'

Alex shoved her pillow under his head. 'You pushed me off just at the moment.' He remembered lying beside her afterwards, but nothing else.

'If it had been our wedding night, it would've been perfect.'

'Perhaps we did get a little swept away, but I have no regrets, and I remember what I said to you. I love you.'

Amelia got out of bed wearing one of Alex's shirts as a nightgown. 'Tea?' He nodded. She walked quietly across the lounge into the kitchen. 'Ah... John...' She blushed. 'Good morning.'

'Tea,' he said as he passed her a jar of teabags.

'You heard us?'

'The walls in this flat are paper-thin.'

She went even redder as she started to make the teas.

'I'm only teasing. You can't hear anything in this solid brick building.' John grinned. 'He's got a great body, hasn't he? I'm almost a little envious.'

'He's really cute.' She smiled as she stirred the tea. 'I like him big time.'

'I didn't know about Alex's fiancé until recently. But I just wanted to say. I think you two are perfect for each other.'

She leaned forward, kissed John on the cheek, then carried the teas back into Alex's room, gently pushing the door closed behind her with her foot. 'Shall we go out somewhere today?'

Alex took the mug of tea from her. 'I've got an idea. How about I teach you how to do sculling.'

She wrapped her arms around herself. 'Am I likely to fall in the water?'

'Not if you follow my advice.'

'But will it be fun?'

'Absolutely.'

'You're on!' She released a broad smile.

They finished their teas, and she removed her chain with her grandma's ring. 'Now we have become more than friends,' she said as she turned to him. 'I would like you to wear this. It's very special to me, as you know.' She fastened it around his neck. 'A part of me close to your heart.'

Alex cooked breakfast as Amelia got showered and changed.

'Over three thousand deaths now in China,' said John, listening to some information on a radio news channel. 'And there was a second death in this country.'

Alex cracked another egg into the frying pan. 'This, I fear, is just the start.' His phone pinged, and he read the text message from Sanjay.

Would u and amelia like to come around for dinner tonight at 7:30? H and lucy r coming.

Amelia walked into the kitchen. 'This looks like good teamwork, you two.'

'Your turn to be chef, my turn to shower,' said Alex taking off his pinny and putting it over her head. 'Before I go, we've had an invitation to dinner tonight with Sanjay and Zahida. Lucy and Hamish will also be there. Are you free?'

'Sure.'

After he had got dressed, Alex took a seat at a small dining table that John had laid up with napkins and a little posy of flowers that he had brought back from his wine bar. 'I'm looking forward to this greasy spoon-type breakfast,' he said as he phoned Sanjay.

Amelia appeared and sat down next to him. John walked in from the kitchen and passed her two plates as Alex continued in conversation with Sanjay. She placed a plate down in front of Alex. He looked down to see a smiley face; two fried eggs side-by-side like eyes on toast with American yellow mustard curved round to make a smiley. He grinned. Amelia stretched out the back of her hand with a small heart drawn in tomato sauce. She leaned over with the squeezy sauce bottle in her other hand and made a letter U next to it. Alex turned to meet her smiling gaze as she folded some loose strands of hair behind her ear.

John sat down and grabbed his glass of orange juice. 'To lasting friendships!' They raised their glasses.

'So, I'll cycle over to Freya's later,' Alex said. 'I'll collect my car and pick you up from college.'

Amelia half-finished her breakfast, got up, and started to put on her coat. 'That sounds awesome. I need to shoot.'

He walked her down to the street entrance door, kissed her goodbye, and went back into the lounge where John was packing a box. 'What're you doing?'

'I started having a bit of a clear-out yesterday.'

'Mm. Don't you want this small picture frame?'

'No, if you want it, take it.'

He went to his room, powered up his laptop, plugged in his phone, printed off his favourite image from the punting trip with Amelia, and mounted it into the frame. He placed the picture on the mantelshelf above the Victorian fireplace in the lounge.

7.20 a.m.

Robert pushed his food around with his fork as Sophie tucked into her breakfast.

'What's troubling you?' she asked.

Robert looked up. 'I'm moving back to Richmond today. Bella is living at the villa in Mallorca.'

'That sounds like great news.'

Robert reached into his jacket pocket, pulled out an envelope, and placed it down on the table in front of her.

'What's this?'

'Can you please just open it.'

She cautiously opened the letter and read it. 'What, you're paying me off. Now I know why you didn't want to have sex last night. You've just used me!'

Robert flinched. 'Keep your voice down, please. I haven't used you – the compensation offer is very generous.'

She glared with anger. 'So that's it?'

'I've given you a very good reference and suggested some organisations which can place you in a good job.'

'I thought you loved me.'

He frowned. 'I will put a personal word in for you. You'll have a year's salary, and you have a separate budget for a new car to the value stated.'

'But I have to sign this non-disclosure document.'

'Of course.'

She reached under the table and began stroking the inside of his thigh. 'Remember the times we've made love in your office.'

He pushed her hand away. 'I'm sorry, but my feelings have changed.'

She promptly got up, grabbed her glass of juice from the table, and went to throw it into his face but froze when he pulled back in shock. She calmly placed the glass back down in front of him. 'I'll accept your compensation offer. If you go back on it, I'll make life very difficult for you.' Their gazes locked. 'I'll wait to hear from your solicitor.' She pushed over her glass towards him, and the juice ran off the table into his lap.

She took a composed breath. 'I'll just get my things.'

3.00 p.m.

Amelia emerged from the changing rooms at the Great Ouse Rowing and Sculling Club wearing a wet suit and Wellingtons. 'You didn't say anything about wearing a wet suit when I agreed to this.'

'It's standard practice for the first time – that's all.' Alex and a club member got a double scull from a rack, carried it down the ramp, and placed it into the shallow water. 'We're just going to take one set of oars,' he said, getting her seated in the stern. He got seated behind her in the bow of the boat.

She gently rowed the boat into the middle of the river. 'Was that the correct technique?'

'That's good so far.'

She felt safe with him as she looked over to a small group of members standing on the ramp. 'Why are all those folks looking over here and sniggering?'

'Just ignore them.' He used his hands to turn her head to face the stern. 'Concentrate. I need to ask you some questions before we set off. Can you swim underwater?'

'Sure, but shouldn't you have asked me that before we got into the boat?'

'Just club protocol. However, there are a couple of rules which you must remember. So, repeat back to me, please. One, get free of the boat, and two, get out of danger.'

She repeated the rules. 'I've got that. What now?'

He pulled the two oars out of the water and rested them parallel on the boat hull. 'We're now going to practise capsizing.'

'Heck – what!' she shouted. The crowd on the water's edge started laughing.

Alex held the rigging and leaned over to one side, forcing the boat to roll around in the water.

'Don't you dare…' she screamed, gulping air just before she went under. Alex checked underwater that she'd freed her feet, and then they both surfaced. She was gasping for air and shaking as she clung to the upside-down boat. The crowd on the ramp was clapping and cheering.

Alex held onto her tightly. 'You're hyperventilating. Breathe easy; it's okay. It's just the cold that's hit you.'

Her breathing started to settle. 'Boy, you're evil,' she spluttered.

He laughed. 'Sorry, you have to practise capsizing before you can go out in a boat. Club rules. I was afraid if I mentioned it, you wouldn't have come.'

'Damn right, I wouldn't. I thought this was going to be a fun day.'

Alex laughed. 'It is, but stay calm, please. You've just been officially inducted into sculling safety.'

'You said, if I followed your guidance, that I wouldn't be falling in.'

He grimaced. 'Technically, you rolled in.'

She took in a deep breath and became focused. 'I'm calm now. What next?'

'Good, that's more like it. We're going to do stages two and three – where we upright the boat because it becomes our life raft. We need to get out of the water and then get it back to the ramp.'

She heeded Alex's instructions, positioning the oars at an angle, turning the boat over, and following the technique of getting back aboard before making their way to the water's edge. The crowd applauded as she stood up with the water at waist level. She narrowed her eyes at him. 'You're so bad.'

A couple of club members congratulated her on a good boat recovery as she stepped out of the water.

Alex grinned. 'The small crowd enjoyed watching your initiation, but there was another reason why I wanted to capsize us together.'

'Go on.'

'Using your Christian theme, we've now been baptised – cleansing us both from our past relationships. So, what do you say to no more emotional baggage from ex-fiancés?'

She smiled. 'A fresh start for both of us.'

4.30 p.m.

Amelia's hand stroked the back of Alex's neck as he drove back to Cambridge. 'That wasn't so bad in the end,' she said.

'So, all forgiven then?' he asked, feeling relaxed.

She tilted her head around. 'Well, it'll take some more sucking up to me for the next few weeks, a few more dinners out, and a huge promise that you'll never do anything like that to me again.'

'I promise, I really do.'

She leaned over and kissed him on the cheek. His phone pinged, and he awkwardly pulled it from inside his coat and passed it to her. She held it as he unlocked it. 'It's a text from Freya,' she said. 'You have two missed calls from her as well.'

'I'll call her back when we stop.'

He parked his car in the multi-storey nearest to his home in the city centre and walked with Amelia back to her college.

'Alex, I'm only a few minutes from college,' she said as they waited at a pedestrian crossing. 'I can walk the rest of the way by myself, and I'll see you later when I've changed.' They kissed and parted.

Amelia had just walked past the porter's lodge at the college entrance a short time later when she felt Alex's phone vibrate in her coat pocket.

'Damn it,' she said, pulling out his phone and answering. 'Hi Freya, this is Alex's friend, Amelia. So sorry, but he's not here. He accidentally left his phone with me.'

'Oh, Amelia. Errr… When are you seeing him again?'

'Tonight, at seven. He's picking me up. Is there something wrong?'

'Please just tell him to call me immediately when you give him his phone.'

'Sure, of course.'

'Please don't forget, it's important. It's good to speak to you.'

She stared at the phone for a moment, turned, and hurried to the porter, leaving her backpack before she walked to Alex's home.

Alex smiled to himself, feeling pleased with how the day had gone as he walked through the streets back to his home. He sprung up the stairs to his flat, unlocked the front door, and froze. The colour drained from his face.

'Hello, Alex,' said Evie, putting down her cup of tea as she sat opposite John. 'I hope it's not a shock seeing me?'

Alex shook his head, walked in slowly and sat down near her.

'I came across this.' She rested her hand on one of Alex's books. 'I thought that I should return it to you.'

Alex listened, but didn't engage in conversation. He got up from his seat as soon as he noticed that she had finished her tea. 'Thank you for dropping off my book. Let me show you out. We can talk more outside.' He followed her down the stairs, onto the street, and stopped with his back to the door.

She turned around to face him. 'It would be really nice to meet up again sometime as friends.'

'Mm, okay… Friends.' He offered out his hand.

She calmly took it and moved in closer. 'A farewell hug?' They embraced.

Amelia walked past shoppers along Green Street towards Alex's home, stopping dead in her tracks when she noticed Alex in an embrace. Evie caught sight of her, gripped Alex's head between her hands, and planted a firm kiss on his lips.

Amelia walked a few metres up to him and held out his phone.

Only now spotting her, he tore himself away from Evie. 'This isn't what you think,' he said as she passed him his phone. 'Evie, explain to Amelia that you're just saying goodbye!'

Evie gave a lopsided gaze with feigned innocence.

He sensed the betrayal in Amelia's eyes as she backed away. 'There's nothing going on here, I swear!' She turned and ran back the way she came. He followed her but gave up, turned around, and marched up to Evie. 'You shouldn't have made out that we're still an item!'

Evie suddenly screamed at him like a cornered cat defending herself and lashed out with her hands. Her nails whipped his face, breaking the skin on his cheek. 'You've had it all your own way – you and that American bitch!' He put up his hands to defend himself as he backed away. People passing gave them space while others stopped to look. 'I noticed that picture on the fireplace of you and her,' she screamed.

Shocked and dazed, he grabbed her wrists. 'Calm down!' He gently slapped her on the cheek. She stilled. Her lips quivered, and her eyes welled up.

Her gaze fell on him like a hawk. 'Why should I?' She swung her fist hard around into his gut. Winded, he dropped to the ground clutching his stomach, and rolled over, coughing and wincing into a fetal position. She gave him a solid kick in his backside. 'And that's for dumping me at the church!' She stomped away in the opposite direction to Amelia.

7.50 p.m.

Alex steadied himself inside Sanjay's home porch and rang the bell.

Sanjay opened the door. 'I'll excuse you for being late if you've brought… What the hell have you done to your face?' Alex staggered past him into the lounge. Hamish, Lucy, and Zahida stared at him in shock. 'Is Amelia not coming? And is that dope I can smell?'

Chapter 29

Monday, 9th March 2020, 6.06 a.m.

Alex was asleep and dreaming of the capsize practise the previous day when Amelia started to hyperventilate, but she suddenly started attacking him and shouting…

'Wake up, Alex,' said Freya shaking him by the shoulder. 'Wake up; you've overslept.'

His eyes blinked open. 'Ah, heck! What's the time?'

'Just gone six.'

He rubbed his eyes. 'Damn. I'm going to be late again.'

Freya sighed. 'I kept reminding you last night to set the alarm.'

'I thought I had.' He sat up and checked his phone.

'No messages, then, I take it?' Freya asked. He shook his head. 'Sorry to state the obvious, but she must be feeling really hurt. You could send her some flowers later with a message.'

'I like that idea.'

'We are talking about Amelia and not Evie?' she asked.

'Of course.'

'Just checking.' She gave him a reassuring rub on his shoulder.

Alex passed Freya a bowl from beside his bed. 'At least I didn't need this.'

She took it from him. 'No, thank goodness. But you need to phone Hamish and thank him for bringing you here.' Freya sat down next to him. 'We've never seen you like that before – you were stoned out of your head. How you ever managed to drive your car to Sanjay and Zahida's home and not have an accident – well, it's a miracle.'

'To be honest, I've only got a vague memory of eating some food and then Sanjay shouting at me when I vomited everywhere.'

'All your clothes are in the wash, by the way, and your shoes are outside the back door.'

'I remember Hamish and Lucy helping me out of the house.'

'Never mind all that now,' said Freya. 'You need to get yourself in the shower. Are you going to be alright cycling into work?'

7.10 a.m.

Alex secured his bike in his usual spot at the hospital. He went to his locker, put on his work scrubs, shoved his stethoscope in his side pocket, and went to the reception desk.

Alice cocked an eyebrow at him. 'Late again; Sandra won't be impressed! You really don't look well.'

'Where should I be?'

'You're down to be working with Doctor Patel in treatment areas C and D.'

'I guess I deserve this.'

'I wouldn't be surprised if Sandra did it on purpose.'

'I think you're right.' He left for the treatment areas and found Doctor Patel examining a patient.

Doctor Patel turned around and lowered his glasses. 'My goodness... If I didn't know better, I would think you were suffering from the coronavirus.'

'It was a late night. Can you just brief me on where you want me working?'

'Speak to the staff nurse back there.' Doctor Patel nodded in her direction. 'She'll get you sorted with our priority patients.'

Alex became focused as he started examining a young three-year-old girl with boiling water burns down her arm. He pulled his finger puppet from his scrubs' pocket as a distraction in one hand, entertaining her with funny voices and actions whilst examining the child with his other hand. The little girl and her mother both laughed. 'The paramedics have done a really good job,' he reassured the child's mother, and then he switched back to the character of the puppet.

Sandra arrived as he was explaining the after-treatment to the child's mother. 'Excuse me. When you have a moment, please, Doctor, in my office.'

A short while later, Alex appeared at Sandra's office and tapped on the window by the open door.

'Hello, Alex. Come in and take a seat.' She sat back, her penetrating gaze bored into him. 'It wasn't so long ago when you were last sitting in that same chair, and your fiancé was in Emergency.'

'I remember.'

'We gave you some time out, but clearly, there are concerns, and they need to be addressed because they're impacting on your work.'

'How so?'

'You're constantly late, and I have it under very good authority from some members of staff that, at times, you've been found to be under the influence of drugs and alcohol.'

'That's just gossip!'

'Everyone is worried about you.' Sandra's voice softened. 'If you could just see how you look. You're visibly not well enough to be working, and you could possibly be alarming the patients. In fact, you're potentially a danger to them and to yourself.'

'I'm fine…'

'Doctor Hardson, Alex. I'm actually trying to help you, and I've made a decision. I want you to go home and properly rest.'

'Please don't do this.'

'I'll have a letter sent out today. It will explain that you've been temporarily suspended pending a full medical assessment before you can return as a medical practitioner.'

'I don't believe it!'

'I'm very concerned for you. I'm doing this before it becomes really serious. There's a protocol procedure.'

'This action isn't helping.'

'I'll be the judge of that. Otherwise, the next step is probably being investigated by the General Medical Council, which could lead to a full-suspension order being placed on you, and your doctor's registration revoked. Is that what you want?'

He shook his head as he slumped forward.

She leaned on her desk. 'I hope your conditional suspension is only temporary because, up until your return from holiday, you had a lot of potential. So, make sure you attend the evaluation and get some counselling.' Alex became emotional, wiping his finger under his eyes. She got out of her seat. 'You're no good to us like this. Please sort yourself out… Get some rest, and I hope to see you return in the near future – back to the diligent, focused Doctor Hardson that I used to know.'

He went to the staff area, changed, and collected his backpack from his locker. He cycled out of the hospital grounds along the cycle path towards the city centre and stopped after a short while by a bench. Opening his backpack, he took out his hip flask and emptied the gin into his water bottle. He sat back, drinking, and pulled out his weed pouch from his bag. Looking around to make sure he was alone, he rolled a joint, lit it, and took a long drag.

7.45 a.m.

Robert sat in a taxi just along from Freya's home. He could see her small car parked on the drive and had tried calling her mobile and the home number, leaving a message each time. He asked the taxi driver to wait and then went to her front door with a bunch of flowers and rang the bell.

Freya opened the door and was taken back on seeing him and immediately tried slamming her door shut, but he instinctively grabbed the door frame.

'Arhhh... That really hurts. Can you at least take the pressure off my hand and open the door?'

'Go away. I don't want to speak to you.'

Robert groaned in pain. 'May I just come in for a short while, please?'

'You've got nothing to say that I want to hear.'

'I helped you out with this place after your divorce... Please, Freya, we need to talk.'

She fully opened the door and stood to one side as her father stepped through, clutching his hand.

Charlotte ran up. 'Granddad!' Robert knelt and embraced her. He picked her up, went into the lounge, and sat down with Charlotte on his lap.

Freya's face was full of disdain as she walked towards him. 'These are for you,' he said, holding out the bunch of flowers. She kept her arms folded. 'I'll just leave them down here on the floor.'

'I'll get you some ice for your hand while you have a few minutes with Charlotte. But then you have to go.'

'A cup of tea?'

Freya went to the kitchen, and he started reading a story to Charlotte. Freya returned a short time later with an ice pack and a tray with two teas. 'Charlotte, sweetie, can you go play in your bedroom, just for a bit while Granddad and Mummy have a little chat?' she said, placing down the tray. Charlotte disappeared upstairs. 'I don't want you coming around here, just turning up like this.'

'You're my daughter, for goodness sake. You won't take my calls, so you left me with no other choice. You know I will always love you.'

'What, in the same way you always loved Mum? Being unfaithful to her.'

He grimaced. 'I feel ashamed of what I've done. Look, all I want to do is make amends – that's why I'm here.'

She scowled at her father. 'You've tried to live a double life. Now you're sorted with your floozy, as Mum calls her. You can get on with your life, and Mum can get on with hers.'

'I've come to realise that I do love your mother, but we'd drifted apart. I know I've done a bad thing, but is there any way you think she'll forgive me and take me back?'

'What about your floozy?'

'Sophie was a mistake. It's over.'

'Oh right, just a mistake. We're all expected to just forgive you?' Freya glanced away. 'How are we to know this mistake won't be repeated? You've broken our trust in you.'

'But I'm hoping after all our years together, she'll find it in her heart to give me a second chance? I swear it won't happen again.'

'It's not me who you have to swear to. It's Mum.'

He clutched the icepack against his hand. 'I need your support and help.'

'Let's just say I won't be an obstacle between you and Mum getting back together if that's what she also wants.'

'I'll be a loyal husband if your mother has me back… and a reliable father from this day forward. I want to do the right thing by you all.'

Freya looked deeply into her father's eyes. 'Like I said, I won't be an obstacle, but don't hurt Mum ever again.'

8.00 a.m.

Amelia was sitting at her desk in her room, trying to work on her laptop, when her phone rang next to her. 'Hi Daphne, I know it's early there, but thanks for calling me back.'

'What's wrong? You sound down in the dumps.'

'I just want to know how Dad is?'

'He's having the chemo-treatment; what more can I say.'

'I feel so useless here. I should be doing more to help.' She wiped a tear from her eye.

'There's nothing you can do, but I'll keep you informed if there's any change.'

'Well, that's just it.' She drew a breath. 'I've not long received an email from the University Vice-Chancellor explaining that the university is closing due to the coronavirus situation. He's advising all students to leave Cambridge as soon as possible. I've managed to book a flight to Milwaukee, just one way this time, and I've already packed.'

'That's sudden. But if you're really sure. But what about Alex?'

'I'll explain more when I see you.'

'I'll pick you up from the airport. Just text me your flight details.'

Amelia checked her messages: three texts and four voice messages from Alex. She blocked his number on her phone. There was a text from Jake. She texted back. *I'm on my way back home. We can meet up soon. A X.*

8.20 a.m.

Robert was sitting in the back of the taxi on his way back to Cambridge railway station when he called Evelyn. 'Hello, Mother. I just wanted to let you know that I met Freya. Let's just say it went better than I deserved. I enjoyed seeing little Charlotte and reading a Peter Rabbit story to her. I'll be honest with you; it made me realise how much I've missed spending quality time with her.'

'Good, but when are you going to speak to Alex?'

'I phoned, but it went straight to voice message.'

'Alright, Robert, but you should probably get yourself out to Mallorca sooner rather than later. There is talk about stopping flights to try and control this awful virus. You've probably heard on the news that the infections in Spain are dramatically increasing. So be hasty making plans.'

'I know. Leave it to me.'

8.25 a.m.

Alex sat on a bench just half a mile from the hospital, smoking cannabis and drinking alcohol. He tried to focus on his surroundings, but everything was blurred. His phone calls to Amelia had gone to voicemail. He texted her. *Please can we meet and talk? Alex XXX.*

He shoved his tin, bottle, and hip flask into his backpack, pulled up his scarf, got back on his bicycle, and cycled off unsteadily along the cycle path. He could just make out the traffic lights ahead through his blurry vision. Not waiting for green, he traversed into the road and became confused when a car came directly towards him. He didn't feel his bicycle being wrenched away from under him or his shoulder thumping the windscreen before his whole body hit the ground with a thud. He lay motionless. A car on the other side of the road screeched to a halt, stopping just in front of him. Opening one eye, he saw a blurred face, and then it went dark.

He became semi-conscious as he was put into the back of an ambulance. The paramedic leaned over him. 'Hello, Doctor. I recognise you. You've had an accident.'

'I feel numb and sore.'

'I'm not surprised. I can see in your eyes that you have a concussion, and you're intoxicated. It's a good job you were wearing your cycle helmet.'

He grunted. 'My arm and hand are sore.'

'You've taken a heavy blow to your shoulder, and you've a broken finger. It was bent right back, but I've reset it. I'm just going to strap it up to your ring finger.'

A short while later, the ambulance pulled into A&E. 'Shit. This isn't going to go well,' he mumbled.

'We've brought your bike back with us,' said the paramedic as he pushed Alex's bed into A&E. 'It's a bit twisted. I'll leave it by the staff bike rack.'

A triage nurse and an emergency nurse immediately recognised Alex as the paramedic briefed them in A&E. Sandra, the manager, arrived as Alex waited. She gave him a disappointed glare and then read the paramedic's notes. Alex turned his head away. He knew she would read that he was intoxicated.

9.10 a.m. Mallorca.

Annabelle was busy doing some cleaning at Villa Francina, music playing in the background. She heard the side drive gates open and went to the window. Emilio drove in and parked his van. He stepped out in his shorts and tee shirt and waved as he caught sight of her at the window. She walked out under the porch as he walked up the path and went to kiss her on the lips as they met, but she kissed him on his cheek instead.

He gazed into her eyes with a puzzled look as he held her. 'What's with the polite kissing?'

Smiling awkwardly, she pulled away from him. 'We need to be discreet – understand?'

'You're a married woman. *Si*, I understand.' He mimicked having a drink. 'I'll get my tools and make a start on garden.' He walked back to his van, fetched his gardening tools, and started digging up the area he had marked out with wooden stakes and string two days earlier.

Annabelle returned with two drinks. 'I've also brought the plans and a sketchpad.' She passed him an iced lemon drink. He stood next to her as they discussed the planting scheme. She was suddenly aware of his muscular arm going around her waist; he embraced her and started kissing the side of her face. His affectionate touch made her desire him; she let her pad fall to the ground and closed her eyes as she soaked up his tender kissing. Her hat fell back onto the grass, and she kissed him back. Passion rose up unhindered within her, and she pulled him in. His hand slipped inside her blouse, but she suddenly heard a car pull into the drive. It parked next to Emilio's van. She quickly pulled herself free and, breathing anxiously, readjusted her clothing. Emilio picked up her hat and pad, casually passing them to her. She slowly walked down to the drive and greeted Teresa.

Chapter 30

Tuesday, 10th March 2020, 6.50 a.m.

Robert was in a taxi on his way to Heathrow Airport when his phone rang. 'Hello, Mother.'

'Have you heard the news?'

'If you mean the announcement that all flights to Italy have been cancelled – yes. But my flight to Mallorca is still scheduled to leave.'

'But you might struggle to get a flight back if you stay too long.'

'I know…'

'And the new government guidelines here state that you will have to self-isolate on your return.'

'Mother, if I didn't know better, I would say that you're actually concerned for my welfare.'

'I'm concerned for the well-being of all my family,' said Evelyn. 'That's why I was conscious of the long-term effect of your selfish actions. Please don't mess it up with Annabelle.'

He looked out of his cab window. 'I can only be myself.'

'That's what I fear. Have you informed her that you're on your way?'

'I don't think that's a good idea. I'll speak to you later when I get into Palma.'

12.30 p.m.

Alex was sitting back in an armchair at his flat with his bandaged left hand elevated on a cushion. Soft soul music was playing on his phone. 'John. Any chance of a fresh ice pack, please?'

'Why didn't they do a scan on you?' Hamish asked, sitting opposite him, reading *Rowing And Sculling*.

'I haven't told you the full story. Doctor Bianchi wanted to do some tests to check if the blood flow to my brain had been interrupted, but I didn't give her the chance.'

'How come?'

'When she left me alone with just the nurse, that's when I fought the pain and got myself out of bed. The nurse helped me put my shoes on, and I just walked out.'

'But you had a concussion. You should've had a scan.'

'I know.'

'You ought to take another painkiller,' said John, handing Alex a tablet and then a glass of water. He strapped a frozen pack of peas to Alex's badly bruised shoulder.

'You'd make a good nurse, John,' said Hamish. 'If you ever got bored with running your bar.'

The front doorbell rang, and John went down. Freya entered the lounge and sat next to Alex. He could sense her disappointment.

'When I said, sort yourself out yesterday,' she said, shaking her head, 'I didn't mean you should try to commit suicide by riding your bike into a car. You're lucky you've only got bruising and a broken finger. You're causing the whole family a lot of worry with all these accidents you keep having.'

Alex exhaled. 'Have you quite finished?'

Freya looked up. 'I don't mean to nag, but seeing you like this and hearing about your job. Well, it's not exactly good news, is it – you're a mess.'

Hamish closed his book. 'I've just broken the news to him. Amelia flew home last night. The university has closed because of the virus.'

'Did you manage to send her flowers?' Freya asked.

Alex raised his bandaged hand. 'It appears I was too busy getting myself injured.' He fidgeted in his seat from discomfort as he fingered the ring around his neck. 'How about you and Hamish help me get a flight organised to fly out to her? I know roughly where she lives.'

Hamish chuckled. 'You gotta be kidding.'

'You're bloody serious, aren't you?' Freya rolled her eyes. 'You're not fit to go anywhere.'

'What am I going to do then?'

Hamish stood. 'I'm all out of ideas, and my shift is starting soon. I'll see myself out.' He put a hand on Alex's shoulder as he left.

Freya held his hand. 'You need to get yourself well again. I'll be coming around every day from now on to check up on you.'

His head slumped. 'It's all gone wrong – everything. I can't even do my sculling.'

'Stop feeling sorry for yourself. You'll bounce back.'

'Freya's right,' John said. 'You just need time.'

'And what about Evie in all this?' Freya asked.

Alex frowned. 'Evie is history after what she did. I can only think about Amelia right now. I'm worried I've blown it with her as well.'

8.30 p.m. USA CTZ.

Amelia was greeted by Daphne with a hug as she came out of Arrivals at Milwaukee Airport. She stroked Daphne's tummy affectionately. 'Your bump has grown.'

'Really, that much? It's only been two weeks since you last saw me.'

'You've got a healthy glow, but your eyes are telling me a different story.'

'And yours,' Daphne retorted as she placed her arm around Amelia's shoulder. 'You can spill the beans and tell me all in the car.'

Daphne drove north on Interstate 43 towards their parents' home. 'So, what's happened with the super fit doctor guy with the cute smile?'

'I thought he was genuine. He made me believe in him, but he turned out to be like Jake.'

Daphne glanced around. 'What, you caught him sleeping with someone?'

'Not exactly. I caught him hugging and kissing his ex-fiancé.'

'Oh, so she's not so ex.'

Amelia reached into her handbag and pulled out a packet of tissues. 'He said it was a misunderstanding, but he's let me down.'

Daphne reached over and placed a comforting hand on her sister's knee. 'I'm so sorry.'

'I just wanted to get away. Closing the university turned out to be a blessing.'

'Well, everyone is really looking forward to seeing you. Being home will help take your mind off that at least, but...'

'How's Dad? Be straight with me.'

'Not good... You might be shocked when you see him. He's deteriorated a lot more since you were last home.'

Amelia twisted herself around. 'I thought the tumour was shrinking?'

Daphne reached down and clasped Amelia's hand. 'I'm sorry to say it's not working anymore. He was getting a really bad reaction from one of the chemo treatments, so they felt it best to stop. We had an open conversation as a family; Mom, Dad, Uncle Dex, Greg, and myself. Dad made the final decision not to tell you. He said it would interfere with your studies and everything you've been working towards.'

'Oh, my goodness. I don't believe it.'

'I'm pulling off here at the gas station.' She took the turning and stopped the car opposite a diner. 'I'll tell you what he said, "Amelia can't change the situation, so don't say anything just yet." But it really was a relief when you said you were coming home. It just meant I didn't have to watch my words anymore over the phone.'

Amelia released her seat belt and stepped out of the car into the cold night air. She stood still, her arms wrapped tightly around herself as the tears started to flow down her cheeks.

Daphne got out of the car, walked around, and wrapped her arms around her. 'They did warn us that there would be side effects and that he could have a bad reaction. Sadly, that's what has happened. The doctors said it just happens sometimes – every patient reacts differently to the treatment. Cancer sometimes mutates and becomes more aggressive. I will tell you more tomorrow, but not tonight.'

They held each other for a short while, both feeling comforted in each other's arms.

Daphne released her embrace and gripped Amelia's shoulders. 'We have to be strong for Dad and for Mom, right?' Amelia nodded; they then got back in the car. 'You know Dad won't want a fuss. He wants us to be as normal as possible. So, try to be as positive as you can.'

Amelia gazed at her sister. 'Does this mean that Daddy is dying?'

Daphne nodded. 'The doctors are not sure how long he has, but it's not long. They think it'll only be a matter of two or three weeks. They have to keep draining fluid every few days from his lungs so he can lay back and sleep.'

Amelia started to sob again. 'Is there really nothing they can do?'

Daphne shook her head. 'Let's go inside the diner and have a hot drink.'

They both had a long conversation over coffee, sharing their feelings about their father's illness, and then Amelia started to get emotional again.

'Remember, we need to be strong for Dad,' said Daphne.

'I know, but there's something else.'

'What?'

'I've been so stupid. I gave Grandma's engagement ring to Alex as a sign of my love for him.'

'I'm sure he'll do the right thing and give it back.'

It was just over an hour later when they pulled up in front of their parent's garage. Amelia unloaded her bags from the car and went into the house, dumping everything down before she hugged her mother.

'Hey, here's my other girl,' said Bradley resting in the sitting room. Amelia struggled to hold back her emotions as she sat on the arm of his chair and hugged him. 'Hey, none of that teary stuff. Have a drink with me and tell me all what's been happening.'

'Dad, what's this? You're drinking strong beer.' She turned and looked at her mother. Connie raised her eyebrows back at her and then went into the kitchen.

'It's okay. The doctors have said so.' Bradley reassured her and turned to Daphne. 'Have you told her?' She nodded in reply. 'I can have a drink of whatever I fancy as I'm no longer having the treatment.'

Connie brought in a tray of drinks and passed a glass of lemonade to Daphne. She went and sat on the other armrest next to her father. Connie passed a glass of wine to Amelia.

'Now I've got both my girls with me again,' said Bradley with a slightly croaky voice. 'Let's have a toast… To family!'

7.00 p.m. Mallorca.

Robert's taxi pulled up at Villa Francina. He got out and gazed over the boundary wall up towards the villa entrance and asked the taxi driver to wait as he checked the gate – it was unlocked. He walked up the path and pulled the handle to the doorbell, pulling it again when there was no reply. He walked around and peered through some windows, but there was no sign of life. So he went back to the taxi.

He sat in the taxi rubbing his chin and wondered where she could be. 'Villa Esencia,' he said to the driver. 'It's a kilometre up the road.'

7.10 p.m.

Annabelle poured the last of the wine into Teresa's glass. 'I wonder if Robert is with his floozy tonight?'

'Best not think about him. Try one of my prosciutto and olive puff appetizers,' said Teresa.

'I'll just go and get another bottle of wine first.' She got up from the sofa and walked into the kitchen. The front doorbell rang. 'Visitors!'

'Who could that be at this time?' Teresa said as she went to answer it.

Annabelle came back into the lounge smiling with a fresh bottle of wine and grabbed the corkscrew.

Teresa appeared at the door from the hall, staring anxiously.

'Cheer up,' said Annabelle. 'What on earth is the matter?' Teresa stepped to one side as Robert walked into full view. Annabelle took in a breath. 'What are you doing here?' She narrowed her gaze. 'Never mind, just go!'

'Could I have just a few minutes in private with Bella, please?'

'I've got nothing to say to you, Robert.' Annabelle folded her arms. 'Your actions have spoken louder than any words you can possibly say.'

Teresa walked out of the room and closed the door behind her.

'Bella, please hear me out. I've been so selfish and stupid – I can only apologise for all the hurt I've caused you. But, if you could just let me back into your life again and give me a second chance, I promise I will always remain faithful.'

Annabelle could barely look at him. 'So, what's happened to your floozy? Has she dumped you?'

'I broke it off with her, and she's left the company. You are all I need – you always have been. It's just that I've been too shallow to realise it, but I see it now. I lost my way.'

'That's an understatement. And you also lost me.'

'I'm asking if we can at least be friends, and then, given time, maybe you can learn to forgive me and love me again.'

Annabelle's eyes slowly met his gaze. 'I'm doing very well without you in my life, thank you.'

'Don't be hasty. I'm not sure if you've just heard what I've said. I've ended it with Sophie because I want you back.'

'Oh, you want me now – just like that! So, I'm expected to come running to you?'

'I didn't mean it like that,' he said. 'You know I didn't.'

'Teresa, I know you're listening on the other side of the door. Please come through.' Teresa opened the door and walked in softly across the room, and sat down on the sofa. 'Robert has nothing more to say and is leaving now.'

Chapter 31

Wednesday 11th March 2020, 7.00 a.m.

Robert awoke in the spare bedroom at Villa Francina. He got up, drew the curtains, leant on the windowsill, and stared out over the garden just as the sun was rising. Picking up his smart watch, he checked notifications for work emails and then went to the kitchen. He switched on the coffee machine, opened his laptop, and immediately started reading through his emails, only pausing to pop a coffee capsule in the machine. He sipped his coffee as he pinged out email after email. Annabelle walked in wearing her dressing gown.

'Good morning,' he said, getting up from his stool and closing his laptop. 'Let me make you a tea.'

'Remember, I reluctantly agreed to you staying just the one night. Don't get too comfortable.'

'My airport taxi won't be here for another two hours. I'm happy to make breakfast for us, just like old times.' He felt her eyes bore into his back as he waited for a reply.

7.40 p.m.

Alex limped alongside Freya towards her car. 'What are you cooking for dinner?' he asked.

'First, we're going to The Old Dog and Duck. I've arranged a meeting with Evie.'

Alex froze. 'What? No… She's a bloody psycho.'

Freya turned and faced him. 'We are having dinner afterwards. You both need to put proper closure on your relationship.'

He frowned. 'I'm not sure about this.'

'Who would've thought that she would've reacted like she did?'

'You know she's got a nasty side when she feels cornered.'

'Seeing Amelia was the catalyst, but no one could have foreseen that.'

He shook his head. 'You shouldn't have given her my address.'

'I gave it reluctantly. Evie convinced me that it would be amicable.'

'Ha, that's a joke.'

'You should've taken an interest in her wellbeing. I told her that you knew she'd tried to commit suicide.'

'So, she was aware that I knew. Shit…'

'Look. It'll be alright. She's been having some counselling. We had a nice conversation last night, and she's been feeling really bad about what happened.'

8.00 p.m.

Alex eased himself out from the passenger seat in the pub car park. He leaned on the car and watched as Freya walked around the pub peeking through the windows.

'I've spotted Evie,' said Freya as she walked back over to him. 'She's with three friends at a table on the left side of the pub. We'll go through to the other side, where I've noticed some spare tables.' They walked into the pub and got seated. She ordered a lemonade with the barman. 'I'll leave you alone now,' she said, passing the drink to Alex.

'What, you're not staying?'

'It's between you two. I'll be watching from outside.' She pointed to a window.

'Look at the condition of me. I'm really still not sure about this idea.'

'It'll be alright. I'll hurry around if anything happens, but it won't. I've just texted Evie.' Freya went and stood in the darkness of the pub garden watching through the window from a few metres away.

He was anxious as Evie approached. 'Can I get you a drink?' he asked.

Evie smiled. 'No, thank you. I have one in the other room. What've you done to your hand?'

'It doesn't matter.'

'Did I do that to your face?' He nodded. She put her hand to her mouth. 'I'm so sorry.' They gazed at each other. 'Don't worry, I'm feeling better with myself, and I'm not about to do anything irrational,' she said.

'I'm the one that should be apologising after what I did to you at the church.'

'I was really hurt and felt embarrassed.'

'I can't find the words to say how sorry I am for what I did.' He took a breath. 'I heard about the incident.'

'I was so depressed. Taking an overdose seemed like the only way out.'

'Oh… Evie…' They sat in awkward silence for a moment. 'I can't change what's happened or the way I feel. But you're better off without me.'

'I know that now. I've accepted the situation.'

He felt a deep sadness. 'Who are you here with; anyone I know?'

'Some of my teaching friends.'

'It's good that you're getting out.'

She nodded. 'I wasn't trying to trick you when I said I changed my mind and that I was prepared to have a go at starting a family.'

'I think I knew that, but I was all mixed up myself.'

'I just need you to tell me that you don't love me, and then I can move on.'

He rubbed his forehead. 'That's hard.'

'I need to hear the words from your mouth.'

He dragged his fingers across his lips. 'Sorry, but I don't love you.'

She digested his words. 'I hope you find happiness with Amelia or whoever it will be.' Tears started to well up in her eyes. 'I've got my family and friends; I'll be alright.' She reached inside her coat pocket and pushed his cufflink box across the table to him. 'By the way, I came across this.' She stood. 'I should go back to the others.' Alex slowly levered himself to his feet, using the table to steady himself. She kissed the palm of her hand and reached over and touched his scratched cheek. She blinked, and a tear fell from her eye. 'Goodbye.' She walked back through the bar entrance.

Freya continued to watch from outside as Alex remained motionless, leaning against the table, for what seemed like ages to him before he left his drink and joined her outside.

Freya helped him into the car. 'I guess it went alright by what I could see?'

'Short and amicable.'

Have you thought about joining Mum in Mallorca to recuperate before everything shuts down?'

8.30 a.m. USA CTZ

Amelia was sitting with her family eating breakfast and listening to her father recall past family holidays – adventures on the coast and canoeing with the girls when they were little. He nibbled at the corner of his toast and left the rest.

Amelia studied his emaciated appearance – his sunken eyes – and stroked his thin arm. 'We're gonna have a good day today, Daddy. Come for a short walk with me and Daphne later?'

'I'll see.'

Connie placed a hand on Bradley's shoulder and smiled. 'Are you not going to finish your toast, dear?'

He grimaced. 'I can't eat anymore.'

Amelia could feel her phone vibrate in the pocket of her jeans. She excused herself from the table and walked to the far side of the house. 'Hello, Jake.'

'It's good to speak to you. Are you free later?'

'I think so.'

Amelia and Daphne helped get Bradley settled in the sitting room after breakfast. Connie joined him as he watched the TV. Daphne and Amelia returned to the kitchen, cleared up, made two teas, and sat opposite each other.

Daphne cradled her tea. 'Dad was getting more poorly because of the aggressive nature of the cancer and needed blood transfusions. He's had awful constipation and skin infections – he's really been quite unwell.' She paused as Connie joined them.

'Your father is asleep.' Connie sat down. 'Are you bringing Amelia up to date with your father's condition?' Daphne nodded. 'It's important that you explain everything.'

Daphne took a sip of her tea. 'The doctor called us into his office to give us Dad's prognosis.'

'Was Dad with you?'

Daphne nodded. 'He explained that although the tumour had originally shrunk, it had got bigger again, and the chemotherapy wasn't working. So they decided to stop any further treatment.' Connie started to get tearful. 'Do you want me to stop, Mom?'

'I'll be alright.' Connie wiped her eyes. 'Basically, the doctors have said… that there is no more they can do. It was now about quality of life verses length of life. Your father has accepted the situation. His faith has given him the strength to face what's ahead. Speaking of which, Pastor Warren will be around in about an hour to counsel and pray with your father.'

Pastor Warren had been talking with Bradley alone in the sitting room before he asked the three women to join them for family prayers. Afterwards, the family walked with Pastor Warren to his car. Bradley joked with him about how he used to always beat him in fishing competitions. They waved goodbye. Daphne and Amelia watched Connie help Bradley back into the house before the sisters set off for a walk.

'This friend you're seeing tonight – it's Jake, isn't it?' Daphne asked.

'He's taking me to some new fancy wine bar in Algoma.'

'Mom has already worked out that you're seeing Jake. Tell me what happened between you and Alex.'

'It was an interesting day. We did this capsizing practise in the middle of a river. He treated the dunking as a metaphor for a baptism – to cleanse us from our past relationships.'

Daphne glanced around and grinned. 'Like a clean, fresh start.'

'Only, he was kissing his fiancé later back in Cambridge.'

'Mmm… Not good. But, do you think you should give him a chance?'

'Nah.' Amelia shook her head.

7.30 p.m.

Amelia parked on a street in Algoma near a wine bar and got out her phone.

Jake tapped on her side window and made her jump. 'I was just texting you,' she said, opening her car door. They walked into the bar together and sat at a small round table in the corner that Jake had reserved.

'Let's order drinks,' he said. 'Are you having your regular wine?'

'A juice cocktail for me.' A waitress took their drinks order and left. 'Jake, I have to be direct, and I have to tell you.'

'If this isn't good news, I don't wanna hear.'

'Sorry, I really wanted our fresh start to work.'

'Wait... It is working.'

'I don't want you to waste any more of your time on me.'

'But we're moving on and putting the past to rest.'

Amelia shook her head. 'I have come to realise that we can never be an item again; that's why I'm here. I apologise if you thought there was a chance of us getting back together.'

Jake's shoulders slumped. 'No, please. I made that one mistake. I was a dork, but I've changed. I will always be true, I swear. I just need you to give us another chance.'

She struggled to hold eye contact. 'The thing is, well, we've both changed. I've come to realise that my feelings towards you could never be the same again. I'm sorry.'

Jake stretched out his hand over the table and took hold of hers. 'I'm prepared to wait... If you could at least think about it.'

She retracted her hand. 'Do you remember what I said to you after I discovered you with Melanie? I said, "You've destroyed my trust in you and our future dreams by your unfaithfulness."

'We learn from our mistakes. Please, can you give me a second chance? Amelia – I need you.'

'The thing is, I would always live in fear of you doing that again. If only you knew what you put me through – you nearly broke me.'

'Is there someone else?'

She looked down and fiddled with her scarf. 'I thought there was, but it's over now. Jake, please find someone who will love you and then be faithful to that woman.'

They stared at each other for a moment. He nodded, stood, and left.

She sat alone for a while longer, just staring into the candle flame in the centre of the table. Then, she blew it out.

Chapter 32

Thursday, 12th March 2020, 8.55 a.m.

Alex laid back in his bed, staring at the ceiling. He didn't hear the door chime or John speaking to Freya in the lounge on the other side of his door.

'Are you decent?' John asked as he slightly opened the door. 'Your sister and niece are here.'

'Sweetie, can you sit and read your book, please, while Mummy has a word with Uncle Alex?' Charlotte nodded. Freya's nose twitched as she entered his room. 'C'mon, Alex, you need to get up. Urgh. It smells rank in here. Is that dope and drink spirits I can smell?' She pushed back the curtains and threw open the sash window. 'This won't do. It won't do at all! I don't want to sound like Mum, but you can't carry on like this. Being hit by a car should've been a warning to you.'

Alex squinted. 'That's what Hamish said.'

'Seriously though, you need a complete change of scene. We need to get you out before Spain goes into full lockdown due to the thousands of Coronavirus cases.'

'And do you still think it's a good idea I go?'

She exhaled. 'Mallorca has a zero infection rate because of its isolation, so you'll be fine at the villa. You know we're only a couple of weeks behind Spain. It's coming here.'

John walked in with two cups of tea. 'It's here already. Eight deaths now in the UK. I'll just leave your teas here. The LBGTQ mug is yours, Alex.'

Freya helped Alex into a sitting position before she sat down on the edge of his bed. She took her iPad out of her bag and researched flights to Mallorca.

John sat next to Charlotte in the lounge, taking an interest in her book. 'I'll hold your room because you'll still be paying rent!'

'Cheers, John!' Alex said loudly towards his door entrance.

Freya checked flight availability. 'The morning flight is full...' she mumbled as her fingers scrolled down the screen. 'The evening flight is too late. Here we go. There is availability on a flight out Saturday morning.' She turned to Alex.

'But what about Amelia?'

'You said yesterday that you've got her address. You could send her some flowers through Interflora with a message.'

He sipped his tea. 'And you'll help me sort that out today?'

'Of course.'

He put his tea down and held up the ring from around his neck. 'And what should I say about this?'

'Ah, the ring. Just ask her if she wants you to send it to her by recorded delivery or if she will be back to collect it?'

He nodded. 'Let's get that flight booked.'

9.10 a.m.

Annabelle sat down in the kitchen opposite Robert. 'How do you know that your flight won't be cancelled again – like yesterday?'

'I don't,' he said. 'But I can only try. We're in uncertain times.'

'I meant to say I enjoyed breakfast. The omelette was delicious.'

'I'm pleased. Can I get you anything else while I'm waiting for my taxi to arrive?'

'I'm still trying to adjust to this new you. It's a little bit unnerving. But I'll have a tea, thank you.'

He made the drinks, and they went and sat out on the veranda. 'The garden is looking great,' he said, sitting back and checking the time.

'I've been thinking,' she said slowly. 'If I don't go ahead with pursuing a divorce and we were to try and work things out between us, will you promise to always put me first before your business and making money?'

He sat up. 'Most definitely – I genuinely promise.'

She betrayed a hint of a smile.

'How do you feel about me cancelling my flight and staying on here for a bit?'

7.40 a.m. USA CTZ

Amelia heard a knock on her bedroom door. 'Come in, I'm awake,' she said, sitting up.

Daphne walked in and placed a coffee down beside her bed. 'You're late getting up. We're all having breakfast.' She sat on the bed holding her baby bump. 'I'm feeling exhausted already. Helping Mom get Dad out of bed and get him dressed. It's also a struggle now to get him downstairs.'

'I'm so sorry; I should've been helping.' She took a sip of her coffee. 'I'll take over as soon as I'm dressed.'

Daphne fidgeted, trying to get comfortable. 'How did you sleep?'

'To be honest, not good. Stuff kept churning around in my head. Worrying about Dad and Mom. Then I was thinking about Jake, and the evening I finished it between us.'

'You can be so unforgiving.' Daphne raised herself off the bed. 'But what about giving the doctor guy, Alex, a chance?'

Amelia took another sip of her coffee. 'When I was overthinking everything in the night, I tried clasping Grandma's…'

'Ring,' said Daphne, interrupting. 'But it wasn't there. He's got it, and you need to talk to him. Surely, you realise that?'

8.50 p.m.

Alex was sitting in a lounge chair when Sanjay entered and sat down opposite him.

'Can I get anyone a drink?' John asked.

'No, I'm all good, thanks,' Sanjay said. 'So, what have you been doing with yourself?'

John put his head around the kitchen door. 'Nothing, he's been sitting there all day just watching daytime TV.'

Sanjay turned his gaze back to Alex. 'This isn't good.'

'Thanks, John,' said Alex sarcastically. 'Actually, there's a lot of good stuff on TV during the day. It's another world.'

'How do you fancy going out for something to eat?' Sanjay asked.

'Why not?' He got ready with a little help from Sanjay.

Alex limped slowly along Green Street with Sanjay beside him. 'I should be off to Mallorca early on Saturday morning, all barring the flight not being cancelled.'

'Let's hope you make it.' They turned into Sidney Street and continued walking until they came to a pub and ordered a pint of beer each and a burger.

'Have you managed to do any sculling?' Alex asked as he sipped his beer. Sanjay's phone rang. Alex knew it was Hamish on the other end when Sanjay said the name of the pub.

'Hamish and Spud are on their way,' said Sanjay.

Alex gazed out of the window. 'I'm not in the mood for banter.'

'It's exactly what you need. We're all concerned about you.'

Alex gulped back his drink, called over a waiter, and ordered a whisky.

'Look, we've all had relationship problems. But the amount you're drinking and what with smoking dope – well, it's not like you.'

'Don't judge me. If this is about the other night when I was sick over your carpet – well, I would like to pay for the cleaning.'

'It's not about that. We want to help.'

'Oh look,' said Alex as Hamish and Spud walked in. 'Here comes Mars and Venus.'

Hamish and Spud sat down at the table and ordered drinks. 'Lucy got a text from Amelia,' said Hamish. 'She was meeting up with her ex-fiancé. Sorry, mate. But I thought you should know.'

Alex gulped back his drink just as their food arrived. He ate quickly, not saying a word as he listened to the others' banter.

'I just knew that someone would grass on you to the *Trust*,' said Hamish.

'But I always tried to be clear-headed at work.'

Sanjay raised an eyebrow. 'I understand that part of the investigation will be based on a medical evaluation after you've had some counselling. When is that due?'

Alex stopped eating. 'I can't be doing with all of this questioning.' He got up and walked out. The others scrambled to follow him. Sanjay hurriedly paid the bill.

'C'mon, man,' shouted Spud. 'We just want to help.'

Alex reached his apartment street door. 'Look!' He snapped at them. 'I don't appreciate the interrogation.' He unlocked his door. 'I've messed up my job and my relationships. I'm just a bit pissed off and not good company. I'm going to bed.' He slammed the door on them and stood behind it in the stairwell, waiting for them to leave.

Several minutes later, he re-emerged and hobbled through the streets until he found a tucked-away bar and ordered a whisky. He sat alone at a table thinking about Amelia – how she entertained the little baby and played with the children at Becky and Oliver's reception. He put in his earbuds and listened to music in between watching video clips of sculling races. He had another drink, then another, and a few more.

11:40 p.m.

Alex staggered out blurry-eyed and struggled to get his bearings to find his way home. He felt hopelessly lost after a while until he heard a voice in a shop doorway.

'Alex, it's me, Rose.' Her small black dog Gertie emerged from under her blanket and barked.

'Oh, hi,' he said as he propped himself against the wall. 'I'm lost.'

'And very drunk.'

'Can I sit down here with you, please?'

'Of course,' she said. 'Gertie, we need to move up and make room.'

'You have a friendly voice, Rose,' he said, slurring his words.

She laughed. 'And you have more of a drunk voice.'

'I haven't seen you in ages, sorry,' he said as he fumbled a £10 note out of his wallet and gave it to her. 'For breakfast.' He pulled out his pouch and rolled a joint. 'Where is this place?'

'Jesus Lane.'

'I'm sozzled.' He lit the joint and offered it to her. 'Can I ask you, Rose, what's your story? How did a nice woman like you become homeless?'

She lifted Gertie onto her lap and took a drag. 'I don't mind, as you've paid for my breakfast tomorrow.'

'Only if you're sure.'

She took another drag. 'It all comes down to some shitty, disruptive relationships I've had in my life... That, and an abusive stepfather who caused me to have mental health issues.'

Chapter 33

Friday, 13th March 2020, 00.02 a.m.

Alex listened as Rose told her story. 'But why didn't your mother get the police involved?' he asked.

'She never knew what my stepdad was doing to me,' said Rose as she stroked Gertie. 'I didn't say anything to her because I believed I was protecting her by keeping quiet. He said that he would hurt Mum if I said anything to her or anyone.'

Alex took a drag of his joint as he tucked himself into the corner of the shop entrance. 'How old were you when it started?'

'Thirteen. It was like a never-ending nightmare for two years. Mum found out what was going on when I was fifteen. But what made it worse was that she believed him, and she sometimes hit me. I left home when I was sixteen and didn't do my school exams.'

'Why didn't you go to the police?'

'Ha! Who were they going to believe, with my mum supporting him and no evidence?' She took a deep drag of the joint.

'That's awful.'

'You asked me how I landed up here – now you know. Do you want me to carry on?'

He nodded. Tiredness made his eyes heavy.

'It gave me depression and plagued all my future relationships.'

'Wasn't anyone helping you?'

'One partner I had beat me from time to time because I struggled with intimacy. He reminded me of my stepdad. I don't know what I saw in him in the first place,...'

Rose continued to talk about her past relationships, and he started to fall asleep. He slumped over with his head resting down on her bedding, almost against her thigh. She dragged some of her bedding over him.

00.58 a.m.

'What's... happening?' Alex stirred awake on hearing Gertie barking and could feel a warmth seeping onto his skin. He glanced up at a man urinating over him. The man sniggered and redirected his piss over Alex's head. Coughing and dazed, Alex tried to make sense of everything.

'Get off, you bastards!' Rose shouted as Alex noticed two or three people dragging her out onto the pavement away from him. Gertie continued to bark. Suddenly the dog yelped and started to whimper.

'Urhhh!' He felt his body jolt from a kick into his back. Another kick went into his side and then into his stomach as he rolled over. Winded and reeling, he tried to crawl towards Rose. He could only make out blurred silhouettes of men.

A man's head came over her face. 'Fuck off!' she shouted. The man clamped her mouth shut with his hand. She couldn't move; her head was pressed hard back against the pavement. She felt his breath on her forehead. Two others held her arms and body down as another dragged off her boots and stripped off her jogging bottoms and knickers.

Coughing, Alex tried to get his breath from a couple of metres away as they exposed her naked lower body. The man started to undo his trouser belt as he stood just out of reach of her lashing feet. Alex tried to prise himself up, but the man turned and kicked him hard in the head.

Alex started to hear Gertie growl and bark again as he regained his senses. Opening an eye, he tried to focus as he lay flat out on his side. He saw a man on top of Rose trying to get between her legs, but then he lost consciousness. 'Alex, Alex. They've gone now,' said Rose kneeling over him. 'Are you alright?'

He blinked repeatedly, trying to clear his vision as he remained on his side. 'My head.'

She felt his head. 'You've got a large lump.'

He grimaced. 'But what about you? That bastard was on top of you.'

'I kneed him hard in the balls, which made him roll off. But one of his arsehole mates booted me. Fortunately, they didn't want to hang around. They pulled him up and buggered off.' Her dog whimpered beside her. 'Gertie has been hurt. But let's get you sat up against the wall.' She could hear voices. 'Hey, can you come and help us, please!' Two young men came over, and one got out his phone.

Alex waved his good hand. 'Don't call emergency services,' he mumbled.

'Nor the police,' she added. 'They're useless in these situations. But we need to get you medical help.' She turned to the stranger. 'Can you call the Night Shelter here in town that looks after the homeless? I know their emergency number.'

The man phoned the number that Rose gave him, and she told them their location and an explanation of what had happened.

An estate car soon arrived, and a man and a woman from the shelter helped Alex, Rose, and Gertie into the car. They thanked the two men for their help as they gathered up all of Rose's belongings and bundled them in the back before they drove to the shelter.

They supported Alex and helped him walk through the front café entrance and then continued through to a medical room out the back. The woman put on some PPE, a plastic apron, and gloves and then examined Rose. The male worker took Alex into a side booth and helped to remove his clothes, down to his underwear. Alex swayed as he tried to sit upright on the bed.

'Are you okay with taking this?' The worker asked as he held out some pain relief tablets. Alex swallowed them back. The worker put on a face mask and gloves and started to examine Alex's bruised body. 'So, you're not homeless.' Alex shook his head slightly. 'I'll find you some clean clothes in a moment. Did your attackers cause all this bruising?'

'No. I got knocked off my bike; that's how I got a broken finger.'

The worker finished cleaning Alex with some wet wipes and helped him put on some new underwear. 'You should really go to A&E to be examined. Why didn't you want those helpful guys to call an ambulance?'

'I'm not in trouble with the law, but I have my reasons.'

'Some of our homeless prefer medical help from us if it's not too major. I'll leave your phone and wallet on the side here.' The shelter worker sniffed Alex's pouch of weed.

Alex tried to get up and winced.

'You're welcome to stay here the night. But no drugs.'

He nodded. 'I do need rest.'

The female worker knocked and entered. 'Rose is going to stay, she's having a shower. I've given her dog some pain relief. I'll ask the morning team to arrange for an appointment with a vet.' She gazed at Alex with a pressed-lip smile. 'How are you doing, young man? You've got an awful lot of bruising.'

The worker bundled Alex's clothes into a bag. 'Alex is also staying the night.' The worker helped get Alex into some clean clothes before he joined Rose in the café. They chatted over mugs of tea and hot buttered toast.

After a while, Rose went to the female dorm, and Alex was assisted up some stairs to the male dormitories, which had rows of small makeshift plywood cubicles, each big enough for a single bed. The worker quietly showed Alex along a corridor to the last unoccupied cubicle and helped him to bed, covering him over with a duvet.

7.05 a.m. Mallorca.

Annabelle started to set the table for breakfast at the villa.

Robert finished replying to some emails on his laptop. 'Do you remember when we first met thirty-six years ago? You used to stay over in my flat after the odd wild Friday night out.'

She smiled. 'Oh my god, yes... You would make Saturday morning breakfast. Eggs benedict and sometimes eggs royale. You made an excellent hollandaise sauce.'

Robert held out his hands. 'You do remember. They were good times. We would be out drinking and dancing.'

She glanced over at his closed laptop. 'And we've been having conversations like a normal married couple, without you being fixated on work and money.'

'Would you prefer to sit outside to eat?'

Annabelle stretched her arms around herself. 'I think inside. I'll watch the sunrise from here with a cup of tea.'

'A cup of tea coming up,' he said, putting on the kettle. 'And runny poached eggs on toast?'

'Thank you, that'll be lovely.'

'I was catching up with the news earlier. It said that the number of confirmed cases is still rising rapidly. There's talk that Spain will go into quarantine measures tomorrow.'

She reminded herself of how he was before coming to Mallorca. 'Robert, I just want you to know… I do need time. I'm finding it all a bit difficult.'

Robert stirred a pan of boiling water on the hob. 'I understand…'

'Ah… I almost forgot. I received a text from Freya last night. Alex met up with Evie. They had an amicable conversation and seemed to have parted on good terms.'

'That's a relief.' He cracked an egg into the pan.

'But more importantly, Freya has managed to coax him out here. He needs a complete change of scene to recuperate.'

Robert spun around and narrowed his eyes. 'Recuperate?'

'There's been a whole load of stuff going on with him. Let's have breakfast first, then we can go for a walk afterwards along Formentor beach, and I'll explain everything.'

1.20 p.m. USA CTZ

Amelia heard the front doorbell ring. 'Daphne… Can you, please?' she shouted from the landing.

Daphne opened the door to an Interflora delivery person. She was surprised to see a beautiful basket flower arrangement. She checked the name on the card, signed the receipt, and walked through to her parents, who sat in the kitchen, placing the basket in the middle of the table. 'For Amelia, from her friend in England.'

'Who was that at the door?' Amelia called out, coming down the stairs and walking into the kitchen. There was silence in the room as Amelia gazed around at her family and then at the flowers. She nervously opened the attached envelope and read the printed message. Leaning over, she took in the scent. 'They do smell nice. They'll make a lovely display in the sitting room.' She picked them up and turned.

'Hey, wait a minute, pumpkin,' said Bradley. 'Who's the admirer?'

'It doesn't matter,' she said, walking away into the sitting room. She placed the flowers on one side of the fireplace. Daphne followed her in and put an arm around her. She lifted the message out of Amelia's hand and read it.

Amelia, please accept this small gift as an apology for any hurt I unintentionally caused.

PS. I have your ring. How would you like it returned?

With love

Alex

X.

7.30 a.m.

Alex awoke to the sound of voices in the hostel corridor. Upon turning his head, pain stabbed at his neck, and he abruptly reconnected with his senses. A face appeared through the cubicle pull-curtain.

'Time to get up, mate,' the worker said. 'Breakfast.'

Alex gingerly raised himself up on his elbow. Using his good hand, he felt down the side of his bruised body and checked his bandaged broken finger. Pushing the cover back, he swung his legs over the side of the bed. Aching clawed at his every movement. He pressed a lump behind his ear; soreness made him slump forward and hold his head against his knees. As he did so, a sour smell stung his nostrils. His gaze drifted to an open bin-liner on the floor containing his dirty clothes, and then he remembered the man urinating over him. He ran a hand over the spiral-patterned jogging bottoms the hostel worker had given him, not quite believing his own eyes. He forced himself to his feet, twisted a knot in the bin liner, and dragged it along as he limped towards the dormitory door. He slowly eased himself down the stairs, discomfort clinging to his every step as he clasped the banister rail. The smell of freshly cooked bacon encouraged him towards the dining area which was full of hungry people tucking into their meals. Over at the kitchen servery, he recognised Rose wearing a bright blue jumper with Gertie lying nestled in her arm.

Rose's small willow figure turned to greet him. 'Alex…'

He was momentarily taken aback by how fresh and tidy she appeared after a shower – her face and short auburn hair had a healthy sheen. 'How did you sleep?'

'I got some rest.' She twisted some strands of hair in front of her ear. 'Are you good?' She examined the bruising to the side of his forehead.

'I'm feeling sore,' he said, trying to maintain eye contact and mask the surge of pain shooting through his shoulder. 'But what about Gertie?'

'Pretty whacked out on Paracetamol.' Rose showed him the bandage around Gertie's leg. 'The guys here are taking us to the vet after breakfast.'

'Poor thing.' He observed four red marks on the side of Rose's mouth from where the man had gripped her face. She appeared unmoved now by what had happened. 'Gertie's barking helped save us from those three drunken scumbags.'

'There were four of them – three were holding me down and urging on their mate.'

Alex recalled being kicked, Gertie barking, and Rose trying to defend herself. Only now did he notice a large butterfly tattoo on the side of her neck in an array of blue colours.

'What would you like, dear?' asked the women at the servery.

Rose pointed to the fried eggs, hash browns, toast, and baked beans. Alex settled for a couple of slices of toast, then found an empty trestle table at the corner of the room. He grasped a jug of water from the centre of the table, filled two beakers, and gulped down his own. Meanwhile, Rose stroked Gertie's black matted fur with one hand as she forked down her food with the other. A helper brought them steaming mugs of tea.

Alex pulled out a blister pack from his pocket. 'Like Gertie, I, too, need a bit of pain relief.' He washed down a couple of pills with his tea. 'Do you mind if I examine her?'

'What? Are you a vet or something?'

'I've got some medical experience.'

Rose got up and placed Gertie in his lap, all the time stroking the dog's head as Alex examined her.

'Her leg's fractured,' he said. 'The ulna bone. The vet will fix it.' He carefully re-bandaged Gertie's leg.

'She'll be all right then?'

'Yes, but they might want to keep her in for a few days.' He gazed up at Rose. 'After what happened last night, what about you?'

'I'm fine.' She forced a smile. 'I showed that vile creep you can't go messing. You should've seen how he reeled off me doubled up in pain.'

Alex's phone buzzed in his pocket. 'I'm just going to take this. Hi John.'

'Where are you? Your sister has been trying to contact you.'

'I'll be back within the hour. I'll explain then.'

'Have you heard the news about flights?

'No.'

'Loads of flights across Europe are being cancelled. Check your flight as they've just announced on the radio that Spain is going into lockdown tomorrow.'

Alex digested the information. 'I have to go.' He ended the call.

'Is everything alright?' Rose asked.

Alex nodded. 'Are you sure that you're going to be alright without Gertie for a few days?'

'I'll be fine. Everyone has to be out of here after breakfast. What're you gonna do?'

'I've got things arranged.' He rubbed the side of his aching head. 'Will you stay here in the city for the next few weeks?'

'Why do you ask?'

'I just want to know where I can find you again – if that's alright?'

She moved her fingers to his ear and drew a line along the contour of his jaw towards the centre of his chin. He reclined his head slightly. 'You're idealistic, a little stubborn at times, but willing to listen and understand people.'

'Not bad. Where did you learn all this stuff?'

'My grandmother, bless her. She was a bit of a mystic. But to answer your earlier question, I'll be in the city, somewhere. If you ask – someone here should know roughly where to find me.'

'It might be a few weeks.'

'I'll be around.'

He stood up uncomfortably. 'I have to go, but I'll find you…' He grabbed his bag of clothes, thanked the hostel staff for their kindness, and moved towards the main door. He turned just as he was about to enter the street and caught Rose's gaze. She pointed a finger at him. He knew what she meant; don't forget.

He lumbered along the street a short distance before stopping. 'Am I doing the right thing?' he said quietly to himself as his eyes searched the morning sky.

11.00 a.m. Mallorca.

Robert sat in the lounge, reading the latest news online. 'Spain has already started some social restrictions in preparation for full quarantine tomorrow.'

Annabelle turned around. 'I'm worried about Alex making it out here.'

'Hm… His flight might be cancelled.

'That wouldn't be any good. Freya is convinced he needs a complete change of scene. She thinks he's suffering from depression.'

Robert sighed. 'We can only hope then there are no problems.'

'I know you're working here at the villa for the foreseeable future while we try and rebuild our marriage. Well…'

'What is it?'

'When you are back at your office after this crisis, and the company is interviewing candidates for your new PA, I want to discreetly be involved and have the final say.'

'What, you don't trust me or the interview process?'

'Look what happened last time. I want to see the shortlist of the applicant profiles before the interviews. To be honest with you, I have my own criteria.'

'Let me guess. The successful applicant will need to be suitably old and unattractive, but efficient?' She smiled. He rolled his eyes and gulped back the rest of his coffee.

Robert heard a car pull in and went to the kitchen window. 'Emilio is coming up the path.'

Annabelle quickly went and opened the door. Her eyes read like alarm bells with a hesitant shake to her head as Emilio moved forward to embrace her. She stepped backwards.

'Emilio!' Robert sang out before he could see the gardener. 'Hey, Emilio!' Robert stretched out his hand. 'What's the matter? You're not shaking my hand?'

'Social distancing. Coronavirus.'

'Of course,' said Robert, retracting his hand. 'Can you take us for a tour around the grounds in ten minutes? I want to see all the changes you've been making since I was last here.'

'*Si*, I understand,' said Emilio as he turned and walked away.

'Emilio isn't his usual jovial self,' said Robert, turning to Annabelle.

'This coronavirus thing is worrying everyone.'

'But he gave me a bit of a disdainful look.' He pushed his hands in his pockets. 'Strange...'

She blinked. 'He's also probably worried about future work.'

'Talking about future work. I've noticed the design plans for the flower bed. They're impressive.'

'Thank you...' She smiled. 'I'm pleased you like them.'

Chapter 34

Saturday, 14th March 2020, 4.40 a.m.

Alex moved uneasily through his dark lounge and pulled back the curtain at the sash window. A mist hung in the night air above the sleepy city. A single streetlamp glowed through the shadows on the wet grey pavement. Feeling a little nauseous, he rested his forehead against the windowpane and felt the coolness of the glass. It soothed him.

He peered towards the street entrance and used his shirt sleeve to wipe his hair off his clammy forehead. Reaching into his pocket, he took out a blister pack of pain-relief tablets, swallowing a couple with a swig of water from his clear plastic bottle. He went into the kitchen cupboard and stared at his bottle of gin next to the whisky. He emptied some water into the sink and topped up his bottle with gin. He took a large gulp. Pulling out his phone, he checked his flight-tracker app – no cancellation of his flight. He lifted the ring from inside his top and watched as a soft kaleidoscope of light reflected from the diamond stones. Clenching the ring in his fist, he grunted through gritted teeth and kissed the ring before tucking it back inside his tee shirt. He went to the window, opened it, leaned through onto the Victorian metalwork, and breathed in the cool air. Still feeling nauseous, he stared towards the road entrance and then down onto the dark, wet street. The cobbles appeared animated, like black beetles, as they shimmered under the street lighting. His senses were jolted by car lights at the top of the street, and he threw himself sharply back against the underside of the window. Grabbing his head, he hummed the pain.

John walked out of his room yawning and switched on the lamp on the mantlepiece. 'What's with all the noise?'

'Sorry, said Alex rubbing his head. 'My taxi is here.'

'I hope everything goes alright.'

He picked up his flight bag. 'And I'm sorry for being a pain this last week.'

'By the way, you still look like shit.' John grinned.

'I'll stay in touch.' He noticed the photo beside John of the selfie taken with Amelia on a punt, and hobbled over and picked it up. 'I still don't understand why she wouldn't let me explain.'

'Forget about her and get yourself well again.'

Alex placed the photo frame face down, hugged John, and was out the door with his small case and bag. The nausea made him feel dizzy as he bumped his way down the narrow staircase and along the hallway to the street door. Taking a moment to compose himself, he opened the door, stepped out, and stumbled over the doorstep, falling sideways over his case onto the pavement.

The taxi driver was standing by the open tailgate and rushed over. 'Are you alright, sir?'

'Do I look alright?' He levered himself into a sitting position. His groaning echoed around the street.

'I take it that you're, Mr Hardson?' Alex nodded in reply. 'I must inform you that I will not take drunk and disorderly persons in my taxi. It's against company terms and conditions.'

'I'm not drunk. Sorry.'

The driver helped Alex struggle to his feet. 'Do you need to change out of those clothes?'

'Let's just go.'

The driver placed Alex's case in his taxi and helped him into the rear seat with his flight bag. He got into the driver's seat and put on a face cover. 'A new company policy – we've been advised to wear masks.'

'Your company is wise, despite what the government advises.'

Alex was still feeling nauseous and clammy during his journey to the airport and started to assess his own condition. He checked his pulse. *Increased heartbeat.* He tried to ignore the pain that he was feeling from his aching head and body. He pulled his phone out from his back pocket and texted: *Mum, I'm on my way to the airport. There r no flight delays so far. Love Alex. X.*

'What lousy weather,' the driver said as he increased the speed of his windscreen wipers. 'Are you off to somewhere warm and sunny?'

Alex looked up and caught the faded view of the driver's eyes in the rear-view mirror. 'How long until we arrive?'

'Around twenty-five minutes.'

Alex opened his flight bag and took out the letter from his NHS *Trust* employer. Frowning, he read the contents using the light on his phone. *You are being placed on non-voluntary sick leave for six weeks... to be assessed and deemed medically fit to return as a medical practitioner.* He read on... *returning to work on a probation period.* Feeling nauseous, he pressed the letter down against his lap. *I need to be positive.*

5.30 a.m.

Alex awoke as his taxi pulled up outside Stansted Airport.

'Excuse me, sir!' said the driver gazing around. 'We're at the airport. That's a hundred pounds exactly, please. I'll come around and help you out.' The driver opened the door. 'Should I try and get you some medical assistance?'

'I'll be fine. I don't need any help.' The driver cocked an eyebrow. Alex reached into his side pocket and offered his open wallet with shaky hands. 'Can you pull out what I owe you and an extra twenty for your troubles.'

'Thank you.' The driver helped him out as people hurriedly moved around them, trying to get out of the heavy rain. The driver placed Alex's case onto the pavement and then scurried back into his cab. The taxi was gone within a flash, leaving Alex standing like a statue by the curbside, getting soaked.

Alex turned his face towards the dark sky as if he could feel the healing power of the cold rain. He drew a breath, dragged his case into the airport, and waddled past a group of people with Italian flags on their bags, wearing face masks. Gazing up at the departures board, he identified his flight among all the red flashing lights and headed for the check-in. He noticed that many of the different airline counters were closed as he shuffled forward.

He took a gulp from his bottle and slouched over in front of a female check-in assistant.

'Have you packed your luggage yourself?' she asked.

He coughed. 'Of course. Who else do you think packed it?'

She narrowed her eyes. 'There is no need for rudeness.'

'Sorry, but can we please hurry?' He took another gulp.

'By the way,' she said firmly. 'You cannot take the bottle through security.'

'Sure.'

'Have you got your passport and e-ticket, please?'

Another wave of nausea came over him as he handed over his documents. Swaying slightly, he gripped the edge of the counter as she examined his passport. Dizziness swept over him. He swayed and, like a pack of cards, collapsed to the floor with a thud.

The check-in assistant launched herself out of her seat, came around her desk, and stared down at him. Other people that were queuing rushed around him. A woman leaned over, fanned him with her passport, and then stepped back as two security personnel arrived.

'Sir! Are you alright?' asked one of the security men.

Alex stirred. 'Urrr…'

'You fell, sir. Don't try moving.' The security man took off his jacket and propped up Alex's head. 'How many fingers am I holding up?'

'Four.'

'Good. A wheelchair is on its way.'

'I'll be fine now – I don't need… a wheelchair.'

The two masked security personnel knelt on either side of him. 'Have some of your water,' said one of them, handing Alex his bottle. A medical person and an airport assistant arrived pushing a wheelchair.

'I don't need a sodding wheelchair,' said Alex trying to push himself to his feet, but immediately needed steadying and was seated into the wheelchair.

The medic checked Alex's blood pressure and temperature. 'You're intoxicated, but I'll allow you to proceed. You'll have to stay in the wheelchair. The assistants will take you straight through.' He gave the assistants a message for the plane cabin manager.

Alex didn't respond; his face was void of emotion as he was wheeled through the automated check barrier for flight tickets. He gulped back the contents of his bottle before one of the assistants deposited it in a bin. The assistants got him swiftly through security and manoeuvred him through the service corridors, boarding gate, and onto the plane.

One of the assistants handed the cabin manager the message from the medic.

'Alexander Hardson. No alcohol!' The cabin manager pointed to an aisle seat five rows back from the front, and they helped Alex into his seat.

The cabin manager stood back in the aisle. 'I'm not sure about this,' she whispered to a colleague. 'Just look at his condition. Keep a watch over him.'

The assistants departed with the wheelchair as the manager locked the cabin door behind them before the plane taxied onto the runway for take-off.

A young mother sitting by the window in the same row was trying to entertain her two-year-old son with a cuddly toy. She called the flight attendant over. 'No offence to this gentleman, but how do you know he doesn't have this coronavirus? He's clearly not well.'

Alex cringed at the woman as the flight attendant listened.

'The gentleman had an accident before boarding the plane and has been assessed by a medic,' said the flight attendant through his mask.

Alex slumped down in his seat as he listened to the discussion. Trying to ignore the increasing nausea he was feeling, he closed his eyes and fell asleep.

An hour into the flight, the young mother was quietly reading to her son who was sitting on her lap, when Alex stirred from his sleep.

'Mummy, mummy,' said the child, giggling, pointing to Alex's trembling hand. The mother pressed the button for the flight attendant.

The flight attendant walked over to Alex. 'Can I get you anything, sir?'

He looked up. 'Have you got some pain relief, please?'

The attendant got some pain relief tablets, put on some gloves, and held a glass of water to Alex's lips before helping him get more comfortable.

'I would like a large gin and tonic.'

'Only water or juice – sorry.'

'It's for medicinal purposes.' His voice was cracking as he argued. 'Do you understand? I need a G&T or a whisky.' he insisted. 'I need to stop these sodding hands of mine from shaking!'

The cabin manager arrived. 'What's the problem?'

'I've explained that he can only have water or juice.'

The woman next to Alex was trying to comfort her crying son. 'Please stop quarrelling – you're scaring my little boy.'

Alex rubbed his head as he slouched. *What's wrong with my head?* He quietly rested. The woman's child stopped crying, and the cabin staff returned to their duties.

Alex's condition eased after a while, and feeling better, he started to entertain the little boy by pulling amusing faces as the child sat on his mother's lap. The boy giggled out loud. His mother was smiling with approval. The cabin manager surveyed the scene from the flight galley and smiled to herself. Even some of the passengers seated around the mother were amused at her child's infectious laughter.

Nausea suddenly hit Alex again. *What's wrong with me?* He slumped back in his seat. He watched the young mother as she played with her child. She tucked some loose strands of hair behind her ear. It triggered a memory from a week earlier when Amelia served up breakfast. He didn't want to think of her, but he couldn't help it. Tiredness weighed on him, and the memory soothed him into sleep.

9.20 a.m. Mallorca.

Alex stirred as the flight attendant crouched over him. 'Wake up, Mr Hardson. Are you alright? We're disembarking.' The rest of the passengers collected their luggage. 'Apologies,' said the attendant, turning to the woman with her son. 'You'll need to wait a little longer.'

The cabin manager arrived after saying goodbye to most of the passengers. 'He really does look unwell. The captain has radioed for medical assistance.'

Feeling confused, Alex looked around with one open eye. He grimaced and then unexpectantly grabbed hold of the seat in front with his good hand and levered himself upright. He swung around and fell against the flight attendant, who eased him down onto the aisle floor.

'Let's get him up to the front,' said the cabin manager. The crew supported Alex towards the open cabin door. Airport ground staff and a medic hurried up the passenger stairs carrying an evac-chair into the aircraft cabin. Alex mumbled incoherently and suddenly lunged himself forward on his good leg towards the stairs.

'Wait!' shouted the attendant as a ground staff person sprung forward and grabbed hold of him. Three ground crew assistants and a flight attendant secured him in the evac-chair and steadily brought him down the passenger steps. The cabin manager walked down behind them, carrying his case and flight bag. An airside ambulance arrived near the base of the steps. Two airport paramedics wearing face visors took control of the situation and settled him down in the ambulance.

'Alex, *señor* Alex… can you hear me?' asked one of the paramedics. 'Was someone going to meet you?'

'Hm…' he replied, clutching the ring and holding it tightly to his throat.

'Do not close your eyes! Have you got a phone with a contact?' asked the paramedic in his broken English. The paramedic pulled it from Alex's pocket and held the phone up to Alex's face. 'Can you unlock it?' Alex swiped across the screen. The paramedic found Alex's mother's phone number and dialled.

'My mother should be waiting…'

Annabelle answered. The paramedic briefed her on Alex's situation and told her to go to the information desk. The ambulance pulled up alongside the airport building, where a police officer boarded. The paramedic continued to assess Alex's condition as his parents arrived with an airport official.

'Alex, Alex…! What's wrong with him?' Annabelle asked as Robert gently restrained her at the open rear door of the ambulance.

'We must go to the hospital immediately,' said the paramedic, waving them both forward into the back of the ambulance. The other paramedic secured the doors after the police officer had completed a passport check and stepped out.

Annabelle crouched down near Alex and held his free hand. 'Alex darling, I'm here. Please speak to me.' The ambulance lights pulsed as it raced away.

10.36 a.m.

Alex didn't hear the sirens blazing as the ambulance rushed through the traffic towards Palma hospital. The paramedic pulled back Alex's eyelids one at a time and shined in a penlight. He turned to Annabelle and Robert. 'Your son has unequal size eye pupils. It is a strong indicator that he's had some sort of head trauma. I'm going to give him some medication intravenously.' The paramedic also attached a cardiac monitor to his chest.

Annabelle held Alex's hand between both her palms.

The paramedic examined Alex's head. 'It appears that he has taken some severe hits to the back and side of his head recently.'

Alex was being pushed along a hospital corridor on a casualty trolley and became semi-conscious. His eyelids flickered under the bright lights passing overhead, and he noticed a nurse pulling his trolley bed on one corner as he tried to process everything.

He sensed his mother holding his hand and flicked an eye towards her. 'Mum…' he said in a shallow voice.

'Can you hear me, Alex?'

He couldn't process her words, and her image started to fade. Another person appeared, and he felt pressure on his chest as a hand came above his face. A sudden bright light appeared in his eye as consciousness slipped from him.

11.14 a.m.

Annabelle sat on one side of Alex's bed in an emergency assessment cubicle, and Robert stood next to her.

The curtain was pulled back, and a female doctor and a nurse entered. 'Hello, I'm Doctor López,' she announced in perfect English. Annabelle looked up through smeared mascara eyes. The doctor picked up a clipboard at the base of the bed and looked over the top of her glasses, examining the wave lines on the care monitor above Alex's bed. 'Your son is stable. We're going to carry out further blood tests and have him sent for a brain scan to help us determine what type of stroke he's had.'

'Do you know what caused it?' Annabelle asked.

'The results from the blood tests and the brain scan should indicate exactly what happened. He had low blood sugars, possibly caused by toxins. He would've felt very confused.'

Robert squinted. 'Is our son still in any danger?'

'As I said, he's stable, and he's responding to treatment.'

'What treatment has he had?' Annabelle asked.

'A clot-busting drug delivered intravenously by the emergency medical personnel in the ambulance. The physician correctly identified the symptoms. It was important that the drug was given promptly.'

Annabelle's eyes filled with tears. She took hold of Robert's arm.

The doctor shone a torch into Alex's right eye. His pupil immediately contracted. 'That's a good sign, and there is also random eye movement. His mind is active. The nursing staff will now get him along to the MRI unit, and then he'll be transferred to a hyper-acute stroke bed for special monitoring.'

12.45 p.m.

Annabelle followed a nurse into a room and tensed at the sight of Alex wearing an oxygen mask and hooked up to an ICU monitor. Robert followed behind her. She looked at the waveforms flowing on the monitor screen as she approached him.

A nurse made an adjustment to the drip that was attached to Alex's arm. She gave Annabelle a reassuring smile.

Doctor López entered the room and immediately examined some paperwork she took out of an envelope. 'I have the results back from the tests and the head scan.' She flicked through some of the information and the MRI images.

'How serious is all this?' Annabelle asked.

Doctor López looked over the top of her glasses. 'One scan shows that there are some abnormalities to his cerebral vessels, and the others show some disruption to his blood flow causing sudden insufficient oxygenation and energy supply to parts of his brain.' The doctor paused as Annabelle became emotional. Robert put his arm around her. The doctor gazed at the paperwork again. 'Your son had high levels of alcohol in his blood and other drug toxins.'

'That doesn't sound like him,' explained Annabelle.

'The scans and the blood tests show that he has had a transient ischemic attack.'

'What does that mean?' Robert asked.

'The next three days are the most important while we wait to see how he responds to the treatment and rest.'

Chapter 35

Monday, 16th March, 10.15 a.m.

Annabelle straightened herself up in a chair next to Alex's bed as a nurse entered the room. She watched as the nurse carried out some observations on Alex.

A female doctor in an open white coat strolled in shortly afterwards. 'My name is Doctor Ramira Torres,' she said through a mask. 'I'm a speech therapist and rehabilitation specialist. I work mainly with patients recovering from strokes.' The doctor moved beside Alex's bed. 'We all have to wear masks now due to the new coronavirus regulations, even though there are no infections here in Mallorca.'

'They're still recommending not to wear masks back in the UK if you're a healthy person.'

'Interesting. I'm pleased, therefore, that you're wearing yours.' The doctor turned to Alex. 'Good morning, Alex.' He stirred. 'Please follow the tip of my finger with both your eyes.' She made some notes. 'A very good start, Alex. I'm going to assess if you're suffering from dysarthria, which can affect your speech.' She paused. 'If you understand me so far, please raise your fingers on your right hand.'

Annabelle leaned forward and rubbed the side of Alex's arm. 'His speech has been slurred for the last two days, but I thought he sounded better this morning. His general movement has improved.'

'The massage treatments would've helped. His general health needs to have improved enough before he goes home with you.'

'And if he doesn't respond well?'

'It all depends,' explained the doctor. 'The main concerns are his cognitive communication and if he has any problems swallowing. I'm going to remove the cannula tube and start the assessment.'

10.25 a.m.

Annabelle was ushered outside the room by Doctor Torres. 'Alex is making a good recovery,' said the doctor. 'But before we speak in front of him again, there are some long-term neurological concerns. We need to have a conversation about some counselling to aid his recovery.'

'I understand.'

'We cannot offer it freely as he's not a Spanish resident, but he'll now be in Mallorca for a few weeks due to quarantine. Have you any personal medical insurance?'

'Not for Alex. But my husband can cover the costs.'

'Counselling will also provide a full psychological assessment.'

'I see,' said Annabelle. 'How quickly could a transfer be arranged?'

'As quickly as today, providing all the paperwork is in place. You can let us know what you've decided later.'

Chapter 36

Tuesday, 17th March, 8.30 a.m.

Alex was awake and resting in a private hospital. Annabelle was slumped over, fast asleep in a chair by the side of his bed, having been awake most of the night since he was transferred.

A nurse walked in with a physiatrist practitioner. 'She's exhausted,' said the nurse through her mask.

'Mum…' he mumbled. Annabelle blinked and jolted upright.

'Let me introduce myself. I'm Doctor Graupera. I hope you can understand my English. Please only speak when guided, Mr Hardson.'

Annabelle rubbed her eyes, quickly put on her mask, and moved out of his way. 'Where's my husband?' She looked at the nurse and pointed to an empty chair.

The nurse's eyes suddenly widened. 'Ah…' She mimicked sleep, putting her hands to one side of her face. Annabelle nodded. The nurse elevated Alex's bed and made him more comfortable.

'I'm a physiatrist,' said the doctor as he faced Alex. 'I'll be coordinating your rehabilitation, assessing what difficulties you have, and helping you make relevant adaptations to assist you. For example, we'll provide you with an exercise regime to become fully mobile again.'

Alex knew his strength and coordination were slowly returning as he listened.

'He's much better.' Annabelle pointed to Alex's face. 'His colour has returned, and he is eating by mouth again.'

'He has indeed made good progress. You should be able to understand that you're recovering from aphasia caused by a mini-transient stroke.'

He gave a hint of a nod.

'I also understand from the notes here that you're a doctor yourself.'

Alex didn't respond, almost disappointed that the doctor knew.

'His speech has improved,' said Annabelle.

'When you're able to speak more naturally, I will need to examine your lifestyle leading up to your stroke. We need to identify any issues or concerns. That's the plan, anyway. Is that clear so far?' Alex gave a thumbs up.

'How long do you think he'll need to stay in the hospital?' Anabelle asked.

'At least a few days, all going well, and then Alex can continue his rehabilitation at home. I'll be coming by twice a day. Our physiotherapist will be along later. I would like to first test your current physical strength.' Doctor Graupera held out his gloved hand. 'Please take it with your good hand and squeeze it hard.' Alex squeezed. 'Good. You're making progress.'

Stuck in the bed, Alex had never felt so useless as he watched the doctor peel off his disposable gloves.

Chapter 37

Thursday, 19th March, 8.50 a.m.

Alex sat up in bed. 'Does my NHS employer in England know that I'm in a hospital here?' he asked, slurring his words slightly.

'Not from me,' said Doctor Graupera. 'This is confidential information – unless you wish them to be informed?'

'No.'

'Let's start then by examining your lifestyle.' The doctor reached for his computer tablet. 'Are you currently in a relationship?'

9.25 a.m.

The doctor checked his tablet notes. 'Your friend's wife gave you some advice at the church after you confided in her. That's what I've written here.'

'Zahida.'

'You were stressed and confused after leaving your fiancé. You had an argument with your father, and then you returned home but had an accident falling down the stairs. Hm…'

'But I recovered.'

'Let's move on. When did you find out about Evie taking an overdose?'

'When the duty manager asked me into her office.'

'How did you react?'

'I was in shock. Afterall, I was responsible. I wanted to go and see her, but I was instructed to go home.'

'And did you?'

Alex shook his head. 'Not at first. I found out that she was being interviewed by a primary care physician to evaluate her mental state. Like you're doing with me, I guess.'

The doctor smiled. 'Following on from what you said earlier. Did you continue indulging in smoking cannabis?'

Alex nodded. 'And snorting.' He looked away with shame.

The doctor stood. 'I feel we're making very good progress, but you should rest before your physiotherapy session. We'll continue this later.'

'I want to carry on for a bit longer, please. I've bottled up everything that has been troubling me. I want to get it all out.'

'If you're sure,' said the doctor, sitting back down.

10.03 a.m.

Alex had one arm around a nurse and the other around Gabriella, the physiotherapist, as they sat him up on the edge of his bed.

'Take hold of the walking frame,' said Gabriella in perfect English as she helped him onto his feet. Annabelle and Robert stood to one side, watching. 'Good, just steady yourself and then try one step at a time.' She and the nurse held his arms and steadied the frame. Alex soon found his confidence after several minutes, moving the frame himself. He was walking slowly up and down the room.

He gazed down at his slightly wobbly feet as he walked. 'I'm really having to focus.'

'You're doing very well,' said Gabriella. 'If we leave the frame with you, do this exercise as often as you can during the day.'

Chapter 38

Friday, 20th March, 4.48 p.m.

Alex was resting in a chair by the side of his bed, thumbing the ring around his neck.

'To sum up,' Doctor Graupera said. 'You've had at least four traumatic incidents with blows to your head in the last three weeks. Any one of them could have caused the stroke – the road accident, falling down the stairwell, being attacked and kicked in the head. And then you collapsed, hitting your head on the stone floor at the airport.' He clasped his hands together. 'Some transient strokes only last seconds or minutes. It's also possible that you had a mini-stroke after the car accident, and because you weren't treated, it's taken longer for you to recover here. I'll invite your parents back in.'

Alex tried to listen as the doctor spoke softly to his parents in the corridor. Then they entered the room. 'What's your assessment, please, doctor?' he asked.

'Gabriella has already given me her report, and I'm satisfied with your progress. I'm pleased to say that you can leave the hospital today.'

Annabelle clasped hold of Alex's hand and smiled at Robert.

'Before I leave you with Gabriella, who will show you some exercises that you should do at home – I would like to impart some advice, if I may. As doctors, we have a duty of care to our patients but also a core duty to ourselves. The patients will suffer if we do not maintain our own mental and physical wellbeing. So, please always remember to take the utmost care of yourself.'

Alex exhaled a breath. 'Thank you for everything.'

'I've prescribed some medication which the nurse will talk you through before you go.'

7.10 p.m.

It was just over an hour's drive to Villa Francina on the north side of the island. The sun had just set behind the mountains when they arrived. Robert walked around to the passenger side door.

'I can do it myself,' Alex said as he levered himself up using his walking stick. Annabelle went ahead of him up the path and hurriedly unlocked the door. Robert followed Alex carrying his bag.

Annabelle walked through the villa, out onto the veranda, and quickly arranged a few cushions on her favourite lounging chair, positioning it with a good view across the bay. 'Come on through, darling.'

Alex slowly went through to the veranda and used his stick to ease himself into the lounger. 'This feels kind of weird being back here without Evie.'

Annabelle shook her head. 'Let's not talk about her now.'

'The air is quite cool out here.'

'I'll get a blanket.' She covered him over and lit a candle arrangement on the table.

Alex sighed. 'It's good to be out of the hospital.'

'I'll make some tea and coffee,' said Robert going into the kitchen and switching on the radio.

Annabelle sat in her rocking chair near Alex and whispered, 'While your father is making drinks, can I ask that you try and get along with him, please?'

'Have you forgiven him?'

'Not fully… But he's making a real effort and has promised that he'll be faithful.'

Alex nodded. 'If it'll make you happy, then okay.'

Robert walked out on to the veranda with a tray of drinks. 'I've heard on the radio – Matt Hancock announced in the House of Commons that all unnecessary social contact should cease on the twenty-third.'

'What does that mean exactly?' she asked.

'The UK will be in full lockdown like Spain's quarantine. We should talk in the morning and decide what we're going to do next. Flights have already been grounded everywhere.' Robert raised his shoulders. 'Alex was lucky to get here. Another flight on the same day had to turn around and go back to Stansted.' Robert placed down the tray and went back into the villa.

'I'm exhausted,' said Annabelle as she took hold of Alex's hand. 'I've been thinking a lot lately while you were recovering. How I've tried to deal with your father's affair, which totally knocked my confidence.' She exhaled and released his hand. 'I haven't dealt with it very well.'

Alex gazed out across Pollensa Bay as the night descended. 'At least your moral compass is intact and pointing north. Dad's went totally south, and mine has wobbled. I've messed things up.' He stared at an anchored yacht silhouetted by its deck lights, bobbing up and down.

8.20 p.m.

Robert had been reading on the veranda for some time before he put down his book. Annabelle lay asleep with her book resting on her tummy. He tucked a cushion under her head and covered her over with another blanket.

'Thank you,' she murmured, snuggling down.

Alex looked at his father. 'I guess exhaustion has caught up with Mum.'

'She has been watching over you, night after night.' He turned off the veranda lights, leaving a single candle burning on the table. He quietly moved his chair closer to Alex and rested back. 'The view from here across the bay is so calming.'

'I can see why Granny bought this place,' he said with slurred speech.

'It was her little bolthole for a while. She now prefers to holiday on the Amalfi coast and Lake Como with her retired friends. But, we've had some great family holidays here.'

'Why did you do it, Dad?'

Robert looked around uncomfortably. 'I know you're still angry with me. I've been totally selfish, not behaving like the father you deserved. It'll always be like a cloud hanging over me. I'm so sorry for all the hurt I've caused.'

'Saying sorry fixes everything then, does it?'

'Of course not,' he replied softly. 'I can't take back the wrong I've done, but I promised your mother that I'll be a faithful husband from now on.'

Alex glanced around and made eye contact. 'How do we know that you won't break your promise?'

'Everything will come second to your mother and you and the family – you have to trust me. Besides, Spain is in quarantine now, and the three of us have to get used to living together for the foreseeable future. It's going to be a very different lifestyle for quite a while until someone comes up with a vaccine.' They stopped talking, and Robert gazed out over the bay for several minutes.

'Thank you,' said Alex breaking the silence.

'I don't understand. What for?'

'Everything – my childhood, the family holidays, my education, supporting me through medical school, and a whole lot more.'

A hint of a smile appeared on Robert's face. 'I'm going to get something stronger to drink. Would you like anything?'

'Some sparkling water, please.'

The sound of soft classical music drifted through the open French doors. Annabelle was still fast asleep when Robert returned several minutes later with a glass of water. He gently squeezed Alex's shoulder and placed the glass into his hand. 'I hear you've made your peace with Evie.'

'That's right,' said Alex.

'That's really good.' Robert rested back in the chair and gazed out at the lights twinkling on the other side of the bay. 'You just need time to rest and get fully well again.'

Chapter 39

Tuesday, 24th March, 7.10 a.m.

Annabelle awoke shortly after sunrise and checked in on Alex. 'Let me help,' she said, trying to assist him in getting out of bed.

'Don't fuss; I can manage.' He slowly levered himself up using his walking stick.

She walked back into the kitchen and pushed Robert's laptop lid down as he sat working.

He pursed his lips. 'What's bothering you?'

'We need an activity for Alex to keep his morale up. We'll all go stir crazy with the three of us here in quarantine.' She started pacing around the kitchen with her arms folded.

'What about the exercises that the physio gave him?'

'They won't be enough. He needs something more.'

'I'm in the middle of something right now…'

She gave him a sideways glance. 'I'm just searching for ideas.'

Robert shrugged his shoulders. 'I'm sure that Alex will work it out, but he could start by going for regular walks around the grounds.'

10.20 a.m.

Alex was ambling around the garden using his walking stick to steady himself. He kept trying to brush thoughts of Amelia out of his head. *Why didn't you let me explain?* He wondered how Rose was coping.

Annabelle sat on a garden bench in the spring sunshine, watching him. After almost half an hour, she walked over. 'Don't you think you've done enough?'

'Another fifteen minutes or so.'

'You're getting tired; you might stumble and fall.' She could see the determination he had to get strong again and returned to her seat. She remembered how determined he was to finish something when he was a little boy.

The temperature was a comfortable 22°C. The three of them had their lunch on the patio in the shade.

'This is so frustrating,' Alex said as he stared at his strapped-up broken finger.

'Only another week,' said Annabelle. 'What're you going to do after lunch?'

'Nothing. I'm keeping in touch with the guys over a Zoom chat later. Some more exercises, some reading, and maybe watch a movie. I'll then repeat the whole routine again tomorrow, the day after that, and the day after that...'

5.30 p.m.

Alex had decided to go for a walk along a path that weaved through sloped grass areas of the 2.5-acre grounds and through a grove of pine trees. He thought of his meeting with Sandra and his suspension. He stopped walking and closed his eyes. He remembered the last time he met with his sculling friends. But then, the words that Doctor Graupera had said to him bounced back. *Doctors like us also have a core duty to ourselves. The patients will suffer if we don't maintain our own mental and physical wellbeing.* Alex opened his eyes and sighed. He felt a sense of shame. He felt that he had let everyone down. *I deserved what's happened to me.*

Annabelle had been following him from a distance and stood watching with curiosity as he just stood about fifty metres ahead. Alex turned around and slowly walked back.

'I'm so pleased you're getting stronger,' she said as he approached her.

'I just wish I wasn't such a physical and mental wreck. I really miss my sculling. I realise now how much it kept me sane.'

'You'll be sculling again soon.'

He decided to try walking without the aid of his walking stick, carrying it in his good hand as they wandered back side-by-side.

Chapter 40

Thursday, 26th March, 11.00 a.m.

Alex was with his mother checking the new island border in the garden when he heard a vehicle pull into the drive.

'I think that's Emilio,' said Annabelle. 'He's still carrying on as if there wasn't a quarantine.'

'It'll be good to catch up with him.'

'I'll leave you both; I'm driving into Puerto Pollensa. I missed the market yesterday. I guess there'll be lots of socially-distanced queuing going on.'

'You used to like your time with Emilio, walking around the garden and discussing ideas.'

'You can talk to him and fill me in later.' She walked back into the villa, and Alex went and sat on a garden seat.

Emilio walked up the steps, around the villa, and across the garden carrying some tools to edge the lawn. He noticed Alex and raised a hand in acknowledgement. Alex sat in the shade and took an interest, watching him edge the flower beds and prune some small trees into shape.

Alex got up and ambled over. 'Hi, Emilio. Sorry I haven't spoken to you much in the past, but how are you – *cómo estás*? Sorry, but my Espanol is limited.'

'I understand more English than I speak.'

Alex grinned. 'I'm interested in why you're pruning off the lower branches of the tree and not the long sides?'

'To make room for shade-loving flowers underneath.'

'I get it.'

'Would you like to help? A little job to help build your strength.'

'I would like that.'

Emilio fetched a small fold-out seat from his van and positioned it in the shade in front of a patch of earth under the branches. He showed Alex how to lightly fork the ground surface from a seated position. Alex paced himself, slowly turning over the surface earth until he was tired.

'Lunch time,' said Emilio, standing and wiping sweat from his brow. He sat on the grass near Alex and opened his cool bag, offering him some of his small tapas dishes.

'Shouldn't we be social distancing?'

Emilio waved his hand. '*Mañana*. There are no cases yet in Mallorca.'

Alex picked at some *tapas*. 'This is really good.'

'*Bueno*.'

'I'm enjoying the gardening. It's actually helped me to forget some women troubles.'

Emilio poured out some water from his flask and passed it to Alex. 'Women can be mysterious at times. I think you say, a paradox.'

'Hm… Enjoyable when a relationship is going well and poisonous when it's not.'

'Where's your mother today?'

'She went into town shortly after you arrived.'

'Is she avoiding me?'

Alex chuckled. 'I don't think so – she enjoys planning projects with you.'

Robert walked across the garden, carrying two glasses of iced lemonade. 'I thought you could both do with a cold drink.' He passed one to Alex. Emilio looked away. 'I'll place yours down here, Emilio. I need to get back to work.'

Alex picked at some olives. 'I guess clients of yours will still need their gardens maintained during quarantine?'

'*Si.*'

'I've got a proposition for you. I'm getting bored hanging around here, and my strength is returning each day. Do you think I could help you out with some gardening at your clients' properties?'

Emilio placed his lemonade down. 'Sorry... I could not afford to pay you.'

'I wouldn't need paying. I just need something positive to focus my mind on.'

Emilio pointed to Alex's left hand and leg. 'You have some physical issues, and it'll be a long day.'

'Just let me try, please?'

'Okay... I'll come and pick you up on Monday.'

Chapter 41

Monday, 30th March, 6.50 a.m.

Alex walked down the villa path with a slight limp, carrying his walking stick, and got into Emilio's van with his lunch box. Annabelle watched from the kitchen window as Emilio did a five-point turn and drove out. 'What's the first job?' Alex asked excitedly.

'A German client.' Emilio parked his van a few minutes later. He set Alex up in a fold-out chair in the rear garden, demonstrated how to do topiary using garden clippers, and left him to it.

After a busy morning visiting three properties, they stopped for lunch, sitting in Emilio's van with the doors open.

'I'm feeling tired, but I'm enjoying it,' said Alex.

'We have a final job for a good client in the Serra de Tramuntana mountains. 'It's about a thirty-minute drive.' They spent two hours at the property, and then Emilio started packing away.

'Amazing views,' said Alex. 'Mountains to the sides and that coastline in front. Wow.'

'You make me money, so I will buy you a drink.' Emilio got in his van and drove on the only road that passes through the mountains on their way back to a small remote bar near Lluc.

Alex eased himself out and gazed around at the dramatic views as Emilio walked towards the entrance. Alex was suddenly startled when Emilio slapped his hand down on his van bonnet. 'No good.'

'Quarantine. I'll hold you to it another time.'

Emilio exhaled as he got back in his van. 'If you're not too exhausted and you want to continue – two days a week, Mondays and Thursdays. I will bring lunch. We can start with Villa Francina.'

Chapter 42

Thursday, 2nd April, 1.40 p.m.

Alex stopped his pruning at the bottom of a long garden in Alcudia and watched Emilio shouting and kicking his lawnmower.

'Lunchtime!' shouted Emilio walking towards his van. 'I need an iced beer.' He grabbed two.

Alex took a can of beer. 'What's with all the shouting?'

'A stone has broken the mower blade.'

'You're normally quite calm about things.'

'Tell me, Alex, is your mother happy with your father? They appear a little distant earlier.'

'I shouldn't be telling you, but to be honest, they're trying to make their marriage work. I feel that I can trust you to be discreet. There was another person involved a short while ago – it was like a three-way thing. So yes, they're a little distant from each other.'

Emilio squinted. 'Do you know anything about this third person?'

'Not really; I only saw them once through a window with their arms around each other.'

Emilio suddenly became agitated. 'You saw us…'

'What are you talking about?' Alex shook his head in confusion. 'I saw a red-haired woman with my Dad.'

'Ah! You were there, that's what I meant to say – you saw them. I get muddled translating my English sometimes.'

'Shall we just call it a day and carry on next Monday?'

Emilio nodded, and they loaded up the van with all the gardening equipment.

Emilio drove through Puerto Pollensa and was waved down at a police checkpoint. A policeman wearing a face mask ordered Emilio out. Alex watched as the policeman questioned him. Emilio pulled some paperwork from the glove compartment and passed it over. He continued to watch as the officer waved his finger and then shook his head. The officer issued Emilio with a fine for not having the correct paperwork for being an *essential worker* before he let Emilio continue.

'It looks like no more gardening until end of quarantine,' said Emilio, taking Alex back to the villa.

'No need to be sorry. You've given me a sense of purpose and helped me get out of a rut.'

'Rut? Is it another of those strange English sayings?'

'*Si.*' Alex walked up the path and watched Emilio drive away. He then gazed at his mother sitting on the bench in the shade, reading. Annabelle waved. He turned back and saw Emilio wave out of his van window.

Chapter 43

Thursday, 9th April, 11.30 a.m.

Annabelle searched the grounds for Alex and eventually found him in one of the secluded areas of the gardens, engrossed in planting flowers among the grasses. 'What're you doing?'

'I got so inspired working for Emilio. He let me have a load of these young flower plugs. He's got hundreds of them that he grew from seeds and were going to waste because of quarantine. I said that we could use them.'

'You're going to plant up all this slope with spring flowers.'

'It'll keep me busy.'

'I'll leave you to it then.'

'Emilio was hesitant at first, but when I mentioned they were for you, he was more than happy to give me as many as I wanted.'

'Well, that's good. Any news from the hospital here?'

Alex moved into the shade. 'My outpatient appointment in Palma has been cancelled. It's not considered urgent under the current situation. I'll only miss minor checks with my coordination progress.'

She slid her sunglasses off her face and over her head. 'You appear to be doing brilliantly – almost back to your old self. You're even using your left hand now that the strapping is off. I'm so relieved.'

He rubbed his hands together to remove some loose earth. 'Being out here has really helped me both physically and mentally.

The problem now is that I'm feeling guilty and a little ashamed that I'm here and not back in the UK, helping at my hospital.'

'You're still not well enough.'

'Hamish and the rest of the frontline crew will be stretched in the current climate. It doesn't seem right while I'm relaxing and planting flowers.'

'But it's out of your control. You still cannot return to work until you've been assessed by the medical council, and there are no flights yet.'

'I know, it's just that…' he exhaled and put his hands on his hips. 'I do miss my life back there. At least I'm not feeling the need to numb my head with drugs and get drunk anymore.'

'Do you miss this other woman that lives in America?'

'I'm over her. I sent her flowers with a message before I left home about this.' He pulled the ring out from inside his tee shirt. 'But no reply – nothing!'

'It is strange, but I still think you'll hear from her at some point.'

'I think about Rose quite a lot. I really like her. I want to try and help her when the quarantine-lockdown thing is over.'

Annabelle tilted her head. 'That's admirable.'

'I've started reading medical stuff online again. My aim is to pass the GMC assessment with flying colours.' A moment of silence fell between them as Alex gazed up at the sky.

'I'll leave you with your planting.' She slid her sunglasses back down over her eyes and went to leave.

'Do you think you'll miss Emilio not coming around due to quarantine?'

She froze and slowly turned to face him. 'Of course. He's an excellent gardener.'

'And a good friend.'

She nodded. 'But hey, I guess we have you now as our gardener.' She waited for Alex to make another comment, but he just stared at her. 'I need to get back and sort out a few things before lunch.'

Chapter 44

Saturday, 16th May, 7.30 p.m.

Alex was in a Zoom meeting with Hamish. 'What's the latest?'

'You'll never guess,' said Hamish. 'Spud has been secretly dating Avani and breaking lockdown rules.'

'I guess they've formed a bubble.'

'That's one word for it. Have you heard from Amelia?'

'No. It's over with her. To be honest, I'm carving out a new life for myself here. But I really do miss our sculling sessions, and I've put on weight.'

'Me too,' said Hamish. 'The club is closed, and there's nothing to do. I've invested in a rowing machine here at the flat.'

'That's great. Send me a picture, but I need to go now.' He finished the meeting, walked through to the kitchen, and grabbed a bottle of beer from the refrigerator. He took a gulp and walked out onto the veranda. 'Are we having a late dinner tonight? He asked his parents. 'Why the sombre faces? He noticed his mother had been crying.

'Please sit down a moment,' said Robert.

Alex pulled up a chair. 'What's happened?'

'It's my mother. She died this morning.'

'Granny is dead?'

Robert nodded. 'She was apparently admitted to the hospital Thursday evening struggling to breathe. She had contracted the

Covid-19 virus. They put her on a ventilator but couldn't save her. Freya couldn't even get to see her before she died.'

'Ah… Poor Granny… Do we know how she caught it?'

'Havers said she wouldn't be imprisoned by the virus and was still popping into shops to get her essentials.'

Annabelle brushed a tear away. 'Unfortunately, she'll just be another statistic, not recognised for all the great things she'd achieved.'

Robert put his arm around her. 'I just hope she didn't suffer at the end.'

'I wonder how many more people have to die before they get this dreadful disease under control,' said Annabelle.

'Almost twenty-seven thousand people have now died on the Spanish mainland alone. The only good news to come out recently is that the death toll has started to drop dramatically. We must try and get back to the UK as soon as flights resume.'

Chapter 45

Tuesday, 9th June, 7.22 a.m.

Robert rested his suitcase outside on the porch and then went back inside the villa and tried enjoying a last-minute cup of coffee. 'I do feel a little safer us travelling, now that the Covid-19 death toll in the UK has dropped to below two hundred a day.'

'I'm pleased that flights across Europe have at least returned to forty percent of their pre-covid levels,' said Annabelle. 'Things are at least getting back to some normality.'

'The taxi will be here soon.'

Alex walked into the kitchen. 'I'll give you a hand down the path with the cases.'

'Will you be alright here at the villa on your own?' Annabelle asked.

Alex rolled his eyes. 'Mum, c'mon.'

'Of course, you will be. At least you'll have your gardening to keep you busy. And your Zoom chats.'

Robert put down his empty cup. 'And not to mention this new job he's starting down at the boatyard on Monday.'

'It's a volunteer job. Otherwise, they wouldn't have taken me on to repair boats. Emilio's local contacts have come in useful.'

'It'll be quite a bit different to fixing up people.' Robert knew that he was going to miss his son's company. 'And you enjoy living here at the moment – it'll be good for you.'

A taxi turned into the drive, and the car horn beeped.

'I'll take your case, Mum.' Alex walked with a slight limp down the path and loaded the luggage into the taxi. He hugged his mother. 'Give my love to Freya,' he said.

Robert was surprised when Alex embraced him. 'Your granny was very proud of you,' said Robert as he got into the taxi. 'And I'll remember to place your farewell letter in my mother's coffin.'

Chapter 46

Tuesday, 7th *July, 10.00 a.m.*

Annabelle was in her home. 'Robert! It's no good. For some reason, the login for our Zoom meeting isn't working.'

'Okay, let me have a go.' Robert swapped seats with her. 'I'll check the code again. Hang on... There's an email message from Evelyn's solicitors.'

'Let me see.' She swapped seats again, staring into the laptop screen. 'It says, as we are the main beneficiaries, they would now like a meeting at their office. The Zoom meeting now only applies to her friends and some other associates.'

11.50 a.m.

Annabelle arrived with Robert at Evelyn's solicitor's office, wearing face masks. They were guided through to a large waiting room. Havers was already seated to one side. He gave a polite nod. They found two chairs on the opposite side of the room to Havers and took their seats.

Evelyn's lawyer entered the room and took his seat at a desk a few metres from both of them. 'Good morning. I am named as the executor of the last will and testament of Evelyn Hardson's estate.' He removed his mask and took a sip of water. 'As the two main beneficiaries of Lady Evelyn Hardson's will, I thought it best, considering some sensitivities involved, that I should go through the specific details in person.'

'What do you mean sensitivities?' Annabelle asked.

'I do apologise, but I deemed it necessary to have a separate meeting with you away from the rest of the beneficiaries.'

Robert narrowed an eye. 'Shall we just get on with my mother's will reading, please?'

'Of course... Friends of your mother's were left paintings, other works of art, antiques, personal belongings, and some money, as stated here in these documents. You'll both have copies.'

Annabelle took hold of Robert's hand as her breathing quickened.

'Havers has been gifted Evelyn's Jaguar for being her trusted loyal driver,' said the lawyer. 'He is also to inherit her Chelsea apartment.' Annabelle and Robert both straightened up in their chairs with a look of shock on their faces as they glanced at each other with questioning eyes.

'Furthermore,' said the lawyer. 'Mrs Annabelle Hardson is to receive the title deeds to Villa Francina.'

Annabelle released her breath and drew another as she smiled with satisfaction. She felt relief from inheriting the one thing she wanted. 'I wonder what's left?' she whispered.

The lawyer went on to explain how Freya was to receive jewellery and an equal amount of money along with her brother.

'Now for the final part. Mr Robert Hardson, only son of Mrs Hardson, is to inherit her beloved pet, Percy, the parakeet.'

'What....' Robert snorted. 'I don't believe it...'

'Hence, the sensitivities, Mr Hardson,' said the lawyer, slightly embarrassed. Havers grinned.

'Trust Mother to pull a stunt like that.'

'It comes with a dowry of six hundred pounds per month to cover Percy's essentials, including any veterinary costs.'

***

The Balearic Islands continued with the gradual easing of quarantine restrictions in July. Mallorca started encouraging shop owners to reopen their businesses, and the ports remained busy due to its dependence on mainland Spain.

Alex's parents remained in the UK, but he decided to stay in Mallorca. His week settled into a comfortable routine, where he worked at the boatyard until lunchtime and then, in the afternoons, read in the coolness of the villa. Emilio started to call by again, and between them, they completed a couple of wildflower landscaping projects to encourage more birdlife into the villa grounds.

Alex looked forward to his evening Zoom meetings with his friends and family, which had become a regular feature. His parents would be on a Sunday; hospital colleagues on a Monday; Freya (and occasionally Charlotte, who loved pressing the mute button) on a Tuesday; John on a Wednesday; and his sculling friends on a Thursday. Fridays were movie night, where he would download a film to watch. He kept Saturdays clear to read and go for a walk along the Pine Walk, enjoying the tranquillity.

Self-isolation restrictions were lifted in the UK and in other low-risk countries, including Spain, from the 10th of July 2020. A period of normality returned to Mallorca. Puerto Pollensa was quieter than usual, but that suited Alex.

Chapter 47

Thursday, 23rd July, 6.40 a.m.

Alex walked down through the pines to the rocky beach and stood on a large rock at the water's edge. Remaining motionless, hands in his pockets, he gazed out across the bay into the morning sunrise as it broke across the horizon. His mind drifted like a rudderless ship as he reflected on the events that brought him to the island. He tried to make sense of it all as the sound of the water gently lapped against the rocks. Birds were tweeting in the pines behind him as the sun rose. It reminded him of his sculling days on the River Great Ouse. He glanced at his watch. It was time for him to leave and go to work.

Alex was lying underneath a wooden boat outside the boatyard using a powered disc sander to remove old loose paint. He finished his shift, sat up, threw back his face visor, and pulled off his breathing mask from his sweaty face. Grabbing his water bottle, he took several refreshing gulps.

His supervisor walked up and ran his hands along the underside of the boat where Alex had been working and nodded with approval. He patted Alex on the back and pointed to his watch. 'You finish now – two o'clock.'

'*Gracias*, Pablo,' he said, wiping his mouth and forehead with the back of his hand. 'I'll complete this task tomorrow, and then I'll start on the decking.' He went to the changing rooms and showered.

Cycling home on his mother's bicycle, he stopped at a mini supermarket, bought some provisions, and placed them in the front basket. He arrived back at Villa Francina whistling a tune, pushed back the entrance gate, parked his bicycle against the wall out of the sun, and lifted out his bag of shopping. He started to walk up the path to the front porch when he became aware of a person sitting in the shade on the far garden bench. He froze. She slid on her sunglasses as she stood and stepped out into the bright sunshine wearing a lime-green shoulder-strap top and white shorts. Narrowing his eyes, he recognised her as she approached. He went and sat on one of the bench seats just inside the entrance porch and took a breath.

The woman walked up and stopped a few metres away from him. 'I've taken you a bit by surprise – sorry,' said Amelia, taking off her sunglasses and putting them into her shoulder bag. 'Is it alright if I sit here?'

He nodded and noticed her slightly rounded tummy as she came forward. She slowly sat down opposite him, two metres away. His gaze flicked between eye contact and her tummy.

'Thank you,' she said. 'I didn't let you know I was coming because I was unsure if you would want to see me. After all, I didn't return any of your calls or messages or even reply to your very kind letter. The flowers were beautiful, by the way.'

'How did you find me?'

'I arranged it all with John, and I got on a flight from Canada to London.'

Alex frowned. 'I only spoke to him last night on Zoom – he didn't say anything.'

'I asked him not to.'

He folded his arms. 'So why are you here?'

'I wanted to see you and explain.'

'Explain what, exactly?'

'I felt hurt... I should've made time to listen to you. Family issues completely absorbed me.'

He made eye contact. 'The thing is, none of it matters now.'

'Is that because you're involved with somebody?'

He shook his head. 'I'm just rebuilding my life.'

'Please tell me how I got it all wrong that day outside your home. I'm ready to hear you say that I made a huge mistake.'

'It's not important anymore.'

'I have a problem with trust. And what with everything else going on in my family back home, it was all too much.'

Alex glanced around and then pulled the ring out from inside his tee shirt and unfastened the clasp. 'I haven't taken it off since you put it on me. I can now safely return it and feel that we have closure.'

Amelia hesitated for a second and then reached out her palm. 'Remember that last night we spent together – you showed me some of your old vinyl soul albums. We were both silly and completely trashed.' She giggled, but tears started to fill her eyes. 'Something like my soul desires your soul... I want to dig deep into your soul and make you happy forever.'

'You tore my soul out when you just left without a word.' He released the necklace, and the ring fell into her hand. He watched as she slowly fastened it around her own neck before he gazed down at her tummy. 'And what's this?'

She blinked, and a tear fell. She put on her sunglasses.

'Ha! I get it now, of course,' he said with mock laughter. 'You ran back to the ex-boyfriend and fell into his arms, and hey, you seem to be in the family way. But I'm guessing it just didn't work out with him. So, you thought you would track me down and try to pick up where we left off.'

More tears ran down her cheeks and out from under her sunglasses. 'My sister and Mom thought it would be a good idea for me to meet up with you. "The right thing to do," they both said. "You should explain in person."' She stood and wiped the tears away with her fingers.

'Go on then – explain.'

'I was over-sensitive and didn't give you a fair chance to say what had really happened.'

'Okay, you've explained. So, what happens now?'

'I've gone to a lot of trouble to be here. I'm trying to rebuild the bridge between us, but this conversation isn't going quite as I'd hoped. So, I'll go now. Thank you for looking after my grandma's ring. I won't bother you again.' She turned and started to walk down the path.

'What things were going on with your family that were so important that you couldn't reply to my letter or any of my texts?'

Amelia stopped. 'My father was dying. He passed away shortly afterwards.' She didn't wait for a response and walked down the path.

He felt knotted up inside as he watched her walk out of the gate. Something reignited inside him. He swallowed down his stubbornness and then set off after her.

Amelia ignored him when he caught up with her. Something had hardened within her heart as she continued walking.

'I'm sorry to hear about your father,' he said, following her from a short distance. She walked on in silence for a few minutes until she reached the bus stop. 'I don't think you heard me. I'm sorry...'

She couldn't bring herself to look at him. She studied the bus timetable, then checked the time on her watch before sitting on the bench.

He stood a short distance from her with open hands. 'I really am sorry.' He moved a little closer to her. 'I had no right to talk to you like that. I was confused with you turning up out of the blue.'

She sat there like stone as she tried to process all her shattered future hopes that pivoted on her meeting with him. She had made an effort to build a bridge between them, which now appeared to have collapsed into the depths.

He checked the bus timetable and then the time on his phone. 'Is that it then? When the bus comes, you'll be gone for good?' He started to rub his temple.

She didn't answer but glanced down the road and nonchalantly checked the time on her watch again.

'Is that what you want?' No reply was given. He drew a breath. 'Please don't go. I've been a mess ever since that day you walked away. I want to share my life with you.'

The hardness within her started to melt, and she turned her head towards him.

He sat down near her. 'I did embrace Evie as a final farewell, but then she literally pulled herself right into me.' He went through the sequence of events. 'You couldn't have turned up at a worse time. Half a minute earlier or later, and you would've seen the situation for what it really was...'

'I felt crushed inside when I saw you with her.'

'But you know now that she's history.'

A hint of softness appeared in her eyes. 'John told me about her attacking you.'

'I haven't seen you since that day, and I so wanted to put things right.'

She noticed the bus coming up the road. 'You were like the dawning of a new day when you came into my world – you swept away all my grey clouds.' A tear rolled down her cheek. 'That's why I gave you all of me.' The bus pulled up, and there was a hiss of air as the door folded open. She stood. 'I should go.' She moved towards the bus, pulled her face mask out of her bag, and took hold of the handrail.

'Don't go,' he said as he grabbed her free hand. She placed one foot on the bus step, but he held her hand tight. 'I behaved like a right plonka back there – please stay.'

'Why?' she asked, feeling torn and unable to face him.

'*Hola*,' said the bus driver through his mask.

Alex placed his other hand over hers. 'I need you...'

She slowly turned towards him and removed her sunglasses.

'*Hola, hola*!' said the driver again.

'Don't go,' Alex said. 'We're right for each other. And... I love you... I want to spend forever with you and do crazy things with you...'

She stepped away from the bus and fell into his embrace. 'I've missed you,' she said.

The bus driver grunted as he closed the bus doors and then pulled away.

Alex held her tightly, kissed her cheek, and whispered. 'I don't mind becoming the father of the other man's baby.'

She placed his hand on her tummy. 'You're the father…'

His eyes twitched as he processed her words. 'Just from that one time when I…'

'I was surprised as much as you are now.'

9.40 p.m.

Alex lounged back on the sofa with his arm around her. They laughed as they watched a streamed comedy film. He'd gotten so used to his own company in the evenings that he almost couldn't believe she was with him.

'That's just the tonic I needed,' she said when the film credits rolled. 'It's been quite a day, but I should be getting back to my hotel in town. I'm on a flight back to London Stansted tomorrow.'

'Nonsense,' said Alex. 'You must stay. Pick up the rest of your stuff from the hotel tomorrow.'

Her eyelids fluttered. 'Are you sure?'

'Absolutely. So long as you let me wear that symbol of love around my neck again.' He grinned.

She nodded. 'I'll feel more comfortable in the spare room. We've been apart from each other for so long.'

'I understand. I'll show you the room.' They made up the bed together. 'I hope you sleep well,' he said, leaving her in the room and closing her door as he left.

11.50 p.m.

Alex had not long been asleep in his own bed when he awoke on his side, feeling the soft touch of her fingers on his neck. He tingled as she stroked his back. He became aroused as she softly kissed his shoulder blade. He rolled over and pulled her into his arms. Their bodies and their love at last fully entwined.

Epilogue

Alex had been lying awake for ages. He couldn't stop smiling to himself as he lay back contentedly on his pillow, watching the warm orange glow of the sunrise fill the room. His arm was wrapped around her as she lay asleep nestled up beside him.

He contacted the boatyard when he got up and explained that he wouldn't be returning to his voluntary work. They were disappointed but understood. She rescheduled her flight, and the two of them spent the following week hardly leaving each other's side. They would walk down to the sea through the pine trees before breakfast each day, leaving their towels at the top of the beach and swimming out into the calm water of the bay. They started making plans for their future as they relaxed. He was still coming to terms with the fact that he would be a father and regularly placed his hand on her tummy.

She joined him each evening that week in his Zoom meetings with his friends and family, introducing her to his mother and sister. So, in turn, she introduced him to her mother, Connie, and her sister, Daphne, along with Daphne's little baby girl, Faith.

He and Amelia returned to the UK and lived together at John's apartment. He was assessed by the British Medical Council and was eventually allowed to continue to practise as a junior doctor.

Amelia returned to her studies for her Ph.D in Biological Sciences. Alex and John set up a desk in the lounge so she had a place to work. John treasured their company and friendship like an extended family.

Evie started dating a divorced science teacher from her school and found happiness.

Spud and Avani became an item and went to Hamish and Lucy's engagement party in the autumn, along with Amelia and Alex, Sanjay, and his wife, Zahida. It was almost like old times.

Emilio continued to be the gardener and handyman at Villa Francina. He still lived in the hope of a relationship with Annabelle but was hired in the autumn by a French widow. She was a few years older than him and passionate about gardening. They fell in love just before the next quarantine in 2021.

The position for a new PA for Robert was advertised; Annabelle scrutinised the applicants' CVs and sat in on the interviews. She was overjoyed when the organisation went with her recommendation and promoted internally – a well-spoken man from the HR team.

Sophie got herself a marketing job in the City and soon set her sights on promotion, flirting with the Head of the department – a married man.

Rose was placed in a small hotel in the city of Cambridge as part of the government emergency plan that recognised that the homeless were a vulnerable group during the pandemic. Alex found where she was staying and managed to set her up with an office cleaning job. Robert found her a flat that accepted pets. He offered to pay her rent and utility bills on the condition that she would take care of Percy – the parakeet he had inherited. She thought it was a good idea to have Percy keep Gertie company when she was out. Alex and Amelia would sometimes go for park walks with her and Gertie.

Amelia and Alex never managed to travel back to America before their baby girl was born at The Maternity Hospital in Cambridge on the last day of November 2020. Instead, Connie flew over for the birth. They named their baby girl Bradleah, in memory of her father. She weighed 7lb 4oz.

Amelia and Alex married at her family church near Maplewood in July 2021. Her Uncle Dexter gave her away. She held Bradleah in her arms during the ceremony. All of Alex's close friends and family were there. Daphne and John were joint *maids of honour*, and Hamish was Alex's best man.

Acknowledgements

My heartfelt thanks goes out to all the people who have supported me during the writing of this book. Especially to my wife Amanda, who has very patiently allowed me to disappear into the house office after a busy day at work and at weekends.

Furthermore, a special thanks to my sister in-law, Louise Birch, who read the first completed draft of my manuscript and for giving me a woman's perspective on the characters of Amelia, Becky and Evie.

I would also like to thank the author David Simons at the Blue Pencil Agency for professionally editing the story from my initial concept, to the almost finished article. David was very encouraging during the whole process with tips and advice for a new writer. And to BPA for all the correspondence and liaising with David.

Further thanks goes to Becky Monk for her initial proof reading at the start and my friend Peter Flowers for inspiration for Oliver and Becky's wedding reception. Bob Lloyd; toastmaster language.

I would also like to thank the novelists, Jojo Moyes and Liz Fenwick, who have unknowingly inspired me to write about the struggle in finding true love… Jojo probably won't remember the time when I was one of only three men in the audience of otherwise, all women, at her book launch of Still Me in Harts bookshop, Saffron Walden, Essex. I was the one male asking questions in the front row, trying to get into the mind of a successful author.

I would like to thank Walter Krasniqi at Amazon for convincing me to publish with them. Liz Hales, for project managing the final editing and production of the story into a book.

Motivation for Writing This Novel

I wanted to write about relationships and the breaking down of barriers between the *haves* and *have-nots*. The homeless character is based on two young vulnerable women from my own experience talking to homeless people, having empathy with their plight.

I wanted to use a close fellowship of a few friends to link the well-being of the protagonist through a shared interest in a sport. I decided to use my son's rowing experiences when he rowed for his university in training and competitions. I've observed rowing teams while out walking along the embankment of the River Great Ouse, where the Cambridge University rowing teams practice. Further inspiration came from a part of my life spent in Cambridge; being at Homerton College, punting on the River Cam and walking out to Grantchester. Extra inspiration came from several holiday visits to Pueto Pollensa, situated at the end of the Serra de Tramuntana mountain range on the island of Mallorca. I wanted to use the location as a reviving source for my damaged protagonist. Additionally, I've drawn on my friendship with an American woman living in Wisconsin as character stimulus.

About the Author

He has a passion for writing short stories inspired by true events, but especially about the most powerful emotion – love… He has been inspired by reading powerful love stories written by authors; Jojo Moyes and Liz Fenwick.

The author is a high school teacher and sixth form tutor in Hertfordshire, England. He says, 'You feed off the energy of young people.' The author is also a Duke of Edinburgh expedition assessor.

Mary Anne and the rest of the supporting team who have made it possible. I would also like to thank Clare Webber, independent graphic designer in Saffron Walden, for producing the front cover book design from my conceptual idea.